PASSIONATE PRAISE FOR CHERYL ANNE PORTER

PRAIRIE SONG

"Cheryl Anne Porter writes with the same spirited individuality that tamed this land. Her star is on the rise!"
—Debra Cowan, an author of the anthology *Every Breath You Take*

"Heartwarming and tender. Cheryl's best book yet!"
—Georgina Gentry, author of *Apache Tears*

"In the grand style of Edna Ferber and LaVyrle Spencer, Cheryl Porter has crafted a sweeping tale of passion and betrayal during the Oklahoma land run. A must read for history buffs and true romantics at heart!"
—Merline Lovelace, author of *River Rising*

"PRAIRIE SONG has complications, captivating characters and a compelling story you can't resist."
—Sara Orwig, author of *Comanche Passion*

"PRAIRIE SONG is a rare gem of a book. It's simply terrific. Full of twists and turns and the kind of emotion that goes straight to your heart, the book is one you simply can't put down."
—Patricia Potter, author of *Star Keeper*

more . . .

"Spine-tingling suspense combines with a poignant love story when a hardened gunfighter and a determined young woman embark on a high-stakes journey into the Oklahoma land run."
—Maggie Price, author of *Most Wanted*

CAPTIVE ANGEL

"Porter keeps readers on the edge of their seats with this action-packed, fast-paced western romance."
—*Publishers Weekly* (starred review)

"CAPTIVE ANGEL grips you from the get-go and never lets up. A top-notch romance from a top-notch writer!"
—*Romantic Times* (4 1/2 Stars, Top Pick)

"CAPTIVE ANGEL will captivate the hearts of western romance fans . . . The story line is exciting, romantic, and loaded with who-done-it that enhances a warm novel."
—Harriet Klausner, *Painted Rock Reviews*

Prairie
Song

Cheryl Anne Porter

St. Martin's Paperbacks

PRAIRIE SONG

Copyright © 2000 by Cheryl Anne Porter.

ISBN: 0-312-97291-1

Printed in the United States of America

St. Martin's Paperbacks edition / May 2000

St. Martin's Paperbacks are published by St. Martin's Press, 175 Fifth Avenue, New York, N.Y. 10010.

10 9 8 7 6 5 4 3 2 1

To my esteemed agent "First Mate" Pattie Steele-Perkins ... friend, mentor, guide, cheerleader, and expert career navigator.

And to Captain Jeremy Steele-Perkins ... as fine a British sea-faring gentleman as I've ever met, a man not unwilling to call himself "Cheryl's porter."

Prairie Song

Chapter One

~~~~

BEGIN A NEW LIFE IN OKLAHOMA.
PRESIDENT PROCLAIMS TWO MILLION
ACRES OF RICH AND BEAUTIFUL LAND
JUST WAITING TO BE CLAIMED!

Salvation. That's what it was, pure and simple. Salvation. Her body rocking along to the musical rhythm of the train's motion, Kate Chandler closed her eyes and hugged the much-read, crumpled advertisement to her chest. In her mind's eye, she tried to picture the vastness that was two million acres, but found she couldn't. *Why, it must go on forever.* Which made it the perfect place, this strange-sounding Oklahoma, for her to lose herself in, never to be found.

Never to be found. Just the thought, the very idea that she *might* be found, had Kate's heart pounding. She opened her eyes, sending furtive glances all about her in the crowded passenger car. Not detecting anyone paying her any undue attention—after all, these were the same people she'd been riding with for days on end—she lowered her gaze to the soul-saving piece of paper she now smoothed across her lap. *You're safe. Just remember that,* she told herself. *You got away, and you're safely on your way to Oklahoma and a new life.* But immediately she slumped, not even believing her own self. *Safe? Maybe for now. Maybe even for the next few days or weeks. But after that?* She shook her head, knowing the truth. She'd never be safe. Not as long as Mr. Talmidge was alive to have her hunted down and either brought back . . . or killed.

Kate's throat constricted and she clamped a hand over her mouth, swallowing convulsively, forcing back the rising tide of her morning sickness. Just the mere thought of the man intensified her nausea, had her remembering again the past few harrowing months of her existence. She could see him now, in her mind's eye . . . the socially prominent, politically powerful figure who'd had no qualms about using her for his own dark purposes. Again she saw him suddenly yanking her away from her upstairs-maid duties and imprisoning her in his own private suite of rooms in his New York City mansion.

She'd been terrified, had no idea what she'd done, what to expect, no time to scream—not even when he threw her on his bed. She'd begged him to stop, to let her go, but he'd taken her . . . without mercy and against her will. But that hadn't been the worst of her ordeal. Or even the end of it. Because thereafter, he had kept her in his locked room and used her over and over . . . until she conceived his child—

No! Not his child. My *child. Mine*—

Instantly aghast, fearing she'd shouted out her desperate litany, Kate fisted her hands in her skirt's folds. Her gaze skittered to those seated around her. But all about her in the narrow car, no one stared quizzically her way, no one questioned her. Kate exhaled her relief, concentrating now on *not* reliving the past few months of her life, months spent crying out for help . . . help that never came. But just as her actual cries back then had fallen on deaf ears, her present determination not to relive those moments fell on the deaf ear of a mind driven to recount the terror. Because the next unbidden image that popped into her head, the face so unnervingly like her own, was that of Norah Heston Talmidge . . . the barren wife of Edgar Talmidge.

It was because of her uncanny resemblance to Mrs. Talmidge—the same black hair and green eyes, Kate now realized—that she'd been . . . chosen. *What to make of that woman?* Kate wondered for the hundredth time. Somehow, in her quiet way of moving, her quiet way of speaking, Mrs. Talmidge was more terrifying than her husband.

Everyone—even Kate, at one time—thought her kind and good-hearted. But now Kate knew better.

No, she harbored no sympathy, no forgiveness in her heart, for the delicately boned woman unable to conceive a child, a child so desperately needed by her husband for him to hold onto his fortune. That was the rumor among the servants. Everyone in the household knew that his younger brother, Justis Talmidge, with his three sons, stood to inherit control of the family wealth when their father died . . . unless Edgar, as first-born, produced an heir before the sick old man went to his reward.

That had to be what was driving the high-society lady to go along with such awful goings-on, ones against every law of decency. It had to be. Because there'd also been rumors that Mr. Talmidge wasn't above ridding himself of his own wife. A shiver of cold chills assailed Kate. *Such evil in this world.* Evil that had pitted her life—that of a poor girl with no family—against that of a society lady with no choice. Even so, Kate saw no reason to forgive her. Wrong was wrong, no matter what your intentions were. No one had to tell her, Anna Catherine Chandler, about the ways of the world. Even at twenty years of age, she'd seen enough to know that were she to disappear—were she to be killed—the law would look the other way, wouldn't even care. But it would if Mrs. Talmidge were suddenly gone.

That explained everything. Because the society lady knew what was going on, knew how Kate—a girl forced to submit or to die—was being held and being used. So that she and her husband could have a baby out of Kate's body—one that would favor both Talmidges—which they were already publicly claiming as their own. Mrs. Talmidge had quietly announced to friends and family alike—once it was confirmed by Kate's symptoms that she had conceived—that she, this rich and barren woman, was at last with child. All this pain and treachery . . . in the name of an heir. All for a child who would mean nothing more to them than a way to secure their wealth.

Her chest constricting anew with the awful memories, Kate saw again the day when Mrs. Talmidge, as usual toting a tray of food for Kate, had come into her husband's bedroom and told her how sorry she was about all this. And that's when terror had been born in Kate's heart. *About all this?* As if she'd been apologizing to a guest for the dust on a bedside table. And there Kate had been sitting . . . manacled by a wrist to that woman's marriage bed. But sheer desperation had her begging the unfeeling woman to turn her loose, to let her go. Again Kate heard herself swearing that she'd never, ever tell anyone, if only Mrs. Talmidge would release her.

And that was when Mrs. Talmidge had told Kate how shocked she was. And how honored Kate should feel to have been *chosen* to carry the Talmidge heir. Why, she should be proud that her child would be so well taken care of, so indulged in ways Kate could never provide for it. Kate saw herself again—half naked, abused, sore and raw—staring at the woman who stood at the foot of her own husband's bed, saying those things. Kate had actually felt sorry for her. Because Mrs. Talmidge had never said the child would be loved. Cherished, indulged . . . yes. But not loved. It was then that Kate realized the woman had no soul, no idea even what it was to love someone, to put someone else above yourself. And she never would.

It was then that Kate had experienced another moment of blinding truth, even in her battered and fevered state. *If you don't fight, if you don't survive, Kate,* a tiny voice inside her head had whispered, *what will stop them from simply doing away with the child when it's no longer needed?* She remembered now the chill that had swept over her body, the way her heart had throbbed dully. And she also remembered her answer to the voice. *Nothing. Nothing would stop them.* Because to the Talmidges, this child she now carried under her heart was simply a pawn, a possession, no more than a piece of jewelry or a bit of money that they needed.

And so it was the thought of this sweet, innocent baby—

her baby—in the hands of such ruthless people that had driven Kate, kindled her fighting spirit, and had her swearing she'd never accept. From that moment, she stopped caring what happened to her body, what she had to endure. She'd cared only about surviving and somehow escaping, somehow getting away with this child she carried. And then getting lost in the vastness that was America, just her and her child.

Exactly how she would do that, she'd had no idea. After all, what plans could she make, a prisoner in that upstairs suite of rooms, with nothing but her smallclothes to wear and no money and no one to help her? But then, when the miraculous, mysterious opportunity presented itself—a dark night, an unlocked door, a knapsack by the bed with money stashed inside it—she'd been almost too stunned to take advantage of it. She'd feared a trap. But no one had tried to stop her.

And yet she remained, even to this April day in 1889 and on this train, troubled over her escape being so easy. Who had helped her? And why? Not that it mattered, really. All that mattered was that her angel of mercy had helped. That night, Kate now recalled, she had been blind with terror, even as she ran. And was still running. All the way to Oklahoma. Because to turn back now, to lose her courage, or even to make a mistake that would give her away, meant certain death. Not only for herself. But also for her baby.

Oh, the Talmidges had made that very clear to her. If she ran away with the baby, then both she and her baby would be found and killed. Because Mr. Talmidge would tolerate no loose tongues, he'd said. And no bastard claiming his name or his wealth. He'd told Kate the baby would be surrendered to him and his wife . . . or he'd see to it that Kate and her baby didn't live to tell any tales. But Kate didn't believe Mr. Talmidge would have her killed. At least not while she carried his heir. Because, despite what he said, he needed this child. But still, she couldn't be sure.

My baby. A stab of now-familiar despair assailed Kate,

had her wanting to give in to the tears of ultimate defeat that threatened to spill over. For how could she hope to win against such a powerful man? Well, she couldn't. Not on his own ground. It remained nothing short of a miracle that she'd made it this far without being caught. But she had. And when that didn't frighten her, it gave her hope. At moments she actually believed she could succeed. Maybe out here in the untamed, wide-open prairie land of the Oklahoma country, among the throngs of folks pouring into the area daily, she stood a fighting chance. And that was all she asked for. A fighting chance. For her and her baby.

Kate exhaled a breath, thinking, *Will we ever really be safe?* She smoothed a hand over her still-flat abdomen, telling the child within her, *I'll do my best to never let anyone hurt you, little one. I swear it to you.* Then, suddenly feeling better for having made that promise, having reclaimed the sense of hope that had grown inside her every minute of every day that she remained free, Kate savored the rising giddiness that rumbled through her belly. Her new life awaited her just around the next bend when the train pulled into the station in Arkansas City, Kansas.

Her determination ringing anew, Kate folded the paper and stuffed it back inside her knapsack. Her plan was a simple one. Once she arrived in the Oklahoma country, she would go to the land office and claim her 160 acres of "rich and beautiful land," as the advertisement stated, and start her new life on her own. She believed in herself. She'd make a good life for herself and her child. She would. She alone.

The conviction brought a rare smile to Kate's face. Accompanying it were the heart palpitations of sheer freedom. Freedom . . . for the first time in her life, the life of an orphan who'd worked hard and long in someone else's home since her own childhood. Well, not anymore. And not her child. Her child would know the freedom of choosing its own life's path. She'd see to it. She'd make that future possible.

With that conviction comforting her, Kate turned to stare

out the open window next to her, saw the passing country-side, and took in a deep breath of air. She really couldn't believe she was actually this close to Oklahoma, to what folks were calling the Promised Land. A smile touched Kate's mouth. *The Promised Land.* She liked the sound of that. Because in her heart, it was the land of her future—the only future she could lay claim to.

And now that she thought about it, it seemed downright providential that on the night of her escape, once she'd gotten free of the Talmidges' home and made her way to the street, as she'd stood there, panicked, trying desperately to think what to do next . . . her gaze had lit on the very advertisement she now carried in her overstuffed knapsack. Someone had posted the notice—a godsend to her—on a storefront. She'd snatched it off the board and headed for the nearest train station.

Once there, using most of the stash of money she'd found in the knapsack left her, she'd bought a one-way ticket to Oklahoma. Thinking again of the money inside her knapsack, of how she'd awakened from a sleep of exhaustion the night of her escape only to discover the manacle holding her in captivity had been unlocked, that a side door to the bedroom was ajar, and the Talmidges were out for the evening, Kate spared another thought for her unknown savior.

She suspected Hudson, Mr. Talmidge's kindly valet. Since he was the only servant with permission to enter that suite of rooms, Kate felt certain the old man, in carrying out his duties, at some point had heard her cries for help. But if not, wouldn't he—as well as the remainder of the staff—have wondered who the trays of food going upstairs were for, since both Talmidges took their meals downstairs? And too, would he have believed Mr. Talmidge's story to the staff that she'd been dismissed for stealing?

After all, Kate reminded herself, Hudson had befriended her years ago, and so would know her better than that. Being a smart man, he'd no doubt put it all together, she thought, and had hunted for the keys, found them, and then plotted and arranged for her escape. That had to be it. Because here she sat on a train bound for freedom.

Reliving all this, trying to find answers, yet knowing all she had were guesses, Kate felt sure enough of her conclusions that she sent up a prayer for the nice old man. She only hoped he hadn't been dismissed, or punished, when the Talmidges came home and discovered her gone. *Poor Hudson.* But he'd done a brave thing, if it was him, by making her escape possible with his money.

Kate sighed . . . money that was all but gone, except for a few coins. Worried about that, too, and wondering how she'd get more anytime soon, she bit at her bottom lip, even knowing she'd spent it well, having used it for food and clothes. *Well, all things in their own good time. I've made it this far. I'll make it when I get to Oklahoma, too. I just have to.* Thus encouraged, she smiled down at herself now, fingering the moss-green traveling costume she wore. It was beautiful, and the only nice thing she'd ever owned.

"Yer thinkin' about that land again, ain't you, Miss Chandler? Having second thoughts, maybe?"

Her musings interrupted, Kate looked up, even managing a smile for Mrs. Jacobs, one of the many like-minded land seekers who shared the crowded rail car with her. The woman's warm but knowing gaze had Kate looking away, staring out the grimy window at the framed countryside rocking by. "No, ma'am. No second thoughts for me. The closer we get, the more excited I am, it seems."

With that, Kate turned back to the care-lined face of the woman who sat across from her. She held a baby to her breast. Her three other children huddled silently around her and watched Kate. Their clothes were of a homespun material, threadbare but clean. Hunger and hard times haunted their eyes, just as it did their mother's. Then the woman smiled tiredly. "I s'pose a young thing like yerself would think this is excitin' and not see the danger."

Kate sobered. "I know all about danger, Mrs. Jacobs."

"Be that as it may, my offer still stands. You can join me and my man when we get there. We'd be right proud to have yer company. Ain't nobody sayin' you cain't take care of yerself, neither. We just don't want you comin' to no harm, bein' a woman alone and all."

A woman alone. Kate thought of her baby, and knew she'd never be alone. But she'd had this same talk with Mrs. Jacobs maybe five times already. So, keeping a firm but friendly note in her voice, she again turned her down. "I do thank you. You're very kind. But I'll be fine. The papers say the land is free to anyone who cares to come claim it. And that's what I intend to do."

A loud guffaw from the large man two seats away from Kate on the same cramped bench had folks staring his way as he leaned forward and thrust himself into the conversation. "I keep telling you, missy—you and ten thousand other people intend to do the same. And most of 'em are men. You'd best get you a man to make the run for you."

Kate narrowed her eyes at him. The last thing she wanted was a man. Ever again. But judging by the wolfish looks this rough-looking sort kept sending her, Kate thought she knew exactly which man he meant. "I have just as good a chance as anyone, Mr. Simms. I'll do this by myself, and I'll be just fine. I don't need a man to take care of me."

"Now, we don't mean to pick on you," came Mrs. Jacobs's hasty interruption, and Kate looked her way again. "You got as much right to be on this here train as the next body. Just be careful, child, is all I'm sayin'. A slender woman like yerself, with all that black hair and them green eyes, is fair game for all the bad sorts. Just have a care about yerself when we get to Arkansas City, if you will."

Kate nodded, murmuring, "I will," and felt her mood slip a notch as she again looked away, out the open window to her right.

Yes, there was danger out here. But it couldn't be anything like what she'd just escaped in New York City. Yet the strangers on this train kept telling her that she'd most likely find herself killed or worse before the day of the land run ever came. But what they didn't know was she'd already faced death. And had lived through the *worst.* So whatever lay ahead, Kate knew she could face it. She had to. Because in only a few minutes, they'd be in Arkansas City—the last jumping-off point on the rail line leading into the Oklahoma country.

Putting past fears and worries for the future aside, Kate focused on the present, and the practical. First thing, she'd find a place to sleep, and then she'd hire on somewhere doing chores or waiting tables to earn her keep until the run on April 22, six days away. It was a good, simple plan—life for her and her child. On her terms. She'd show them all what Anna Katherine Chandler was made of. She'd show them all.

Cole Youngblood nudged his black Stetson up with his thumb and exhaled sharply as he stepped outside onto the crowded boardwalk. Closing the door to the Arkansas City sheriff's office behind him, he stood there a moment, looking all around, thinking about what to do with the information the lawman had just given him. Not that the sheriff had welcomed Cole to town, or had been more forthcoming than the situation warranted. Cole's mouth quirked. No tin badge was happy to see a gunslinger of his reputation ride into town. Even if it was for personal business. And even if he did have three kids in tow.

He hadn't lied to the sheriff. He *was* in town on business. Family business. His own . . . and Mr. Talmidge's. But that second part, as Cole saw it, wasn't anything the sheriff needed to know. Because a promise of complete confidentiality to those who hired his services was a stock-in-trade of Cole's. That, his fast gun . . . and quick results. Still, he felt silly as hell with two boys trailing him. And judging from the looks he was getting from the throng of folks who jostled by him as he stepped out into the wagonwheel-rutted street, he figured he looked that way, too.

But not on the second looks, the double-takes. Cole knew that even in a town lousy with hucksters and gamblers, a man of his notorious reputation still warranted a nod, coupled with a respectful sidestep, from the folks who passed by. But seeing one man's startled expression as recognition dawned in his eyes and he frantically pressed himself against a wooden building to make way, Cole's mood rankled. It wasn't every day that a law-abiding citizen was likely to see Cole Youngblood at high noon toting a three-year-old girl in his arms and being followed by two ragamuffin boys who held each other's hands.

They *were* still following him, weren't they? Cole chanced a quick look over his shoulder. They were. Two sets of somber brown eyes looked up trustingly at him. Stopping and turning to face them, staring down at them, Cole felt his heart flip-flop. The boys looked just like their mother. *Charlotte.* Had it really been two weeks since his only sister had succumbed to that fever? Yeah, it had to be, because here they were already in Arkansas City. Him and three kids he had no idea what to do with. Realizing the boys were still staring up at him and that he hadn't said a word yet, Cole adopted a serious frown and said, "You keep close to me in this crowd, you hear?"

"Yes, sir, Uncle Cole," seven-year-old Joey said. "I got Willy's hand real tight-like."

"Yeah, an' it hurts." Five-year-old Willy frowned to prove it.

Cole frowned right back at him. "Well, you let Joey hang on to you, boy. Better that than being lost among all these folks."

Willy scowled, much as if Cole had just told him to jump naked into a hot bath with a bar of soap in his hand. But he did finally nod and quit trying to jerk his hand away from his brother's.

Shaking his head as he turned away, as much at Willy's expression as at the dilemma he found himself in, Cole started them all off again. How had it come to this? From age sixteen on, once Charlotte had married, he'd made his own way in the world. But now he had her younguns in his care. Fourteen years of keeping his own counsel and living by his gun were hard to undo. He kept forgetting he had three kids dogging him, that he couldn't make a move without considering them, or without tripping over one of them.

"I want my mama."

Cole glanced at the ringlet-fringed face of the three-year-old girl he carried. Her little fingers at the nape of his neck worked absently at the longish hair that spilled over his collar. With a brusque motion, he wiped a smudge off her chubby cheek. "You can't see her, Lydia. She's . . . in heaven, like I said."

"Then I want Papa. I don't like you."

Cole huffed out a breath. "You don't have to like me. But you know about your pa, Lydia. It was only yesterday that we buried that son of a—I mean, he's in heaven, too."

Lydia didn't say anything else, just poked out her bottom lip far enough to trip over. Cole didn't blame the little girl one bit for not liking him. She barely knew him, and yet she and her brothers had watched him bury both their parents in less than two weeks' time. But not being one to share his own feelings, much less his own grief, Cole knew he was scant comfort to the hurting kids.

Kaleidoscopic images of himself riding onto his sister's farm, noting with alarm its rundown condition, and seeing the kids tumbling out of the wood-frame house and begging him to help their mother still had the power to tighten Cole's chest. He'd found Charlotte dying of a fever, and her husband nowhere around. She'd been able to tell him that Mack had come here to Arkansas City to make the run. She'd said she hadn't been sick when he left, and that he was supposed to come back for her and the kids once he staked their claim. *Like as not the shiftless man wouldn't have made the effort,* Cole suspected. But still, there hadn't been much he could do for his sister but comfort her and promise to bring the kids here to their father.

Burying Charlotte had done nothing to warm Cole's heart toward his brother-in-law. Mack Anderson was one lucky son of a bitch that he was already dead before Cole arrived two days ago with the man's kids. Getting himself robbed and beaten to death by ruffians was only a mite worse than what Cole'd planned for the dirt farmer who'd never provided much for his family. If it hadn't been for the money Cole made hiring out his gun and bringing it himself to Charlotte all these years, she and her family would have starved to death.

Should have shot the bastard years ago, Cole fumed. But, as worthless as the man had been, his sister and the kids had loved him.

But he was dead now, and that left Cole responsible for Joey, Willy, and Lydia. For now. At least until he found a married female cousin of his, a mother herself from what he remembered, who might take them off his hands. If he could remember her name. *Something with an* m *in it.* It would also help if he could remember where exactly, here in this southern part of Kansas, she lived. *Dammit, could it be harder?* A sudden image of himself roaming the area to look for her and keeping up with three kids at the same time nearly undid him.

Close to cussing out loud just thinking about it, he comforted himself with the thought that he would, by God, remember her name and where exactly she lived. He also felt sure he could get her to keep Charlotte's kids for good, once he told her he would pay for their keep.

A recurring prick of conscience, telling him he should keep his sister's children with him suddenly bit at Cole again. But he dismissed it immediately. Him, a for-hire gunslinger, raising these kids? Hell, he couldn't fill a boot with what he knew about taking care of kids. Especially a girl child.

"Where we headed now, Uncle Cole?"

Cole pivoted, saw the anxious expression on Joey's face. And knew he was right to search for that cousin. Because the kids needed . . . something warm and reassuring that Cole just didn't know how to give, much less name. And that made him feel as if he'd done something wrong somehow. Not liking that feeling, he frowned and spoke more sharply than he'd intended. "To the wagon. Now you boys get on up here in front of me where I can see you."

They obediently scooted ahead of him, glancing back over their thin shoulders as they continued walking and listening to Cole's plans. "We're going back to the wagon we came in. And then out to the camp at Walnut Creek. The sheriff said your pa's wagon and belongings turned up there. We'll bed down in one of the wagons tonight and then get out of here tomorrow."

"I don't like yer wagon. I just like ours."

Cole considered the pouting girl in his arms. "Lydia, are you sure you're not just a little bitty woman?"

"Nope. I'm a little bitty girl. But yer not."

He tipped his hat to her. "It's right kind of you to notice, ma'am."

Certain as ever that he was in over his head, Cole herded them all safely across Summit Street, figuring he looked like a mother duck with her trailing ducklings. Pushing past men and women whose faces reflected the land-grab fever, Cole likened Arkansas City to a tipped-over beehive. A man couldn't turn around without knocking into some preoccupied soul whose eyes were on a distant point. The sooner he cleared out of here, got the kids settled in with his cousin, and then got on the trail of that runaway maid of Talmidge's, the better he'd feel.

The better he'd feel? Hardly. Another prick of conscience, this one of a different, even more troubling nature, snapped at him. Because he didn't like one damned thing about this job he'd taken. It wasn't the sort of thing he'd ever hired on to do before, that of finding and killing a woman, no matter what she'd done. But much less over some stolen money and jewels.

True, he'd killed a lot of deserving men in his time. Been paid handsomely to do so, too. But not women. Hell, it just didn't set right with him. Especially tracking down a woman who just got greedy. Didn't hardly seem like a killing offense, not for someone with as much money as Mr. Talmidge had. Which told Cole that something else, something he hadn't been told, was going on here. Because Mr. Talmidge, a man Cole had never met but communicated with through the telegraph, hadn't indicated in his wire that he cared about getting the money or the jewels back. Or the maid. He wanted her dead. And to assure that, he was paying Cole almost three times his usual fee to see it done.

That was strange, too. And troublesome. But he'd accepted the job, Cole now reminded himself, so he'd do it. But first he had to tend to his own personal matter, that being the kids. Which was the hell of it, really. It was his niece and nephews being in need of a home that had finally prompted him to agree to track down a woman. Because Talmidge, a powerful man with a lot of enemies and always some little detail that needed cleaning up, paid well and paid quick—two things Cole needed right now. Quick money and a heap of it.

But he hadn't been given much to go on. The wire awaiting him in Wichita, one of his usual checking-in points, held only scant details. That, and the telegraph operator's apology for the message being so spotty. Some problem along the wires somewhere, as the edgy little man had said, that had left him to piece together what he could for Cole and to figure out some of the spellings of names and such. But with the hefty advance awaiting him at his bank, Cole hadn't worried then about equipment problems and apologetic clerks.

Because the operator had gotten the essentials that Cole needed. Namely, what the woman's name was and the fact that she was apparently heading this way to the land run. That made sense to him. All this open country. Untold numbers of folks milling about. A body with a reason to get lost and stay lost could do so easily. Still, he'd be damned lucky, Cole knew, if she showed up here in Arkansas City, instead of one of the numerous other jumping-off points along the run's borders.

But here he was, so it was the obvious place to start. However, with the crowds hereabouts, he surely could use that description of the woman that hadn't come through. Cole hadn't had time then to wait around for days for the line problems to be worked out, either. Couldn't even send one back telling Mr. Talmidge he'd take the job, but that he first had to see to his own personal problem—meaning the kids—and finally to request a description . . . because the telegraph lines were down altogether when he got there. He hadn't bothered to leave a message to be sent later, either, because he wasn't about to head back to Wichita, and wouldn't be there to get his answer.

But at least, Cole figured, Mr. Talmidge would know he'd accepted the work when the bank reported his withdrawing the money. That'd have to be good enough, because here he was in Arkansas City, where there was no telegraph. And too, he'd worked before with less information than he had now and had gotten the job done. He could do it again. Still, he hoped like hell he didn't run into this Anne Candless, the name given him by the Wichita telegraph operator, while he still had the kids with him. They'd seen enough of death. The last thing they needed was the sight of their uncle gunning down a woman. They'd be terrified of him after that.

Yeah, they would. But gunning down a woman? Damn. The very thought made him queasy. And if the thought alone did, what then would the actual doing of it be like to live with? Could he really shoot down a woman? Cole had no answers for himself, only the hope that this Candless woman would turn out to be some hellcat of a big vicious woman. An *armed* hellcat of a big vicious woman. One who drew on him first. After cussing him. And spitting on him. Maybe then, after all that, he could stand the thought of killing her.

Cole's scowl, much like Willy's of a moment ago, deepened. *It's plain unnerving, is what it is.* But what was most unnerving to Cole was his sudden realization that, yes, he had a heart. And convictions of a moral nature.

With that, Cole stopped beside the wagon he'd bought in Wichita to get the kids here from their dirt farm of a home. Before lunch, he'd hitched the mule team in front of the cot hotel where they'd been sleeping for the past two nights. Tied to the back of the wagon was his big roan gelding, which turned its head and nickered in recognition when Cole smoothed a hand over its muscled shoulder.

Going to the wagon's front, he set Lydia on the buckboard seat. She gripped the wood under her and dandled her legs back and forth, singing softly, apparently content now that her stomach was full. Cole motioned the boys to climb onto the wagon bed. Willy scooted in obediently with some help from Cole and settled himself cross-legged.

But Joey hesitated. Shading his eyes with his hands, he stared up at Cole. "What about our mules and all of Pa's tools and lumber? Are they with the wagon?"

"Yeah. You heard the sheriff say so. The army's been keeping an eye on the gear." Knowing that Joey felt very keenly his responsibilities as the oldest, Cole talked to the boy as if he were already a man.

Joey nodded, thoughtfully tipping his tongue through the gap where his two front teeth had fallen out. "What are we going to do with the wagon? We don't need two wagons and two teams."

Cole nodded his agreement, even as he reflected that this kid held him accountable for every decision he made regarding them. But every day his respect for this practical little boy rose another notch. Seven was a tough age to start being a man. "I believe we'll look them over, keep the best of the lot, and sell the rest. Folks here wanting to make the run will pay a good price for it all. Especially the mules. And the tools and lumber to build a cabin."

Nodding as if giving due consideration to that answer, Joey finally said what Cole knew, from countless other conversations with him, was really on the boy's mind. "Pa was gonna make the run and get us a clean start in Oklahoma. Our land was about farmed out. Wouldn't nothin' grow anymore."

Cole looked down at the boy's pinched face. He knew what Joey was really asking him, and it made Cole curse the boy's dead father yet again. *Damn you, Mack Anderson. If you were alive, I'd fill you full of lead.* How could the man have been so stupid, Cole wondered, as to get drunk and wind up in a crooked card game with the hucksters here who almost outnumbered the decent citizens? And then get himself killed and leave Cole strapped with his responsibilities?

Lifting his Stetson to wipe at his damp forehead with his sleeve, Cole then resettled his hat and told his nephew, "I already told you I don't intend to make the run, Joey. I'm not a farmer or a family man, son. And you, better'n most, know I don't know anything about caring for kids. Besides, in my line of work, I don't stay in one place any too long."

A stricken look claimed Joey's features. The boy looked down at his feet. Cole narrowed his eyes and tried to deny the emotions that gripped his stomach. Chief among them was a building rage against the unfairness of this situation to him and to the kids. Hell, yes, he saw how his words had affected the boy. And he knew what Joey was thinking— that Cole could change, that he could settle down and stay in one place . . . and quit killing people for a living. But Cole wasn't so sure that he could. He'd been doing it for too long. Feared it was in his blood. But still, he wanted to cuss at the heavens.

Just then, Willy sniffed and gave Cole the reason he needed to turn away from Joey's accusing pose. The younger boy sat on the wagon's bed, hunched forward, his shoulders shaking, his hands covering his face. Cole rubbed a hand over his mouth and chin. *Dammit.* Acute frustration with the situation had him all but growling at the five-year-old boy. "Now what's the matter with you, Willy?"

Willy looked up at him. A world of hurt and tears was reflected in his dark, baby eyes. "You gonna leave us, too, Uncle Cole? Like Ma and Pa done?"

Cole's heart constricted with the truth. Leaving them was exactly what he was going to do. But he found he just couldn't voice the words right now. Not to these kids.

They'd already had enough hurt and worry to last them a lifetime. And so, for the first time in his adult life, Cole Youngblood hedged his answer. "I don't want you to worry about that right now. Later on, we'll figure something out."

To Cole's relief, Willy nodded with the easy acceptance of a trusting child. But just then Cole's sleeve was grabbed and tugged. He pivoted around, facing Joey again, whose face contorted as he struggled with gathering tears. "Yer leavin' us, ain't you? Why don't you just say it? We ain't goin' ta be no family. So don't tell Willy and Lydia that it's so."

Willy and Lydia immediately burst into tears. Cole looked helplessly from one to the other of them. The overwhelming urge to hit something hard, like the wagon, nearly sent him stalking off. Instead, he put his hands to his waist and stood his ground. Deliberately, he towered over Joey, establishing his word as law. "I didn't say that, now did I? And we are a family . . . for now. I suppose. Unless you've got a better plan, boy."

The moments silently ticked by. Then Joey said, "I don't reckon I do."

Cole exhaled a relieved breath, realizing that he'd half expected this kid to come up with a workable plan. "Well, then, that's settled. Is there anything else we need to get out in the open?"

The kids quit their sniffing, enough to exchange questioning glances among themselves and say, together, "Nope."

"All right then, let's load up." Cole again made a swiping motion with his hand, indicating for Joey to join Willy on the wagon's bed.

This time, Joey climbed somberly onto the wagon to sit beside his brother and stare back at Cole. A sudden realization stung Cole—Joey was someone he didn't want to disappoint. Never before had Cole cared a damn for what any man thought of him. But this kid? He made a man feel he had something to live up to in his eyes. Dammit, he didn't need this. To prove it, Cole stalked to the hitching rail and untied the team, finally hauling himself up beside Lydia on the narrow seat. He glanced down at her. She was fiddling with the hem of her dress.

But the tiny girl had apparently been doing some thinking of her own. "Are you goin' to be our new papa?"

Cole stopped in the act of backing the team into the muddy street's bustling traffic. Looking down at his niece, he saw her rosebud mouth pucker. She was now twisting a dark curl around her chubby finger. With huge brown eyes, she considered him, a doubtful expression puffing out her rounded cheeks. Cole flicked the tip of her button nose with his finger and grinned. "Yeah, Lydia, I suppose I am. For now, anyway."

When she didn't say anything further, but bent to pick at a burr in her stocking, Cole let out a relieved breath and began his maneuvering of the team. Just as he set them on their course for Walnut Creek, a train's whistle overrode the other street noises and had Cole turning toward the sound and puckering his mouth in disgust. *Another trainload of land grabbers.* All he wanted to do was get his brother-in-law's affairs settled and get out of town before the seams burst in this overrun frontier settlement.

Since the wagon path out to the Walnut Creek camp— a settlement the sheriff'd said had literally sprung up under a dense grove of trees at the creek's bottom—paralleled the train tracks, Cole couldn't help but see the big engine come to a stop and begin to disgorge swarms of people from its long string of cars. He guided the mules around the sea of disembarking people and shook his head at all the noise and bustle. A twinge of some emotion, one that tugged at him, assailed Cole. *Not for me. Not any of these trappings of civilization.* Just then, he felt a tug on his shirt.

"Papa Cole?"

Sparing Lydia only a glance as he kept an eye out for the milling newcomers, he smiled at her calling him "Papa Cole" and figured it was easier for her to say than "Uncle Cole." "What, baby?"

"Where's our new mama?"

Chapter Two

Startled by the child's question, Cole gaped at her, forgetting for a moment the disembarking folks. A split second later, yelling and whooping directly in front of his wagon spooked the team into half-rearing and jerked Cole's attention back to the street.

"Watch out!"

"Whoa, there! Whoa! Mind your team, mister!"

Cursing, Cole sawed back on the reins, finally bringing the agitated mules under control. Immediately he jumped up and called out to Joey, "Take the reins, son. Willy, keep a hand on your sister." Waiting only to see that the boys jumped to do his bidding, Cole dismounted as nimbly as if he'd been on his gelding. Hurrying around to the front of the wagon, he found himself confronted with a knot of gawking onlookers. Looking from one upset face to the next, he asked, "Was anybody hurt?"

"Not as much as they could've been, young feller," an old codger barked out, pointing to a young woman off to Cole's right. "You danged near ran down this here little lady. You're lucky all your team trampled was her belongings."

Accepting the deserved chastisement, Cole looked in the direction the bewhiskered old man pointed. And found he couldn't look away. He forgot the old man, along with the rest of the bystanders, because . . . there she stood at the front of the crowd. An arresting woman . . . tall, slim, black-haired, dressed all in green from her hat to the hem of her mud-splattered skirt. But it was her eyes that captured his attention, that took his breath away. He'd never seen eyes the green of hers, eyes that gleamed all the more for being set in such a pale face.

Cole instantly realized that he'd put that look on her face and so roused himself to inquire, "You all right, miss?"

She blinked, as if startled by the sound of his voice. Then, staring at him for a moment too long, she finally said, "I am. I'm fine. I just need my knapsack." She pointed to the trampled earth under his team's hooves. "It's under there."

Cole nodded at her, hypnotized by her voice. Low yet melodic, it played over his skin like a soft spring breeze. Frowning now at his school-boy thoughts, he said brusquely, "Let me get it for you."

Turning, taking hold of the nearest mule's bridle and, with Joey's help, urging it back until the woman's ruined bag came into view, Cole bent over and hauled it out of further harm's way. He straightened up and offered it to her. A look of dismay settled on her features as she reached for it and hugged it to her bosom. Her actions prompted Cole to speak. "I'm right sorry this happened. I can pay you for the damage done if you—"

"No," she interrupted, shaking her head, which caused the feather on her hat to dance nervously. Then, glancing about, as if only now aware of the crowd and how they pressed in around her, she sent Cole a wide-eyed—and fearful—look. "No," she repeated. "Thank you, but it's okay. I've got my property, so I'll just be on my way."

"Yes, ma'am," Cole replied, tipping his Stetson's brim to her, but with his mind busily assessing her reaction and wondering at it. "You sure you're okay, that's there nothing I can do for you?"

Sudden tears sprang to her eyes. "I'm fine. And there's nothing anybody can do for me. I mean, I don't need anyone's help. I'm fine."

More than curious now, Cole nodded at her. "If you say so. You know best, miss."

Her chin came up, revealing a slight quiver there. "Yes. I do, don't I? I do know best. Thank you." With that, she turned and shouldered her way into the crowd, which parted for her and then closed around her, blocking her retreat from Cole's sight.

Once she was gone, and the crowd began dispersing, he shook his head and turned back to the wagon and the kids. *She was acting mighty strange,* he thought as he hauled himself up onto the buckboard seat and settled in next to Lydia. Turning to the little girl, Cole asked her, "What'd you think about all that, Miss Lydia?"

The ringlet-crowned child shrugged her shoulders as she turned her face up to him and said, "Her was more scared than me."

Cole found himself nodding and agreeing. "Yeah, she was." Then, to himself, he added, *But scared of what? Or who?*

Only recently had Kate become afraid of approaching darkness. Because of the horrific events back in New York, she now associated the long shadows of day's end with that of Mr. Talmidge's appearance at the bedside, his face bloated with a mixture of hatred and desire for her. Even now, in this wide-open faraway place, the early evening shadows creeping up on her took her back to that bad place.

No! Gritting her teeth, she fought back the wrenching sobs that threatened to overtake her. Instead, she forced herself to concentrate on the practical, on her present predicament. And a mighty big one it was.

Exhausted, her spirits low, she dropped her muddy, torn knapsack to the ground as she sank down on an abandoned wooden box under a blackjack oak tree. She called the tiny square seat under her the only welcoming thing she'd found all this long afternoon, since she'd stepped off the train only to be almost trampled to death. That memory sent a shiver frittering along her nerve endings. But it wasn't the memory of the rearing mules that had her shaking again. No, it was the dark eyes of the big, square-jawed man whose team she'd walked in front of.

Again she saw him looking her up and down . . . and giving her that considering stare, one that said she couldn't hide her secrets from him, a look that had made her turn tail and run from him.

Since then, things had only gotten worse for her. And the way she saw it, it was all her fault. Why, she wanted to know, hadn't she at least suspected there might not be even one empty bed in a frontier town thronged with would-be settlers like herself? Couldn't she have, on the days-long train ride it'd taken to get out here, at least guessed what it would be like? Not that knowing would have stopped her or changed her plans. No, she'd had no choice but to continue her journey, what with the ticket bought and her money supply dwindling. But even so, she had no right to be so surprised and upset to find that even that ornery Mr. Simms was right. There must be over ten thousand people here, like he'd said, waiting to make the run.

Kate shook her head. Talk about town had it that every border into Oklahoma country was just as crowded as Arkansas City. And Mrs. Jacobs had been right, too. Meaning, what chance did she, a lone woman afoot, have of beating mounted riders to a suitable claim? Why, she hadn't given much credence on the train to the men's bragging on whose horse was the fleetest and on how they planned to get first to the choicest land. She'd listened with only half an ear, as tangled up in her own fears and troubles as she'd been for most of the way here. But now she understood, and all too painfully well, why the run was referred to jokingly as "Harrison's Hoss Race," after the new president.

It was all true. The land run, the race for her future, only days away, was already lost to her. Why? Because she probably wouldn't even survive until then. Right now, she couldn't even see to her most basic needs. Such as money. She had none left, after paying for a meager supper at a cot hotel's dining room. A place to sleep? A humorless chuckle escaped her. She was sitting on it. And work? There was none to be had anywhere. Nothing to keep her body and soul together until the blasted run. Which was a *real* run. An actual race, with the best land going to those with the fastest horses.

Now where was she going to get a horse? It'd taken her all day just to find this wood box to sit on. And she'd thought it would all be so easy. *Just get here,* was all she'd been able to think. *Just get here and you'll be fine,* she'd promised herself. Well, here she was . . . and she wasn't fine. If she didn't come up with another plan, and soon, she and her baby were as good as dead. A plan, she firmly told herself, that wasn't as silly as the picture she'd had in her head of simply stepping up to the land-office window and picking out her parcel of land from a map.

A wave of overwhelming futility crashed over Kate with a suddenness that swamped her remaining courage. And robbed her of hope. She buried her face in her arms and began to cry, sobbing quietly with all the desperation in her soul. She didn't care about all the folks walking by, either. Nothing mattered—

"Lady, can I help you in any way?"

Kate jumped, quickly wiping at her eyes and cheeks as she looked up. She sucked in air. *It's him.* The man whose mules had nearly trampled her. And here he stood now, a hand outstretched to her, as if he meant to touch her. She shied away from the contact and managed to stare up into his face. "I don't need any help."

He pulled his hand back and stood up straighter, staring down at her. "That may be. But I keep hearing different. Talk around town and out at Walnut Creek camp says you're all alone. Got no place to sleep. Been looking for work you can't find."

Kate's heart thumped erratically. *Folks are talking about me?* Must be. And apparently he, for one, was listening. Again she had the sense that he knew her whole life, that he could see into her soul. Somehow she knew she had to put him off the scent right here and now. "Talk's cheap, mister. But true or not, like I said . . . I don't need any help from you."

His expression clouded. "I see. Well, I'm sorry to have

bothered you. But I . . . well, I was passing by and heard you just now."

Mortified that he'd find her in this state, Kate struggled for control, which made her voice sound high and tinny, even to her own ears. "Well, you're right about that. It was me . . . as you can plainly see."

He didn't say anything. But he didn't have to. Because somehow his standing there in front of her, so tall and in control, only made her feel more guilty for having been so unprepared to take care of herself. Just as that realization came to her, he spoke again. "Is it true, the talk? About your not having a safe place to sleep?"

Kate tensed—the last thing she needed was some stranger, a man, concerning himself with where she'd sleep. "No, it isn't," she assured him. "And I do have some place to be. Now, if you'll excuse me." With that, she came to her feet and grabbed up her knapsack, holding it close to her chest. Wide-eyed and slowly backing away from him, she stared at him. He suddenly loomed larger, seemed to float toward her. Kate swallowed, tasting her fear . . . and the danger.

Before a few months ago she wouldn't have seen this trap, at least not as vividly as she did now. "Leave me alone," she warned him, feeling herself slip toward panic. "I'll scream. I swear I will."

"Whoa. Hold on there, lady," the man protested, holding up a cautioning hand. "There's no need to scream. I don't mean you any harm. I was just asking, that's all."

Kate stopped where she was—pressed against the tree trunk at her back—and stood her ground. "Well, now you know. I have a place to sleep. Not that it's any of your concern."

"You're right. Like I said, I'm sorry I bothered you. I just thought that—Well, never mind." The man then took his leave of her and tipped his hat as he turned on his boot heel and stalked away.

Slumping with relief, Kate watched his retreat, telling herself she wanted to make sure he didn't double back on her. After a moment, though, she realized she was noting his broad shoulders and his long-legged stride that was rapidly putting a respectable distance between them. But it wasn't until he stepped up onto the boardwalk that fronted Summit Street's wooden buildings, and rounded the corner, out of her sight, that Kate exhaled the breath she'd been holding. *That was a close call,* she told herself, now heading back to the wooden box she'd been sitting on until a moment ago.

But she'd no more than squatted back down on her perch before her conscience went to work on her, accusing her of sending away the only helping hand that'd been held out to her since she stepped off the train. But his offer was one she couldn't accept, she argued right back. For one thing, he was a man and a stranger to her. For another, from what he'd said, she was already the subject of gossip about town. What then would folks think if she suddenly took up with him? Why, they'd think the worst. And she'd deserve it.

Because there was just no telling what was involved in his offer to help her. What might he want from her? Maybe nothing. Maybe he truly was only a kind man thinking to help a woman in need. There was a time in her young life when she would have believed that. But not anymore. Harsh experience had taught her to be wary. Suspicious. Not so trusting. And even now, those same emotions had Kate sitting up taller, had her feeling stronger. But just as suddenly, she slumped, knowing the reasons she'd just given herself weren't the only ones for sending the man away.

She'd also pushed him away because . . . he was *him.* Why, he'd fairly taken her breath away earlier today when he'd jumped off that wagon and come to stand in front of her. He was quite easily the handsomest man she'd ever seen. So tall, dark, and muscled. And such feelings, so startling and unsettling to her after what she'd been subjected to by Mr. Talmidge, scared her. It was that simple. Hadn't she been shaking like a leaf after their set-to this afternoon? And no, it hadn't all been from fright, either. The truth was,

the man's nearness shook her up. And that was enough of
a reason to send him away. She wasn't studying any man
now. She had her baby to think of.

Dismissing the man from her thoughts, Kate recalled
Mrs. Jacobs and her brood of hungry kids. If only she could
find the kind woman and her mister. She'd swallow her
pride and take them up on their offer of shelter and food.
But where in all this people-clogged madness could they
be? Out at that Walnut Creek camp she'd been hearing
about all day?

She pivoted on her wooden box, away from the town's
center, until she could see the trees that sheltered the camp.
They were most likely out there. But did she dare try to
find them, now that it was getting dark? From what she'd
seen today, the creek was among a thick stand of trees.
Anything could happen to a woman alone out there. And
probably would.

With that fear holding her firmly in place, Kate's slump
deepened, had her resting an elbow atop a skirt-covered
knee and rubbing tiredly at her forehead. What was wrong
with her? Was it the growing baby that kept her tired, hungry, and sick? And full of tears? Then, as if just the thought
of crying could bring on a jag, Kate felt her chin tremble
and her eyes fill. Blinking rapidly, sniffing, she swiped at
them. *Why, now I'm just being plain silly. There's not a
thing—*

"Get up. You're coming with me."

Kate jerked around. And froze. It was him. Again. Gulping back her tears, she silently stared up at him. Why, he'd
walked right up behind her—and she hadn't even heard
him. Her heart pounded in her throat. She couldn't even
speak, she was so terrified. All she could do was . . . be
afraid.

He stood there in front of her, his thumbs hitched in the
gun belt that rode low on his narrow hips. There was no
doubt in her heart, from seeing the way he wore it, that he
knew how to use the huge Colt revolver holstered there. "I
said . . . you're coming with me, ma'am."

"I'm not going anywhere—"

"Fine. Then you can sit here and wait for all those men over at the saloon to get good and liquored up and come looking for you."

Kate's gasp was accompanied by her swiveling atop her box until she was staring in the direction of the saloon. Loud music, loud chatter, and laughter spilled out of the bar . . . along with several lurching, singing men, among them that horrid Mr. Simms from the train.

"You can see it's like I said, ma'am."

Kate pivoted back around to look up at the stranger in front of her. "I was passing by there," he said, "heading for the general store, when I heard them talking about what a fine figure you cut in that green dress. They aim to see what's under it. So, the way I see it, the choice is yours. You can come with me. Or you can wait here for them and their . . . tender mercies."

His words froze her insides. The way she saw it, what he offered her wasn't salvation, but a choice between death sentences. Finally, she found her voice. "How do I know that you're not . . . just as bad?"

That got a humorless chuckle from him. "Well, I don't guess you do. All I can tell you is . . . I didn't have to come back. But I did."

Kate realized that was true enough, but still . . . "Why would you do that? You don't even know me."

"I have my reasons," he said. And that was all.

Not the least bit comforted, Kate could only stare up at him. Until a horrible thought occurred to her. "Are you the law?" she blurted out. "Am I under arrest for loitering? I saw the signs about not—"

"I'm not the law." With that, he leaned over and took hold of her arm. His hand on her arm, even through her clothing, was warm . . . but his grip was unyielding. Kate tensed, wanting to pull away, but sensed that if she tried, he'd only grip her harder. Then, as he hauled her to her feet, still holding on to her, but bending over to pick up her much-maligned knapsack, he asked, "Is this box yours?"

Kate took the knapsack from him and clutched it to her heart as if it offered protection. She then looked back down at her perch, the box he'd just asked her about. "No, it's not mine. Well, yes, I guess it is. I mean, it was just sitting there."

Sliding his hand down to her elbow, he bent again to pick up the box. Straightening up to tower over her, he looked into her eyes. "Now, I take it you're of a mind to accompany me, right? You won't be screaming or anything?"

Kate knew she ought to, but she thought about the drunks over by the saloon . . . and weighed their intent against this man's hand on her. She hated it, but the truth was . . . right now she had to trust somebody. And as he said, he hadn't had to come back for her. She made her decision. "I won't be screaming. But just so we both know, I'm coming with you only because I don't have any choice."

He nodded, his dark eyes sparking with some emotion. "Fair enough," was all he said as, still holding on to her, he set them in motion, away from the crowds and the drunks on Summit Street. And toward the crowds of families out at Walnut Creek camp.

Kate breathed a little easier for that, having already figured that was where the decent folks were. Decent folks who wouldn't let a man harm a woman, folks who would come to her aid. And besides, maybe she could still find the Jacobs family once they got out there. "What are you going to do with me?" she asked.

That stopped him. "*Do* with you?" He stared down at her, his expression that of dispassionate granite. Kate had all she could do not to cringe. Then, tugging on her arm, he hauled them out of the flow of the foot traffic on the walking path where they'd been, and said, his voice low, "What exactly *do* you think I'm going to do with you?"

Kate's heart knocked against her breastbone. Too afraid

to speak, she looked up at him, not feeling any more safe for realizing that despite her height, she barely came to his shoulder. Finally, she managed to say, "I . . . I don't really know. Like I don't know where exactly you're taking me. Or what your intentions are when you get there. Or even who you are. And I think, under the circumstances, I have the right to know those things. Or to scream for help."

A huff of breath left him. He shook his head and kept on walking with her. "All right. Fair enough. I'm taking you to my wagon, where three kids are waiting. My intentions are to make a proposal to you. And my name is Cole Youngblood."

When he said his name, Kate forgot about the wagon, the kids, and the proposal part. *Cole Youngblood?* Her blood ran cold. *Mr. Talmidge's hired killer.* Servant talk below stairs had spread this man's reputation, along with those of the other killers their employer hired from time to time. But especially of this man. Even back East, chilling tales were told of his feats and exploits. And now, here he was, holding on to her arm and leading her away into the night.

Stiff with fear, yet still marching along at the hired killer's side, Kate's desperately plunging thoughts worked in circles around themselves. What should she do? Jerk her arm out of his grip and run away? He'd only catch her. Besides, where could she run, if she did get away? To the sheriff—who had his hands full, along with the army of cavalry sent in by the president, with keeping order among ten thousand people bloating his small town? How accommodating would he be for one lone woman?

Not at all, Kate realized. But finally, her thoughts began to sort themselves out, unraveling enough to become logical and thus calm her some. *This gunslinger doesn't know who I am. Or I'd already be dead. He could have shot me out there by that tree, off alone like I was. But he didn't. So maybe Mr. Talmidge hired another of his paid killers to come after me. And not this man.* Which meant that maybe the safest place for her was, unbelievably enough, with him.

Especially when the real hired killer came looking for her.
And she knew one would.

So, she was thinking, if she stuck by Cole Youngblood
now and got to know him, maybe even became useful to
him in some way—she shied away from thinking in what
way—then maybe he could come to respect her. And if
that happened, then she could take him into her confidence,
tell him what had really happened. Why, he might even
take her side and help her, when the time came. It sounded
crazy, she knew, but really . . . why not? He'd stepped in
now, this evening, to help her. Or so he'd said. She still
didn't know yet if he was telling the truth.

Kate glanced over at Cole Youngblood. Could she trust
him? Did a hired killer have a heart? And what could he
really want from her? For that matter, what did she have
to offer him? She knew. Only herself. But she wasn't about
to be offering herself to a man, any man, anytime soon.
Maybe not ever again. Not that he'd want her, whether she
wanted him or not. Because she was carrying another man's
child. Sudden anger swelled Kate's heart. *So what am I
supposed to do? Continue to be pulled around by the hand
by every man who takes a notion that he needs me? But
only until he's done with me and decides to do away with
me?*

Sure, she *could* allow that to keep happening. Or she
could put a stop to it and start living her life on her own
terms. Wasn't that the notion that had gotten her this far?
Yes, it was. And so she would. She didn't know what this
hired killer wanted with her—something about kids and a
wagon and a proposal—but one thing she did know was,
no matter what it turned out to be . . . it'd be on her terms.
Because, push come to shove, she could just walk away.
Nobody had her tied up in his bedroom right now. Or
would ever again. Because she was a free woman. And a
free woman she would remain.

There. Now she felt better . . . even being pulled along
by a man who, as the legends had it, had ice water running
through his veins. Again she glanced over at him, furtively

noting now—against her will—just how handsome a man he was. Dark eyes and hair, high cheekbones, clean-shaven, a full pleasing mouth. *Well, handsome he may be,* Kate fumed, *but that doesn't change a thing.* Mr. Talmidge was a handsome man, too—and it hadn't stopped him from being heartlessly cruel.

Just then, Kate stumbled and pitched forward over a huge exposed rock hidden in the grassy edge of the wagon path. Cole Youngblood saved her from falling by whipping an arm around her waist and steadying her against his side. "Whoa, there. Easy. Watch your step."

"I'm fine," was Kate's terse answer as she shrugged out of his embrace and stepped back, away from the feel of the man's hard-muscled body against hers. Then she just stood there . . . scared yet defiant, her senses alert to the growing yet dispassionate clanking and groaning of the big wagons now passing by within mere feet of where she stood. Alert to the sweating scent of the plodding teams of mules hitched to the schooners. Alert to the cramped closeness of the hungering humanity flowing around her like a strong wind current. And . . . alert to the forbidding presence of the hired killer facing her.

Who narrowed his eyes, considering her as if she were some curiosity he couldn't figure out. Then he shrugged. "You don't look fine, but if you say you are . . . then, fine." Without another word, he turned and left her there. Along with the hundreds of other folks sharing the path with them and intent on the same destination, he walked on toward the tree-sheltered camp.

That surprised Kate . . . that he'd left her standing there. She was free to go. She truly was. She didn't have to follow him. He wasn't making her do so, that much was plain. She looked back toward town. Remembered the drunks. And pivoted to see Cole Youngblood's retreating figure being swallowed up by the crowd. Her mouth quirked as she considered the hard realities, the tough choices, that were her life. But again she did the sensible thing, the only thing she could.

Clutching her knapsack under an arm and holding up her skirt's hem, she took off after him, finally catching up to him and slowing down to a walk at his side. For his part, he said or did nothing to acknowledge her presence, just kept walking. That was fine with her. She'd learned her lesson. Being too much in her own thoughts right now, when she needed instead to be minding her feet, could have her misstepping again and maybe pitching herself into the muddy ditch to her left. Which meant he'd think he had to help her out. Which meant . . . he'd have to put his hands on her again.

That thought alone had Kate concentrating on the moment, on her surroundings. And suddenly marveling at the sights and sounds. Not two minutes ago, this people-choked path had seemed overwhelming to her, had made her fear being swept away. But now she pronounced it wonderful and exciting. It was true, she realized, feeling her spirits lift. For, even at this early evening hour, the narrow road she trod—one still muddy from a recent rainstorm, as evidenced by the downed branches that littered the ground— was clogged with an endless parade of would-be settlers in white-canvased wagons, all making their way out to Walnut Creek and the camp there.

Despite herself, her uncertainties, and even her fears, Kate found herself suddenly invigorated by all the hustle and bustle around her. Amazing. A most wonderful sight to see. Uplifting. Finally she recaptured the sense of something outside herself, of an event bigger than her problems. An event that could absorb all these people, a land that could hold them all. A land that was to be her salvation. She must never lose sight of that, she warned herself. Must always remember that.

Just then, the temporary settlement finally came into view, began to take shape, to sort itself out into clusters of campers. The sight of so many families prompted Kate to speak the one thought uppermost in her mind, the one that had nagged her all the way out here.

"Those children you mentioned." He looked over at her,

his hard-eyed gaze like a hawk's. She swallowed, but managed, "Are they . . . yours?"

He shook his head no. "My sister's."

"Oh. Then she's here with them?" Everything would probably be okay if another woman was with him.

"No. She's dead. Same as her husband."

Comfort fled from Kate, at the same time that a rawboned, skinny dog out on the wagon path suddenly yelped, drawing Kate's attention, as he shied away from the massive rolling wheels of a particularly large schooner. Unharmed and unbidden, the yellow dog fell into step with Kate and nudged her hand with his wet nose until she let go of her skirt and patted its head absently. She then glanced up at the no-nonsense man striding along at her side. "I'm sorry about your kin."

He nodded his acknowledgment of her condolences, but didn't say anything. Kate swallowed, not so easy to do with her throat constricting. This Cole Youngblood was a difficult man to talk to. How was she ever going to get into his confidences?

"What's your name?"

Kate jumped, felt her heart do the same. Before she could think better of the impulse, she answered. "Kate Chandler."

He stopped, turned to her. Folks bumped into them, finally moved around them. At her side, the hound dog stopped, too, and sat down. Kate spared it a glance before meeting Cole Youngblood's gaze. The man's expression could have been chiseled from marble. "Chandler? Not Candless?"

"No. Not Candless. Chandler. Kate Chandler," she was forced to repeat, even though she already realized her mistake. With fear running amok inside her, she reminded herself that despite all her rationalizations to the contrary, he could still be the very killer sent to end her life. She needed to remember that. His reaction to her name told her that he was most likely on the trail of someone. But maybe only someone who'd cheated him at cards, for all she knew. Not that she believed that for a moment . . . given the way he was silently watching her even now.

His somber gaze considered her face, her expression, from all angles. "Where'd you come here from?"

More on her toes now mentally, Kate said, "Kentucky." It was true. She'd had to change trains in Kentucky to get here to Arkansas City.

"Where in Kentucky?"

Kate blinked. *Now, where in tarnation had that train station been?* Then it came to her. She blurted it out, along with a little white lie. "Russellville. I have family there. An aunt and an uncle."

Again he looked her up and down . . . in much the same way an undertaker would size up someone for a coffin. "What's a woman like you doing here by yourself?"

Kate swallowed, felt a trickle of sweat run down her spine. "Same as everyone else. I'm here to make the land run."

His dark eyebrows rose. "The land run? A woman alone?"

Kate's temper surged to the fore—which instantly pleased and comforted her. She'd feared she'd be cowed forever. But apparently not. "Yes, Mr. Youngblood. A woman alone. What's wrong with that?"

His expression changed, became mocking. "You tell me. You were the one sitting on a box and crying."

Kate felt her face heat up. Her chin notched up. "Instead, Mr. Youngblood, why don't you tell me what *you're* doing here?"

"Family business."

And Kate knew somehow that's all he would say about it. But it was fine with her. She didn't intend to answer any more of his questions, either. Besides that, she was nearly out of breath from scooting along beside him. But if he noticed her breathing hard, he didn't care because he again took her arm and set them off along the crowded path. Kate grabbed up her skirt and again had to hop over a rock big enough to trip her. The skinny yellow dog bounded effortlessly over it.

In another few moments, they reached the cover of a stand of black willow and river birch at the creek bottom. Low, overhanging branches further lengthened the evening shadows around them. Lanterns winked on in some of the near wagons. Men gathered in knots, maps spread out before them. Children ran among the wagons and between the different campsites, laughing and hooting. Women chatted over campfires as they tended babies and cook pots.

But still, Cole Youngblood walked on with her. As she passed by the families, Kate expected to feel comforted by their relative closeness. But the feeling didn't come. How could it . . . with Cole Youngblood being even closer?

As if he read her thoughts, felt her discomfort, the man stopped and faced her. The yellow hound dog stopped with them. It lay down and rested its large head on its front paws. Kate looked around and saw they were now standing off to one edge of the congested camp under a knot of sycamores, isolated somehow in the forest of humanity around them. She then met the gunslinger's cold gaze . . . and refilled her lungs with deep breaths of courage. The good Lord alone knew what would happen now. With no choice but to wait for the man in front of her to speak, Kate renewed her grip on her knapsack, shifted her weight . . . and waited.

"You need to know," he stated abruptly, "that it was no mistake I found you just now. I've been looking for you off and on for most of the afternoon."

A jet of fear chased down Kate's spine. In her mind, there was only one reason why Cole Youngblood would be looking for her. "You were . . . looking for me? Why?"

Grimacing, as if the answer to her question didn't come easily to him, he yanked off his Stetson and hit it against his denim-covered thigh, knocking a dust cloud loose from the hat. Even in the long shadows, Kate could see the red line striping his broad forehead where the hat's band had pressed tightly against his skin. Resettling his hat on his head, he finally said, "Because of the fact that you *are* here alone."

Kate's heart leaped. She thought of the baby she carried. She wasn't alone. But out loud, and forcing calm on herself, she said, "Yes. I'm alone."

"And you're here for some land."

A sense of wonder, and no small amount of relief, washed over her. *He truly doesn't know who I am.* "I've said as much, yes."

"And you have no way of getting it."

Sudden vexation—*Why is everyone so all-fired determined to point that out to me?*—caused her to burst out, "Mr. Youngblood, I don't see how any of this is your bus—"

"I've made it my business, Miss Chandler." Then his eyes narrowed as he looked her up and down consideringly. "How old are you? You don't look like much more than a schoolgirl."

Kate bristled. "My age has nothing to do with—"

"It does. The Homestead Act states you have to be twenty-one to claim land. And you have to sign that it's so. Are you twenty-one?"

Shock widened her eyes. "That's not true. I would have heard that by now. You're making that up, Mr. Youngblood."

His features set in hard lines. "I don't make things up, Miss Chandler. If you'd gone to the land office today to register for the run, anyone there would have told you the same. You have to be married, if you're not of legal age. Or the head of a household. Now, are you any of those?"

Again, Kate thought of her fatherless child, of her unmarried state. And of her youth. But still, pride had her wanting to lie to this man, although she realized that it would make no difference. He had nothing to do with the truths of her life. Or the death of her dream of freedom, her salvation. Sudden despair tugged her mouth down at the corners. What was she going to do now? What *could* she do? "No," she heard herself say around a sniff of gathering emotion. "I'm none of those things."

"I didn't think so." His quiet words and his soothing tone of voice lulled Kate, softened her into not resisting when he tucked a finger under her chin and raised her head until she peered into his eyes. Some emotion she couldn't name edged his dark gaze as he said, "I'll make the run for you."

Chapter Three

The merest gust of wind could have knocked Kate over. Her heart stumbled, as did her feet when he let go of her chin and stepped back. She clutched at her knapsack as she righted herself. "*You'll* make the run for me? Why would you do that?"

He shrugged, all business now. "Because you're a woman. And there's something I want in return from you."

Outrage combined with abject shame—yes, she knew she'd been used cruelly and unfairly by Mr. Talmidge, and in her heart . . . there was that shame . . . and the fear that others could see on her the dirt of her degradation—burst through Kate like a liquid fire and had her lashing out, aiming for his hateful face with her open palm.

With lightning-quick reflexes, Cole Youngblood caught her wrist in a grip so strong that the shock of contact rocked Kate's shoulder joint and ricocheted through her body. From the corner of her eye, she could see the dog come to its feet. A low growl rumbled from the depths of its chest.

"Whoa there, ma'am. Not that," the gunslinger assured her. "You've no cause to hit me. Maybe I said it wrong. Because what I'm proposing is a business arrangement between me and you, regarding my sister's kids. And nothing else. Are you hearing me?"

Her heart hammering, the tears only moments away, Kate was still able to nod that she had heard him. A couple of men passing by only glanced curiously their way before going on about their business.

Cole Youngblood eyed the men, too, and then looked down at her, keeping his voice low. "I'm going to let go of your hand now. Don't try that again. You understand?"

Kate locked gazes with him. The hard, black glitter of

his eyes reinforced his words. He meant what he said. Again, she nodded that she understood.

Finally, he released her arm. Swallowing hard, Kate found she couldn't look away from the gunslinger's set jaw and dark eyes, even as she rubbed at her aching wrist. The stray dog chose that moment to sit down again at her feet. Finally Kate found her voice. "I'm sorry if I misunderstood. What . . . what about your sister's kids?"

The man's expression shadowed, as if due to a passing pain. Then Kate remembered . . . earlier he'd said his sister had passed on. Despite herself, Kate felt bad for speaking so abruptly. After all, he'd suffered a loss, too, same as the children. But when he spoke, no apparent emotion tinged his voice. "The kids lost both their folks in the last two weeks. And now, they . . . well, they need something more than I can offer them. A home, I suppose."

Kate nodded. "Yes. Children do need a home." She knew that feeling. This wasn't the first time in her life that she'd been adrift. In her mind's eye, she saw herself at the age of twelve, saw her parents being robbed and killed by street thugs. Even now the fear and helplessness she'd felt then as she'd hidden in an alley unsettled her. It was then, alone and vulnerable, that she'd gone to work for the Talmidges.

Returning to the present, Kate said, "My heart goes out to those children, Mr. Youngblood. But what exactly is it you want from me? This . . . business arrangement you spoke of?"

His expression never changed. "I'm getting to that. It's a proposal of sorts, I suppose you'd call it."

"A . . . proposal?" Kate gulped out. "Of sorts?" Surely this feared and respected gunslinger wasn't asking her to marry him on the first day he met her. Then she remembered what he'd said only a minute ago. About the kids needing a home. She put her fingers to her mouth and stared at him. *Oh, no.* Lowering her hand, she ventured, "And you think that in this home those kids need . . . that *I* should be their mother?"

He frowned as he looked her up and down. Kate had the distinct impression that she'd been judged and found lacking. He quickly confirmed that for her with a terse, "No."

Stung despite herself, and acutely aware of her own state of impending motherhood, she stiffened. "Then just what is it you're asking of me, Mr. Youngblood?"

Looking suddenly unsure of himself—to Kate's surprise—he looked everywhere but at her, even going so far as to nod at a group of older women who spoke respectfully to him as they passed by. Finally he met Kate's eyes. "I've got a cousin. A female cousin with a family of her own. She lives close by here in Kansas. I need to find her and get her to take my sister's kids. But I can't do that in any timely manner with the three of them tagging along."

Kate nodded, not seeing a proposal in his words. "I guess not."

He nodded back at her and went on. "My final aim is to settle them permanently with her. But for now, until I find her—"

"Wait," Kate blurted out, holding up a hand to stop him. She was surprised that she'd dared to interrupt him. But somehow, since he needed a favor from her and they were talking about kids and family, he didn't seem so fearsome. Maybe that had given her courage. "You said *find* your cousin. You don't know where in Kansas she is?"

His expression hardened. "No. Had no need to until now. But until I *do* find her, Miss Chandler—and I *will*—I need you."

His statement prompted Kate to take a step back. "I see." But she didn't. "You need me to do what, Mr. Youngblood?"

Mr. Youngblood swiped a hand over his mouth . . . and mumbled something under his breath. Finally, he said, "To keep the kids with you out at your claim."

Kate stiffened, shook her head. "Oh, no. I couldn't possibly—"

It was his turn to hold a hand up, to stop her protest.

"Only for as long as it takes me to find my cousin. In exchange, remember, I'm offering to make the run for you. And after that, the kids would be with you only until I find . . . her."

The way he said *her* caused Kate to have misgivings. "You do know her name, this cousin of yours, don't you, Mr. Youngblood?"

The look he gave her was probably the same one he'd have on his face if he slipped in manure. "It'll come to me."

He didn't know her name. Kate put a hand to her chest. "Dear heavens, Mr. Youngblood."

"I said it'll come to me. And I will find her. And you won't have the kids for long."

Kate nodded, more than willing to agree. "I believe you. But . . . how do you know she'll take them?"

Still frowning, he put his hands to his waist. "You're just full of questions, aren't you?"

Kate straightened up to her full height, still woefully short of his. "I believe I have every right to be, Mr. Youngblood. After all, I'll be the one with the children in my keep once you ride off."

Something sparked in his eyes. Kate thought about her words. Had she just agreed to his proposal? Her eyes widened . . . she must have. Because he went right on talking.

"They're not bad kids. Hardly any trouble at all. And I'd pay you in advance for your time and your trouble. I'll even throw in a wagon, two mule teams, and enough lumber and tools to build yourself a decent cabin."

A cabin? Kate's eyes widened.

A chuckle from the gunslinger told her he'd correctly interpreted her expression. "You hadn't thought about that, had you? Once you get the land, Miss Chandler, you still need a home on it."

"I know that, Mr. Youngblood," she fussed, having no idea at all how to go about building a cabin. But still, her heart leapt with joy. If she said yes to this man, he'd make the run for her, and her dream of life on her own would come true. And if she said no? Well, she'd get her wooden box back, and nothing more. Put like that, the decision seemed obvious.

But Kate thought she needed to know a bit more before committing herself. "Even as desperate as you know I am, Mr. Youngblood, tell me why I should say yes. Because it seems to me that . . . in your line of work . . . you, um, could get yourself killed. And then where would I be?"

His eyebrows slowly rose, his gaze seemed to penetrate hers. "In *my* line of work, Miss Chandler? Then you've heard my name before, and know what my reputation is?"

Realizing what she'd just revealed, Kate's mouth dried, her throat threatened to close. There it was. The one reason she should say no to him. But if she did have his sister's children with her . . . wouldn't he be more inclined to see that she was safe? To see that no gunman hired by Mr. Talmidge would be successful? Pleased with her cleverness, Kate admitted a piece of her truth. "Yes, I do know your reputation. But I suspect just about everyone else around here does, too."

His slash of a grin did nothing to settle Kate's stomach.

"You're right. So where you would be . . . if I got myself killed. First off, I won't get myself killed. I've been tracking men for fourteen years and I'm still here. But let's say I did, Miss Chandler. You'd be sitting pretty on your own land. In your own cabin. With mules, a wagon, and a lot of money. That's where."

"True." Protectively, she folded her arms under her bosom. "But I'd also have three children to raise. That's a big undertaking for a woman alone, Mr. Youngblood. Now, I love children. But I—"

"Then, knowing my reputation, how I make my living, would you be the first to agree that I have no business with three kids, Miss Chandler?"

He had her there. "Well, yes. I suppose. But—"

"So all you'd be out is a little bit of your time. Because after I find my cousin, I'll be back for the kids. And then we'll all be gone. Forever. And you'll still have your land."

"That I would." But there was another thing Kate wanted clarified. And she didn't quite know how to ask . . . without getting herself shot. Screwing up her courage, she decided to forge ahead with it. But as she spoke, her gaze insisted on skittering away from his. "I need to know, Mr. Youngblood, purely for accounting purposes, just, um, how much money we're talking about. For me to keep the children."

A muscle tic in the man's jaw worked furiously. "Enough so that you'd not want for anything. For a long time."

Kate's breath left her in a rush. His offer was so tempting. She bit her bottom lip, wanting to accept, yet hesitating. She peered down at the rawboned hound still sitting there. Absently, she rubbed his velvety ears and got a big sloppy grin from him for her efforts. And found herself grinning right back.

Just then, the gunslinger spoke again, capturing Kate's attention away from the dog. "For someone with no means of fixing herself a bed for the night, ma'am, I'd think you'd jump at the chance of such help as I'm offering you."

Well, there it was. "You're right. All right. I'm listening."

"That's more like it." Then he looked all around them, at the folks fixing their suppers, at the dog—eyed it critically—and finally settled his gaze on her. "I stopped us here because I don't want the kids to—well, they don't know my thoughts yet."

Kate frowned. "Your thoughts?"

"My aim to leave."

"I see. Is there a reason why you haven't told them?"

He shrugged. "I didn't see any need to, until I found you."

"You mean until I *agreed*, don't you?"

He grinned at her . . . probably the same one he had on his face a second before he pulled the trigger. "Both. And have you agreed? Because the kids are over at the wagon by themselves."

A sudden rush of concern had Kate's hand to her bosom.

"By themselves? No one's looking after them?" She did recall seeing children in his wagon this afternoon when his horses had reared and startled her.

Mr. Youngblood scowled at her. "I'm not a fool, Miss Chandler. I've asked some people to peek in on them. But mostly, Joey is seeing after them."

Wanting that scowl off the man's face, Kate resorted to pleasantries. "I see. Who's Joey?"

The gunslinger's expression smoothed out, relieving Kate greatly. "He's my nephew. And the oldest of the three."

"Oh." Kate nodded, a tentative smile on her face. "How old is he?"

"Seven."

Her smile fled. She couldn't believe this. And told him so. "Joey is the oldest at seven, and he's watching two younger children—alone, in the dark, in a strange camp with all sorts of folks wandering the area? Mr. Youngblood, don't you realize that anything could happen to them?"

Mr. Youngblood's face darkened more quickly than the falling night. "I said other folks are looking in on them. People around there know who I am, and no one is going to mess with those kids. Besides, Joey's nearly a man. He'll see to his brother and sister."

Unconvinced—especially about any seven-year-old boy being almost a man—Kate frowned, but wisely chose to say nothing further. Because she really didn't relish the thought of pushing this man any farther. Just thinking about who he was set her knees to knocking and her heart to hammering. Why, she wasn't even sure she'd have the courage to tell him no . . . if that was her answer.

"Do we have a deal, Miss Chandler?"

Kate's heart thumped dully in her chest. "I just don't know, Mr. Youngblood. This is an awfully big step. I mean, three little children. Why, anything could happen to one of them. Something awful. And then when you came back, and found out, you'd shoot me."

He stiffened, looking insulted. "I wouldn't shoot a—"

He cut off his own words, clamped his lips together, and stared down at her, looking her up and down. Finally he said, "I wouldn't shoot you, Miss Chandler."

Kate didn't believe him for a minute. But she kept that to herself. "I'm sorry if I spoke in haste. I just . . . well, I just don't know what to say. About any of this, Mr. Youngblood. I can't see how—"

"Let me tell you how I see it. I leave the kids here with you, go make the run, stake your claim, register it, and then come back here to get all of you. Then, we'll—"

"Wait. That means the land will be registered in your name. Not mine. And another thing, how do I know you'll even bother to make the run? How do I know you won't just ride off, never to be seen again?"

Kate watched in fearful wonderment the effects of her apparently ill-advised words. Cole Youngblood drew up like he was getting ready to retreat from his own words about not shooting a woman. The dog drew up, too, standing and eyeing the gunslinger, flattening its floppy ears against its scruffy head.

When Cole Youngblood spoke, it was in the clipped, quiet tones that bespoke an underlying honor and decency. "I can't do anything about the land laws. But I know myself, Miss Chandler. I'll come back for those kids. They're the only thing in my life I care about, and I'm trying to do what's right by them."

Chastised, and rightly so, with her face heating up considerably, Kate again looked at her booted feet and then back up at him, seeing him now as a human being with emotions and not just a killer with a gun. "I apologize, Mr. Youngblood. Go on with what you were saying."

But he didn't. The dog sat down and perked his ears up, looking from Kate to Cole Youngblood and back to her, as if he were having trouble following along. When the hired gun still didn't say anything, Kate felt worse for her unthinking remarks and prompted, "You were coming back to me and the kids."

His eyebrows rose. But finally, he said, "Right. You and

the kids. I'll come back here after the run to get all of you, and—"

"Why can't we just go with you in your wagon to make the run? I didn't come this far, Mr. Youngblood, to sit back now and watch. And besides, you don't know what I'm looking for in a claim."

His brow furrowed. "You're staying here, like I said. The run'll be too dangerous for a woman and kids, even in a wagon. You can just tell me what and where you're hoping to settle, and—"

"Too dangerous? Plenty of whole families are making the run together."

"Yeah, and plenty of whole families will be too slow to get a claim. And they may even get themselves rattled to death in those heavy wagons, for all their effort. Besides, even if that wasn't so, it'd be too rough on Lydia. She's only three."

Kate's mouth opened, she stiffened. "Lydia's only three?" she all but whispered, so appalled was she. "Sakes alive, Mr. Youngblood, we've been standing here talking while there are babies out there somewhere alone? You show me to them right now."

The dog came to his feet again and barked his agreement.

Not waiting for the fearsome gunslinger, Kate made an about-face and stalked off determinedly in the direction of the gathered wagons. The dog followed her.

"Miss Chandler?"

She whirled around, causing the loping dog to run into her. He skittered back on his haunches and righted himself with only a slight loss of canine dignity. With one hand at her waist and the other one on the dog's head, Kate faced her fears, her worst nightmare . . . and Cole Youngblood. "Yes?"

"Does this mean we have an agreement?" If he'd been anyone else, he would have looked ridiculous to her, standing there all big and tall and . . . clutching that silly box she'd been sitting on earlier. But he was who he was. And he didn't look silly at all. Especially not when he pointed off to his left and said, "Because if we do, the wagon's this way."

Huffing out an agitated breath, she and the dog stalked back to him and turned with him to his left. Riding a wave of righteous indignation that the man would be so callous as to leave three small children alone at dark, no matter who was keeping an eye on them, she mentally harangued him while following a step behind him as he led the way. The dog came in a close third behind her.

"I will admit, Mr. Youngblood," she said to his back when she could no longer hold her tongue, "that you definitely need help with those children. *And* I agree that they'd be better off with me while you roam Kansas. But I think I should have some sort of pledge, or commitment, on your part that will give our arrangement some standing with the law during your absence. Just in case. I mean, the land *will* be in your name, and there *are* three children involved. And I'm not their mother or even kin to them, like you are. So, if something did happen to you, then the law could take—"

He stopped abruptly. Kate ran into his back. The dog ran into her legs. Kate grabbed at the tall man in front of her for support, and garnered for herself a handful of cotton shirt covering warm, solid male. The unaccustomed feel of him, combined with the heady scent of his masculinity, brought a sharp stab of awareness to her, an awareness she had no interest in feeling. Mr. Talmidge had seen to that. She let go of Cole Youngblood as if he were a hot skillet.

When he pivoted around and stood staring down at her, looking like a hawk that had spotted its evening's supper, she took a step back. So did the dog. And yet Kate still felt the heat of Cole Youngblood's body.

"I hadn't thought about what you just said. But I suppose you're right. The law could take the land and the kids from you. So what do you have in mind?"

She had no idea. As a distraction, one that would give her time to think, she looked at the dog, who was furiously scratching at fleas and ignoring her. But Cole Youngblood wasn't. With the man's attention trained on her so keenly, she suddenly became aware of the feel of her toes in her stockings and boots. Became aware of the long pin that secured her straw hat to her hair. Became aware of the flushed heat of her blood coursing through her veins. She was desperate for an end to his intense scrutiny.

She also was desperate not to think about why she was accepting this man's proposal, a man she knew only as a fabled gunslinger, when only a few weeks ago she'd escaped the evil man he worked for. When even now she carried that man's baby in her womb. And wanted nothing to do with another man ever. But even so, with no other options open to her—as he'd just gone to great lengths to point out to her—she blurted out the first thing that came to her, the first thing that seemed to her to be binding. "We could get married."

Cole stiffened, much as if he'd just felt the cold steel of a gun barrel poking into his back. *Married?* He wasn't marrying anybody. Ever. Still, he couldn't stop himself from looking her up and down. And being well pleased with what he saw, from her thick, silk-black hair . . . to her glittering green eyes . . . to her curvy woman's body. And being even more pleased when he imagined her under him, naked and moaning out his name.

Incensed by his strong and unexpected attraction to the rumpled, defiant woman-child standing before him, he adopted a fierce tone. "Miss Chandler, this isn't about getting married."

Wide-eyed, her voice shaking, she nevertheless stood her ground. "I understand that," she said. "And I only proposed it as a legal, in-name-only arrangement. Because, believe me, Mr. Youngblood, I have no taste for being tied to a man. Any man. Now or ever."

Now that's a mighty strange thing for such a young woman to say, was Cole's distracting thought . . . when he blinked and realized that she'd picked up her skirts as if she meant to walk away. Even the hound dog stood up with her. "Well, if you can't, you can't," she was saying. "But I would need something that binding if you expect me to take on three children not my own, and not knowing when or if you'd ever come back—"

Cole's raised hand cut off her words. "Now, hold on a minute, Miss Chandler." He couldn't believe this opportunity was slipping away so quickly. "Give a man time to think. There might be another way."

She tilted her head, as if considering his words, and finally relaxed her grip on her green skirt. The dog sat down on his haunches, his floppy ears perked up the slightest bit as he too stared at Cole. "Another way?" she repeated. "All right. I'm willing to listen."

"Good." Surprised at the depth of his relief, Cole found that all he could do was stand there and stare back at her. Because her marriage proposal was perfectly logical. And he had no other suggestions. All he knew was what he couldn't tell her, that he couldn't get married—to her or to anyone else. Not in his line of work. Not when it was too late, when killing for a living had taken from his heart everything good and fine. When hiring out his gun had tainted his soul with the blood of too many dead men .... men he'd killed.

But the worst part was, all too soon his soul would be forfeit. Because all too soon, it would be tainted again ... with the blood of a woman. Cole scowled at his thoughts, at the depths of the badness in him. He couldn't forgive himself for taking on this job, despite knowing that he'd had no other practical choices left to him, since he needed the money to feed and house three little kids. But his reason didn't matter, not even to himself. He'd still taken the work. He shook his head, knowing it would be too late for him to be saved once he carried out his mission.

"No? Your distaste for my idea is plain to see. Good evening to you, sir."

Miss Chandler's words snapped Cole back to the moment. She was grabbing up her skirts again. "While you've been standing there trying to think of a way around all this," she went on, "I've been hoping you'd realized that if we *were* married, the land would be registered in my name as well as yours. I'm just thinking to protect myself, Mr. Youngblood. Because I sure don't have any personal designs on you. But if you can't see the benefit to you of marrying me, well then, I'll just be on my way. So if you'll give me my . . . box . . ."

She held out her hand, to take the wooden crate from him. Cole stared at her hand, then at her face. And sudden realization dawned. She was exactly right. There were benefits to him. Big, practical benefits. He ran a hand over his mouth to keep a triumphant grin off his face. Her own words had trapped her. And freed him to take advantage of them . . . and her. "All right," he said, not handing over the box. "You're right. I'll marry you. I accept."

She met his words with wide eyes and silence. Then, surprised, she said, "You do? You will?"

"I just said I will." Before she could protest, he stalked over to her, took her arm, and turned her with him. "Now, come on with me back to the wagon, back to those kids you're so all-fired worried about."

Frowning at the unsettlingly pleasant tug he felt in his gut whenever he touched her, he wordlessly wove them through the maze of wagons in the gathering dark. And pretended he wasn't adjusting his gait to allow for her smaller steps. And that he wasn't thinking that if she was married to him, then not only was the land hers, but so were the kids. Permanently. Her marrying him, even in name only, legally tied her to Joey, Willy, and Lydia. Hell, once he married her, the kids would have that home and the new mother they needed and he wanted for them.

Which meant he could go off and live his life the way he always had, the way it had to be. Not only that, if he were married to her, he needn't go look for that cousin he didn't know the first thing about. Which meant that right here in the coming week, after the run, he could get on the trail of that thieving maid of Mr. Talmidge's. Because he'd still need the money for the kids. And for Miss Chandler. Cole glanced over at her, taking in her youth and innocence. And realized his chest had tightened. Married. Only a moment ago he'd told himself never. And now here he was, preparing to marry this innocent girl he didn't even know. All so he could rush off and kill some other woman he didn't know. For the money on her head.

All right, Cole fumed at his raging conscience, *I committed to the job. And I'll do it.* But, dammit, he had to get to it quickly, before the guilt over killing a woman, no matter what she'd done, ate him alive. He just couldn't spend any more time idly thinking about it. He needed to act, to do it—as soon as possible. That being so, he told himself now, he'd just find this Anne Candless, take care of . . . business, get the rest of the money from Mr. Talmidge, and bring it back to this young woman at his side. And then he'd move on. *Life sure as hell hasn't presented me too much in the way of good choices,* was Cole's next thought. Except maybe for this one, he conceded. Because marrying her was perfect.

It was also deceitful. He knew and understood that, so maybe he wasn't as far gone as he thought himself to be. He glanced again at his . . . soon-to-be wife out of the corner of his eye. And exhaled sharply, guiltily. She was a pawn in his game. And appeared to be as innocent and trusting a little thing as Lydia was. The truth was, Cole knew, he sure as hell wouldn't mind making Miss Kate Chandler his in more than name only. But he wouldn't. Hell, she wasn't that kind of woman. No, her kind would have to fancy herself in love with a man before she gave herself to him. And Cole didn't need that . . . some clinging wife pining after him, wanting him to be a real husband to her. No. Not for him.

Still, the unsavory aftertaste of his intentions toward her nagged at Cole—until he remembered that this marriage idea was hers. All he was doing was giving her everything she wanted, everything she'd asked for . . . the land, a home, money. Everything she'd asked for, and more . . .

meaning Willy, Joey, and Lydia. Another stab of guilt, this one for the kids, had Cole cursing himself and these trying circumstances. The more time he spent in the company of women and children, it seemed, the more he disliked himself, the more he questioned himself. And that wasn't good. A hired gun who doubted himself, who thought twice, would soon be a dead gunslinger.

And then what good would he be to them all? Because he didn't intend to abandon them, any of them, Kate Chandler included. Of course, he meant to bring money back to her and the kids on a regular basis, just as he had done for Charlotte. So nothing would change. Nothing in his life. Yet everything was already different, and Cole could no longer deny it. Because the silent girl at his side wasn't his sister. Far from it.

Narrowing his eyes at the slender, black-haired woman next to him, and feeling her tug on his masculinity, Cole purposely tried to find fault with her. She was too skinny for his taste. He liked buxom blondes who knew how to use their womanhood. The last thing he needed was some frail, dark, little thing who possessed no earthly notion of how she affected a man. How she made him want to crush her to him and kiss her and keep her safe. Like now . . . when her brow knitted with worries he could only guess at.

Which only highlighted for him that Kate Chandler was a stranger to him. A stranger who would soon be his wife.

Chapter Four

What have I gotten myself into? Kate stared mutely back at the three rumpled and wary children who peered at her from inside the crowded confines of a large schooner. With its heavy canvas cover pulled up and tied back to make the most of the cool evening breeze, the wagon hunkered in the midst of the crowded boomer camp, close to the rushing rain-swollen waters of Walnut Creek.

A flatbed wagon, apparently also belonging to Mr. Youngblood, was parked at an angle to the tongue of the schooner, forming an intimate V-shaped enclosure. Several yards away, and downwind, a knot of mules and a big roan-colored horse stood tied, remuda-style, to a rope strung between two young sycamores. A cookfire had been stoked to crackling life between the two wagons, but no supper pot bubbled over it. And darkness was rapidly descending.

Kate watched as the gunslinger set down her wooden crate and then faced the children. "Now, mind your manners and say hello to Miss Kate Chandler. She—"

"Hey, that's the lady our mules about killed." A dark-haired boy of about five years pointed to her, his face alight with recognition.

At Kate's side, Cole Youngblood stiffened. "They didn't nearly kill her, Willy," he said. "Now, listen to me, all of you. Miss Chandler is . . . joining us now. So, I want you to treat her nice and—"

"Is her our new mama?" A chubby-cheeked little waif of a girl with dark, tangled ringlets eyed Kate critically.

Kate's heart beat fast at the child's question. And even harder at Cole Youngblood's answer. "No. It's more like she's your . . ." He turned to her, imploring her mutely to help.

"Just call me Kate," she quickly said to the waiting children. "All my friends do." And then she made a determined effort not to look at the man beside her, whose black eyes she felt boring into her. Maybe he was thinking that she'd extended no such friendly invitation to him. And here he was going to marry her.

"We ain't your friends."

Kate gasped at the older boy's unfriendly bluntness. But Mr. Youngblood did more. Pointing a finger at the child, he warned, "You mind your manners, boy. Or I'll remind the seat of your pants of them."

Into the embarrassed silence, the younger boy, Willy, looked anxiously from his uncle to his older brother, telling him, "I want to be her friend, Joey."

Joey rounded on him. "Well, you can't, Willy. We don't know her. And we don't need her."

As Willy frowned at his brother's words, Kate wished she could crawl away somewhere, mortified and fearful that these children would never accept her. Just then, Willy brightened as another thought occurred to him. "Can we keep her dog, then, Joey? We need a dog."

My dog? Kate looked down at her side. The skinny yellow dog sat by her and was returning her stare. His tongue lolled cheerfully out the side of his mouth. "He's not my dog," she felt compelled to announce.

"What do you mean he's not your dog?"

Kate stared up at Cole and shook her head. "I mean he's not mine. I thought he was your dog. He was following you."

"That skinny, ugly thing?"

They stared at each other until the baby girl spoke, pouting. "I don't like dogs. I want a cat."

Cole opened his mouth to answer her, but it was Joey who replied. "You can't have no cat—nor no dog, Lydia. It ain't ours."

Lydia rounded on him. "I can so have it, Joey. You're not the papa. I can have it. And I can name it Kitty." She turned Kate and Cole's way. "I can so, huh, Uncle Cole?"

Again, Joey cut off his uncle's response. "You can't keep it. And you can't name no big ole skinny yellow dog Kitty, Lydia."

"Yes I can."

"No you can't."

"Yes I can."

"No you—"

"All right now, stop it. All of you!" And Cole Youngblood meant it, too, Kate knew. That was clear from the heightened color in his face . . . and the blood in his eye. "Not one more word from the lot of you. Especially you, Joey. Now here's the way things are. I'm marrying Miss Chandler. And then I'm making the run for her. After that, I'm going to settle all of you on her claim. And after that, I'm"—he cut his eyes over to Kate—"going to go find my cousin here in Kansas for you kids to live with."

An intense silence followed his words, broken only by the gurgling, splashing water of the creek and the skinny dog's whining yawn. Numbed by his bluntness with the children, Kate stared at Cole Youngblood.

"Any questions?" He put his large, square hands to his waist and stood with one knee bent. His fierce expression said any questions had better be on the subject at hand, too.

Willy had one. "Why can't we live with you and Miss Kate, Uncle Cole . . . if you'll be married and all?"

Kate's heart wrenched dangerously. *Poor, sweet babies.* There was no way they could understand this grown-up arrangement between her and their uncle. She might be marrying Cole Youngblood, but they would not be living together as man and wife. But for all the kids knew, their uncle was settling down with her and didn't want them with him.

Before Cole could answer, Lydia cut in plaintively. "I don't want me an' Kitty to live wif no cuzzin. I just want you an' Kate for my papa an' mama."

Cole opened his mouth to speak, but was again cut off by Joey's sharp words. "You don't want us. Nobody wants us. I wish we was dead, like Ma and Pa."

Willy looked shocked, as if he were afraid that just by Joey's having wished it, it would be so. "I don't want to die, Uncle Cole. I'm just a little kid."

Kate, like Cole, had been busy looking from Willy to Lydia to Joey, and then back again to Willy, whose last outburst reduced him and his sister to tears. Their older brother fought the trembling of his chin and gathered his siblings to him. He stared accusingly at Cole and Kate.

Cole Youngblood muttered his cursing assessment of the situation. And Kate stood rooted to the spot for what seemed an eternity. Adding to this pickle of a situation were the many unanswered questions between herself and Mr. Youngblood that kept her from telling the whole truth to the children. But she knew that these children needed comforting and reassurance right now. And they also needed their supper. The devil take the future. Having decided all that, she looked up at the gunslinger, even dared to lay a hand on his arm . . . and capture his dark-eyed attention. "Let me. Please."

He made a gesture toward the kids. "Please do."

So, with her heart thumping erratically, and uncertain of her reception, Kate approached the wagon. Reaching in, very much aware of how she'd want some stranger to treat her own child, she lifted out the little girl. Despite Joey's halfhearted attempt to maintain his hold on his sister, Kate took the child in her arms. The girl clung pathetically to Kate, wrapping her baby-chubby arms and legs around Kate's neck and waist.

Hushing Lydia's whimpers and rocking her from side to side, Kate held out an arm to Willy. He quickly scooted out of the wagon and flung his arms around Kate's hips, clinging to her every bit as fiercely as did his sister. Kate patted his narrow back with her hand and then smoothed her hand over his mop of black hair. Very nearly weighed down with the two children, she turned her gaze on Joey. He sat with his arms and legs crossed, his face a mask of mistrust. This one would be a battle.

Kate knew of no other way but to speak from her heart.

"I know all of this is hard for you, Joey—and for Willy and Lydia. But I'm not trying to take your place with them. And I'm not trying to take your mother's place, either. I can't do that, I know. I'm just hoping we can be friends. You see, your uncle and I . . . well, we came together because of our needs. He needs help with you, and I need someone to make the run for me. That's why we're getting married. And that's the only reason."

The older of the dark-haired boys, who held himself so rigidly, looked from her to his uncle and back at her. He raised his chin stubbornly, but interest flickered in his dark eyes.

Kate rushed on. "But we—your uncle and I—won't be . . . living together like your parents did, like real married folks. He'll get my land for me, and then move on—once you're settled with your cousin."

Joey didn't say anything, but bright tears flooded his eyes. Hoping she was getting through to him, Kate finished. "Now, I want you to know that right now nobody's going to make you do anything or go anywhere you don't want to. And nobody wants you dead, least of all your uncle. He's doing everything he can to see that you have a good life. And he deserves better from you than what you're giving him."

Joey's mouth worked furiously as he fought the tears. He gave a vicious swipe of his sleeve to his eyes. Kate wanted nothing more than to wrap her arms around him and tell him not to worry. But he didn't move, didn't respond to her or to her words. Kate nodded, smiled. "It's the best I can do, Joey." She had to content herself with the thought that she'd opened the door if he felt like walking through.

Then, thinking maybe if she enlisted Joey's help he might be more open to her, she turned to practical matters. "Now, I need you to help me get together fixings for some supper. We're all tired and hungry right now, Joey. And we're bound to say things we don't mean. But I promise you this—everything will look better in the morning."

Joey still didn't say or do anything for a moment or two. He just stared at her, his throat working convulsively. As the seconds ticked by, Kate felt Lydia rub her little button nose on her shoulder. Willy did the same with her skirt. Suddenly she became aware that Cole Youngblood had come to stand by her side. Without looking at her or saying a word, he put his arm around her shoulder. Kate swallowed hard around the lump of fear in her throat, telling herself his gesture was intended to show Joey that they were all standing together, rather than from some desire to be affectionate with her.

Finally, when Cole Youngblood spoke, it was to his nephew. "So, what do you think, Joey? You want to try things the lady's way? Or do you have a better plan?"

Kate looked up at Cole. He was grinning at his nephew. Feeling the warm weight of Cole's arm around her, and refusing to think how she felt about that, she looked back at Joey and added her smiling encouragement to him.

At long last, the boy sniffed and rubbed his sleeve under his nose. Adopting a fierce expression, he said, "I don't reckon I've got a better plan."

Relief brightened Kate's smile. "Good," she said cheerily. "Then I can count on you to help me? I'm going to need you, Joey."

"Yes, ma'am. I'll help you." He got up solemnly and stepped around bed rolls and heavy traveling chests to get to the back of the wagon.

Kate looked up at Cole. Not for anything was she going to remind him that he still had his arm around her. Keeping her voice down, she asked, "Does that child ever smile?"

Cole released her and took Lydia from her, saying, "I'll take her and Willy to wash up at the creek." With the little girl perched nonchalantly on his arm, Cole then answered Kate, his voice low enough not to be overheard by Joey. "Joey smile? Not that I've seen of late."

Feeling sorry for the little boy, Kate shook her head as she gently loosened Willy's arms from around her and handed him over to his uncle. "Then we'll have to work on that."

Cole took Willy's hand and turned to head toward the creek. Looking back over his shoulder, he winked at her. "Whatever you say . . . Kate."

Someone was shaking her shoulder. Kate went from dead asleep to instantly awake the next morning. At first, her heart pounding, her hands fisted around her covers, she couldn't remember where she was. But the sight of Cole Youngblood leaning over her in her bed in the big schooner refreshed her memory. Still, she had all she could do not to scream . . . and to remember that he wasn't Mr. Talmidge. And he wasn't here to hurt her. She hoped.

"Wake up, Kate. I've got some news for you," the gunslinger was saying. Removing his Stetson, he hunkered down beside her . . . and waited.

As Kate struggled to a sitting position, she belatedly remembered she was cradling Lydia's warm little body to her own. But barely disturbed, the girl muttered in her sleep and snuggled back into their nest of blankets while Kate slid to the end of their makeshift bed, as far away as she could, so as not to awaken the child with their talking. Then she spared a thought for the girl's brothers, assuming they still slept on in the other wagon, where Cole had also slept.

"What? What is it?" She rubbed at her eyes and shoved her heavy hair back over her shoulders. Not getting any answer, she looked up, marked the gunslinger's expression, and then looked down at herself.

Dear Lord. Not only was her hair hanging loosely down her back—a sight usually reserved for husbands—but she was also undressed, all but exposed from the waist up, wearing nothing but her cotton chemise. A sudden chill from the cool April-morning air washed over her bare skin, puckering her nipples under her thin garment. She quickly grabbed up a loose quilt and draped it around her, but too late to stop the hot flush that claimed her cheeks.

And apparently also too late to stop the hot, slow look

she was getting from Cole Youngblood. Kate sucked in a tortured breath and rushed to remind him of their arrangement. "I'll thank you to remember that our union is no more than a business deal, Mr. Youngblood—"

"You may as well call me Cole. Especially under these circumstances."

Kate stared at him, fearing he might decide to define what circumstances he meant. Their imminent marriage. Or his being in here now with her half-naked. She remembered that he had called her Kate last night, something she hadn't invited him to do. But she was going to marry him, so how could she protest? That left her with nothing to say but, "All right . . . Cole."

A slow grin claimed his features. And the air seemed to still around them. Maddeningly, he didn't say anything. And Kate couldn't. Not with him looking at her that way. His expression spoke of desire. For her. And it shamed her. "Please don't do that," she quietly asked, her gaze steady, despite the gathering tears. "Please don't look at me like that."

The man's expression turned quizzical. "Like what?"

Kate swallowed, felt the words stick in her throat. "Like . . . like you want me. I don't like it."

His expression darkened, asked a hundred questions. But what he said was, "You don't have to worry about me, Kate. I know our arrangement. I won't stray across any lines."

She nodded, her hand fluttering up to her temple to brush away her sleep-tangled hair. "Thank you."

"You're welcome," he said, even as he suddenly reached out and inexplicably crossed a line by capturing her hand, raising it to his mouth, and kissing her palm . . . warmly, tenderly. Before Kate could do much but try to tug it back, his gaze met hers . . . and locked, holding her there, wordless in the moment. "I just meant to reassure you, nothing more. Who hurt you, Kate? Someone did, I know it. I see it on your face. Who was it?"

She said nothing. For many reasons. Pride, for one.

Shame, for another. And because, finally, there was nothing she could say. Or wanted to say to him. She could only stare at him . . . and know he was who he was. And she was who she was. And wonder if one day their paths would cross . . . and he'd have a gun in his hand. One aimed at her heart. Because this man worked for Mr. Talmidge, who wanted her dead.

Just as suddenly as he'd taken it, Cole Youngblood relinquished her hand, which Kate instantly curled into her lap. He pulled himself to his feet and stood looking down at her. Sheer awareness raked his features, just as his hand did his jet-black hair. Sitting there, wrapped in a quilt and feeling the heat of his kiss searing her palm, Kate looked down, slowly shaking her head as she picked at a loose thread in the quilt's fan pattern.

"Kate?"

She looked up, but not directly at him. She couldn't quite manage to keep her gaze in one place.

"Kate, look at me."

She did. And took a deep, unsteady breath. His presence overpowered the cozy den of the wagon's covered interior. Big, dark, muscled, intent. Armed. He exuded raw masculinity that shrank the narrow space so that it seemed to Kate that only he and she existed in all the world. She found it difficult to breathe.

"You don't have to tell me a thing," he said, breaking the silence. "But I want you to know that you're safe with me. I won't hurt you. Or expect anything from you. And once we're married, my name will protect you." A shadow of an emotion flickered across his expression, and he added, "Even when I'm not around."

Kate nodded, thinking that much was true. He wouldn't be around. But she shied away from how she'd feel when that day came. Because she just didn't know, as surprising as that realization was to her. She should be relieved and glad, she knew that much. And she would be, she told herself. But looking up at him now, she felt the weight of his presence, of his protection, like a palpable thing in the space between them. Well, to imagine being without that . . . the days that lay ahead of her would be so empty.

But then Kate's mind latched on to what else he'd said. About his name protecting her. It was true. Once she married him, her name would be his. And so would her baby's. She tested it in her mind now as the gunslinger bent over to check on Lydia, to better cover the little girl. Watching his every move, noting his tenderness with his tiny niece, Kate mimed his name. *Youngblood.* A feared and respected name. She and her child *would* be protected.

She then thought of Mr. Talmidge. Obviously he hadn't sent Cole Youngblood to kill her, or she'd already be dead. But Kate wondered, when Mr. Talmidge did send someone—or came after her himself—would Cole Youngblood stand by her . . . given all the lies she'd told him?

The gunslinger straightened up, turned her way. "You're staring at me. What are you thinking so hard about, Kate?"

Kate shook her head and managed a wavery smile for this man who was going to be her husband, even if in name only. "I'm sorry. I didn't mean to stare." Then she suddenly realized he was also her salvation . . . as much as was the land he would get for her. And so she heard herself saying, "I guess I ought to . . . well, thank you for everything you're doing for me. I hope someday to be able to pay you back."

His expression never changed. But Kate thought she detected a flicker in his eyes, maybe of uncertainty. But then he said, "Well, first off, you're welcome. Your end of the bargain, though, is payback enough. And it's why I'm standing here now."

Kate's brow furrowed. "I don't know what you mean."

"I know you don't. But it's what I came to tell you." He hesitated, and then said, "We can't get married right away like you wanted."

Kate sat stock-still and stared up at him. Having to keep her voice low, so as not to awaken Lydia, only made her words sound that much more plaintive, even to her own ears. "I don't understand. Why can't we? You just said—"

"I know what I said, about my name protecting you. And I meant that. But"—he settled his Stetson on his head— "some things have changed. With the land run. Not with me. While you and the kids slept, I've been at the land office, registering to make the run for you."

Kate bit her bottom lip and tried to remain calm, to allow him to explain. "I see. Thank you. Was it difficult to do?"

He blew out a breath, as if recalling the ordeal. "Not if you don't mind standing for hours in a long line. But I finally got your numbered stake, so I can register your claim afterward. But while I was there, word came from the army that people can start moving down tomorrow through the Cherokee Outlet and go as far as the actual border to the Unassigned Lands."

Kate frowned her bewilderment. "Tomorrow?"

Cole nodded. "Yes. That's the new word from the Interior Department. But only those of us who were in line this morning know that right now. But word will spread fast enough, I expect. And folks will start heading down there directly."

Excitement quickened in Kate's belly. "Is that what we're going to do? Move down there ahead of them?"

His disbelieving chuckle killed Kate's giddiness. "No. Not we. Me. I'm going to go on down to the border tomorrow. My horse is a fast one, has a lot of stamina. So I should be able to get in a front-line position to grab you any claim you want."

His face fairly beamed with anticipation. For the coming horse race? Or for riding off, never to come back? Kate didn't like any of this. Because she simply didn't trust him. "So, is this why you say we can't get married first? There's no time, as you see it?"

His expression hardened. "It's not just how I see it, Kate. It's how it is. I didn't move the time up. The Interior Department did. Look, you want a good claim or not? It's up to you. I can go on ahead. Or I can wait here, and we hunt down the Justice of the Peace, get married, and then I leave and arrive late at the border. And be at the back of the crowd when the gun sounds—with you and a wagon of younguns to slow me down even more."

Kate knew what he wanted her to say. "And in that case, I might not get anything. Isn't that what you want me to realize?"

He nudged his Stetson up. "I'm saying it's a possibility."

She knew he was right. The best land—maybe even all of the land—would go to the swiftest. But she had other concerns. "All right. I believe you. But the way you want to do it, the land can't be in my name. Because we won't be married. And that was our deal. Why can't we just go find the justice today, right now, and get married?"

"I'd like nothing better myself, Kate. But who do you think is at the head of that long line of settlers waiting on numbered stakes and certifying every document? The JP. He's going to be busy every minute. That line goes on for miles. And it'll only be worse once the word spreads about moving out early."

Acute disappointment, tinged with fear of her salvation slipping through her fingers, had Kate scarcely able to take in what Cole was saying. He wanted to leave, to go on without them to the run. Or maybe just go. And never come back. All she could think was . . . *he's leaving us.* Suddenly she knew how the children felt. Alone. Scared. What if he didn't come back? What would she do with four mules, three kids, two wagons, a skinny dog, and no money?

But she couldn't find the courage to say any of those things. So she fell back on skepticism. "And just how do I know that you're telling me the truth?"

Cole Youngblood straightened to his full height. His narrow-eyed gaze raked over her. "Are you calling me a liar, Kate?"

Seeing his black-eyed stare under his equally dark Stetson, Kate swallowed hard. And shook her head no.

"Good. Then cover yourself and get outside this wagon, so we can talk further without waking up Lydia."

As soon as he stepped out over the wagon's gate and disappeared from view, Kate let out her breath and got dressed in a quiet frenzy, quickly pulling on her moss-green skirt and high-necked white habit shirt from yesterday's traveling costume. Next, she tugged on her boots, laced them, and raked her hands through her sleep-tangled hair.

Within moments, she climbed out of the wagon bed, and after going off privately to relieve her bladder, she rounded the schooner and stopped, seeing Cole squatted by the campfire and pouring hot coffee into a mug. Next to him, the big skinny yellow dog lay on its side, deigning to raise only its head at her arrival. No doubt his full belly from last night's supper scraps had rendered him lazy.

At the dog's acknowledgment of her presence, Cole turned his head, spotted her, and then shook his head, as if he were disgusted with her. "You can come over here, Kate. I don't bite. At least, not until after I've had coffee."

Feeling a bit silly for having hesitated, Kate crossed her arms. "Maybe not. But you do shoot people. You said so yourself."

He considered her a moment longer but apparently chose to ignore her comment in favor of taking a swallow of the steaming brew. He made a face, as if it were too hot or too strong. "You want some coffee?"

She started forward, nodding that she did. Invigorated by the bracing air, she rubbed her hands up and down her arms and glanced up, surprised to see the sun so high in the cloudless sky. "You let us sleep."

Cole shrugged away his good deed. "You were tired."

"I was. But I didn't realize until now just how late in the morning it is. But I guess I should have when you said you stood in line for hours." Kate took the mug he held up to her. She was as careful as he was not to let their hands touch. She sipped at the black brew. Hot, strong, biting. Looking over the mug's rim, she caught Cole watching her.

He looked away and then reached around to drag her wooden box from yesterday around to the fire. He stretched to place it at arm's length from him. "Sit here."

Hesitating only a moment, Kate walked to the box and sat down, knees together. She perched her mug on her knees, and turned her gaze to Cole. And prayed her morning sickness wouldn't take hold of her just yet.

He sucked in a gulp of his coffee, looked up at a point in the distance, huffed out a breath, and turned back to her. "What are you looking for in a claim?"

She realized she had no idea. And it was hard to think with his black eyes boring into her soul. So she said whatever practical-sounding thing came into her mind. "Water, I suppose. And trees."

"Water and trees. That's all?"

Refusing to squirm, she quickly added, "And grass and good soil."

"Grass and good soil."

Kate clamped down on her back teeth. "Do you intend to repeat everything I say?"

His chuckle further unnerved her. "Kate, who in hell let you get on a train bound for Oklahoma country with no idea what you're getting yourself into?"

She raised her chin a notch. "No one *let* me. I'm my own woman, Mr. Youngblood. Just like you're your own man. And I don't take kindly to people who think they can *let* me do anything." *Not after Mr. Talmidge,* she added to herself.

"Is that so? You're your own woman? That's not how you looked when I saw you under that tree last evening, sitting on that very box there and crying."

Stung by further evidence of her unpreparedness, Kate lowered her gaze, concentrating on staring deep into the tin mug of coffee cupped in her hands. Quietly, she said, "I know what I was doing. And I've said thank you for helping me."

Then she looked up, capturing his knowing gaze. One that said he knew she was just as aware of him as he was of her. Kate took a deep breath and reminded him, "We're not accomplishing anything here, Mr. Youngblood."

He blinked; the look was gone. "You're right." He took

another pull from his coffee mug. "So, I'm to find you a claim with water, trees, grass, and good soil, right?"

Finally. They were back on the subject. "Right."

"Which city you want it to be close to?"

She frowned and lowered her mug, which she'd been raising to her lips. "City? I didn't know there were any cities in the Unassigned Lands."

Cole gave her a sidelong look. "I swear you'd be dead now if I hadn't come along when I did. Kate, there are cities staked out and marked by the government already. Not everyone here wants to farm the land. A big number of these folks are businessmen and tradesmen, expecting to get rich off the building of this territory."

Kate slumped with the realization of how little she knew of the world, of how sheltered—except for those last weeks—her life in the Talmidge mansion in New York had been. She'd been so preoccupied with getting out here that she hadn't noticed a single thing going on around her. There was so much to learn. But the good news was a city close by meant work, something she knew how to do. Unlike farming. So finally, all she said was, "I see. Whole cities. Go on."

"All right. I'm going to suggest that you settle near the railroad's Guthrie station." He pulled a folded-up piece of paper out of his shirt pocket, unfolded it and showed it to her. "I found this map that my brother-in-law had marked a likely spot on right here." He pointed to it. Kate studied it intently. "It's close to the Cherokee Outlet border, near the junction of the Cottonwood and Cimarron rivers, which means I can get to it in a hurry on Monday. And being that close to water, the land should be good for farming. And if you're near Guthrie, you'll likely be close to neighbors, which will be good for a woman alone."

Kate nodded, her thoughts winging ahead several months from now. To the dead of winter, when her time would come due. And of just how much she would need these as yet unknown neighbors. What if she couldn't get to them when her time came? And if she was alone, as she suspected she would be, who would she send to get these neighbors, assuming they were inclined to help her? A shard of sheer terror of the unknown sliced at Kate. What would she do, she and her baby?

She glanced over at Cole Youngblood, saw his hard profile . . . and wondered if she should tell him of her condition. And make up yet another lie, this one about her baby's father. Or barring that, could she come up with enough reasons to keep him with her until her condition showed itself? Even then, would he stay? Would he even care, married to her or not? Finally, realizing the silence between them had stretched out, and feeling certain that he had purposely allowed it to, she quickly said, "You've thought of everything. It all sounds grand."

"Yep. Grand." Cole Youngblood straightened up, refolded the map, and stuck it back in his pocket, all the while eyeing her. "When are you going to tell me what it is you're really thinking about? Something's eating at you. Something big and raw and ugly. And don't tell me it's not. Because I can see it in your face. What is it, Kate?"

Chapter Five

Kate's breath caught. She couldn't tell him. She just couldn't. Not when she didn't know if he was merely curious, or scouting for details that could get her killed. Well, she hadn't gotten this far and kept herself alive by making strangers privy to her deepest thoughts and darkest secrets. And she saw no reason to begin doing so now. And especially not with this man, a Talmidge hired-gun.

So, raising her chin a notch, she lied. "There's nothing eating at me. Go on about this Guthrie station, please. I'd like to hear more."

He steadily considered her. Tension coiled in Kate's belly. She fought against just blurting out the entire truth. Then, just when she thought she'd break, he said, "All right. The talk is that Guthrie might be the new capital city, which would make your land that much more valuable. But for now it's been designated as a land office for the run. And if I can get that plot of land for you, I'll be able to register your claim right away and then get back here quickly to you and the kids. I don't think I'd be gone for more than one, maybe two, nights."

Kate stared at him, envying this man his knowledge and experience and confidence. Darn him, he just made everything sound so reasonable and so easy. And he did sound sincere, as if he really did intend to make the run for her and come back. She looked over at the man's saddled horse, which was tied to the remuda line. So he had been out and about, like he'd said. Perhaps her stake was in one of those saddlebags.

She hated how hard it sounded, but getting the land was her priority. Just as getting his sister's kids taken care of was his problem. Immediately, Kate's guilty heart tugged at her. She already cared about Joey, Willy, and Lydia. Hadn't she held the baby girl all night long? And hadn't she gotten Joey to give in enough to help her with supper? And didn't Willy dog her every step, just like Kitty . . . as Lydia had named the skinny hound dog who'd adopted them all? Yes, it was true.

But Kate also knew that her first priority, even above the land or another woman's children, was her own child, the one she carried under her heart. So she couldn't come to care too much for any of these people. And especially not for this man sitting quietly beside her, his gaze fixed on her. She couldn't get used to letting him direct her actions or do her thinking. And getting her out of scrapes. How was she ever going to learn to do for herself if she didn't start now?

After all, he'd made it plain enough all along that he didn't intend to do much but stake her claim, settle her on it with the kids, and then leave to go find that cousin of his. And after that, they'd all move on . . . without a thought to her. So she couldn't afford to need him. He didn't want to be needed. And she didn't want to need. And she surely didn't want to cry, which was what she suddenly felt like doing. How was it possible, she wondered, for a body to be surrounded by as many people as she was and still feel all alone?

To keep from giving in to this foolishness, this self-pity, and sure that Cole's assessing stare was partly responsible for her tumbling emotions, Kate blurted out her thoughts. "Mr. Youngblood, I appreciate everything you're doing for me. I truly do. But I didn't come all this way not to make the run for myself. I want to see my claim firsthand, where my home will be. And I want to see the city of Guthrie, all staked out. So, the kids and I . . . we're going with you."

Well, she'd surprised him with that. He glared at her and pushed his hat back. "I already told you why you can't. It's pure folly, Kate. The wagon would—"

"I know all about the wagon slowing you down."

He didn't appreciate her interruption one bit. His narrowed eyes said as much. "And about the kids being shaken to death in the back of it? Do you know about that? And yourself maybe being knocked off the buckboard seat and trampled in the rush?"

Good points, all. She couldn't deny any of them. And she didn't intend to do anything as uncalled for as getting those kids, herself, or her baby killed. But she persisted. "I'm not saying I have to be on the front line, Mr. Youngblood—"

"Cole. You're to call me Cole. If I'm going to marry you, you're going to call me by my given name."

Momentarily taken aback, Kate could only stare at him . . . and remind herself that, yes, she was going to marry this man. The very idea, though, still seemed so foreign to her. Imagine. Her, married to Cole Youngblood. She couldn't believe it. And his insistence on her calling him by his given name. It had her wondering just how many people in his life he'd invited to call him Cole. She'd bet, outside of his family, he could count those people on one hand. Was that why he wanted her to do so now? Was he lonely? Did he want something more than he had? Kate's thoughts about the gunslinger unsettled her. But especially unsettling to her was how his name on her lips seemed so right.

But finally she did as he wished, even though she felt her face heat up. "All right . . . Cole." Then she rushed on. "All I'm saying is I'm the one who came here to make the run. And I'll be the one living on the land the rest of my life. So I think I should be the first one to see it. I'll go slow, so the kids aren't—"

"You know how to handle a team? How to drive a wagon that size?" He jerked a thumb over his shoulder to indicate the lumbering schooner behind them.

Kate didn't have to look at it to know how big it was. Or to know that she'd never driven one. "No," she reluctantly admitted. "But you could teach me."

Cole Youngblood's eyebrows rose . . . slowly. Very carefully, he placed his coffee mug on the ground beside him. Then he ran a hand over his mouth and looked off through the trees at nothing in particular. And finally, he looked at her. "When, Kate? When am I going to teach you how to handle a team?"

Kate shrugged, but inside she was shaking like a willow in the wind. "I'm not doing anything now. Are you?"

His stare intensified. "You're not making the run. That's my wagon, my mules, and my niece and nephews. And I say you're not doing it. There's no time to teach you. Be reasonable."

Kate's determination increased tenfold. She didn't like his tone of voice. "I am being reasonable. I'm thinking we still have to get married, even though you said there's no time for that, either. So why don't we do both things? Take the kids with us in the wagon ... and you can teach me to handle the team on our way into town. And while we're there, we'll find the justice of the peace and get married. I'm betting that when you tell him your name, he'll be glad to give you the few moments a ceremony takes."

In one smooth move, Cole Youngblood stood up. Kate held her breath, half fearing he'd pull his gun and shoot her. But all he did was put his hands to his waist and stare down at her. "No. There's no time. For either one."

Disappointment ate at Kate. And had her trying yet another tactic. "I see." She stood up, the better to be on his level ... well, the better to look up into his eyes. "So if you don't teach me, then when you make the run and afterward marry me and ride off to go find that cousin of yours ... who *will* drive this wagon and team you've promised me?"

His eyes narrowed. "Joey."

Kate nodded. She'd thought he'd say that. Yesterday she'd seen Joey handling the team while Cole had come around his wagon to see if his horses had trampled her. "But Joey won't always be with me. You're taking him to that cousin of yours. And then what do I do?"

Cole's gaze flicked away from hers and then back. "It'll take me a while to find her. In the meantime, Joey can teach you."

Kate wondered at the hesitation in Cole's manner and voice. That was unusual for him. But she didn't dwell on it, wanting instead to make her points as quickly as possible. "I suppose he can. But I'd rather he didn't have all that resting on his shoulders. He's just a small boy and there'll be plenty else for him to help with. But still, how long did it take him to learn how to drive that wagon?"

"Longer than the one day you have, Kate. And will you look around you? This ground is muddy and rutted. And what's worse, there're trees and roots and ravines to navigate around. All those things make mules skittish. Now, I admire your gumption. And I understand your wanting to make the run. But our deal was, I'd make the run and you'd—"

"And I'd stay here with the children. If we were married . . . first." Even though her heart pounded, Kate refused to look away. She'd won. She could see it in his eyes. And he didn't like it one bit. And so again she rushed on with her real point, with what she really wanted. "You're not my husband yet, Cole."

He crossed his arms over his broad, hard-muscled chest. "But if I was, you'd have to obey me, right?"

The trap door slammed shut. And she'd done it to herself. Then she had a sudden, devilish thought. Maybe not. She let the thought roll around inside her mind and finally take hold. Her decision made, she fought desperately to keep her expression neutral and sincere under his intense scrutiny. "Yes. You're absolutely right. If you and I were married, I would have to listen to you."

Cole lowered himself to the ground, sitting with his knees bent. Again he picked up his coffee mug and sipped at it. But over the rim of the tin cup, he watched her.

Kate began sweating under the man's silent scrutiny. And knew this trait of his was probably what made him so good at his profession. Quietly watching and waiting, a whole store of patience, time on his side. It worked, too— on her anyway. He made her want to scream and tell him everything she knew. Just then, he lowered his mug to the

ground and laced his fingers together, dangling them between his spread knees. Kate was sure she would get a
headache from purposely keeping her eyes so wide and
innocent-looking. She didn't even allow herself to blink
until he spoke again.

"You're right. That was our deal," he told her. "I'll go
get the kids up and ready. You fix us some breakfast and
then fix yourself up. On the way into town, once we're out
of this bog here, I'll turn the team over to you."

Kate's spirits perked up. "You will? You'll show me
how to drive them?"

He looked everywhere but at her, as if he were embarrassed to be caught doing a good deed. "I said I would,"
was his fierce reply. "And while we're in town, we'll find
the justice of the peace and get . . . married"—he cut his
gaze over to her, as if he too were having trouble coming
to grips with that notion—"if that's the only way I can be
sure you'll stay put and not get your fool neck broke."

"It is," Kate assured him, even knowing she was lying.
But when had she not been lying to this man? And what
choice did she have except to continue to lie to him? Because right now lies were the only way she could get what
she wanted . . . and still keep herself alive.

He nodded, saying, "I thought as much. But get this
through your head, Kate Chandler. After we're hitched, I'm
leaving to make the run. By myself. And you're staying
here with the kids while I do. You understand that?"

She knew his last words were a test—one she didn't
intend to fail. So she blinked, and exhaled . . . softly,
slowly. And flashed a very demure smile to her husband-
to-be. "Yes . . . Cole."

That got him. He cocked his head sideways—assessing
her sincerity, and no doubt her sudden submissiveness.

Kate finally had to look away. She quickly sat down and
picked up her own mug of now-cooled coffee, raising it to
her lips to take a deep drink from it. Not that she wanted
any of the bitter brew. But she wanted less for him to see
the truth in her eyes. And the truth was . . . she wanted this

marriage to Cole Youngblood more than she'd ever wanted anything else in her life. That, and the coming lesson on handling a team and wagon. Because those were the tools she needed.

And wasn't it he, after all, just last evening, who'd told her a married woman with the means to do so could make the run herself? Well, in less than a few hours, she'd be both. Married. And with the means to do so . . . the buckboard wagon, the lighter vehicle of the two she'd soon own, and two of those very mules right behind them now.

The land run. She'd come here to make the run . . . and she still intended to do just that.

"You ready to take the reins?"

Giddy yet afraid, Kate swallowed and nodded to Cole, who was seated to her left on the spring-supported buckboard seat. Sandwiched among dozens of others, their wagon lumbered along rhythmically on the narrow path leading out of the Walnut Creek camp. From here on out, Kate could see, there wouldn't be much to do but keep the mules nosed in the right direction, toward the clapboard buildings of Arkansas City.

Still, she wanted to shout, no, she wasn't ready. But she had to do this, she told herself. She couldn't let fear get the best of her now. Not with her whole life depending on the next few days, if not hours. Exhaling, she said, "I am. I'm ready."

Cole's answering grin said he'd heard the catch in her voice. Kate bravely met his gaze. "You look scared, Kate. You sure you want to do this?"

That was all she needed to hear. Her chin came up a notch. "I said I did. I have never let fear stop me before. And I'm not about to start now." She held her hands out. "Give me the reins and show me what to do."

He didn't, though. Not right away. Instead he pivoted to look over his right shoulder. Kate did likewise, looking over her left to see the newly scrubbed Joey, Willy, and Lydia seated on the wagon bed . . . and holding on to each other for dear life. Sitting opposite the kids in the bed, and taking in all the sights, was Kitty, the skinny old hound dog Lydia had adopted. Of the four in the back, he was the only one who didn't appear to be concerned. Kate had to grin . . . and didn't blame the children one bit.

"I'm going to give the reins over to Kate now," Cole warned them. "You kids stay put, you hear?"

"We hear ya, Uncle Cole," Joey answered for them all. "I got Lydia real tight-like. And Willy's holding on to the sides."

Kate chuckled. "I'll try my best not to send us all to our deaths. Especially on such a fine sunny day as this."

Sober as a hanging judge, Joey nodded his thanks and told her, "We'd be purely thankful if you didn't, Miss Chandler."

Miss Chandler. Of the three, Joey was the only one not already calling her Miss Kate. *Maybe one day,* she mused, grinning at the dark-haired little boy and then turning around to face his more formidable uncle. "I'm ready," she announced.

"All right, then." He put the reins in her hands. There must have been a hundred of them. And they all felt thick and heavy to Kate, whose expression fell. Immediately her palms began sweating. Especially when she was jerked and pulled along with the mules with every thudding hoofbeat. One particularly nasty jounce nearly sent her over the wagon's footboard and into the bracings.

Cole immediately encircled her middle, his strong, warm hands all but spanning her waist as he held her steady. "Whoa there, Kate. Relax, or your bones will get rattled loose. That's better. Now breathe. Just take it easy. Let me show you what to do."

"Please do. And I am . . . I'm breathing"—she gulped in some fine April air to prove it—"and it's okay. I'm fine. Just don't let go of me."

"I won't. You're doing fine. Just relax. Move your arms with the rhythm of the reins. There. That's better." He then divided his time between watching the mules' plodding progress and Kate's blundering attempts to navigate them along the quagmire that was the road. When finally Cole did release her, it was to show her how to thread the leather leads through her fingers in such a way that she gained more control over the laboring team.

Kate marveled at how long and strong his fingers were . . . and how they felt holding hers. And how confident they were. Whereas she was all frustrating thumbs and clumsiness.

Cole seemed to divine her thoughts, too, as he met her still-panicky gaze. "Don't worry. No one catches on right off. Just remember, most of the work is done by the team. They know what they're doing. All you have to do is guide them."

"The same as with children, right?" was Kate's shaky observation, offered without looking at him.

"Right. Just steady as you go. Don't saw back on the reins or jerk them suddenly. You don't want to startle the team. Now, the one on the left—that's Duke—he's your lead mule. Boots, there on the right, he'll do whatever Duke does."

With her bottom lip held firmly between her teeth, Kate nodded that she understood. She was too terrified to take her gaze off the slow-going and dependable mules long enough even to glance over at Cole. She just knew if she did, Duke and Boots would sense it and suddenly bolt out of the string of wagons making their way into the city and send them all careening around the next bend in the worn and muddy path. And tip the wagon over and kill them all, just as Joey feared.

"You're good at this, Kate," Cole encouraged, letting go of her hands, thereby turning complete control of their welfare over to her. Again he pivoted to face the riders in the back. "How're you kids doing?" They chorused that they were fine. Apparently satified with that, Cole again faced forward and asked Kate the same thing. "How're you doing?"

Kate darted him the briefest of glances. "Good. Fine."

Cole chuckled. "You'll get used to it. After a while, you won't even think about it. It'll come as easy to you as getting yourself dressed." Then he suddenly sat forward, tensing and pointing. Kate nearly jumped out of her green travel costume. "Watch that puddle there. It could be pretty deep. Go around it, like the others did. We don't want to get stuck." Again he put his hands atop hers, helping her, expertly tugging on the multiple reins. "Here. Like this."

With his help, the mules smoothly responded, skirting around to the left of the puddle . . . and Kate finally exhaled. Looking at his hands covering hers, she was no longer able to deny how safe she felt in his presence. Nor could she help feeling guilty for all his patient help, knowing as she did that she had her own selfish reasons for learning how to drive a wagon today. Kate glanced over at him. His face, in profile, was amazingly handsome. Her belly knotted. And she quickly said, "You're a most patient teacher, Cole. I do thank you."

He shrugged, his dark eyes warming. "You're a quick learner." Then he tipped his hat's brim to her. After that he fell silent, leaning back with his boots up on the footboard and his hands braced atop his knees.

For her part, Kate concentrated on the team and the wagons ahead of her and on the looming buildings of Arkansas City. In only minutes, she reminded herself, she'd be standing in front of a justice of the peace. Marrying a man she barely knew. A man who might be looking for her, if he knew the truth of her identity. But to kill her. Not to marry her.

Just then, as if he'd picked up on at least one of her thoughts, Cole said, "You look nice, Kate."

Surprised by his kind observation, she glanced over at him, a tentative smile at the ready. But then her gaze locked with his as she noted his truly admiring expression. He really meant it. He did think she looked nice. Kate's smile bled from her face. She didn't know what to say, couldn't even get her mouth to say a decent thank-you.

Then, out of the blue, Cole said, "I expect that this isn't

exactly how a young girl pictures her wedding day, is it? Three kids, a hound dog, a town full of strangers. No ring or flowers or family."

Suddenly shy, even despite this being no more than a marriage of convenience, and moved that he'd think of her feelings, Kate found her smile again and sent one his way. "I didn't expect such as that. Besides, I don't have any family, anyway."

Cole's brow furrowed. "What about your aunt and uncle?"

Kate couldn't think who he meant. "My aunt and uncle?"

"Yeah. The ones you told me about. In Kentucky. Where you come from."

With her heart pounding, Kate's mouth dried, her spine stiffened. She'd just learned a lesson about letting her guard down around this man. "Oh. Them. Of course. I forgot about them. We're just not very close."

Cole nodded . . . and silently watched her. Kate immediately faced forward and denied to herself that her face was heating up guiltily. And pronounced herself thankful that driving the team demanded her full concentration, even if the jouncing around was beginning to upset her stomach. Feeling suddenly lost and vulnerable, Kate wondered what else could go wrong.

"What're your aunt and uncle's names?"

Kate's insides churned. She felt hot. "Their names?"

"Yep. Their names. You do know them, don't you? Even if you weren't that close?"

Kate tried to laugh, as if that were funny—but her mouth just wouldn't cooperate. "Of course I know their names. Don't be silly. They're, um, Ephraim and Ruth . . . Cobb." Instantly she felt better. And embellished her lie. "They're on my mother's side. She's her sister . . . Ruth is."

Cole Youngblood just nodded. "Tell me about Kentucky. What's it like there?"

Kate's stomach flopped over as she darted a guilty glance Cole's way. "Oh, there's not that much to tell." Because she didn't know the first thing about it. All she'd seen were the blurred images of towns and forests and farmland through the train's windows. "It's a pretty state."

He nodded soberly. "Yes, it is. I've been there a time or two myself."

He knows. "You have?" *He knows, and he's just stringing me along.* "It's a wonder I didn't run into you, then." Kate's breath came too fast. She began having trouble getting air into her lungs. Her lips and her fingertips began tingling. She felt hot all over.

"I feel sick," she blurted out, shoving the reins into Cole's hands about one second before she leaned over the side of the wagon, held on for dear life . . . and retched out her entire breakfast. The children were shrieking and hollering, and Kate realized from the wagon's movement that Cole was taking them off the path and leading them out into the grass.

She also heard the calls of concern from those still on the buckboard-rutted path into Arkansas City. Was there anything they could do to help? Cole hollered back that they were fine. And Kate also realized something else. She was crying. And ready to give up. And about to fall off the wagon, which mercifully lurched to a stop.

In less time than she could have imagined, Cole loomed into sight, sprinting around the wagon by way of the mules' heads, only to stand to one side of her. Reaching up, he held her hair back as Kate again heaved and cried and gagged. From a pocket somewhere, Cole produced a big red bandanna and wiped at her sweating brow and then her mouth. "Joey," he called out. "Come here, boy, and go wet this in the creek. Willy, you and Lydia stay put."

"Yes, sir," Joey called out, already leaping out of the wagon. Kitty the hound dog scrambled out right after him, flying through the air to land on all fours on the grass. Kate watched helplessly as Joey snatched up the bandanna and took off at a run, the rawboned yellow dog hot on his heels and finally passing him.

Then Cole was reaching up to her, gripping her under

the arms and gently tugging her from the wagon. When he swooped her to the ground, away from her sickness, and set her down, her legs wouldn't hold her. She went to her knees and fell forward, her hands squishing in the mud, her beautiful moss-green skirt now ruined with mud. Defeated, weak as a newborn, Kate cried . . . while Cole held her hair back and patted her calmly between the shoulders. "I think the worst of it's over. Easy now. Just a case of nerves. And all that bouncing." Then he straightened up, yelling out, "Joey, hurry it up, boy."

Kate looked up, saw the boy and the dog on their way back. Kitty was again outdistancing Joey's pumping little legs. But in only a second or two, the racing duo skidded to a stop. Joey tossed his uncle the soggy bandanna and then bent over, his hands to his knees as he gasped in and out, trying to get air into his lungs. As Kitty trotted around them all, barking for all it was worth, as Willy and Lydia called out from the wagon, wanting to know if Miss Kate was dying like their mama had, as Cole yelled back that no she wasn't . . . Kate slumped sideways to a sitting position, resting her weight on her hip, her knees bent, her legs out to one side, her palms flattened against the grassy ground.

Cole immediately squatted in front of her, brushing her hair back and wiping at her cheeks and brow. His fingers against her skin were damp and callused, but gentle. Then, calmly, as if this were an everyday occurrence in his life, he asked, "You okay?"

Kate almost laughed as she shook her head no. And then almost began crying again when she realized in how many ways she meant it. In more ways than he could ever imagine. But finally, she began feeling stronger. Instinctively clutching at him and using his rock-solid arm for leverage, she sat up straighter and pulled the bandanna from his grip. In a voice not surprisingly hoarse and croaky, she assured him, "I'm better now. Thank you."

Then she refolded the wet cloth and, holding her heavy hair up off her neck, swiped it across her nape. Its cool dampness further revived her. Finally . . . she had to meet Cole Youngblood's dark-eyed, steady gaze. To allay any questions he might have, and for about the tenth time today, Kate thanked him. "I appreciate your help. I think I'm okay now."

She then heard Willy and Lydia crying about how Miss Kate was dying. "Why don't you go see to the children? I just need to sit here a minute. And then I'm going to go rinse my mouth out. And wash my hands. And maybe try to get some of this mud off my skirt."

His hand on her arm squeezed gently. "You sure you're okay?"

Kate nodded, wiping at her mouth. "Yes. This happens all the time now."

" 'All the time now' . . . What does that mean?"

Kate froze. Then she snapped her head up, her gaze locking with his. "Nerves. Like you said. Since I left . . . home. All the excitement."

He nodded. But he didn't believe her. It was there in his eyes, and in the lines that bracketed his mouth. "I see. Well"—hands atop his knees he levered himself up to a stand—"I'll go calm Willy and Lydia. You take your time here, then wash up. We'll go when you're ready." He started to turn away and then stopped, looking down at her again. "I'll get you some peppermint out of the back of the wagon. I got the kids a stick of it in town yesterday. It'll settle your stomach some. And give you a better taste in your mouth."

With the wet bandanna over her mouth, Kate nodded silently, grateful for his care with her. She wondered if he knew what a good man he could be. But given his line of work, she somehow doubted that he did. Or would like being told he was.

Just then, Cole turned on his boot heel and, as Kate watched him, stepped to the back of the wagon, reaching up to hold on to the wagon's sideboards as he talked in a low voice to Willy and Lydia, no doubt assuring the chil-

dren that she would live. Further evidence of his decency
. . . his care with his sister's children.

Kate closed her eyes, exhaled softly . . . thinking of her
own baby, and wondering who in the world would ever
love it and care for it if she died. Or was murdered. The
thought snapped her eyes open. Joey wasn't three feet
away. His hands still to his knees, but with his head now
cocked at a considering angle, he stared at her, curiosity
alight in his brown eyes. He looked like a miniature of his
uncle, even flanked as he was by Kitty, who ignored them
both in favor of scratching his fleas.

"I'm all right, Joey," Kate rushed to assure the boy. "Just
a little . . . sickness, I suppose."

Joey nodded. "I've seen this before. My ma did this
when she was carrying Lydia. Maybe you're just going to
have a baby, Miss Chandler."

". . . I now pronounce you man and wife."

Complete silence followed the justice of the peace's final
words of the civil ceremony. Inside the sparsely furnished,
one-room-square, weathered-wood building that served as
the land office, the short, rotund official—who only moments ago had introduced himself as Mr. Franklin Voorhies—now stared from Cole to his new wife and back to
Cole. No one moved.

"You may kiss the bride," the man said, his brown eyes
owlishly round behind his spectacles. His balding head
beaded with sweat as his nervous gaze flitted from the bri-
dal couple to the others present for this momentous occasion, the crowd behind them and those outside around the
open window of the land office.

Cole glanced down at his pale, mud-caked bride. Katherine Chandler. She clung to his chambray shirtsleeve as if
afraid she'd fall through the planked floor if he let go of
her. Her hand on him shook, her nails dug into his flesh,
even through the shirt's material. And she looked straight
ahead. At the justice of the peace. Mr. Voorhies.

"Kate?" Cole suddenly said.

She gasped, as if she hadn't known he was here. And then turned her face up to him. "Yes?" she whispered.

She looked like a china doll, all smooth skin, tautly stretched over her high cheekbones. Green eyes the color of jade. Hair as black as midnight. It wouldn't take much, Cole knew, for him to forget that this ceremony was only a little more binding than a handshake to seal a business deal. But what stopped him from acting on what his body urged him to do was the certainty that she deserved better. Better than this. Better than him. However, with business to conduct, Cole carried on with the moment. "I think," he said softly, "that the justice wants us to kiss. And then get out of here so he can register these men's stakes."

"Oh." Kate looked around, over her shoulder, to the men standing behind them. Cole watched the play of emotion over her face. Then she looked up at him and caught him doing so. She blinked, her face colored, finally tinting the pinched paleness that had remained after her bout of nervous illness. "I suppose we . . . ought to . . . do it, then," she said gamely.

Cole grinned. He was now the only man in the world with the right to kiss Kate Chandler. *No. Kate Youngblood.* Cole was surprised by how that made him feel, her name being the same as his. Protective. Territorial. Proud. She was his. Legally. In the eyes of society. But not in her heart, where it counted. He knew that. So what the hell was he thinking about? *Just kiss the girl and move on. Get to the next job.*

Cole circled Kate's waist with an arm, his hand against the small of her back as he pulled her to him. Then he tipped her chin up . . . and lowered his head until his mouth covered hers. She gave a start of surprise and stiffened, her hands clutching fistfuls of chambray shirtsleeves. But she didn't pull away. Cole deepened the kiss, tasting her pepperminty breath.

Men shifted their weight, making the floorboards creak. Self-conscious sniffs and coughs filled the air. Childish gasps and giggles and shushing mingled with the rest.

Cole was aware of the sounds only as he would be of a waterfall dimly heard as it cascaded in the distance. Because his senses were filled instead with his first experience of his new wife. He found he couldn't pull away. He only wanted the kiss to deepen, to go on . . . but her painfully obvious innocence, evidenced by her clenched teeth and stiff posture, had him breaking off their contact. Pulling back from her, he stared down at her . . . and saw the fear in her eyes. And saw that her cheeks were wet with tears. She was scared to death. Of him. Of a man.

Cole tightened his hold on her and his expression hardened. He wondered not for the first time just who had hurt this girl, and what he'd done to hurt her. He didn't know those answers, but he did know this much . . . if he ever crossed paths with the son of a bitch, he'd kill him.

Chapter Six

"Are you my new mama now?"

Her heart melting, Kate pulled Lydia's worn dress over the child's curly-topped head and tossed it aside. Then she met the hopeful brown-eyed gaze of the three-year-old girl sitting with her atop the pile of makeshift bedding in the schooner. Reaching for Lydia's nightgown, Kate held it in her hands and managed a smile. "No, honey. I'm now your aunt . . . I suppose. Since I'm . . . married to your uncle Cole."

It was all so new, only half a day old, this new identity of hers. So the words didn't come easy yet. Kate wondered if they ever would, since this marriage wasn't a real one.

Lydia's mouth puckered, dimpling her tiny chin. "I don't gots a mama. Uncle Cole says she's in heaven. So's Papa."

The child was just so heartrendingly accepting of her fate. Kate couldn't stand it and instantly gathered the little girl into her arms, holding her close, rocking back and forth with her, and kissing the top of her curly head. "I may not be your mother, but I'll love you, Lydia. I swear it."

Even as she spoke the words, Kate knew she had no right to say such a thing to the little girl. Because Cole intended to hand Lydia and her brothers over to that cousin of his. He'd leave in less than a week, since the run was only five days away, to go hunt her. Kate suspected he'd make short work of locating this kin of his, since finding people was what he did for a living. And then he'd come back here and take the children away from her. Once again, they'd be wrenched away from their home and handed over to a stranger.

Suddenly, Kate wasn't sure she could stand by and

watch Cole ride away with Joey, Willy, and Lydia. Any more than she could stand the thought of someone taking her own child away from her.

With that thought came another. Kate's head snapped up, and she held Lydia all that much tighter, as she asked herself why she was taking on responsibility for three children when a hired killer was on her trail? Who would take care of these children if that gunman found her before Cole got back from hunting his cousin? Would that gunman also kill these babies? And why in God's name hadn't she thought of any of this before now?

Kate distractedly rocked the baby harder, cradling the nestling girl to her chest, as she told herself, *No. I can't tell him. Not the whole truth, anyway.* Lying to him, using him because she had to, was one thing. He was a grown man and was using her, too. She knew that. They both had needs that the other one fulfilled. Practical needs, and not those of the heart. But her heart was having none of her denials. Instantly she saw again Cole Youngblood's smile, felt his warm hands atop hers as he'd helped her with the reins, heard him saying how pretty she looked . . . relived his kiss after the ceremony, and recalled how she'd panicked. But not as much as she'd thought she would, given everything Mr. Talmidge had put her through.

That sobered her, just thinking the awful man's name. Snapping back to the moment, banishing all thoughts of the man who was now her husband, Kate forced her mind back to her present dilemma. That of telling Cole why she had to back out of their bargain. It couldn't be helped. Because it was, to her, an unforgivable sin for her to keep quiet and thus endanger children as innocent as her own unborn child—

Then it hit her. She couldn't tell him who she was, couldn't risk him killing her. Because that would kill her baby, too. Why, she couldn't even risk him simply taking her prisoner and turning her over to the Talmidges. Because then all would have been for naught. Her desperate run to freedom, her overwhelming urge to protect her child, to give it the life and the love it deserved . . . all would be for nothing. She couldn't do it, couldn't tell Cole the truth. But she couldn't keep her bargain, either.

Kate's head began to hurt as much as her heart did. What had she done? Was there no simple answer that would save them all? There had to be. And she had to come up with it. She had to get past this, had to think her way out, had to assume that Cole was Talmidge's man. And act accordingly.

Talmidge's man. That had her recalling Cole's searching questions about her family and about Kentucky earlier today when she'd been learning to drive the wagon. Wasn't that proof of what she feared? *Yes, it was.* She must have thought so even then, too, because she hadn't given her full name, Anna Katherine, for the wedding vows. She again heard herself hesitating just before saying "Kate Chandler." Kate now took a deep breath, exhaling it slowly as she cuddled Lydia protectively, and turned her thoughts to Cole's sister's children. These poor children. Hadn't they been through enough hurt to last them a lifetime? Thinking of them had Kate again recalling Joey's earlier observation.

What if he should go tell his uncle that maybe Miss Chandler—Mrs. Youngblood now—was carrying a baby and that's why she'd gotten sick? Kate could just see that. She'd have no more of an answer for Cole than she'd had for Joey, except for the weak denial she'd given the boy. Would Cole so easily accept a shake of the head and a laugh?

Somehow, she didn't think so.

So what to do, then? Because if she couldn't really take the chance of telling Cole the actual truth, then what *could* she tell him? Was there any explanation he'd accept as good enough? As she mulled this over, Kate looked down at the little girl in her lap. And saw she was asleep. A mother's smile lit her face. The poor tiny little thing.

Lydia just went at it full-tilt all day long, trying her best to keep up with her brothers and that dad-blamed dog Kitty. Even now, Kate knew from checking earlier, the dog lay stretched out on the ground right outside. He was never more than a few feet from Lydia, and most of the time was right up against her as she walked with her arm draped around the hound's neck and sang songs to him.

Thinking to lay the child down without waking her, and forgoing the notion of the girl's cotton nightgown—tonight her one-piece smallclothes would have to be enough—Kate eased herself and Lydia forward, finally managing to place her atop the bedding and cover her with a thick quilt. Then, smoothing the child's ringlets away from her face, Kate stood. But on impulse, she bent over and kissed Lydia's forehead. Straightening up, and feeling the sudden welling of tears in her eyes, Kate wondered why she'd done that, why she'd kissed Lydia.

But more than that, she wondered at her sadness. It was as if she were already—her head came up, her eyes widened—*saying good-bye to the children. Oh no.* Her frown mirrored the bewilderment she felt inside. *Am I? Am I saying good-bye? Why now?*

Not even sure herself what she was thinking, why she was behaving this way, or what lay at the root of her sadness, she sat down heavily atop a wooden chest. Folding her hands in her lap, she stared at the sleeping little girl only a few feet away. And knew. *I am. I'm saying good-bye. I'm leaving. But how? Why? I can't leave.*

But the truth was . . . she couldn't stay. She had to leave. It made perfect sense for her, for these children, and for her own child. *But maybe not for Cole.* Kate immediately suppressed any thought of him, telling herself he was a grown man and could take care of himself. Just as she was a grown woman and had to take care of herself. And could. Because now she was a married woman, had a numbered stake, was registered with the land office, and knew the location of the land she hoped to claim.

All of that thanks to Cole Youngblood.

Kate bit her bottom lip, hating how the man kept intruding himself into her thoughts. But Cole was the one who'd given her everything she needed to survive. Yes, he'd given it to her . . . or still had it. Kate turned, looking out the back of the wagon, and found what she sought. Cole's big roan. He'd said it was a fast horse. She'd need a fast horse. Not that she knew how to ride one. But she did know which way to face on the animal. And she'd learned how to handle the team today. *Cole taught you how to do that.*

Stop it! Kate rubbed furiously at her forehead, as if she could erase her conscience, as if she could stop it from telling her right from wrong. Was it right to stay and get herself and her own baby killed? Was it right to stay and get these three children killed? No. It was right that she left. But she couldn't go naked and unprepared. She needed money and that numbered stake, both of which she knew were in Cole's saddlebags, along with the map to the claim. She'd seen him put it in there earlier.

But getting to the bags wouldn't be easy. If they weren't thrown across his horse's rump—which they wouldn't be, it being night now—then they'd be in the buckboard where Cole could keep an eye on them. At night, he slept with them, she knew, putting them under his head for a pillow, and for safekeeping.

It'd be hard. And foolhardy, she knew. But what choice did she have? None. So that settled it. Somehow she'd get the saddlebags. She hadn't made it this far by giving up at the first sign of difficulty. *So now I'm a thief, too.* She was going to take the man's money and his horse. No, she told herself, shaking her head. *I'm not a thief. Cole is my husband, even if in name only.* She couldn't steal from her own husband, could she? She didn't know what the law might say about that, but she did know how it made her feel. Like she was stealing. But she had no choice, as she kept having to remind herself.

And that being the case, she may as well come up with a plan. All right. She'd gather what she needed, pretend to go to bed, and then steal away—once Cole was asleep—with the man's horse, some of his money, the all-important numbered stake, the map to the claim his brother-in-law had drawn, some food . . . and a gun. A gun. Kate shook her head. She was a complete innocent out here. She had no idea how to fend for herself. The city's dangers were one thing. Those she understood. But all this open prairie and ten thousand strangers? No.

Why, she'd never even held a gun in her hand. But she now knew enough to know that she'd need a weapon, being a woman alone. As for using it . . . well, she knew which end to hold. And push come to shove, she didn't think anybody would want to stand around in front of her if she just pointed it and began firing wildly.

With her shopping list concluded, Kate turned her mind to coming up with a practical plan. Obviously, she'd have to hide out, and hide well, once she got away from here. But first, before she left Arkansas City proper, she'd need to purchase some supplies, like more food. And clothes. Something more suitable than her filthy moss-green traveling costume. She supposed she could get all that at the general store come first light. With any luck, she wouldn't be missed before then. But right after that, she'd have to hightail it out of here, maybe join all the settlers going down to the border tomorrow.

Kate paused. Was she forgetting anything? She blinked, her gaze lighting on the sleeping Lydia.

The children. Kate put a hand to her mouth, rubbing her fingers over her lips as she thought. Lydia'd be safe enough. Kitty was right outside. And Cole slept in the buckboard wagon with the boys and wasn't more than a half-dozen yards away if Lydia woke up and fussed.

Suddenly ill, Kate sat sharply forward, her heavy dark hair falling forward as she tucked her head between her legs, held on to her knees, and concentrated on breathing deeply. If Cole Youngblood caught her, he'd kill her, Mr. Talmidge's orders or not. But leaving was the only thing she could do. She had to get away before these kids were hurt because of her.

With her hands still braced against her knees, Kate swung herself back up to a sitting position, blinking, pushing her hair back, and waiting for the dizziness to pass. Yes, it was bold, what she planned to do. But it was boldness that had gotten her out of New York City and all the way here. And so, she'd do this, too. Starting now. Taking a deep breath, Kate stood up. And told herself it was time— time to put her plan into motion, beginning with securing what she needed from the saddlebags before Cole went to sleep atop them.

Afraid for herself, but thinking first of her own child and of Cole's niece and nephews, Kate edged her way around chests and wood crates until she could climb over the wagon's gate and then down off the end of it. As she touched the ground, Kitty came to his feet and stretched. In the lantern-lit darkness, Kate looked all around, didn't see Cole anywhere. *Good.* Unless he was already asleep in the buckboard. Or was gone.

She peered into the dark, searching the remuda line. No. Still there, that big fast roan of his, along with the four mules. If he was going to abandon her and the kids, he'd have done so atop that roan. She knew because that was what she herself intended to do, wasn't it? She shook her head in wonder. *Look how far gone I am already. Accusing him of doing exactly what I intend to do. Well, enough of that,* she told herself.

For the moment, she turned her attention to the rawboned, yellow-furred hound in front of her and scratched at his floppy, velvety ears. In a voice just above a whisper, she ordered him to stay put. "You stay here and keep an eye on Lydia, you hear me, Kitty?"

Kitty whuffed and sat down, staring at her, his tongue lolling out the side of his mouth. Kate grinned at him, but knew somehow in her heart that he would, with his last breath, protect them all, but especially the child inside the schooner. He seemed to love that little girl. And why wouldn't he? She had pretty much saved him. Because when the rest of them had wanted to shoo him away last night, Lydia had raised an instant ruckus until she'd gotten her way. Kate grinned again, this time thinking of how fast they'd all given in, too. *Why, if we aren't careful, we'll all spoil that child until she's unbearable.*

No. I mustn't think those things. I won't be here to spoil her. Fearing she'd lose her courage if she didn't hurry, Kate worked fast to draw the canvas covering tight, tying it as much to keep Lydia inside as to keep the cooling night air outside. And all too soon it was done. She turned around. A sudden gust of wind whipped her hair out and flapped her skirt around her legs.

Kate grabbed for her hair and smoothed a palm down her once-lovely but now dirty moss-green skirt. But to no avail. The wind would have its way with her, she feared, and would continue to do so until she purchased more suitable clothes early tomorrow morning. Before she lost herself in the crowd of settlers moving toward the land run border.

"Well, Kitty," she told the dog, keeping her voice low as she turned to him. "Wish me luck." She held her hand out, pretending she wanted to shake his paw. "It's been nice knowing you."

Surprisingly, the dog held his big rough paw up to her. Kate chuckled . . . and took it, shaking it. Someone had once spent time with this dog, training him. Kate briefly wondered what else he might have been trained to do as she released his furry paw and focused on the pressing but very unsavory tasks ahead of her.

She took the few steps over to the buckboard wagon and peered into the back of it, looking for the all-important saddlebags. Slowly, quietly, she moved around the wagon, looking and lifting and sorting through the items in its bed. Everything else was here, including the sleeping Joey and Willy. But no saddlebags and no Cole Youngblood. Frustrated, she stopped, standing with her back to the campfire, her arms crossed atop the wagon's side railing. And stared down at Joey and Willy, saying a silent good-bye to them.

Barely two little lumps under their shared quilt, they were sound asleep. Kate smiled and pulled their covers up around their necks. Such good little boys they were. *Sweet children.* Kate could only hope her child—given who its father was—would turn out to be half as kind and well-behaved as these three were.

"They're good kids, aren't they?"

Kate spun around, her hand to her pounding heart. "You scared the life out of me," she hissed, mindful of the sleeping boys.

Cole Youngblood stood there, as tall and sturdy in the night's shadows as one of the nearby oaks. "Yeah. I saw that I did."

Kate swallowed. Had he seen her searching through the wagon? Not saying anything, she eyed him, taking in his appearance, his hands to his waist . . . his saddlebags flung over a broad shoulder. He stared back at her. "What were you looking for, Kate?"

"Looking for?" She bit her bottom lip. "Nothing. I was just . . . checking on the boys. Lydia's asleep now, so I thought I would check on the boys."

"So you said." He moved past her then and hefted his saddlebags—Kate's gaze never left them—over the tailgate, laying them as quietly as possible in the wagon's bed.

She marked their location and then turned to Cole—and saw his hawklike gaze resting on her. The pressure was too much, causing her to blurt, "How long have you been watching me?"

"Long enough to see you shake the dog's paw," he drawled, as if he hadn't heard the accusing tone in her voice. "Come over here"—he startled her by taking her arm and directing her steps—"away from the wagon. So we don't wake the boys. I want to talk to you."

The last thing she wanted to do was talk to him. But forced to do so, Kate allowed him to pull her along toward their banked camp fire; she felt her face heat up with guilt and fear—and was glad for the evening's covering darkness. And for the chirping crickets and the hooting owl. That way Cole couldn't see her heightened color or hear her thumping heart as she asked him a question she really had no desire to hear the answer to. "Talk to me about what?"

"About tomorrow."

Relief on more than one score washed over her. He could have said, *About your real identity and why I have to kill you.* Or, *You're my wife now, and I think we should share a bed.* But she was none too happy with this topic, either. "Oh. Tomorrow. Um, where were you just now? I didn't see you when I climbed out of the schooner."

Kate stopped at the fire's stone-encircled rim and, with him still holding her arm, still assisting her, sat upon a thick branch he'd evidently pulled over here sometime this evening. He sat beside her and finally answered her. "After I made sure the boys were sleeping, I went to talk to some of the other men close by. About tomorrow, like I said."

"I see." Kate refused even to think of her own dangerous plans for tomorrow as she commented, "About moving down through the Cherokee land to the border?"

"Yep. Most everyone's planning on doing that, on going down early."

Kate nodded, knowing she planned to do the same thing . . . if she lived that long. "I guess, um, you'll be going with them?"

He nodded, eyeing her, his expression quizzical. "That was the plan, Kate. You knew that." Then he sobered. "There's some talk going around about how some are sneaking in sooner than they're supposed to and staking their claims before the official run."

Fearful disbelief—in her mind the land Cole had only this morning described to her was already hers—had Kate's heart thumping leadenly. "But they can't do that. It's wrong. That land is mine."

Cole chuckled—the first time she'd heard him do so. But the sound of it said plain enough that he thought her an innocent. "Well, not yet. But try telling them that."

She tsked at that. "Won't the army stop them?"

Cole shrugged. "I expect so. If they see them. But there're hundreds of miles of border all around that million acres, Kate. I imagine some will get through and get their land in an underhanded way."

Kate fell quiet, knowing she was planning on doing the same thing. Not going in earlier than the law permitted. But certainly her plan for getting her land on her own was underhanded, from Cole's point of view. She swallowed, staring at him now as he leaned over to stoke the fire back to life. She tried not to notice how big, how strong, how intimidating he was. Her chest tightened, and she could only breathe through her open mouth. What a mess her life was. She'd give anything for someone with a calm mind to talk to, someone she could trust. Then she blinked, again seeing Cole sitting right here next to her. Wasn't a woman supposed to be able to turn to her husband with her problems? Well, maybe so, but not in this case—

"You're awful quiet, Kate. What's eating at you?"

He'd been watching her again. Her eyes wide, Kate cast around desperately for a subject. "Tomorrow," she came up with. "It's, um, a big day . . . I suppose."

Reflected firelight had flames dancing in Cole's eyes. It terrified Kate. He almost looked like a kind of scary imaginary monster, the kind mothers conjured up to frighten young children into behaving. Except this man wasn't imaginary. He was all too real. And onto her, she was sure. He was playing a cat-and-mouse game with her, waiting for her to let her guard down, waiting for her to blurt the truth, tell him who she was . . . so he could kill her.

He opened his mouth to speak. Terrified, Kate half expected brimstone to issue forth. But all he said was, "Nice evening, huh? Hear it won't last, though. There's talk of rain later."

Relieved, Kate exhaled sharply, then looked up and gasped for more air.

Cole immediately put a hand to the small of her back. The warm, firm pressure of his touch did nothing to calm her. "You okay? You sick again?"

"No. I'm not sick. I'm fine," came her raspy answer.

"You don't sound fine," Cole Youngblood—her husband—said.

"Well, I am. I'm fine. I'd know if I was fine or not, wouldn't I?" Kate froze, hearing the snappish tone in her voice, hearing her desperation. Had he picked up on it?

Apparently so. Because there was only silence between them following her outburst. And Cole's hand stayed where it was. Finally, he spoke. "Joey has a mighty interesting notion about why you might be getting sick like you did this morning."

"Does he?" Kate's heart pounded like a racehorse coming down the home stretch.

"Yep. He thinks you're . . . well, going to have a baby."

"Me?" Kate feigned surprise, putting a hand to her chest. A shaking hand. "A baby? How funny. And what did you tell him?"

Cole considered her for a moment and then moved his hand away from her back, resting it now atop his thigh as he turned, directing his gaze off into the night. "I told him that couldn't be. That until today you didn't have a husband. So you couldn't be carrying a baby." Then he leaned over, scooped up a tiny twig from off the ground, and gave his attention over to rubbing it slowly between his hands, hands that intimately knew the working end of a gun.

He knows. Kate's throat all but closed. She stared at his face under his Stetson. Shadows, planes, and angles. The curve of his cheekbone, the stark straightness of his nose, the firm set of his mouth. She was as good as dead. So why not tell him and get it over with? Because she just couldn't do it, couldn't go through with her own plan. The truth was, she was about as well equipped to take care of herself as Lydia was. So, once again, she changed her mind. "A woman," she said into the quiet space between them, "doesn't always have to have a husband to have a baby."

Cole's hands stilled, then he edged them apart, wide enough for the twig to drop away and fall to the trampled grass of the ground. "No, I don't expect she does," he finally said, now looking her way, his black eyes boring into her soul. "But it was enough of an explanation for a seven-year-old boy."

Almost numb with fear, Kate still managed to nod assent. And then further tested the troubled waters with her next statement. "I wasn't quite truthful with you earlier."

Cole chuckled . . . as if he'd known that all along, too. "Oh?"

With her cheeks warming, Kate firmed her lips together. "Yes. Just now, over by the wagon, you asked me what I was looking for. I was looking for you."

"Is that so?" He tugged his Stetson off, ran a hand through his black hair, and then settled the hat atop his bent knee.

Kate watched, fascinated despite herself. What he'd done seemed so intimate somehow, as if he'd taken off his shirt in front of her. He now turned to her, catching her staring at him. Embarrassed, not understanding her reaction to him—she'd been so sure, after Mr. Talmidge, that she'd never, ever want to see another man disrobing—she looked down at her hands folded in her lap.

"Go on," he urged. "You wanted to talk to me. About what?"

Kate cut her gaze over to him. "I, um, wanted to speak with you about the children."

"The children. They behaving for you?"

"Yes, they're behaving just fine," she rushed to tell him. "Like you said earlier, they're good kids."

"Yes, they are. They've been through a lot, to be so young." His jaw set, his expression hardened . . . and Kate felt certain, even though he hadn't moved, that he'd locked a big hand around her throat and was squeezing. "I'd hate to see them go through any further upset, Kate. In fact, I'd probably do more than just hate it. A lot more."

The snapping twigs in the fire crackled. An owl asked *whoo-whoo*. And Kate stared silently at Cole. The words wouldn't come. She knew what she wanted to say, what she needed to say, but her mouth wouldn't form the words. And her heart, beating above where her unborn child was even now forming, wouldn't allow her to speak the words that could cause her to lose her own life. She had more to think about, it reminded her with every beat, than her own self. More to protect than only Cole Youngblood's—her husband's—niece and two nephews. *Her* niece and nephews now.

All of that meant she had to go through with her desperate plan, the one she'd come up with in the schooner. The one where she left.

"What about the kids, Kate?" Cole prompted.

"Um, yes. The kids. Well . . . it's nothing." Her decision made, her fate sealed, Kate braced her hands atop her knees and made as if to stand up. "Nothing that can't wait until the morning. So I believe I'll turn in now." She levered herself up and stood there, looking down at Cole, at the man who had every legal right to tell her where she'd sleep tonight. Again her heart picked up its drumming beat. She feared he could hear it, could divine her thoughts . . . and would hold her to her vows.

"Wait a minute." He plucked up his Stetson and came to his booted feet in one smooth-muscled motion. A good six inches taller than she, and broad-shouldered enough to block the night, he held his hat in one hand and held her gaze with the sheer force of his own dark eyes. "If you'll remember, I said I wanted to talk to you, too."

"That's right. You did." Kate twisted her fingers together nervously and stiffened her knees against a sudden urge to flee into the night. Aiding her urge was another gust of wind, with its captured leaves and dust, which flirted around her hem. "What about?"

"About . . . today. Partially, anyway. About the justice of the peace. And our being married.".

Kate licked at her suddenly dry lips. "Yes?".

He edged his Stetson's brim around in his hands, slowly turning the hat in a complete circle. "It appears that word has spread around the camp—most likely by those men in the land office—about us getting married. And me being who I am. And what with folks worried about you yesterday. Well, something like this, even with all the land-grab fever, is news."

"I hadn't thought about that."

"No, I didn't suppose you had. But anyway, folks know. They might say something, like congratulations. Or they might not. I didn't know how you'd feel about that. But still . . . I thought you should know."

Kate nodded, felt a smile tug at her mouth. He actually sounded shy. "Thank you. It'll be okay, if they do. I'll just smile, if you will."

He nodded and settled his Stetson back on his head, fitting it low on his brow. "I also wanted to talk to you about something else. About tonight's sleeping arrangements."

Chapter Seven

"Sleeping arrangements?" Kate finally choked out. Her worst nightmare come to life, even despite her earlier moments of attraction to Cole. Taking its place now were shock and fear and a flashback memory of New York and Mr. Talmidge. Kate put a shaking hand to her mouth and stared at Cole—her husband, a man with complete legal rights over her, no matter the nature of their private bargain. Finally she gathered her courage and challenged him. "It's not that kind of a marriage. You know that. And you promised me."

His eyes narrowed. "Promised you what? I don't know—"

"Yes you do. You do know. This is a business arrangement between us. Nothing more. You're not sleeping with me. Or doing anything else with me." Kate had just realized, as well, that she'd never get away tonight if he were with her. And tomorrow would be too late. But right now, tomorrow was the least of her worries. Because this night's implied intimacies ruled her growing panic. And had her stepping back, away from the gunslinger just then bracing his legs, settling into his stance, and facing her.

"I know our arrangement. You don't have to spell out the particulars for me." Cole's expression could have been cast in stone. "I'm talking about the weather, the wind coming up just now. It's getting cooler, and there's talk of rain. I was thinking of moving the boys into the covered schooner with you and Lydia. That's all. I meant no disrespect to you."

The boys. He means the boys. Nothing more. Relief washed over Kate. She took a deep breath and turned away, fighting the weakening in her knees. Putting aside her added worry about getting away tonight in the rain, if it came to that, she said, over her shoulder, "I'm sorry. I spoke before I thought."

"No harm done," he said from behind her. And then, more quietly, "I wouldn't force myself on you, Kate. Or any other woman."

Kate's breath caught. She pivoted, turning to face him. "I didn't think you would. It's not you. Not that you're not. . . ." *Desirable.* She couldn't say that. "Not that you . . . It's me. I can't—I won't—"

"I said it's okay. No harm done."

She took another breath, rubbed at her forehead, felt awful—for him and for herself—and then met his gaze. Black and glittering, it almost took away her nerve. "Where . . . um, where will you sleep . . . if it starts to rain?"

Silence met her words. Then, his voice quiet, his gaze steady, he asked, "You worried about me?"

Kate stiffened, began fiddling with her fingers. "Well, no. I mean, yes. I mean, you're a grown man and all. But still, I—"

He held up a hand to stop her. "Don't worry about me. I know how to find dry ground." Then he looked her up and down. "Unless you just want me to sleep in the wagon with you. Do you?"

Intense discomfort, on more than one level, tore at Kate's insides. For one thing, she didn't want to trip over the man in the dark as she stole his horse and money. But she also knew that wasn't the only reason she'd asked where he would spend a rainy night. Surprisingly, she did care. She did feel bad about him possibly taking a drenching while she and the children slept high and dry in the wagon . . . when there was room for one more. But she'd be darned if she could bring herself to suggest it. She just couldn't, married or not, caring or not. Thinking all this, she shook her head no—

"I didn't think so." His expression mirrored some emotion . . . disappointment? "Just help me with the boys.

Or I can get them, if you'll untie that canvas flap for me."

Kate nodded, glad for the suggested activity. Doing was better than thinking. Feeling as if she walked on surer ground now, she started for the wagon. "I'll do that and then get them a place ready. Give me a minute to move some things around."

But Cole stepped to her side, keeping pace with her . . . instead of heading for the buckboard. "Let me help. There're some mighty heavy things in that wagon."

The last thing she wanted was Cole Youngblood that close to her in the narrow confines of the wagon. A protest came to her lips, but before she could get out the words, Cole surprised her by chuckling and shaking his head. "I have to give Mack Anderson—he was my sister's husband—his due. I was certain he didn't intend to come back for my sister and the kids. But with all this evidence here—everything a body would need to stake a claim and then build on it—I have to rethink the man. Because I swear Mack brought everything that wasn't nailed down."

Kate chuckled, completely disarmed by this personal insight he'd shared with her. Caught up in the moment, she heard herself say, "Well, I'm glad he did bring everything. I'm going to need it all to make me a place to live."

Too late, Kate caught her slip. Her expression fell. She'd said *me,* not *us,* not her and the kids. Just her alone, once she slipped away tonight. Never mind that she wouldn't have access to or be using any of the building materials that Mack Anderson had brought. Cole Youngblood didn't know that, either. Nor was she going to tell him. But would he notice her slip-up? He sure as shooting noticed every other thing she said and did.

But luck was with her. Because Cole didn't react, not that she could discern. Maybe he was lost in some thought of his own. Which proved to be true when he suddenly stopped and gripped Kate's arm, startling her and stopping her with him. As instantly as he'd gripped her arm, he released her and put his hands to his waist. "I hadn't thought about that. Damn. How are you and three kids going to build a place to live? Do you even know how to do that? How to construct a house? Even a one-room one, Kate?"

Before she could think, she shook her head no. An honest response. And the wrong one. She knew it instantly. Just as she knew he'd have no reason, after tonight, to worry about sticking around to build her a cabin. Because she wasn't taking the kids or the wagon. No, come tomorrow, he'd still have both. And she'd have his name, his horse, and most of his money. The only thing, then, he'd want to build for her—if he found her—was a scaffolding with a hangman's noose swinging from it. But he didn't know any of that, so she either had to say, yes, she did want his help. Or come up with a darned good reason why she didn't. And all that without giving away the truth. "We'll be fine, I expect. I can—"

"Like hell." Then he stood there, silent and shaking his head. Kate had only long enough to note the agitated outline of his body before he added, "I can't leave you like that, with only a wagon to live in. You need a decent place to keep yourself and those kids."

"No I don't. I mean, yes I do. But I really think I can make do—"

"No. It's settled. I'll stay and build you a decent place."

Kate licked at her dry lips. "What about your cousin?"

Cole's expression mirrored confusion. "My cousin? What . . . ?"

"Your cousin. Remember? You're going to go find her and then take the kids to her? That's what you should be concentrating on. You don't know how long that will take you. And I don't think the kids should be with me all that much longer, but they would if you stick around to build a cabin before you go hunt for her. Because I'll only come to care more and more for Joey, Willy, and Lydia. And them for me. And then, come several months later"—*when my condition is obvious*—"you'll come back and cart them off, with all of us crying." She was babbling and knew it and had to stop. "And who wants to see that?"

There. She'd gotten it all out. While she concentrated on breathing after all that talking, he blinked and looked . . . bewildered. Because of her speech? Or because he'd forgotten that he'd told her he meant to hunt for his cousin? Kate had to wonder if this woman even existed. And that was Kate's original fear with him, that'd he'd hightail it out of here and never come back. A sinking feeling settled in her stomach. "You are still going to go find her, aren't you?"

Cole's gaze suddenly narrowed, his expression firmed. "I am. But not until after I see you settled in safely. There's a hot summer right around the corner. You need to have shelter and a good supply of food laid in before then." As if his pronouncement alone settled it, he set off again for the schooner.

Kate stood there, watched him walking away, noted his confident stride. Unspoken words remained on her tongue. Because there was nothing she could say. She had her secrets. And apparently he had his. All his talk about building cabins and hunting down long-lost cousins. He was stalling. He never meant to go find that woman. He meant to leave those kids here with her forever. She just knew it. Why, he was no better than—Kate's expression puckered with her realization. *He's no better than me.* She put a hand to her trembling mouth. *I'm a terrible, lying person. No one should ever leave their children with me.*

And then she remembered. She would soon, about the time of the new year, have a child of her own. After this, she swore to herself, after tonight, no more lies. Only the truth. Her child deserved that much, an honest mother. But for now, for tonight, she'd just keep her mouth shut, wouldn't say a thing, truth or lie. Not that she'd intended to tell Cole about her own plan, which was to use the money she took from him to pay someone to build her a cabin. Hadn't he told her there were skilled workmen aplenty here hoping to get rich by building a city? Well, she'd just help them along. And then, after that, to help herself along, she intended to work in town.

Doing what, she didn't know yet. Or for how long, given polite society's views on women in her condition not being seen in public once they began showing. But she'd find something. She'd make do. How soon she had to worry about those things all depended on how much money Cole had. Or, rather, how much of it she took. Of course, her whole plan, as well as her very life, depended on him not finding her and killing her once he realized that she was gone.

But, she told herself, she just couldn't worry about that right now, about how she might have to consider a different plot of land so he couldn't so readily find her. And about how she'd get past him at the land office, where he could simply wait for her to show up to register her claim. The law forced her to do that, and he would know that. But still, as always, he'd have three kids with him. How long could he wait around trying to find her?

Forever, if he was stubborn enough. And Kate figured he was. Fisting her hands around her skirt's folds, she took a deep breath that hurt her worry-constricted lungs and told herself, *One day—and one lie—at a time, Kate.*

Those thoughts finally propelled her into motion and quickly brought her to the schooner with Cole. He'd already reached up and was untying her earlier handiwork. Done with that, he turned to her, wordlessly put his hands to her waist, and handed her inside, helping her over the gate. His hands on her, so strong and confident, made her suddenly feel small and unsure of herself and her abilities. Anymore it seemed like the only thing she was good at was lying. And tonight she'd add stealing and cheating to her skills.

Instantly, Kate berated herself. She had to get over this bad feeling in her gut. Just had to. Had to accept that if she was doing all the wrong things, it was for the one right reason. Her baby.

So, quickly—once Cole walked away, over to the boys sleeping in the buckboard—Kate set about making them a bed. All she had to do was carefully move Lydia over and begin straightening the bedding, allowing room for the boys to sleep with their sister. After all, she herself wouldn't need a bed here tonight. She was leaving.

"Kate?"

She whipped around. Of course, it was Cole. He held his saddlebags. He lifted them over the tailgate and held them out to her, his expression open and honest, saying, "Here. Take these. No sense getting them soaked, too. Too much inside that's important."

How well she knew that. But still Kate hesitated, realizing the quiet statement of trust in her he was making. A trust she was going to betray this very night. *Don't think about that, Kate. Think about these children. Think about your own baby.* Thus fortified, she stepped away from the bedding at the head of the wagon and sidestepped a trunk, making her way toward where Cole stood outside on the ground. When she reached for the leather bags he held out to her, he warned, "Careful. They're heavy. I wouldn't want you to hurt yourself."

Kate froze, her grip on the bags tightening. *He knows.* Otherwise, why would he say that? But how could he be aware of her delicate condition? Not that she felt the least bit delicate yet. No, Kate decided, it must be her guilty conscience weighing on her and making something out of his innocent remark. She tugged the bags in—he wasn't overspeaking himself, either, for they were heavy—and set them just inside the tailgate.

"You ready for the boys?" Cole asked, looking up at her, his hands gripping the raised tailgate, his dark eyes warm, the skin at their edges crinkling with his smile.

Kate's breath caught. The man always took her by surprise. He stirred things inside her, things she'd thought sure had been forever stolen from her. She had to get away from him. She had to. For her own sake. Finally, realizing he was watching her watch him, she forced herself to speak. "Yes. I've made them a place. But you will be close by tonight, won't you?" She worried about the children being in here alone once she left.

He gave her a considering look, one that said he couldn't quite interpret her wanting him so close. "I'll be right outside here with Kitty. Probably sleep under the buckboard with him. But I'm betting it doesn't rain. I don't feel it. Still, there's no sense in not getting the kids out of the weather. Just in case."

"You're right," Kate said quickly, glad for the children's sake that he'd be close. And glad for herself . . . to know where he'd be. But did he have to be so considerate? It made her feel as if she were kicking him in the gut for it, with everything she was getting ready to do tonight. Wasn't he supposed to be the heartless killer? And her the decent person? It was getting hard, Kate admitted, to tell who was good from who was bad.

"Kate?"

She jumped, realizing that again she was staring. And again, he was watching her. Disconcerted, as much by her own behavior as by his nearness, and with her cheeks warming, she blurted, "You want help with the boys?"

He grinned up at her and tipped his Stetson back. "You're awful pretty, Kate Chand—I mean, Youngblood—you know that?"

Youngblood. Kate stiffened, could only stare down at him. She kept forgetting she was now a Youngblood.

Cole raised a hand. "Don't worry. I didn't mean anything by it. It's . . . well, the moonlight in your face. You're . . . pretty, is all. I just thought you should know, this being your wedding night." With that, he winked at her . . . and turned away, making his way back to the buckboard.

Kate never moved. She watched his retreating figure, noting again his broad shoulders, the slim hips and long legs. Such easy confidence in his walk. She wanted to cry. Why now? Why was he opening up to her like this? Why was he so all-fired nice all of a sudden? And worrying about her? Did having a wife do that to a man? To some, she supposed. Her father had been a nice man, that was true. And Mrs. Jacobs, from the train ride out here, seemed to think highly of her husband. But Mr. Talmidge . . . he was another kettle of fish. Having a wife, especially one like Norah Heston Talmidge, certainly hadn't refined him any.

And Cole Youngblood . . . what about his *wife? That's you, Kate. What effect will* you *have on him?* Kate put a hand over her mouth, stifling a cry. She didn't know whether to hang her head in shame. Or raise her eyes to the heavens and say a prayer for her soul, a prayer she'd need once Cole found her gone tomorrow morning.

Just then he approached her again, with a sleepy-eyed, restive little boy held in each arm. Their dark heads lolled against his shoulders. With a thought to her own developing child, worrying about what this heavy lifting might do to it, Kate nevertheless leaned over the tailgate, reached out her arms, and readied herself to take the boys, one at a time. What other choice did she have? She either helped . . . or told Cole Youngblood why she couldn't. Not for the first time did she wish that she'd told him at the outset that she was a widow. That would have covered everything. But she hadn't thought of it then and couldn't simply come out with it now. He'd have too many questions. And he already had enough of those.

Outside the wagon, Cole stopped and looked up at her. "Just help me hand them over. They're heavy and about half-awake, anyway. No sense in you lifting them. Just walk them to the bed. They'll go right back to sleep."

Kate did as ordered, and again wondered if Cole knew, or at least suspected, her condition. Maybe he'd believed Joey's conclusion. Well, it was certainly true enough. But still, if Cole knew or suspected, she would have thought he'd have said something more than he had just now or even earlier. Mulling all this over, Kate walked first Joey and then Willy to the bed. Just as Cole had said, the boys went right back into a deep sleep, the instant their heads hit the pillows.

If only I could do the same thing, Kate mused as she tucked the boys in. She was bone-weary. But the coming night would be a long one for her. And she had no one to blame but herself. And the Talmidges. And Cole Young-blood. And these three kids. And her own baby. As well as some unknown—Kate pivoted to see Cole still standing there watching her, a curious expression on his face. She managed a smile for him and a softly spoken, "Good night."

He tipped his Stetson to her and said, "Same to you. And, um, congratulations, Kate . . . on your wedding night." Then, his expression neutral, he stepped back far enough to tug the tailgate into a closed position. Then, with a final warm and considering look in her direction, he pulled the canvas back into place, blocking himself from Kate's view. But from the interior of the wagon, Kate watched Cole. Thanks to a nearby lantern, she could see him outlined against the canvas as he tied the flap down. She stood perfectly still, even when he turned and walked away, his silhouetted shadow just suddenly gone when he stepped out of the pool of light. But she could still hear the fading crunch of his departing footsteps.

Finally, a tear slid down her cheek. A tear for all she had no choice but to do. A tear for all she'd never be able to do. Or to have.

Hours later, deep in the night, Kate sat up from where she'd been wakefully resting, still fully dressed, at the end of the bedding. She'd feared she'd fall asleep and not awaken until first light. But she should have known better. She hadn't slept a wink. Too scared. Too jumpy. Instead, she'd lain here, her eyes open and staring at the saddlebags only a few feet away, as she tried to calculate time's passing.

But now, here it was . . . time to act. Aided by that outside lantern light that dimly lit the wagon's interior, she looked to Joey, Willy, and Lydia. A tender smile found its way to her mouth. The sweet, innocent children slept on. So did the would-be settlers scattered throughout Walnut Creek. Under the vast stand of trees that sheltered them, the families and their noisy activities had settled down to the occasional snore, clunk, baby's cry, or horse's whinny.

The night air had cooled, the wind blew softly. There was no evidence yet of the rain Cole had mentioned. It was therefore the perfect moment for Kate to make her escape. To begin her life on her own. That *was* what she wanted, wasn't it? Well, of course it was. And yet she made no move to get up and get what she needed out of the saddle-bags. Namely, the money. *Not all of it,* she reminded herself. She wasn't greedy. She'd take only what she figured she might need. That, and the map to the claim ... if she dared still claim that particular plot of land. Well, she'd take the map and worry about that later. She also needed a blanket or two for bedding. But everything else she needed was outside this narrow wagon.

So was Cole Youngblood. The man stood between her and all else necessary for her getaway. Like a horse. Not that she knew how to saddle one, much less ride it. But still, she needed that roan. Her very life depended on getting some land for herself and her baby. And darn that Cole Youngblood, again. He was sleeping too close for her even to get food from the storage box secured to the wagon's side. Why, even lifting a canteen from its peg would most likely wake up Kitty and have him barking.

Kate fumed now, thinking of her foiled plan to get everything together earlier. How could she have done so with the kids right here and Cole right outside? Well, she'd just have to do it. Or go without. Because all she was doing now was sitting here and stalling.

For a moment longer, though, Kate did sit there, trying to think what was the harm in staying put, in letting Cole make the run and getting her land and building that cabin. All of a sudden it seemed silly to her to be running away with no means and no knowledge of how to care for herself. Wasn't she just asking for a wagonload of trouble, being on her own? Wasn't it more sensible to sit tight, get the land claimed and the cabin built, and then tell him he had to take the kids, that she couldn't keep them? Couldn't she simply wait and tell him then? After all, what could he do?

Kill her in a fit of temper, for one thing. But not really.

She'd seen enough of him to figure that he wouldn't lose control like that. But what could he *really* do? Take back the land? No. It'd be in her name, too. Tear down the cabin he'd just built? She didn't think so. In fact, she grinned to imagine a grown man of Cole's reputation doing something as childish as tearing down a perfectly good cabin. No, all he could do was not like it. And then either make other arrangements for the kids, or take them with him.

Kate began to warm up to the idea of staying here, of not running away, and of keeping him with her as long as she could. Because truly, for as long as he was around, the children were safe. Her baby was safe. And so was she ... at least until he found out who she was. But maybe even after that. Because, as she was beginning to realize, Cole Youngblood was many things. But someone to stand by and allow her or his sister's children to be harmed, in the face of a hired killer showing up? No, he wasn't that sort.

But what if Mr. Talmidge himself came here? Kate remained half convinced the awful man would do so. If he did, would Cole Youngblood protect her? Or do the bidding of his employer? That answer she didn't have. But somehow, given what she'd learned of Cole in the past few days, having seen the care and respect with which he'd treated her, she liked to think that maybe he would take her side. If for no other reason than she was now married to him. And carrying a bastard child, a pregnancy she hadn't wanted. But a baby she now did.

Kate's spirits picked up, had her sitting up straighter, even getting excited. She didn't need to run away and hide out, after all. Why, the best thing for her to do was to lie back down and sleep ... and allow events to run their course. It made sense. Because every time she thought of something else she needed to have or needed to know how to do in order to take care of herself, she was forced to realize she didn't have it or couldn't do it. And would only get her fool self killed trying. To make matters worse, even her own body was fighting her now, leaving her sick and tired and hungry. That would only get worse as the baby grew. So would her urgency to relieve herself. As she felt now.

And thus, confronted with nature, decision time arrived. Did she go outside only to do her business and then come back and sleep? Or did she go outside now, never to come back?

Kate slumped. She'd already left behind so much. Had already been forced from the only world she'd ever known. Had already done some unforgivable things, things that had her very soul in jeopardy . . . like marry a man she didn't love, in order to earn a chance for her baby to be safe. So this was no time to fall short of the mark. She couldn't afford now to be wrong. But all she knew was she was tired. Tired of worrying about it. Tired of hiding her intentions. Tired of trying to outthink the world, of trying to be smarter than she was. She just wanted to rest.

Her gaze lit again on the saddlebags. She also wanted to see that numbered stake Cole had secured for her. Did it exist? If it did, wouldn't that answer a lot of her questions about his intentions? Meaning, if the stake was in there, like he'd said it was, then wouldn't that show her he was telling the truth about everything else? It made sense to her.

Her gaze ran over every smooth and worn facet of the leather bags. They weren't locked in any way she could see. Only buckled. And they *were* now partly hers, since she was married to Cole Youngblood. So what could it hurt to look? Why, until this minute she'd fully intended to open them anyway. So what was staying her hand now?

Nothing. Put that way, Kate scooted forward and grabbed them up, quickly kneeling down at the wagon's end, the better to use the outside lantern light to see. She glanced over her shoulder to make sure the children slept on—they did—and then turned her attention to the leather pouches. Unbuckling the first one, and feeling certain she'd burn in hell for doing so, she nevertheless opened it and peered inside. She poked through its contents, moving aside some folded papers.

Then . . . she saw it. Also folded. Money. Her own gasp

of surprise startled her. A lot of money. More than she'd ever seen before in her whole life. Cole Youngblood was a rich man. Kate shook her head in wonder. So this much was true. He'd said yesterday he'd leave her enough money so she'd not have to worry about anything for a long time. He'd meant it.

But besides papers that were of no concern to her and all this money, there was no wooden stake that would officially claim her land for her. Fearing the worst, yet refusing to admit that she did, she quickly rebuckled the pouch and turned the bags over, hastily opening the other side. Blowing out a breath laden with trepidation lest it not be there, she peeked inside.

A thrill of excitement and relief shot through her. There it was. The wooden stake. Just lying there. Tied around its square top was a strip of red cloth—somewhat like a flag to blow in the wind, once it was staked in the ground, and alert other would-be settlers this land was claimed, Kate surmised. Down its length, a number was burned into it to guard against its being changed. This number corresponded with her registry entry in the land office. Her number. Kate realized she was smiling . . . and sniffling back tears. It just meant so much, this stake.

And Cole Youngblood had gotten it for her.

Kate stilled, felt her elation slip away. The man had done everything he said he would. A killer he might be—and she knew he was—but he didn't appear to be cold-blooded, not as the stories she'd heard made him out to be. At least, not in his treatment of her. Instead, Kate knew him as a man of his word. A man she could respect and, surprisingly enough, a man she could have come to have warm feelings for, had it not been for what Mr. Talmidge had done to her.

Her hands resting atop her bent knees, Kate sat back, feeling terrible. Not so much from her urgency to relieve herself, which wasn't painful yet. But about running away. About stealing from Cole. About cheating him. About lying to him. She no longer thought it was something she could do. Because he'd honored his part of their bargain. She would now honor her part. She would stay. And trust that the risks wouldn't be too high, that the good Lord would take into account that she was in a hard place and trying to do the right thing.

Finally feeling better about herself, Kate excitedly reached into the bag and plucked out the stake. She just wanted to hold it for herself. Just once. But caught up in the splintery wood was a folded piece of paper that came with it.

Kate grimaced, pulling it away from the all-important stake. *Does the man keep every scrap of paper given to him?* She meant to stuff it back into the pouch. But something about it, maybe just the way it was folded, stopped her. Or maybe it was the word *Anne*—uncomfortably close to her own given name of Anna—visible on the paper's other side that caught her attention and had her heart pounding.

Licking at her suddenly dry lips, her heart dully beating, Kate held onto the paper, stared at it, and laid the wooden stake down beside her. She knew what this was. She'd seen them before in New York. A telegraph. Suddenly sick inside and not able to draw a deep breath into her lungs, Kate raised her head, stared at the sheltering canvas dome above her, and blinked back tears. *No. Please, no. Please let me be wrong.*

Then, and fearing she wasn't wrong, but knowing it was a matter of two lives or two deaths—her own and her baby's—Kate lowered her head, telling herself she was ready to face whatever was written on this paper. But slowly, as if she'd been ordered at gunpoint to do so, she unfolded the square of paper. And, angling it more to the lantern light outside, read about her intended fate. Instantly heartsick, with tears blurring her vision, she read about how much advance money had been deposited in a bank. And how much more was awaiting Cole Youngblood if he killed Anne Candless, thieving maid to Edgar Talmidge.

Some of the details were wrong. Her name, for one

thing. And there was no description of her. She thought
that odd. But she didn't doubt that the so-named Anne
Candless was her, Anna Katherine Chandler. Hadn't Cole
questioned her about her name yesterday when she'd told
it to him? Hadn't he been full of questions only today about
where she was from? Yes, he had. It was all so awful. And
now so obvious. But the worst outrage to Kate was the
reason Mr. Talmidge gave for wanting her dead. *A thieving
maid.* Anger boiled in Kate's heart. She hadn't stolen a
thing from the rich and grasping man, a man whose awful
touch she knew all too intimately.

Kate felt her expression harden, felt the blooming of
hatred in her soul, a hatred she'd worked hard not to feel,
fearing as she did that it would mark her baby, maybe even
scar it. But how could she not feel it? And how could she
let it go? She hadn't stolen a thing from Edgar Talmidge.
But he'd stolen everything from her. Her innocence. Her
life in New York. Her reputation. Her good name. Her future. Everything but her very life and that of her baby's.

And now it appeared that he wanted those, too. Her life.
And her baby's. For once, Kate allowed herself to carry the
thought one step further, allowed herself to name her baby's
father. Edgar Talmidge wanted the very life of his own
child ended.

A mewling heartsick gasp escaped Kate, had her putting
a covering hand to her mouth. How could he be so heartless? An innocent babe. Fearing her sanity, fearing she'd
simply lay down and die from her own willing of it to be
so, Kate forced herself to think of the money that had already exchanged hands and of the remainder of the money
that awaited only the news of her death before it also was
handed over.

Finally, her spine stiffened with the resolve that also
firmed her lips. At least her life was worth a huge sum to
the man. Somehow, in some sick way, that was comforting.
Mr. Talmidge didn't consider her life cheap. *Good.* If he
wanted her gone, then it was going to cost him plenty.

Because he'd certainly paid Cole Youngblood handsomely to see the dirty job done.

And Cole Youngblood had agreed to do it, to kill a woman carrying a child, a woman who now bore his own last name.

What a wonderful wedding present this is. The thought became an angry grimace. Only then, when Kate looked down at her hands, did she realize she was refolding, along its original lines, the paper that detailed her demise, refolding it with exacting motions, with controlled and murderous rage in her heart and in her surprisingly steady hands. As she did, she determined that she wouldn't die easily. She wouldn't let Cole Youngblood, her husband and her intended killer, just have her life. No. He'd have to take it. Violently. Hurtfully. Bloodily.

Or maybe . . . she'd take his life first. Right now. While he slept. In her mind, she saw herself sneaking up on him, his own rifle removed from its saddle boot and in her hands. She thought she could feel the cold metal, the hard wood stock, could feel its weight, could feel the cool night air in her lungs, the spongy ground under her feet as she stalked him. Then she tried to picture herself firing the rifle . . . into his chest.

Kate gasped, wrenching herself back to reality. She shook her head, desperate to clear her mind of such soul-numbing images, and felt sick inside. She'd eaten the man's food. He'd kept her safe. Given her a place to sleep. Given her a chance. And given her baby a name. Even so, she called herself a coward because she couldn't do it. Couldn't even picture herself killing the man paid to do the same thing to her. She sat quietly, a hand over her mouth, and gave that thought time to take root in her mind. That's what she needed to remember. He'd taken money to kill her. She lowered her hand to her lap. She'd remember that. She would.

But still she sought forgiveness for herself with the realization that she hadn't sunk so far that the notion of committing a cold-blooded murder couldn't still shock her. And for another, she asked herself, what good would it do her if she did kill Cole Youngblood?

Cole Youngblood. Immediately she remembered the feel of his hands atop hers as he'd steadied her first attempts at driving the team. How reassuring and kind he'd been when she'd gotten ill this morning, what good care he'd taken of her then. And how he'd been paid to kill her, this same man. Why couldn't she stay focused on that, instead of giving in to the warm feelings he had no right to make her feel . . . and she had no desire to feel? After all, she still may have to kill him. *But what good would it do?* she argued with herself.

Even if she did, she'd still spend the rest of her life on the run. Because Mr. Talmidge would send someone else. He wouldn't give up, she knew that much. He wouldn't stop until she was dead. And he'd want her dead long before it became obvious to anyone that she was carrying a child.

No one had to tell Kate that getting a hired gun to agree to kill a grown woman had to be a simpler thing to do than it would be to get him to agree to kill a very pregnant woman. Or even one who'd just delivered herself of a tiny helpless infant. Because hired gun or not, she had to believe that somewhere there was a line drawn, a point past which no hired killer would go. Except for Cole Youngblood. Kate sighed her pain, felt the tightness in her chest. It was true. She had proof right here. Cole Youngblood obviously had no problem stepping over that line.

Kate's eyes narrowed. She refused to forgive him, even believing as she did that he actually had no idea that she was pregnant. But what difference did her pregnancy really make? Because he already had, in his saddlebags, the money he'd accepted to kill a woman . . . at the same time he was denying to her that he would do such a thing. She remembered him saying that to her only yesterday evening as they'd stood there in the dark negotiating the deal that led to their marrying. He'd said he wouldn't shoot a woman. And here she'd taken that to mean he wouldn't kill a woman. Well, it occurred to her now that there were other ways to kill. It didn't have to be with a gun.

A sudden start made Kate shiver. Finally, she heard herself, acknowledged her own thoughts. *What am I thinking?* But she knew. And she couldn't believe the paths down which her bloody thoughts had taken her. *Murder. Guns. Killings. Babies.* This path of sin, once followed, just kept getting wider and more twisted. She couldn't believe, either, how one simple lie on her part had brought her to this, to all these lies, to all this thought of sin, thoughts that all too quickly translated into doing, into acting them out.

How had they happened, these images of herself killing a man? Why had it seemed so easy to plot? She was a *good* person, after all. She'd thought so all her life. She'd certainly called herself one. And even Cole Youngblood, given his treatment of the kids and, yes, of her too, was what she would call a good man.

So, how awful this all was. She could scarcely take it in. Then it occured to her that Cole intended to stake her with the very same blood money he'd accepted to kill her. So, how would he see all this, if he knew the whole truth? Would his own plans for her—meaning putting the children in her care—have all been for naught? Is that how he would see it? Or would her death, having to kill her, be nothing more to him than an inconvenience?

Perhaps so. So what was she supposed to do? Just bide her time here with him until one day soon he learned the truth of who she really was and killed her? She shook her head. No. She couldn't do that. But neither could she run away and thereby be forced into doing dangerous things that threatened her unborn child.

Kate put a hand to her still-flat belly, rubbing through her skirt as if she could feel her child there. She could allow nothing and no one to hurt her. Because she had too much to live for. But now that she knew for certain what she had only suspected and feared, now that she knew who she would finally face, what should she do?

What will you do, Kate? What are you capable of doing?

To protect her baby? Most anything, it seemed. So Kate sat for a moment longer, mulling over her options. But a moment became ponderously ticking minutes. Then . . . it came to her, the *what* she needed. With sickening, blinding clarity. The *what* that widened that path of sin for her.

Breathing in deeply, too afraid, too fragile even, to question herself, knowing that if she did, she could never go through with it, Kate replaced the telegraphed message back in the pouch where it had been . . .

. . . and turned her head, focusing on the three sleeping children with whose well-being she'd been entrusted. Cole Youngblood's kin. Here. In the wagon with her. She felt sick. But Kate knew what she had to do, if she had any hope of saving herself and her own child.

And with that knowing, she was lost. Forever. Her twenty-year-old soul was forfeit. Because if it came down to it—came down to her child or someone else's—then someone else's child, or children, would have to be sacrificed. And in the only way she knew how.

Chapter Eight

Cole awakened in the early grayness of the next morning, the day he was to leave the kids with Kate and move with the thousands of other would-be settlers down through the Cherokee Outlet to the actual border of the land run. Instantly, the second he turned over, cradling his head with his bent arm, his mind filled with the numerous details he'd have to consider before he left. Such as his horse's overall condition. Especially that of the roan's legs and hooves.

The gelding was fast, Cole knew that, and he had tremendous heart and stamina. But given the magnitude of this race, with a rumored fifty thousand or more people poised at the different borders and literally ready to give him a run for his land—*no, Kate's land,* he reminded himself—how would the animal hold up?

But knowing that only the race itself could answer that worry, Cole moved on to the next consideration. Food. The roan could graze, like it'd been doing. But Cole needed to take enough food for himself for about a week, he figured, until he got back here after the run, which was still four days away and was only the beginning of the ordeal. Because after getting the land, he'd still have to register the claim at Guthrie Station. No telling how long a wait that entailed, given the untold thousands of others who'd be trying to do the same thing at the same time. And then, after all that, he'd have the ride back here for Kate and the kids. So, about a week, by his best figuring. And that meant he'd need bedding. He'd take his bedroll. No problem.

Muttering about the details of such an undertaking, but not quite ready to jump up and start the long day ahead, Cole lay there, trying to organize everything in his mind. Uppermost was how best to transport what he needed and yet still retain a light enough load atop his horse, combined with his weight and that of the saddle, to keep the roan in the running. It was about to worry him gray-headed. That and the startling fact that he was even making the land run.

Cole considered the uncountable hundreds of wagons surrounding his own. What in the living hell was he doing here, making the land run? It had never been his intention.

Neither had getting married been his intention. And yet . . . here he was, married to a girl he'd met one day before wedding her. A girl he hadn't even done more than kiss, much less take to his bed. She plainly didn't want that. And Cole supposed he didn't blame her. It was different for a young woman like herself. A decent young woman. He could see that. Hell, it was written all over her. Innocence. Good upbringing. Just caught up in hard times. Not someone to be taken lightly, despite what every male instinct he possessed urged him to do.

Last night—her wedding night . . . hell, *his* wedding night—he'd told her she was pretty. But he knew that wasn't true. She wasn't just pretty. She was downright beautiful. He'd never seen eyes that green before. But looking now beyond her beauty, Cole realized that Kate was the perfect type of woman to settle a place like this Oklahoma Country. Young. Strong. Independent.

The perfect type of woman. Cole lingered there a moment in his thoughts. He thought about her closeness to him at this very moment, and knew all he had to do was turn his head to see where she even now slept in the schooner with the kids. She was as untouched as this land they were all getting ready to settle. He knew that from her kiss. She'd been scared and stiff, her teeth clamped against his tongue. He shouldn't have done that, shouldn't have tried to kiss her that deeply. But he hadn't been able to help himself. She stirred something deep within him, something that wanted to protect her, to keep her always with him. To hold her . . .

That did it. Grabbing for his Stetson, Cole rolled onto his back, dislodging Kitty the hound dog from his curled-up slumber right against Cole. "Go on," Cole urged, nudging the dog, trying to get him to stand up. "Get up now, Kitty. I've got things to do." *And no time to lay here and pine for a woman I can't have.*

In a half-crouch, the dog crawled out from under the buckboard wagon and, yawning mightily and stretching, headed off through the underbrush to do his business. Cole followed suit, rolling out from under the wagon and coming to his feet in one smooth motion of hardened muscles. He settled his hat on his head, low on his brow, and then, like Kitty, he stretched and twisted from side to side. *Damn, that ground didn't get any softer last night.*

Around him, the early morning song of folks waking and arising throughout the camp greeted him. The metallic clank of pots and pans filled the air. Babies' cries and children's laughter rang out. Called-out greetings of "good morning" welcomed the slanting sunshine through the trees. Thankful that it hadn't rained, Cole spared a glance for the schooner to his right. No sounds or signs of anyone inside being awake. The canvas flap at the back of the wagon remained tied. Not too surprising. Yesterday had been a big day for everyone. Probably just plain tuckered out, they all were.

Cole chuckled as he went off through the undergrowth to relieve himself. *Damned kids. Just ran till they dropped.* Once he finished his business and was back at the campground, he stood there a moment, taking in deep breaths of fresh woodsy air coupled with the smoky scent of the various surrounding campfires. Cole shook his head as he wondered how his life had come to this. Why, right now, if a stranger were to consider him in these environs, he'd appear to be no different from the thousands of farmers here with a wife and kids trailing him, wanting only a plot of good land and a chance to survive. Or maybe a city plot on which to open his business and make his fortune. All so he could put a roof over his family's heads and dinner in their bellies.

It was amazing. And not for him. Yet here he was,

among them. Cole Youngblood—hired gun, lone wolf—making the land run. That got a chuckle out of him. Life sure was funny sometimes.

But what wasn't funny to Cole about the whole situation was that he liked this feeling. This standing right here and observing and being a part of something. The excitement of it all. Even worse, he liked feeling settled. Liked having kin relying on him. Liked being part of—what?—of belonging to something bigger than his saddle, his horse, his gun, and his bedroll? Maybe. All he knew, as he tugged his bedroll out from under the wagon, was . . . this feeling had better pass. Because before he'd ridden onto Charlotte and Mack's land this last time, and had buried his sister and taken the kids, all he'd ever been responsible for was himself. And he'd liked that, too. Which was good because that was how his life would soon be again, he rushed to remind himself. Alone and on the trail of some worthless scum. That was the only way he could ever be.

But for now—and only for now, a very short time, he promised himself—all that seemed to have changed. How? How had it happened? He stopped in the act of shaking out his bedroll and stared out toward the rushing waters of Walnut Creek. Then he remembered.

His sister's death had started it all. Just thinking about Charlotte had Cole wanting to kick something. Damn, she'd always had a tough life, beginning with their mother dying when she was fourteen and he was seven. After that, Charlotte had been the only real mother he'd ever known. Joey was seven years old, the same age Cole had been when he'd lost his mother. And then, also like Joey and Willy and Lydia had, Cole had lost his father. Suddenly the similarities were too much. And overwhelmed Cole. What he and Charlotte had suffered then, her kids were suffering now.

What was going on here? Cole clutched his bedroll in his hands and looked around, half sure he would find someone else standing here with him. Someone much bigger and smarter and older than himself, someone who was trying to show him what he needed to see, and to teach him what he needed to know. But no one was there. And he felt the least bit silly for having looked. But still, he was left with the feeling that he was supposed to realize something that he just couldn't get. Maybe if he went back to what he'd originally been mulling over. What had that been?

His mother. He'd been thinking about his mother.

Over the years, and to his regret, his memories of her had faded. All he had of Lucinda Youngblood now were the stories Charlotte had told him. The same thing would be true of Joey, Willy, and Lydia. Over time, they too would have only faded memories of his sister, their mother. What a damn shame that was. But a truth he could do nothing about. Because Cole knew he wouldn't be around much to tell Joey and Willy and Lydia about their mother.

You could stay.

Cole stiffened against the truth of the words whispered to him, seemingly by the warm breeze. Then, a far more unsettling memory grabbed at him and had him striding— almost desperately, as if he wished only to get away from it—with his half-folded bedroll back to the buckboard and tossing the blankets inside. Then he stood there, his arms propped up against the worn wood of the wagon's railing. All his life Charlotte had told him he looked like their mother, Lucinda. She'd said he had her ways, her smile. Cole'd never understood what Charlotte had meant by that. Even now, he couldn't fathom it. Surely, their mother had possessed finer sensibilities than Cole's. His had led him to a life of bloodshed. How could he be good and fine like his mother?

But you are.

Cole's breath caught, the hair on his arms stood on end. Where was this coming from? Suddenly he saw himself all those years ago with Charlotte back on the homestead. She'd raised him. She'd had to. Their worthless son-of-a-bitch farmer father hadn't seemed to want to make much of himself or of the place after his wife died. No, within days of burying Cole's mother, that bastard had just up and rode off, telling him and Charlotte that he'd be back, that he had to go call in a debt and get the money he'd need to take them all back East so they could start over there.

And that was the last they'd ever seen of him. There they were, in Kansas, over by Wichita . . . two kids on their own.

But Charlotte had never complained, had never run away from what she had to do. Instead, she'd worked hard, had worked in other folks' homes, doing anything she could to keep them in food and clothes and shelter out on their homestead. And then, years later, she'd married Mack Anderson. A man also from back East. And a man with no skill with the land. But a man who swore he loved her and that he'd try. And so, they were married. Then, sensing he was in the way, Cole at sixteen had taken up with a gun and a way of life that still stood him in good stead. Every penny he hadn't needed to keep himself alive, he'd brought to Charlotte and to her kids as they had come along. But what had Mack Anderson done for them?

Cole's expression hardened, became unforgiving, as he thought of his dead brother-in-law, even as he tried to figure out why he couldn't get himself in motion this morning, why all he seemed able to do was live in the past. *And what good does that do a body? Can't anything be changed.* But right now, at this moment, it seemed that the past wouldn't allow his mind to rest, that like a person, it had something yet to tell him. Something that he had to realize before he could set off on this most important of days. A day, he suddenly knew, that was much more personally important to him than he'd realized until just now. So, giving in, he stood there and told himself to think it through, just get it over with.

So where had he been wandering in his memory's pathways? *Ah. Mack Anderson. Charlotte's worthless husband.* Again Cole's expression hardened. Why *did* he hate Mack so? Even asking himself that question told Cole he was on the right track in his thinking. Because never before had he questioned how he felt about the man. He'd disliked and mistrusted him from day one when he'd stepped onto their homestead. He hadn't been jealous of him with Charlotte. Cole knew she was his sister and not his mother. And that she, a young woman, needed someone other than him, something more than a brother in her life. And she deserved it, too. Deserved happiness, a happiness that Mack Anderson seemed to give her, no matter how hard the times were. And seeing that, Cole had stepped aside, had gone off on his own, had left them be.

It's all mighty strange, came Cole's sour thought. Sometimes he believed that every man he hunted down wore his own father's face. Sometimes he felt certain that in every town he rode through, the possibility existed that he'd find the man. He'd asked around, but nothing had ever come of it. Still, sometimes, when he looked into some old codger's face, he wondered . . . *Could this man be my father?* It was silly, he knew. The old bastard was probably long dead. But Cole just wanted to ask him why. That was all.

He just wanted to know why. Didn't particularly want to kill the man, although he deserved it, most likely. Just the why of it. That was all. Why had he just ridden off and left two kids standing there in the doorway of a small farmhouse with no means of seeing to themselves? Why? What kind of a man did that?

A good-for-nothing one, Cole knew. Then he remembered Joey, Willy, and Lydia. And the fact that he himself was getting ready, after this land run, to do the same damn thing to them that his own father had done to him and Charlotte. Leave them. *Son of a bitch. I'm no better than the old man was.* Cole suddenly felt sick, all the way to his own rotten soul. An angry, aching chuckle erupted from him, and had Kitty woofing at him. Cole turned to the dog. "Go on now, Kitty. Leave me be."

As the dog turned and padded off, Cole returned to his musings. All he could think was, how was this—meaning his situation here with Kate and the kids—for things coming back home to roost? It was true. All his adult life he'd condemned his father for leaving him and Charlotte behind like he had. He'd never allowed himself, after so many years of trying to believe otherwise, that his father had had a good reason for what he did, for not taking them with him.

In his own youth, Cole remembered trying to believe, hoping and praying, that maybe something had happened to him which had prevented his coming back for them. Maybe he'd been ambushed and killed. That was better than believing that the man simply hadn't cared about his own children. Maybe he had meant to come back for them. Why couldn't that be true? Why couldn't he forgive the man? At least give him the benefit of the doubt?

Cole took a deep breath. He really didn't want to think about any of this. But the questions wouldn't release him, wouldn't stop coming, wouldn't go away without answers.

Could the truth be that he'd heaped on Mack's head all the hate and hard feelings he harbored for his own father? Could it be that he'd never given Mack a chance, seeing in him what he'd so despised in his own father? Was *that* what kept him in the saddle and hunting men down? Was that what made him not care about the killing? And why *didn't* he care? What did that say about him? Was it because he maybe thought himself worthless?

After all, how worthwhile could a kid be if his own father didn't love him enough to stick by and see him raised to manhood?

No. It isn't about me. I don't count. I'm a man, and I made my own way. It's about Charlotte. The old man left her, too. But she'd never hated him like Cole did. She'd never said as much as one bad word about the man her whole life. All she'd talked about was how much he'd tried and how much he'd always been kicked down by circumstances. By drought, by flood, by tornadoes, by bad land. Excuses. All of that. Excuses. Abel Youngblood could have made it if he'd tried.

And what about you, Cole? Could you make it? Do you have the guts even to try?

Cole spun around, his hands fisted, looking for the enemy, the one whispering these questions, these . . . *truths* to him. *What about me?* he wanted to yell. But he knew . . . and now questioned himself. *Am I trying to make it? Am I sticking around, trying to do the right thing by my own sister's kids? No. I can't wait to haul my carcass away from here so I can go kill a woman. Some poor little maid who stole some money and some pretty rocks from a man rich enough to buy every bit of land that's up for grabs here in Oklahoma Country. What does that make me, then? I'll tell you—no better than my father. Just like the old man. The fruit doesn't fall far from the tree, does it?*

His breathing ragged, his chest tight, Cole stood there, looking all around. Nothing out here was amiss. The day dawned bright and beautiful. Full of promise. But the ugly truths inside him remained. He still wasn't willing to forgive his father, to do more than briefly entertain the notion that the man, as Charlotte had always said, had tried, that he had loved them, and that she was sure he'd meant to come back for them. She'd clung to that all her life, to the point of staying on the family homestead after her marriage and working that land . . . all in the hopes of being there when their father came home.

And what had that dream, that hope, ever gotten her? was Cole's hard-edged question.

A life as hard as their mother's. And a death at the same age. With her oldest child the same age that Cole had been when his and Charlotte's mother had died. And now—suddenly weak, Cole bent forward, bracing his hands on his knees and staring blindly at the ground—here he was, doing the same thing his father and Mack Anderson had done before him. Running away from their women and children, leaving them to fend for themselves.

Son of a bitch. It's true. Cole straightened up, stiffening his spine. He was worthless, not suited for anything more than hunting down and killing men. Cole didn't pity himself in the least. There was no poor-little-me implied in any of his thoughts or conclusions. Because he was one of the fortunate ones in the world. How many people could say that—that they truly knew why they were put here on earth? It was simple. He was a vulture. An ugly critter meant to live off the bones of other souls. A nasty critter not meant to live among the civilized folks. But still, he performed a service, in his own way. He was useful. He had meaning.

And it hurt like hell. Because this blinding insight into his own soul pointed out to Cole how much he was like his father. He too was a man who ran away. Who didn't have the courage it took to stay and to fight and to make a life in one place with one woman. But he didn't have any choice in the matter, now did he? And he wasn't looking for excuses. Because what did *he* matter? Who, with Charlotte dead, would care if he lived or died? No one. Not really. Which made him perfect for his own fate, now didn't it? After all, who missed a dead vulture?

No one. Except for the past few weeks when they'd been together constantly, the kids barely knew him. He'd pass out of their memories soon enough, just as his own mother had from his. Cole nodded with the rightness of that. Hell, they deserved better than him, anyway. And he had the life he was meant to have, that of a wanderer, a paid killer. It was all he was good for. Then, that being so, the sooner he got out of these kids' lives, the better off they'd be.

And Kate's, too.

There it was, the crux of his present dilemma. It was Kate Chandler, now Youngblood, who'd really brought him to this place on this morning and had him making ready to become a part of history. One woman. She'd changed his whole life, just as his mother had changed his father's life, just as Charlotte had changed Mack's life. Just as Cole knew he'd changed Kate's life. Because they were married. Maybe in name only. But that agreement was only between them, and not upheld in the eyes of the law. The whys and wherefores didn't really matter to the law. Because Cole and Kate were now one. Forever. And nothing but death could change that. It was a scary feeling, this sense of permanence that came with yesterday's brief ceremony.

Not that the ceremony itself had seemed so binding, not even when he'd been standing there and repeating the vows with Kate. Because he'd known, as had she, that theirs wasn't a real marriage. Not one like Charlotte had had with Mack, as worthless as the man had been.

But remember, Cole, he wasn't worthless.

Again Cole stopped, blinking, considering his new conviction regarding the man. His thinking about Mack was undergoing real change. Was it because he now bore the weight and the worry of Mack's responsibilities? That he now walked in the man's shoes? Was that why he was seeing his late brother-in-law in a new, more favorable light? As a man who'd tried to do the right thing. A man who'd stuck by his woman and raised his kids and made a difference in their lives. While he, Cole, had always killed folks for money so he could help his sister keep herself and those same kids alive—without ever giving Mack even a tiny portion of respect for all he did, day in and day out, year round.

That's a hell of a note. The more answers Cole found, the more riddled with questions were his thoughts. Then, feeling a sudden need for activity, Cole reached for some firewood he'd had Willy collect last evening. As he worked getting the morning's campfire going, Cole again found himself reflecting on how what he did for a living didn't seem to make much sense. Essentially, what he did was end one life to keep other ones going. Surely there was more to him than a quick-draw. The fire caught, began to flare up. Cole poked at it with a long stick of wood.

And wondered again where all these thoughts were coming from this morning. But there was still one truth that his mind wanted him to acknowledge, something connected to Mack Anderson. He knew that because every time he thought of the man, something stuck in Cole's craw. Well, he kept trying to get at it. But it appeared that every time he thought he had it . . . the thought slipped farther away, as when a thirsty man thinks he sees water out in the desert and it always shimmers just out of reach. That was how Cole felt now.

One thing he knew, though, was he surely hadn't done as much thinking over the whole course of his life as he'd done in the past forty-eight hours. And especially not along these lines. His present line of thinking, he was convinced, couldn't be good for him. Because if he began to see his jobs, his targets, as individual men, then he wouldn't be so quick to shoot. And a split second's hesitation could cost him his own life. And would leave Kate a young widow.

That's what he'd been thinking about. Kate. Their marriage yesterday. Before then, Cole now acknowledged, nothing in his life had been permanent. Nothing had been forever. He'd always moved on and had kept moving. His life had been built around change, around the next job, the next city, and the next man he'd been paid to hunt down. Cole frowned now, promising himself that soon his life would again be the way it had always been. Lived alone. The way he liked it.

Damn. Cole watched the fire and scrubbed a hand over his mouth and chin, feeling the roughness of his day-old growth of beard. And liked its coarseness. That was something he understood. Just as he was coming to realize he needed to get the hell out of here. Away from this family place. He needed to be on his own, riding alone, seeking his next target.

A woman.

Overwhelmed with that truth, Cole blew out his breath—and determined that his thinking days were over. Whatever he was supposed to realize . . . well, it hadn't come to him yet. So the hell with it. Turning on his heel, as if he'd just turned some corner in his mind, too, he decided he'd be better served seeing to the mules and to his horse than standing here and trying to set the world to rights—something he wasn't having much luck with, anyway. But first, coffee. No. First, he needed to get Kate up. They had a lot to talk

about—more land run details—before he left. And judging
from the already faster pace of movement evident throughout what he could see of the Walnut Creek camp, the
sooner he got her up, the better.

Cole turned in the direction of the schooner, but again
stopped. *Kate.* How *had* she changed him so much in the
course of one day? He didn't know. He just knew she had.
Somehow. And because she had ... he didn't think he
could lie to her about that cousin of his. He'd honestly tried
to think of the woman's name. But he'd be damned if he
could come up with it. Something with an *m* in it. Mary?
Marion? Margaret? Martha? *Who the hell knew?* And her
married name? *No clue.*

Cole firmed his lips, accepted the truth. He stood about
as much chance of finding that cousin as a tender thing like
Kate did of successfully making the run herself.

Which meant he had to tell her the truth. Two evenings
ago, when he'd told Kate he'd marry her and had realized
if he did she'd be the kids' aunt and he could leave them
with her permanently, he hadn't felt the least bit bad about
hiding that fact from her. Because he hadn't cared. But
now, it seemed, he did. And he didn't like it one bit. The
longer he was around her, and around Joey, Willy, and
Lydia, the softer his edge became. So what had he done to
fight that? Hell, he'd signed on to stay longer, long enough
to build them all a home.

Well, what else could he do? He couldn't just leave her.
Not like his father had left him and Charlotte. At least, he
couldn't leave her for a while. He'd do what he could. And
then he'd leave. But not forever. He'd come back by and
check on them, drop off some money. Like he'd done for
Charlotte. But his obligation to Kate, that of marriage, was
different than it had been to his sister. He knew it was.
Kate was his wife.

And that was another thing. He didn't think he could
leave Kate and the kids at all. In fact, he was afraid he
couldn't. Really afraid. He had no desire to go. Maybe it
was just because of the nature of his next paying job. Kill-

ing a woman. Maybe he was just trying to avoid that. But he feared that wasn't so, at least not completely so. *Hell, that Talmidge maid, Anne Candless, could be camped right next to us this very minute and I wouldn't know it, for all I've gone looking and asking.* But Cole knew he hadn't had any time to himself to go off and do that since he'd gotten here. *A man doesn't take three little kids with him when he has dirty work to do.*

Dirty work? Cole frowned, felt troubled. He'd never before termed his profession "dirty work."

But he'd never agreed before to kill a woman, either. Maybe it was getting to know Kate that was at the heart of his conflicting feelings. After all, before her, the only decent women in his life had been his mother and Charlotte. That was all he knew of women. Except for the ones he'd bedded, of course. All of them willing women, women in the trade. Upstairs girls. Women who knew what to do and were paid to do it. Cole realized now he'd never had anything more than a passing thought and some small affection for those women. It was true. In his line of work, in the kinds of places the job took him, he didn't run into too many decent women. Women like Kate. But now that he knew one of the breed, the marrying kind of woman, she sure was making his life hard.

Hell, at this point, and if he had his druthers, Cole told himself, he'd give Mr. Talmidge his damned money back and tell him to get himself another hired killer. But he couldn't do that. For one thing, he'd never gone back on a job once he'd accepted it. And for another, he already had the money, a goodly amount of it already spent or committed. And the rest of it needed. But worst of all, he still— and he couldn't get away from this fact—had three little kids to feed. And a wife.

Son of a bitch. Cole shook his head, put his hands to his waist. And then, hearing something coming through the underbrush, pivoted around, his hand to his gun. It was Kitty. Cole relaxed, chuckling, thinking of Lydia and her insistence on calling this mutt Kitty. *Damned stupid name for a dog.* Who promptly sat down on his haunches and cocked his head, sending Cole a considering stare.

"What the hell are you looking at?" Cole asked the scarred and rangy mutt. "Haven't you ever seen a man standing around and questioning his worth when there's a wagonload of work to be done?"

All Kitty did was woof. And get up and pad over to the schooner's tailgate. He looked back expectantly over his shoulder at Cole.

"All right. You're right. All I'm doing here is burning daylight. When I've got mules and a horse to water. And packing to do." Cole started for the other wagon, the schooner wherein his niece, two nephews, and his . . . wife still slept. *What the hell.* All his musings hadn't changed one blamed thing. Probably why he didn't spend too much time listening to his own thoughts. They never had much good to say. At least, not about him. Cole leaned down enough to rub at the dog's head. "Let's get 'em up and get 'em rolling, Kitty. We've got a long day ahead of us."

Then, standing at the back of the wagon, with Kitty next to him reared up on his hind legs and his front paws resting on the wagon, Cole began untying the drawstring closure that pulled the canvas covering taut and secured it at night. When the dog whined, Cole told him, "Hold your horses, will you? These ties are knotted."

And that was curious. But blaming his fumbling fingers on not having the first sip of coffee inside him, Cole worked with increasing disgust at the disarrayed knots tangling the thin rope.

Then it struck him . . . the realization that he hadn't tied this mess. He knew better than to tangle it so. His hands stilled. He stared hard at the knotted ties and knew the truth. Someone, in the course of the night, had gotten out of the schooner—maybe just to relieve himself—and then had crawled back in and retied it like this. One of the kids? Or Kate? Either way, there was no excuse for this.

"Kate?" he called out. "Are you awake? Are you in there?"

Her answer was immediate. "Yes." And flat.

Cole tensed. "Is something wrong?"

"Yes."

The same flat tone of voice. Cole's insides knotted, just like the stubborn ropes under his fingers. He renewed his efforts with them, working fast and furious now. "What is it? What's wrong, Kate?"

"I don't know," came her plaintive answer. "I'm bleeding."

Chapter Nine

Cole froze, standing there and staring at the knots that kept him out of the schooner. He'd heard Kate's words. But they wouldn't sink in. "You're bleeding? Why are you bleeding? What happened?"

"Shh. Don't wake . . . the children. I don't want to . . . frighten them. And nothing happened. I'm just . . . bleeding."

There was a catch in her voice that tore at Cole. Furiously he tugged on the knots, finally loosening the first one. He only hoped the rest would follow suit. Then, lowering his voice, he hissed, "Kate, who tied these damned knots? I can't even get them undone."

"I did. I . . . had to . . . get out last night. But I couldn't."

Cole frowned. *Now what does that mean? She had to get out but couldn't?* Still, he abandoned that concern for the present one. "How bad are you bleeding, Kate? Do I need to cut these ties and get in there? What's wrong?"

"I—" She was crying softly.

Again Cole stilled, his hands clutched around the knots. "Kate, what the hell is wrong? Talk to me."

A muffled but no less heartrending sob came from inside the wagon. "My baby."

"Your baby?" Cole was certain he hadn't heard her right. She didn't have a baby. "You mean Lydia? Is something wrong with Lydia?"

Silence greeted his question. Cole died a hundred deaths. What in God's name was going on inside this wagon? Kitty suddenly became agitated and began barking loudly and baying and then whining and scratching at the tailgate. Cole could hear the kids rousing . . . and Kate talking to them. But over Kitty's noise, he couldn't hear what she was saying. He turned to the dog and, grabbing a handful of the folds of loose and furry skin at the dog's scruff, pulled him backward, off the wagon, and admonished, "Hush up, Kitty. Shut up."

But Kitty only bayed that much louder. "Hush it up, now. You hear me?" Kitty most likely did hear him, but he didn't shut up. Instead, and whining for all he was worth, the hound pranced and paced back and forth.

Giving up, and cussing, Cole ripped his knife out of its leather sheath at his waist and sawed right up one side of the hopelessly braided ties. "Hold on, Kate. I'm coming."

But it wasn't Kate who answered him.

"Hurry up, Uncle Cole." Joey's voice was high-pitched with fear. "Something's powerful wrong with Miss Kate."

As agitated now as Kitty was, Cole called out, "I know, son. Just sit tight. And all you kids stay back." At last, the canvas came free. Cole ripped out the useless rope and finally pulled the flap back so he could see inside the wagon's dim interior. His gaze instantly sought out Kate. She was on her knees and doubled over, her arms around her middle. *Son of a bitch. What the hell went on in here last night?*

To either side of her, their eyes wide with fright, but obviously fine, sat Joey, Willy, and Lydia. With her chubby little legs stretched out in front of her, the sleep-tousled little girl patted worriedly at Kate's tangled hair and told Cole, "Her's sick. Like Mama."

"No, she isn't, Lydia. She'll be fine. Just you sit tight." Cole wished he could believe his own words. And surprised himself by how much he needed for them to be true. With his heart racing, he quickly resheathed his knife and, employing the smooth motions that spoke of long practice, worked the pinnings that held the tailgate in place. Just as quickly, he had it down and open, and was climbing up onto the wagon bed. Kitty bounded in right behind him and pushed against Cole's legs as he maneuvered his way over to Kate.

With the wagon bed's dimensions being no wider than

four feet and its length about twelve feet, Cole had all he could do to get around without injuring himself. More than once he bumped into some solid object and nearly tripped. Twice he had to clutch at his Stetson as he nearly lost it when rubbed against the canvas covering stretched over the hickory ribs. But in spite of it all, and propelled as he was by concern, in only seconds he was kneeling in front of Kate and gripping her by her arms. Tears streaked her face. White lines of pain bracketed her mouth. And blood dotted her skirt.

Cole's eyes widened. He met Kate's gaze. Pain and fear rode her pale and pinched features. Weakly, she gripped at his hands on her shoulders. "Get . . . the kids . . . out of here."

Cole nodded, standing up as he ripped off his hat and threw it on the bedding. "Joey, take your brother and sister and go wash up at the creek."

"But Uncle Cole," the boy protested. "You might need help with—"

"I'll see to Miss Kate. You do as I say, you hear me?"

Joey scooted to his feet and pulled on Willy as he edged across the rumpled bedding.

"Good. And take Lydia's hand. Hold on to her real tight. There's all sorts of commotion outside, what with the wagons starting to head out for the Cherokee Outlet this morning."

Joey nodded and worked now at pulling the resisting little girl away from Kate. "Are we going with 'em, Uncle Cole?"

Cole firmed his lips together as he watched Kate smooth back the baby girl's ringlets and speak softly to Lydia, encouraging her to go with her big brother. "I don't know, son," he finally answered the boy. "We'll just have to see how Miss Kate is. And take that dog, too." Then Cole began to manufacture chores and duties to keep the kids occupied for a decent space of time while he saw to Kate. "When you get back, start your breakfast. Boil some of that oatmeal for the three of you."

"Okay," Joey agreed. "You need me to get the mules and your horse to water, too?"

Cole cursed under his breath. He'd forgotten about the animals. "No, not just yet. They can wait a bit. Just keep up with Willy and Lydia. That ought to keep you busy."

Another nod from Joey. "I reckon so. You want me to start your coffee?"

And that was when Cole realized how much he relied on this seven-year-old. Also surging through him was the realization of how much he loved this boy, as well as his younger brother and sister. Surprising himself no less than he did Joey, Cole reached out and tousled the boy's hair. "Yeah, son. That'd be nice. Now, you go on."

Joey turned his big dark Youngblood eyes up to Cole. And almost smiled. "Yes, sir," he said proudly, rounding up Willy and the dog Kitty, herding them ahead of him as he gripped Lydia's tiny hand. Then he turned to Cole. "I hope Miss Kate is okay."

Cole winked at the boy, realizing this was the first time he'd used her given name. Until now she'd remained Miss Chandler to him, even though her name was now Youngblood. "She'll be just fine. You go on now. Hurry it up. I've got to see to her."

After that, and with only a minimum of further ado and fussing, the three kids and the dog were out of the wagon and headed—hand in hand, with Kitty the hound dog ambling loose-jointedly beside them—for Walnut Creek. Immediately, Cole turned his attention to Kate. And found she'd lain down on the mussed bedding the kids had only just abandoned. Lying all drawn up on her side, her knees to her chest, she clutched at her middle and cried softly.

Cole dragged his hands through his hair and realized he didn't have the first idea what to do. Although he knew what was wrong with her. She'd said it herself. Her baby. Cole exhaled tightly. Joey'd been right yesterday when he'd said that he thought she was carrying a baby because his mama had gotten sick like that when she was carrying Lydia. Cole exhaled sharply, thinking, his wife in name only, his wife of one day, was carrying another man's child, it would appear. But maybe not for long, the way things looked now.

Cole smoothed a hand over his chin and jaw as he put aside any questions he might have about that. And then sank down beside Kate on the bedding, facing her and putting a hand on her trembling shoulder. "Kate? I don't know what to do to help you. You're going to have to tell me."

She shook her head and sniffled. Tenderly, Cole smoothed her hair back, saw her reddened face and crumpled expression. Fear and concern mixed in his heart. "Can you tell me what to do?"

"My baby," she whimpered. "I'm going to lose my baby."

"We don't know that yet. You might not." Instantly, Kate opened her eyes and stared up at him. Desperate hope blazed from their tear-washed green depths. Cole swallowed. Why had he said such a thing? To smooth it over, he asked, "How long you been bleeding?"

She shrugged her shoulders, shook her head. "Not long."

"Are you . . . well, are you bleeding a lot, Kate?"

She nodded vigorously and began crying in earnest.

"Son of a bitch," Cole muttered, feeling as useless as he'd only minutes ago accused himself of being. "All right. We've got to . . . well, we've got to get your clothes off you, Kate. I'm sorry. But I don't see any other way. If you want, I can go see if I can find a woman to help—"

She clutched at his wrist, gripping it hard, a look of pure panic on her face. "No. Don't leave me. Please. Just you. I don't . . . want anyone else . . . to know. Please."

"All right," Cole drawled as, eyes narrowed, he stared at her hand gripping his wrist and considered her condition. This was mighty strange. But not the time for questions. Or further hesitation because of the niceties. "Let's get to it."

With that, Cole set about gently undressing her. Scooting down to her feet and untying first one shoe and then the other, he realized that she *was* completely dressed, down to her shoes and her green jacket. Which was buttoned up. Cole kept working . . . and thinking. She'd said a moment ago that she'd meant to get out of the wagon but couldn't. What did that mean? Had she needed to relieve herself in the night? If so, what had prevented her? But it appeared to him now that she had gotten out of the wagon and had retied the canvas as best she could afterward.

Only—and this was the curious part—she'd tied enough knots in it to keep herself and the kids in here until the end of time. Much as if she feared being able to get out. Much as if she'd needed to be sure she couldn't get out. Or was it that she feared someone would get in? *Me? Is she afraid of me?* Before this morning and this revelation—her being with child—Cole figured he would have laughed at her tying so many knots and would have concluded she was afraid, on her wedding night, that he'd want to consummate their bargain in such a way as to make it a true union.

But now? Sitting here, removing her shoe, handling her slim ankle and foot through the thin cotton of her stocking? Well, he just didn't know. Yesterday morning, when he'd come into the wagon and had awakened her, she'd been wearing only her smallclothes. But not this morning. He looked at her face, saw she had her eyes closed. Pinched vertical lines between her eyes spoke of pain.

Cole grimaced in sympathy but couldn't banish the suspicious thoughts that kept coming. He gently put her foot down and picked up the other one, working the shoe off her foot. She'd said she hadn't been bleeding long. Which meant she'd had time to undress again after relieving herself in the middle of the night and before all this hit her. That could be. Or . . . had she been thinking of leaving? Cole glanced her way, saw the delicate curve of her cheek. She didn't look to be much more than a child. Why would she leave? Where would she go? It didn't make sense. So there had to be a simpler reason. Maybe she just hadn't undressed because the boys had been in here with her. That sounded reasonable . . . except for her shoes and her jacket.

Cole laid her foot down and pushed her shoes aside. He

then sought her attention. Her eyes were open. She was watching him. He felt his face heat up because of what he had to do next. He'd done this plenty of times with the upstairs girls. But not with someone like . . . his wife. "I'm sorry, Kate," he said, gesturing apologetically, "but I have to reach up under your skirt and pull your bloomers and your stockings down. I just wanted you to know before I . . . well—"

"It's okay. I know you have to."

Cole firmed his lips together and nodded, trying not to think about how he wasn't the first man to put his hands up under her skirt. If he were, she wouldn't be in this condition. Not that he was jealous or mad. He had no right to be, even though they now shared the same last name. This wasn't a real marriage, he knew that. But still . . . he just wondered, was all. Just wondered who'd gotten her like this and then had left her. But maybe she'd left him. Either way, he was just curious.

Thinking all that, Cole carried on with doing exactly what he'd said he had to do. He reached up under her skirt, untied her blood-tinged bloomers, and tugged them off her. Then he rolled her thigh-high cotton stockings down, one leg at a time. She cautiously moved each leg in turn, whimpering a bit with pain but wriggling her foot to help him. Under his hands Cole felt warm, firm, smooth female flesh. And sticky blood. "Son of a bitch," he muttered again as he tugged the hose off and laid them aside, too.

He looked at his hands. His fingers were coated in bright red. He swallowed, ran the back of a hand across his sweating brow, and hurried, now thinking only of helping Kate . . . somehow. But nothing in his life as a gunslinger had prepared him for this, for stopping the flow of someone's blood. Instead, it was his job to cause it to flow. In only minutes, though, and working as gently and as quickly as he dared, Cole had Kate down to her light blue cotton camisole . . . and little else.

As he draped a soft quilt over her nakedness, he couldn't help but observe to himself that she was milky-skinned, slender, and beautifully put together. He could see that much. A fine figure of a woman. But he'd already known that much, too. All he'd had to do was look at her, even fully dressed, to see that it was so. But now her dirt- and blood-stained heap of clothing lay cast aside, at the end of the bedding. She was now free of restrictions on her movements and her breathing. Done with his task, but knowing the ordeal was just beginning, Cole sat back on his haunches, resting his hands on his thighs as he considered her and what next to do for her.

"Kate?" he said softly. Her eyes were closed. He thought she might have drifted off to sleep.

"Yes?" She opened her eyes and sounded alert, maybe even a little stronger, as she turned slightly under her covers until she could see him.

"How you feeling?"

"Better. Thank you."

Cole nodded his "you're welcome." And admitted, "I don't know what else to do. Except"—again his face heated up—"maybe get some rags and water and . . . wash you off. So I can . . . see what's going on."

Kate stared at him, finally blinked. "You know what's going on."

Cole's lips firmed. "I do. But it's not my business." He didn't say anything else, offering this quiet opening for her to explain. She merely stared back at him. After another silent moment or two, Cole gave up. Although he had no idea what he'd be looking for, and wished like hell she'd let him find a woman to help her, he again asked, "Do you want me to clean you up and . . . take a look?"

"That'd be good." She slipped a hand out from under the quilt to swipe a dark sweat-dampened curl out of her face. "I think the bleeding has stopped. I don't . . . feel it . . . coming out anymore."

Cole tried to smile, found he couldn't. Not bleeding anymore could be good. Or bad. "That's good," he said, surprising himself with the realization that he truly wanted it to be so. "I'll go get those rags and some water. They're just outside." He stood up. "You'll be okay while I'm gone?"

She looked so tiny, not much bigger than Lydia, lying there under the quilt and barely making a dent in it. "I'll be fine."

"Good." With that, Cole turned to make his way out of the wagon.

"Cole?"

He turned back to her. "Yes?"

Her expression pinched up. She looked as if she were in pain. Or as if she were hurting inside, in her heart. "I'm scared," she blurted out, gripping the quilt's edge so hard her knuckles whitened. "I can't lose my baby. I just can't. It's all I have."

Cole realized he was nodding . . . and had no idea why. "I know," he said, thinking about himself and the three kids. She had all of them. Well, the kids. She had the kids. Not him. "I'll do what I can, Kate. But you have to realize that, well, it may already be too late." Cole watched the tears slide out from under her squeezed-shut eyelids. Not one anguished sound escaped her. Cole swallowed around the growing lump of emotion in his throat.

"I'm sorry," he heard himself say . . . for the first time in his memory. Maybe even in his whole life.

She hadn't lost the baby. She just knew she hadn't. She would know if she had. In fact, she refused to lose it. It was hers. And it was all she had in the world to love. So she didn't care what anybody said. Not even Cole Young-blood, who even now sat on the chest at the end of the bedding and leaned forward, hatless, his arms braced on his knees, his hands folded together. And questioned her.

"Did you sleep good?"

She nodded. "Yes. I think I needed that nap more than anything."

He nodded. "I expect so." Then his expression changed, showed his concern. "You scared us all pretty bad this morning, Kate."

She looked down, considered her twisted-together fingers in her lap. The pillows at her back that propped her
up only felt bunched and uncomfortable right now. Somewhat like the precautionary clean and wadded-up rags she
had stuffed tight against her woman's place. She'd stopped
bleeding about two hours ago. And the cramping had sub-
sided. But even so, it was his tone of voice that concerned
her most. It sounded accusatory to her.

She figured he had more than one reason to be angry
with her, but she certainly wasn't going to tell him what
all those reasons were. "I'm sorry," she said, looking up at
him, meeting his black-eyed gaze. "I didn't mean to. I
scared myself pretty bad, too."

"I reckon you did." And then he didn't say anything
else. He merely sat up and raked a hand through his black
hair.

He was waiting on her, she knew that. Waiting on her
to tell him about the baby. The baby she *hadn't* lost, no
matter how hard he tried to convince her that she at least
needed to consider the possibility. Which she wouldn't do.
She couldn't. So, instead, she asked a question of her own.
"Where are the kids?"

Cole's eyes narrowed, he looked her up and down. Obviously, this was not the conversation he wanted to have.
Kate swallowed and pulled the quilt up higher over her
chemise-covered bosom. Finally, he answered her.
"They're right outside. Eating their lunch. You want something? You hungry?"

She was. She was starved. She felt better, and she was
starved. That's how she knew she was still carrying her
baby. Her hunger. But she heard herself saying, "No. I'm
fine. I think I just need to rest."

But he wouldn't take the hint and leave. Maddeningly,
he stayed in place, made no move to leave. He also remained silent. Waiting.

Kate exhaled her breath and looked everywhere but at
him. "Have I thanked you yet for . . . all you did?"—heat
blossomed on her cheeks, for all he'd seen of her as he'd

bathed her—"I was in a pretty bad way there for a while."

"Yes, you were. But there's no need to thank me. I did whatever I thought might help. I'm just glad you're okay. Or at least you seem to be okay right now."

Kate's chin came up. She looked into his eyes. "I am okay. And so's my baby." Too late, she realized she'd brought up the one subject she'd been working so hard to avoid.

And he latched onto it. "I hope it is, Kate. I wouldn't wish it any harm."

A sadness filled her heart because Kate knew better. She'd seen the evidence in his saddlebags. He was the killer hired to end her life and her baby's. He may not know it was she he sought, but she did. And so, trapped by that truth, all she could say was, "I never thought that you would. But I can tell, just by looking at you, that you're not saying everything you're thinking."

He sat up straighter and crossed his arms over his flannel shirt, a different one than he'd had on this morning. That other one, like her traveling costume, was no doubt stained with her blood. "You're right about that. But I'm not thinking anything I haven't already said."

Kate's expression hardened. "Meaning you think I lost my baby."

He exhaled forcefully, as if impatient with her. "Meaning I think you need to prepare yourself for that. Kate, you lost a powerful lot of blood. I don't see how it could have . . . made it."

Kate clenched her jaw . . . to keep from crying. "Well, it did. I know. And if anyone would know, I would. I'm the mother." She hated the sobbing breath that followed her words.

Cole nodded; his expression never changed. Could the man be more infuriatingly calm and reasonable? Kate had trouble thinking of him as the same man who, only hours earlier after having bathed her, had lain down with her and held her in his arms as she'd cried herself to sleep. She'd been too ragged and heartbroken then to be afraid of his touch, to be afraid of having a man in her bed. After all, it had been an unwanted man in bed with her who'd gotten her in her present condition. And she *was* still in that condition, too.

Just then, Cole broke the growing quiet between them. "All right, Kate. You're right. If you say you're still carrying your child, then you are. It won't do any good to argue. I reckon time will tell, anyway." Then he cut his gaze to the back of the wagon, as if he thought he should go check on the children outside. Just as hope bloomed in Kate's heart that he would, he swung his gaze back to her. "When were you going to tell me about this baby, Kate?"

Her breath caught. She stared wide-eyed at him. "There was no reason to tell you anything. You're not my for-real husband. You already know that."

His black eyes glittered. "That's not what I mean. And you know it. Don't play with words with me."

A jet of fear lanced through Kate and had her swallowing around the sudden lump of fear lodged in her throat. She'd do herself no good angering this man. "All right," she conceded, slumping, giving in. "I expect you do have a right to know." Then she looked down, smoothed her covers, and thought for a moment. Finally, she raised her head, met his gaze, and said, "I'm a widow."

His eyebrows rose. He sat back, bracing his hands atop his knees. "A widow? What happened to your husband?"

Without blinking, Kate said, "He died."

Cole's expression hardened. "I figured as much. How, Kate? How'd he die?"

"How'd he die?" she was forced to repeat as she concentrated on maintaining eye contact with him. "Um, a horse trampled him."

"Damn. How'd a horse come to trample him?"

She had no idea . . . for a long stretch of quiet moments. Then, "Um, it was mad, and he got in its way."

"Sounds like it. Especially if he's dead."

"He is."

"I see. What's his name?"

"Who? The horse?"

"No. Your husband."

"Oh." *A name. I need a name.* One came to her rescue. Mr. Talmidge's kindly old valet. The only male name she could think of. "Hudson." Then, too late, she wondered if Cole knew Hudson.

But his expression never changed from outright suspicion as he nodded. "Hudson Chandler. Nice name."

"Thank you."

"How long were you married . . . you and Hudson?"

"Two years." The lies were getting easier.

"That's interesting."

"It is? Why?"

"Because as a widow, you could have made the land run on your own. You never needed to marry me. Or anyone else."

Kate's eyes widened, her mouth sagged open. She felt sick. But not like before. Just hot, sweaty, lying-through-her-teeth sick. "I didn't?"

He shook his head. "Nope. Being a widow would make you the head of a household. I asked you that the other night. If you were the head of a household. You said you weren't."

"I didn't know I was. I had no idea—"

"After two years of marriage, you didn't know what 'head of the household' meant? I also told you a married woman could make the run on her own. You were already a married woman then, Kate. Widowed or not."

She couldn't get a deep breath into her lungs. She put a hand to her bosom. "I am. I'm a widow."

He shook his head. "No you're not. You're lying. And I want to know why."

Kate raised her chin, forced herself to calm down . . . and to think. Then she realized she could safely tell part of the truth. "All right. I . . . I was never married. This baby"— she put a hand to her sore belly—"isn't one I . . . asked for. But it's one I want." Then, hearing her own words, hearing herself essentially justifying her own life, and that of her baby's, Kate became angry and clenched her hands around her covers. "It's mine. Do you hear me? It's *my* baby. And I won't let anybody—"

"Whoa. Settle down, Kate," Cole cut in, holding up a cautionary hand. "It's all right. No one's trying to take it away from you."

Kate stared at him . . . and then burst into tears, covering her face with her hands. She couldn't stop the sobs, not even when she felt him join her on the bed and take her in his arms. Not even when she heard Willy's plaintive little voice from outside the wagon. "Is Miss Kate sick again?"

"No, Willy," Cole called back, his voice vibrating his chest and Kate's cheek where she lay against him. "She's just . . . scared. She'll be fine. You and Joey got a hold of Lydia, don't you?"

"Yes, sir, I got her," Joey answered. "I think she's getting tired, though. Like she wants a nap."

"Damn," Cole muttered. Then he called out, "All right. I'll come get her in a minute."

Then, he shifted his position, forcing Kate to move back as he tucked a finger under her chin and raised her head until her gaze met his. Through her tears, she registered the concern etching his forehead and crinkling the skin at the corners of his dark eyes. "Someone *is* trying to take your baby, aren't they? Is that why you're crying, Kate?"

Before she could stop herself, Kate nodded as she wiped at her eyes and scrubbed a finger under her nose.

Gripping her arms, Cole held her firmly. "Kate, look at me."

She did, blinking and sobbing, her breathing affected by her emotions. "Yes?"

"Why would someone want your baby?"

"Because," she sobbed out, "because they can't have one of their own."

Cole frowned, obviously bewildered by her answer. "But that doesn't give anybody the right to take yours. How in the hell did this happen? Is that why you're here in

Oklahoma Country on your own? With no means of caring for yourself? Is that it?"

With her life—what was left of it—unraveling around her, and undone by her own lies, Kate weakened, collapsing against Cole's chest, barely able even to nod her answers. But it was just as well. Because clutching at his shirt as she was, and clinging to him, she didn't dare risk saying anything more. Although hearing his heart beat against her ear, and given how caring and concerned he was being— and how outraged he appeared to be at the very notion of someone taking her baby—she was tempted to tell him the whole truth. Even despite knowing that her death warrant lay in his saddlebag . . .

And that being so, did she dare risk her life with the truth? Or should she stick to the lies that had at least kept her and her baby alive?

Hard questions, she knew. But even harder answers. Because this man, now so tenderly holding her and allowing her these few moments to compose herself, had taken money to serve as her executioner. She needed to remember that. So she found herself wondering . . . would his caring behavior carry more weight with him than the small fortune awaiting him once he carried out his duty to his employer? True enough, he'd accepted the job before he'd met and married her. But now, only two days later, what were his feelings for her? Was he warming up any toward her?

It seemed to her he was. But of course she had to consider that his guard was down around her, since he had no idea she was the one he had been paid to kill. And while she didn't think he found her unappealing, given how he'd kissed her following their wedding ceremony, she didn't think he cared about her in any real sense. Certainly not in a way that could keep her alive if he ever learned who she was. *If* he found out? Most likely, he would find out, sooner or later. Because, as her mother had said when cautioning her about lying, the truth always comes out.

And yet there was their bargain—which was his bargain, too—a business-arrangement marriage. It wasn't a real marriage, one based on love. She didn't love him. And he didn't love her. Nor did she want him to. Him or any other man. That was the last thing she wanted, Kate told herself . . . even as she sat there, resting in Cole's arms and feeling comforted by his nearness. But perhaps the real question was, How would he feel *when*—she could no longer think in terms of *if*—he found out that she'd forced him to marry her, already knowing who he was and that he worked for Edgar Talmidge?

Could she risk his anger in that event? No, she didn't think she could, even though she now believed she knew what drove Cole to do what he did for a living. His sister's children, pure and simple. Seeing that they were well taken care of was behind everything he did. He hadn't ever said as much, but it was there in his actions that spoke of honor, of a sense of doing the right thing. In the way he kept the children with him after their folks died, his marrying her, and then trying to find that cousin. All for the children. Those actions said something good about the man.

Kate admired that side of him, even if she couldn't condone his methods. But even so, she thought she understood. After all, she figured that if she were in his place and as good with a gun as he was, she might entertain the same notions. Because she already knew there was nothing she wouldn't do to see that her baby got everything it needed, no matter the cost to her.

That was all well and good. But there was another, even deeper element of danger here for Kate and she knew it. A deep sighing breath brought to her the musky scent of the man she lay against. He shifted his position, smoothing his hands over her back. He must've bathed while she'd slept because he smelled warm, clean, and woodsy . . . comforting. But comfortable wasn't something she could allow herself to be with him. She must guard against it. Because it was one thing for him to be righteously angered by some stranger's injustices to her, his wife in name only. But it was quite another for him to learn that the stranger was no stranger at all. That in fact it was his employer who wanted her baby. It was his employer who wanted her dead. And it was he, Cole himself, who'd signed on to do it.

So then, once the entire truth was known to him, Cole would be faced with the same choices she'd had. But from the opposite side of the fence from Kate. He'd have to choose between his sister's kids' welfare . . . and that of Kate's and her baby's. But he'd also be faced with the truth that Kate herself had known all that, or had at least suspected it, when she'd forced him to marry her.

But perhaps she might have a chance when Cole learned that the rich Easterner had hired him to kill a pregnant woman—a detail missing in the telegraph she'd read. Kate had to wonder if Cole could do it. Could he kill an expectant mother? And how would he feel about a man like Edgar Talmidge, a man who'd set him up to kill without telling him the whole truth? Not that Cole would be any more kindly disposed toward her when he found out that she'd lied to him.

So . . . who would Cole Youngblood kill, if anyone? Her? Or Mr. Talmidge? Or both? Or would he be so disgusted that he'd simply walk away from them both? He did have that choice, it seemed to her. From where she sat— enfolded in the man's arms—it seemed he could just give back the money and walk away with the kids. He could always get other work. He'd still have his good gun hand.

Yes, he could walk away once he knew the whole truth, it seemed to her. But she also knew she couldn't allow him to do so. Because she needed him. And on so many more levels than he needed her. His need for her was a practical one, for someone to keep the kids while he found his cousin. That and nothing more. While she needed him in order to stay alive.

She couldn't believe it. The very man sent to kill her was now her best chance for staying alive. Because she now shared his last name. She was his wife. That had to mean something to him, didn't it? That fact alone had to make him care just a little bit, didn't it? But even if he didn't, and he found out the entire truth and did walk away, and then Mr. Talmidge sent someone else after her, wouldn't he be inclined to prevent another gunman from killing her, a Youngblood?

All her thinking gave Kate no answers, only more questions and a sick headache. The truth was, she couldn't predict Cole Youngblood's responses. Nor could she believe, with any degree of certainty, that he'd give her a chance to explain all the complexities of the situation before he simply pulled the trigger and silenced her. So, truly sick and weak now, her thoughts tumbling around until they were finally ordered, Kate clutched harder at Cole's shirt. A whimper of fear and aching, for her body, her child, her very life, escaped her.

Cole immediately sat her up, brushing her hair back from her face with one hand as he steadied her with his other. "Kate? You all right?"

She looked at him and smiled, a sad smile. As her gaze roved over his face, as she stalled her answer, Kate thought of last night, in the wagon. She'd made the decision to sacrifice another woman's children to keep her own child safe. She'd meant only that she wouldn't run away, that she'd stay with Cole for her own safety. But that decision, in turn, put the three children he loved in harm's way . . . when the bullets began inevitably to fly.

And now, today, for having decided to risk such a horrible thing, she'd almost lost her own child. In Kate's mind the two things were connected. Her bleeding was a warning. She knew that. So here she sat with no choices and the awful question . . . what would happen to her, to her unborn child, if she persisted in her plan? Would she win her safety for now, only to lose it altogether in the end? Would her life be forfeit for trying to do the right thing, protect an innocent life . . . but at the expense of three other innocent lives?

She sighed. There was nothing else she could do. Her course was charted. Her life set on its path. Everything she'd done, everything that had been done to her, the very choices she'd made, had all brought her to this place, this moment, and this man. So, slowly and still smiling at Cole Youngblood, her husband in the eyes of the law, Kate shook her head. And said, "No. I'm not all right. None of us is, Cole. None of us."

Cole pulled back, staring at her. "What are you talking about, Kate? 'None of us is'? Are you feverish?" He pushed her hair aside to feel her forehead.

Kate tugged his hand down with hers to her lap and held it there, tightly, in both of hers, wanting him instead to listen to her. "I don't have a fever, Cole. I'm not sick. Not like you think."

His eyes narrowing, he looked from her face to their joined hands, and back to her face. "Then what's wrong?"

Kate bit at her bottom lip, fought back a sob, and said, "Before the land run takes place, Cole . . . one of us will be dead."

Chapter Ten

Cole pulled back, tugging his hands free of hers. Kate could only watch him, could only feel sorry for him as worry lines creased his forehead. "What the hell are you talking about, one of us will be dead?"

Kate exhaled her breath, felt terrible . . . but more in her heart than in her body. "Exactly that. One of *us,* Cole. Me or you. I can't say it any plainer than that. And I don't even know how I know. But I do. One of us will be dead. Before April 22. We'll never make the land run."

Cole's black eyes darted as he searched her face. Suddenly, he jumped up and stood over her, his hands fisted at his sides. Through gritted teeth, his voice no more than a low growl, his black eyes sparking fire, Cole warned, "The hell you say. That's the biggest bunch of horse shit I ever heard in my life. You take back those words right now."

Kate shrank back, bracing herself with her hands behind her on the bedding. She'd not seen him lose control before. And she didn't like it now. She was only thankful that he hadn't strapped on his six-shooter. But why had she said such an awful thing, anyway? The words had been out before she even knew she was thinking them. Much less believing them. But now she realized that she did know, and she did believe. "You wouldn't be saying that if you didn't think it was true, too." She waited a moment, giving him a chance to protest. He said nothing. His silence verified Kate's fears. "You know it's true, don't you?"

His face contorted with anger, reddening as if he'd been sunburned. "Like hell it is. I wouldn't kill a woman."

His words slapped her across her face. Kate stilled, could feel her own heart beating in her chest. There it was, what she needed to know. How he felt about killing a woman. Obviously, it ate at him. *Good.* "I never said you'd kill me, Cole. I never even said it would be me who would die. All I said was *one* of us would be dead. I never said how. Or by whose hand."

Breathing hard, his chest rising and falling, his sweat staining his shirt, Cole stared at her. Then, slowly, his hardened expression crumpled. He dragged a hand over his face, covering his eyes, rubbing them hard. "Son of a bitch," he muttered. Then he stood there, staring at her, a world of agony reflecting in his eyes. He inhaled sharply . . . and slowly exhaled. "I can't stand here. I have to go get Lydia. She wants her nap."

He turned away from Kate, but only to jerk back around and lean over her to grab his Stetson from off the bed. In his nearness, his gaze locked with hers. "I have to get out of here, Kate."

"I know." Her words were no more than a whisper. Knowing as she did the source of his torment, Kate lowered her gaze, saw his throat working. Guilt was eating at him. Kate surprised herself with the realization that she wanted to reach out and stroke his muscle-corded neck, wanted to reassure him, to tell him he didn't have to do this. He didn't have to kill her. But she couldn't say that. Because she didn't know if it was true. Maybe he did have to kill her. Or maybe she had to kill him.

That startling thought momentarily flared, lighting her eyes. Instantly she looked down, hiding the truth from him as he again straightened up and towered over her. To her surprise, he spoke again, drawing her gaze his way. "I guess you know, because of this morning—what happened to you—that I won't be moving down early with the others. To the border."

Kate frowned. How could he talk to her of the land run? Hadn't she just told him they'd never make it? Then it occurred to her. Choices. Perhaps he was talking about choices. Not an end, but another path. That was it. There was always another choice, another road. Didn't a different choice mean a different life? Wasn't she living proof of that?

She searched his face, tried to see why he was still standing here now, his hat in his hand, when he'd just said he had to get out of here, away from her. Could he mean if they went together, nothing could or would happen to either of them? Kate fervently hoped those were his thoughts. But still, she proceeded slowly, not wanting him to reject anything out of hand without first listening to her. All she knew was ... if he wasn't closing any doors, then neither was she.

"Yes, I know," she finally answered him, drawing his attention away from the crease in his hat's crown that he'd been worrying, as if it were of utmost importance that he do so. It occurred to Kate then that he simply didn't want to leave her presence. If that were true, then there was hope. If he wanted to be around her, then she was safe. Still, until she could fathom his thoughts, which he kept close to his chest, like a winning poker hand, she had to be careful. "I thank you for staying. I know it caused you to miss a chance at a front-line starting position for the land run. A chance you wanted for me."

He nodded. Kate's heart thumped, steadily picking up its pace. She chanced a smile. "Life sure is strange, Cole. I mean, here you are, ready to make the run for me. And here I am, keeping you from doing it."

Cole's expression, and his stance, relaxed. Suddenly they were having a civil conversation. "I never meant to place any blame, Kate. Especially on you. Not today, not with everything you're going through. That's not what I'm saying. I'm just saying we lost this opportunity."

She clung to his words. *This opportunity.* Not the only opportunity. Just this one. And *we.* He'd said *we* missed an opportunity. They *were* thinking alike. Like a wildfire, the spark of hope flared in Kate's heart, and fueled her words. "We can still make up the lost time, Cole. I'll be fine now. I just know I will."

Doubt flared in his eyes, sharpening his frown. "Well, I

hope you will, Kate. But you don't know that."

Stubbornness had her saying, "I will too be fine. And I do know it."

He held up a hand in an appeasing gesture. "All right. You will. I'm not going to argue the point with you. But that doesn't change the fact—"

"Yes it does. We can still make the land run." Kate sat forward on the bed. "We can do it. Together."

He pulled back. "Together? Like hell, Kate. *We're* not going anywhere. And *I* can't leave you here with the kids. Anything could happen. With most everyone else gone on ahead to find a good starting point, well, you're practically alone here. I can't risk it."

"Yes you can. I mean, no you can't." Now he was getting her all confused. Kate took a deep breath and tried again . . . quietly, calmly. "If we don't join the others today, Cole, then I might not get my land." She allowed a moment for that to sink in before she added, "You promised me."

Cole looked away, shaking his head. His jaw worked. Then he again sought her gaze. "I know that, Kate. I did. I promised. But look at you. Neither one of us counted on this. So it can't be helped."

Kate's stubbornness firmed her lips. "Yes it can. The run itself isn't for four more days. And I'm not bleeding anymore."

"I don't care. You're not making the trip. Especially when all we'd be doing was seeking a better starting position from which to wait."

Seeing that this tactic wasn't working, Kate abandoned her point for the moment, focusing instead on another possibility. "All right. But promise me this . . . if I continue to do better, you'll go on ahead and wait with the others at the border. Even tomorrow or the next day, you could catch up pretty easily on that roan of yours."

He shook his head. "I could. But I'll make no such promise. You might start bleeding five minutes after I ride off. Besides, there are others here to consider, besides yourself. There're three little kids who can't fend for themselves. What if something happens to you, Kate? What about them, here alone? Then what?"

Kate's hands fisted around her covers. She'd been selfish even to think of being left alone here with small children in her care. "You're right. We can't put them at risk. I shouldn't even have said it." She tried a smile and a bit of fun at her own expense. "Even though I do suspect that Joey, Willy, and Lydia know a sight more about seeing after themselves than I do."

But apparently Cole wasn't ready yet to forgive her. "Yes, they can fend for themselves, get a meal together, bathe themselves, chores such as that. But they can't protect themselves. They need an adult around."

One, like herself, who didn't know how to shoot a gun or ride a horse? Kate sobered. "All right. Fine. I'm being selfish. Perhaps I am. But that's because I have to, if I'm going to have any kind of a life ahead of me. I surely don't see anyone else on the horizon and wanting to look after me and my baby. Or am I wrong, Cole? Are you applying for the job?"

His expression hardened. "You know I can't. You wouldn't want or need someone like me, Kate."

Her chin came up. She fought the sudden tears that threatened to spill over. Alone again. She must get used to it. Even if this was her husband—in name only—telling her so. "Well, then," she said, her voice purposely strident to hide her disillusionment. "It seems we have two choices. No one goes. Or we all go."

Apparent surprise stiffened his stance. "No, Kate, those aren't the choices. In fact, there are no choices. And no decisions to be made. Because no one is going. We can't. And you need to face it."

"Well, I won't. I can't. Because we can go. We can do this." Kate tensed, drawing her knees up and leaning over them in her agitation. "I won't hear of anything else, Cole. I won't. It's my land. I want it. And I'm going to get it."

"Dammit, Kate. You—"

"Stop it! Please." He just didn't understand. But maybe

that was her fault. Sudden emotion overtook her. Sobs tore at her throat, tightened her chest. "Don't you see, Cole? This land run isn't some selfish thing I want to do—at my expense or yours. And certainly not at my baby's or your sister's kids'. I have to do it, Cole. I don't have any choice. I'm alone. Just me and this child. Do I have to bleed to death right in front of you before you know it? Look at me. I have nowhere else to go. Nowhere. This is it for me. Right here. This land run."

She took a ragged breath, fought for control. Noting the intent expression on Cole's face, she rushed on. "I can't let my dream, my hope, die. Any more than I can stand the thought of my baby dying. Please, Cole, I'm begging you. Help me."

In the silence following her outburst, as Kate sat there, emotionally overwrought, knowing she couldn't be doing herself or her baby any good with such outbursts, she watched as Cole's expression changed. He blinked, looked down at his boots, then up at her as he put his Stetson on. "All right, Kate," he said quietly. "I'll help you. I'll do it. But you have to tell me how."

Kate's teary gaze locked with his. She'd done it. She'd gotten through to him. He was going to help her. Finally, she could exhale . . . and did. "Thank you," was her breathless response.

He shook his head, his expression sober, resigned. "No need to thank me, Kate. I'm not doing you any favors. I'm just keeping my end of our bargain."

Kate ducked her chin, stared down at her quilt-covered lap. "Still, I'm grateful. I couldn't do it without you." Nor could she believe she'd come to this turn. Or that she was saying such a thing . . . *she couldn't do it without him.* Without him? The man whose job it was to kill her?

"That is so," he agreed, drawing her attention his way. "You *can't* do it without me. But you're still going to have to tell me how we're going to do it, Kate. Because I don't like it one bit. And I don't want you holding me accountable later on. Or saying I didn't warn you."

"Warn me? What are you talking about?"

"I'm talking about all the rain we've had here lately." He began ticking off his several points on his fingers. "I'm talking about muddy trails. About flooding rivers between us and the border. I'm talking about washed-out bridges. And our passage through the Cherokee country, Kate. They're not happy about all the wagons passing through their lands. And we've already missed the cavalry's escort because we didn't leave this morning. But mostly I'm talking about the fact that any attempt—even under perfect conditions—to get down to the border, given your condition, could kill you. Or your baby."

Kate winced at his words. "But Cole, I'm not the only woman here in my condition—I mean, expecting a baby. There are others. I've seen them. Women big with child. New mothers with nursing infants. And even now, they're making their way down to the border with their families. Are you telling me they haven't considered the dangers? That they'll all be dead before they get there?"

"Hell, no, Kate, I'm not saying that. I'm saying they're a sight more healthy right now than you are. I'm saying you're bleeding. And they're not."

Kate took a deep breath. "That's true. I can't argue with you there." But neither did she have another choice. She either took her chances and made the run to secure a future for herself and her baby, or she stayed behind and languished here until she died. Because once she broke her connection to Cole Youngblood, who hadn't offered to stay on and help her any, she was right back where she'd started—alone and penniless and pregnant in the backwoods town of Arkansas City. So there was no sense in arguing. Kate again met Cole's waiting stare. "You know I don't have any choice, don't you?"

He nodded, his expression one of resignation. "I know."

"Well, then," Kate said, smoothing her covers and trying to sound practical and strong, "the way I see it, and as you said, all we need to discuss is the how of it. How I'm going to travel there."

Cole nodded. "There's only one way that gives you any kind of a chance, Kate. And that's in the back of the buckboard, because it has a spring-mounted suspension and will be a sight more easy-riding than this contraption." He gestured to indicate the schooner they were in. "We'll load the provisions and Mack's tools and building materials back in here. And just take both wagons."

Kate didn't know what to say. On the one hand, she was excited that Cole was already working on the details of the trip. But on the other hand, his suggestion sounded so slow and cumbersome. She frowned. "We'll never make it in time like that, Cole."

"Sure we will. Most everybody else is traveling down there in wagons like ours. And they only have a few hours' head start on us. We'll catch up sooner or later. We can do it."

Now it was Kate who wasn't so sure. "But how will we do that? Who'll drive the wagons?"

"Well, who do you think? I'll drive this wagon since it's a lot heavier. And Joey can handle the buckboard okay. And I can tie my roan onto the back of one of the wagons." Then his expression seemed to brighten. "I believe this'll work just fine, Kate. Besides, my not riding the roan down there will save him for the actual run."

Kate hadn't thought about that. Or any of the other things Cole brought up. Which told her she was safe, and in good hands, with him in charge. Well, in good hands until he found out who she was. Still, Kate smiled. "It sounds like a fine plan, Cole. I'm very grateful to you."

Surprisingly, he ducked his chin, looked away. Was he embarrassed? Surely not. Not a man of his reputation. That thought made Kate sit up, had her looking at him with a different sort of clarity. He was nothing like his reputation. They said he was a ruthless killer, with more than twenty names etched on headstones because of his gun hand. A hot temper. A truly bad desperado. But she'd seen nothing of that. Maybe there was a side to him that lived up to the stories told about him. But now, right here, with her and his sister's kids, he was a good and patient man trying only to do the right thing by them all. Which made Kate feel worse for all the lies she'd told him and was forced to continue to tell him.

"I guess," Kate began, breaking the quiet between them, "you'll still be the only one making the actual run, then?"

Cole stood taller, his stance daring her to buck him on this point. "There's only one fast horse between us, Kate. And one numbered stake to plant. I'll be the one doing it in four days. I'll get you there to the border where we're to wait. But then you'll sit tight with the kids, like you promised, while I make the run for you on the twenty-second . . . like I promised." Then he added, "I'll come back for you, Kate. I will."

Her eyes widened. That was the one thing she'd worried about all along. And he knew it. But now, hearing him say it, she realized that she believed him. She truly did. Things were changing between them. Trust was building. She didn't know if that was good or bad. Because the more trust they had between them, the bigger her betrayal of him would seem when the truth of her identity came to light.

But for now, stuck with her truth as well as her lies, all Kate could do was smile and nod. "I know you will. I trust you."

Cole chuckled, a humorless sound. "You'll be the first one who does."

Kate raised her eyebrows at that, thinking she could name five others—namely, his sister, her kids, and Mr. Talmidge—who also trusted him. But just then, she realized that the very air inside the schooner seemed to thicken with the growing silence between them. She didn't know what to make of it. Or what to make of Cole's warming expression as he gazed at her. Kate tried to think of something to say. But no words would come. Then Cole opened his mouth as if to speak. Kate's breath caught. With the look he was giving her, he could say most anything right now—

"Uncle Cole?"

It came from outside the wagon. A child's voice. The

moment evaporated. Cole grimaced and then turned away, walking to the back of the wagon and peering outside. "What is it, Willy?"

Watching Cole and noting how he so appealingly filled out his denims and his chambray shirt—and surprising herself that she had noticed—Kate took note of the exasperation in his voice at the untimely interruption. That more than anything else told her he'd been about to say something important. If not memorable. But now, most likely, she'd never know. And because that made her feel . . . disappointed, she realized she was starting to warm up to Cole Youngblood. That wasn't good, and for more reasons than she could count.

But it also surprised her. Because after New York, after Mr. Talmidge's treatment of her, Kate had been so sure—even as recently as three days ago—that'd she never, ever want another man to put his hands on her or to have control of her life. And Cole had already done both. Now it became clear to her that she was beginning to like and respect him. Another man. But not just any man. This was Cole Youngblood. Hired killer. And . . . her husband.

Kate exhaled sharply, telling herself to beware, to not drop her guard around him. But somehow she knew it was already too late. He'd slipped in under her guard, with all his quiet, confident ways. And so had made her—she cringed at even acknowledging the emotion—care. He'd made her care. Instantly, she denied that to herself. *No. I don't. I don't care.* It was just that she was so painfully dependent on him right now. That's why she felt there was something more between them than the bargain that had led to their vows. That had to be it. And once she got her land, she'd come to realize that was all this was, this sitting here and . . . caring.

No. Stop it. And she did this time. She shied away from the mishmash of her own thoughts by giving her attention over to the conversation between Cole and Willy.

"I am trying to tell you, Uncle Cole," the little boy was saying. "Lydia was fussing and you didn't come out to get her, so Joey lifted her into the buckboard and she fell asleep and Joey is sitting in there with her to make sure she stays put. And he sent me and Kitty to ask you if that's okay. Is it?"

Cole was quiet a minute as, his back to Kate, he stared down at the five-year-old boy. Kate smiled, thinking she knew some of what he was feeling. Then Cole spoke. "That's just fine, son. You tell him I'm proud of him for taking charge. And I'm proud of you, too, Willy."

"You are? What'd I do?"

Kate grinned, heard Cole's chuckle. "Well, you just did a fine job of doing as Joey asked you to do. That shows me you're growing up."

"Yeah. I'm almost growed up now. But I don't like it none having to do what Joey tells me to do. He's right bossy. Like an old setting hen."

Again Cole chuckled. "Yeah, I agree. Only let's keep that between you and me, okay? Now you go on over to the buckboard while I finish speaking with Miss Kate."

"Yes, sir." Then, in a loud whisper, Willy asked another question. "Is she going to die, Uncle Cole?"

Her eyes widening, Kate bit at her bottom lip. She'd like to know the answer to that, too. Just then, Cole pivoted to face her. Their gazes locked. He turned back to Willy. "No. She's not going to die, Willy. In fact, we're all going to go to the waiting area at the border together."

Kate exhaled and slumped against the pillows at her back. At Cole's words, Willy let out a loud whoop that had Kitty barking and Cole hushing them both. Kate heard all that, but only then did she realize that she was grinning. So it was real. She'd done it. She'd gotten herself here. And she was going to make it to the land run. Only now did it seem real, now that he'd said it out loud and to someone besides her. He'd told the children. And so . . . they would all go. She could only hope, as her grin faded, that they would all, including her baby, make it to the border alive.

* * *

Three days later, breathing in deeply of the warm spring air of April 20, 1889, and telling herself she could really and truly smell her own land, Kate stood in the back of the parked buckboard and gazed upon what some called the Promised Land. The Oklahoma Country. The Unassigned Lands. Her new homeland. Right in the heartland. And smack in the middle of Indian Territory. It was incredible. And beautiful. And empty and lonely-looking and nothing more than wave after wave of brown hills and trees and prairie grass. And people. There were more people than trees. More than fifty thousand were rumored to be at the various borders and ready to make the run. "Harrison's Hoss Race," the papers all said, nudging their new president a bit with this jibe at the giveaway of land.

But Kate didn't care what anybody called it. Or how many people stood ready to claim a piece of it. Because out there somewhere were her 160 acres, just waiting on her. She blinked back the sudden tears of emotion and swiped at their wetness on her cheeks. Her piece of paradise. With trees and water and good grazing land. And close to the staked-out ground that would be the new town of Guthrie. Cole had been right about that. Folks were speculating that the small Guthrie station would be the new capital city. In one day, they all said, it would go from a few ramshackle buildings to a fully raised city of tents. And from that would rise the brick and wood buildings of a permanent settlement. And that was good. It was the beginning of civilization.

Civilization. That had her thinking of New York City, and sparing a homesick thought for the place she'd known and loved as a child—the New York before Mr. Talmidge. She was used to making her way alone in civilization. She loved being among the buildings and the people and having law and order and neighbors and stores and churches and schools. That was all good. She'd need all that, plus the closeness of other people, once she was alone, just her and her baby. Kate smiled, put a hand to her belly—she still carried her baby. Morning sickness proved it every day.

But even before the baby came, she had to consider the length of time that Joey, Willy, and Lydia would be with her while Cole rode back up into Kansas to find that cousin of his—

A frisson of fear slipped over Kate, shivering her and interrupting her thoughts. What would he do then, once he'd taken the kids away and had them settled? Most likely, he'd begin hunting down that Talmidge maid. When she— Anna Katherine Chandler Youngblood, Anne Candless to him—was right here and sleeping next to him and his sister's children every night.

No. She'd worry about that later. When the time came. Which wasn't now. Now, today, and the next few days were reserved for planning a better life. Because somehow, despite Cole and the telegraphed message that had made him her mortal enemy, she would have a better life—if he never found out who she was. That's if he were to move on, not be a part of her life. Kate swallowed, hating how empty merely the thought of being alone made her. What would her life be like when she could no longer see Cole's handsome and reassuring figure walking her way?

Stop it, Kate. She obeyed instantly, thinking instead of how she would meet folks who would become her friends . . . if they didn't hold her married name against her. What would the Youngblood name mean out here in this pristine land? She had no way of knowing. But still, this question brought her thoughts back around to what she'd originally been thinking before she'd sidetracked herself with thoughts of Cole. More and more, it seemed to Kate, the man filled her head. But it wasn't him she needed to be worrying over. Instead, she should be concentrating on the other folks out here with her, them and their children. Because children meant a school opening up. And Kate fully intended to see that the boys got their schooling, despite their grumblings. She didn't want Cole's cousin thinking she'd not done her duty while they'd been in her care.

A prick of loneliness had Kate blinking. She was going to lose the children. That might be, but she'd also brought her baby, that sweet and fine promise of the future, that tiny little innocent hope for something beyond herself whose welfare drove Kate past her own endurance. And so . . . she would be fine. As long as she had her baby.

Kate raised her chin again, telling herself she could and would do this, settle in this new land and make a good life for herself. Thus bolstered, she felt satisfied with all that she saw. And smiled for the contentment of the moment. She'd only recently, on the way down here, learned to do that. To cherish the moments, even the tiniest ones, of normalcy and quiet and happiness. Like now, when Lydia was in the wagon with her . . . and pulling Kitty's floppy ears, while he sloppily licked her pudgy face clean. And over there, off to her left, were Joey and Willy, each leading a mule by its leather reins. The two little boys followed Cole, who was leading his roan—Kate's best hope for the land she wanted—and the two other mules toward the water on the other side of a stand of scrub oaks.

We did it. The realization coursed happily through Kate. Together, they'd done it. Like the strongest of families. They'd made it to the border, and in plenty of time. True enough, the hardships had been incredible. Cole had not exaggerated, Kate now concluded as she recalled the most harrowing of them. Like the washed-out bridge that made necessary a river crossing, during which Cole and the mules pulling the schooner he drove had very nearly been washed away—all while Kate and the kids had watched helplessly from shore. And like the rain-swollen waters that had threatened to drown Kitty when he lost his footing in the buckboard and had tumbled into the swirling eddies, yelping and paddling for all he was worth—only to be plucked out by Cole as the hound had washed by him.

And like the wind that had torn Lydia's rag doll from her hands and sent it flying, never to be seen again. She still cried every night for her lost baby. Kate swallowed, refused to think how close she'd come to knowing exactly how the little girl felt. And the rain. Always the rain. It seemed they'd been wet through for days. And after the rain had come the sudden cold spell that hit one afternoon, even though it was the middle of April.

Perhaps some of the worst moments, in Kate's estimation, were when tempers had flared a time or two among some of the men in the wagon train. Everyone not involved had scurried away when the gunplay erupted. But none of the outbreaks had come close to Cole's party, Kate knew, because the folks around them knew his identity and his reputation. As terrifying as those bullet-riddled incidents had been, they'd at least brought home to Kate something Cole had said days ago. His name and reputation would keep her safe even when he was no longer around. All too soon, she knew, that would be all she had of him. His name. And her memories of him. It would have to be enough.

Kate quickly shied away from letting her thoughts go down that road again, the one where Cole rode away for the last time. Instead she remembered what for her had been the absolute worst part of the three-day trip to the border— the jouncy ride she'd had to endure while lying in the back of the buckboard. Also, the time between the near-disasters had given her a chance to talk with the boy and to iron out a lot of their differences. Not that there were many of them. Still, the talking had done some good and Joey'd been most proud to teach her more about handling a team—without making her sick like his Uncle Cole had done. A feat he didn't mind sharing with his uncle every chance he got.

Kate realized again that she was smiling. It seemed she'd done a lot of that in the last few days. *Now why is that?* she wondered. What, besides finally being here, safe and whole, among all these people and their infectious excitement for the land run, was it that had her so happy?

Just then, Kitty yelped and Kate jerked around. Lydia had apparently pulled his ears too hard . . . and the little girl was crying to prove it. "Oh, for heaven's sake . . ." Kate muttered as she knelt down and took the little girl into her arms and held her, hushing her with soothing noises, all while petting the dog's head and trying to smooth the frown from his hound dog face. "Kitty, you poor thing. You shouldn't just sit there and let her pull on your ears. You know she's going to do it time and again." Kate then turned to the curly-haired little waif in her arms. "And you, sweetie. Why are you crying, huh? Did Miss Kitty pull your ears, too?"

Lydia tucked her head into the crook of Kate's neck and shook her head no, inadvertently tickling Kate's nose with her wildly disarrayed and baby-soft curls. And that was when Kate knew. In a moment of blinding clarity, she knew. Knew why she was so happy. And knew why that made her want to cry. She had a family. She belonged to these children. And they belonged to her.

A deep and painful breath assailed Kate. *No,* she quickly told herself. *They're not yours, Kate. They can't stay with you.* She'd been thinking that very thing all the way down here . . . about asking Cole to forget that search for his cousin in favor of leaving the children with her for good. She'd come to care that much about them. *Don't even think that. You can't. Remember who Cole is. And who you are. And what could happen. Nothing's changed.*

But it had changed, she insisted. Everything had changed. The three-day trip down here together and all the dangers they'd faced had changed things. Especially between her and Cole. While he wasn't exactly warm and tender with her—she didn't think that was his nature—he at least showed as much concern for her as he did his sister's kids. And she liked it. Liked him. But feared that what she felt for him was beyond mere liking, had become true caring. She suspected this because she had even entertained thoughts of his hands on her . . . in a good way, a way that didn't cause her to shrink away from the images in her head, and in her heart.

The truth was . . . she wanted Cole Youngblood. And in all the ways a woman wants the man she loves. She just knew that lying with Cole in a marriage bed would be different from the brutal rapes she'd suffered under Edgar Talmidge. It just had to be. Gentleness and tenderness and wanting, a giving between two people who cared for one another, simply had to exist. Otherwise, these fifty thousand or more people who surrounded her and Lydia and Kitty wouldn't even have been born. Because if there was no love, there wouldn't be one woman here who'd want to be around a man. And plenty seemed to want to be.

That much she'd witnessed for herself here on a daily basis and, all her childhood, between her mother and her father. They'd been killed so many years ago, when she was twelve, on the darkened streets of New York City. But she'd never forgotten them. They and their love for her and for each other remained still in her heart and in her mind. *Thank God.* Otherwise, all she'd know of men would be the awfulness of Mr. Talmidge's reddened and bloated face sweating above her as he'd hurt her time and again.

So she knew there was more to life and to love than her experiences with Mr. Talmidge. And now she wanted to have it all. Right here. In this new place. She wanted love in her life. No more running away. She'd done many courageous things in the past few months. But what she was contemplating now—telling Cole the truth and taking her chances based on the caring for her she saw reflected in his eyes—was perhaps the bravest and the most risky thing she'd ever do. But she had to do it, if she ever hoped to live her life to the fullest . . . with or without Cole Youngblood.

Somehow, knowing him now as she did in all but the most intimate of ways, she didn't think he could kill her. Not even for the sum of money she knew was at stake. Truly, she had no idea what exactly he'd do when she told him she was the woman he knew as Anne Candless. But she didn't think it would be anything as drastic as killing her.

Overwhelmed with the enormity of what she felt she had to do, Kate took a breath, felt Lydia tug on her, wanting down from her lap. "All right, baby," she said, helping the little girl down. "But you leave Miss Kitty alone. Don't you pull his ears anymore."

Lydia stood there in the wagon bed, her face puckering stubbornly. "Her likes it."

Kate chuckled. "Miss Kitty's a he, Lydia. And no he doesn't like it. Look at his face."

Lydia did. But putting the lie to Kate's words, Kitty grinned and lolled his wet old tongue out the side of his slobbery mouth. Kate gave up. "All right, you two. Fine. But don't either one of you come crying to me again."

"Us won't," Lydia promised as she threw her pudgy baby arms around Kitty's neck and kissed his furry head.

Kate smiled, shaking her head and watching the two together. Such a pure love they shared, this little orphaned girl and her dog. *So, there you have it, Kate. Pure love does exist. And you have to take a chance on it.* It was much more than a mere chance. The biggest chance of her life. Kate's smile faded. She had to tell Cole the truth. Today. Because the burden of her lies weighed heavily on her heart every time she looked into his eyes, every time she thought of all the things he'd done for her in the past week.

Just then, Kate heard her name being called. She pivoted to her right and saw Joey and Willy bursting forth from the thin stand of oak trees where they'd gone with Cole. As she stood up and waved, she wondered where the mules were. And Cole. But the boys, who threaded their way around all the other parked wagons that separated them from Kate in the buckboard, were grinning and waving as they ran. So everything must be all right. Or so she thought until she heard what Joey was yelling about.

"Miss Kate, Miss Kate! Guess what? We just saw a lady who looks almost exactly like you!"

Chapter Eleven

Norah Heston Talmidge is here.

As insane as she knew that notion to be, fear and dread still washed over Kate, weakening her. She sank dizzily to the bed of the buckboard wagon, instinctively clutching at its splintery wood side for support. Blindly, she stared at Lydia and Kitty as, blessedly oblivious to her reaction, they continued playing at the foot of the wagon. Her breathing labored and her heart pounding, Kate fought for control.

I'm being plumb silly, she desperately reasoned with herself. *Why, it could be anyone. Except for my green eyes, I'm not all that remarkable a woman to look at. And plenty of women have black hair. So it doesn't have to be Mrs. Talmidge. Besides, it just can't be true. Not now. Not when I mean to tell Cole the truth.*

Cole! Kate sat up stiffly, a hand to her mouth. Had he also seen the same woman? But she knew he had to have. If the boys had seen this woman and had made such a commotion that they'd most likely abandoned their uncle with the mules in favor of running to tell her all about it, then surely they would have first shared their discovery with Cole. So where was he? Kate jerked around, scanning the length of the oaks in her aching need to see Cole coming this way, to see him shaking his head and grinning, telling her the boys were wrong. But the gnarled oaks kept their silence and their secrets. Cole didn't break free of them. There was no sign of him.

That scared her even more. Was he even now talking to Mrs. Talmidge? Kate had no choice but to assume it was that hated woman, as much as she didn't want to believe it. But until she knew differently, until she saw Cole's face, she had to think it was Norah Heston Talmidge and had to be ready to defend herself. Then another realization—one that should have come before now—stung Kate. If Mrs. Talmidge was here, then so was Mr. Talmidge.

Kate covered her face with her hands. Hopelessness ate away at her. He was here. He had to be. Because women of Mrs. Talmidge's social class went nowhere unescorted, Kate knew. So if it turned out she was who the boys had seen, then Kate knew that Mr. Talmidge would have accompanied his wife, if for no other reason than a show of husbandly concern, given that their families and their social set believed Norah Talmidge to be at last carrying a child.

Carrying a child. Kate lowered her hands, stared unseeing out over the plains vista before her. *That's it. That's exactly why it can't be her.* Hope burst forth in Kate's heart. Instantly she felt better. Her breathing eased, she felt stronger, strong enough even to stand up and await the boys' clamorous arrival at the wagon. What buoyed her spirits was Mrs. Talmidge's supposed delicate condition. Her former employers were stuck with their own lie. What possible reason could they give for Mrs. Talmidge to undertake such an arduous journey as was the trip here? Wouldn't it seem they were recklessly endangering their long-awaited heir?

No matter that the hills Kate now looked upon were dotted with the fancy tents and carriages and servants of the idle rich who'd gathered to see firsthand the coming spectacle of the land run. Even witnessing such a sight as that wouldn't justify Mrs. Talmidge coming here. So she was just being silly, Kate told herself. It wasn't Norah Heston Talmidge. It wasn't. Because if it was . . . then, Kate knew, she was dead.

Just then, the boys reached the wagon, drawing not only Kate's but Kitty's and Lydia's interest their way. The little girl and the dog both clambered to the wagon's side, edging into Kate in their excitement to peer over it, agog with curiosity. The boys themselves—red-faced, out of breath, excited with their news—all but collided with the buckboard before stopping and latching onto the side rails as they turned their eager faces up to Kate in the wagon.

"Did you hear me, Miss Kate? Did you hear what I said? Did you?"

Despite her remaining trepidations, Kate shushed Kitty's barking and pulled Lydia back from the brink of falling over the side . . . and even managed a smile for Joey. "Yes, I did. Now what's all this about a lady who looks just like me? What exactly did you see?"

Her question was more pointed than the boys could realize, but she hoped for details. And it was Willy who unwittingly supplied them. "She was a fine lady, Miss Kate. Her hat has a feather in it. And she's riding in one of them fancy carriages with a driver. And black and shiny horses pulling her right along, as fast as you please, right back up to that hill over yonder with all them big tents."

Kate nodded, but inside she was dying. The Talmidges' landau carriage was pulled by sleek black horses. But theirs weren't the only ones in the world, Kate was quick to remind herself as, she fought to keep her smile on her face. "Is that so? Why, I expect she was a fine sight to see. But I'll bet she wasn't alone. Fine ladies like that don't go out alone. Was there a man riding with her?"

"Oh, yes, ma'am," Joey cut in before Willy could hog all the glory.

Kate's heart all but stopped. Her smile faded, became wavery. "Oh? And what did he look like? Was he a fine gentleman?"

Joey and Willy traded glances, as if gauging the other's conclusion about the man, and then turned their attention back to Kate. Again Joey got to give the news before his brother could. "He weren't no gentleman at all. He was up front and handling the team. Like Willy said."

"Oh, I see. Her driver." The boys nodded. Instead of relief, a healthy dose of trepidation washed over Kate. Because it didn't mean a thing that Edgar Talmidge hadn't been in the landau. He could be anywhere. Which was scarier than knowing. Still, Kate rushed to remind herself of another truth—she was only guessing who this woman was.

She didn't know, in fact, this fine lady's identity. And right now, there was only one way to find out, so she continued to question the boys. "So tell me more about this lady. Why'd you say she looks like me?"

Willy's frown matched Joey's as the older boy glanced back over his shoulder. But Kate's attention was on Willy . . . and his honest answer. "Why? Because she did, Miss Kate. She looked just like you. Except for them rich-lady clothes of hers, she could've been your sister."

Still holding tightly to Lydia, Kate stiffened her knees against the fearful weakness that shot through her. Her sister. Those were the exact words Mr. Talmidge had used to explain her imprisonment. Because she looked enough like his wife to be her sister, he'd said.

Then it was true. Kate sobered, stared off into the distance. Her new life, her land—wherever it was out there— in her mind became more and more remote. Fleeing with it was her sense of hope, of a new beginning.

Because Norah Heston Talmidge was here.

With his back to the thick growth of scrub oaks that separated him from Kate and Lydia back at the buckboard, Cole stood along the creek's pebbly edge at the watering hole, no more than a wide spot in a thinly running creek cutting canyon-like down the middle of the surrounding green hills. Positioned between his horse and the mules, with their leads in his hands as the tired animals drank their fill, Cole, along with the scattering of other men who were also watering their animals, remained transfixed by the sight that had just passed them by.

The woman, the only passenger in the back of a fancy landau carriage, with its two hoods down, was a beauty. There was no doubt about that. But Cole was more shocked than affected. Because the woman could have been Kate. Except for all her finery that spoke of extreme wealth, from the expensive cut of her dark blue traveling costume to her heavy jewelry . . . and the haughty coolness of her expression . . . she could have been Kate.

The black hair under a plumed hat. The high, smooth forehead. The curve of her cheek, down to a determined chin . . . they were all Kate's. Except he knew this wasn't Kate, even if the rich woman's eyes were the same color as Kate's. Cole frowned at the similarities. It was odd, that the two women had the same color of eyes. Green. Very green. Very specific and unusual coloring.

Cole frowned and shook his head as he dismissed the comparison. But not so easily dismissed was the nagging question . . . could it truly be Mrs. Talmidge he'd just seen? He had no way of knowing, short of stopping the landau and asking the woman. Not the smartest thing to do. He could easily be mistaken, by her armed driver, for one of the hucksters and ruffians who abounded out here. In that case, Cole was willing to bet that he'd be shot dead by the man before he got within hailing distance of the lady.

Realizing how far afield he'd gone in his thinking, Cole asked himself another question. What in hell, besides her uncanny resemblance to Kate, made him think the woman in the buggy was Norah Talmidge? Wasn't that quite a leap? After all, the lady he'd just seen could be any rich man's wife or daughter. True enough, because this border land was rife with the upper class, with their big tents on the hills, their servants, and their boredom, all arrayed for prime viewing of the land run event less than forty-eight hours away.

Cole's expression suddenly soured. To those moneyed folks, the desperation for a better life that ran like water through the crowds of would-be settlers down here on the flatlands was no more than a sport to be witnessed. It sickened Cole, the stench of the powerful that tarnished the fervent hopes of the good folks here for an honest reason. Suddenly, Cole heard himself and stiffened his stance. He was identifying with the settlers. How could that be? He'd never cared before. And in fact, less than a week ago, he'd been impatient as hell to get away from them and their family ways. That meant . . . he was changing. It was that simple. And now it shamed him that he made his living with the money of folks just like those on the hill. Folks just like that handsome woman, with her nose in the air, who'd just ridden by.

Not liking himself at all right now, Cole swore that this contract with Edgar Talmidge, the one he'd agreed to, could very well be his last. When he had to start killing women, it was time to get out of the business and to find another way. But not ready to explore what that way might be, Cole instead forced his mind back to the moment, back to the lady in the landau. The odds were the lady wasn't Norah Talmidge. But odds weren't the same thing as truth. Cole knew that. He hadn't survived all these years of earning his living with his wits and his gun by not looking at a thing from all sides or by discarding a fact or detail that seemed even remotely connected.

And these details were connected . . . somehow. He just knew it. *All right*, he told himself. *Then suppose the Talmidges are here. Why would they hire me to find their thieving maid—if they intended to be out here and could find her themselves?*

The answer was . . . they wouldn't. So either the lady he'd just seen wasn't a Talmidge. Or she was, and Edgar Talmidge had lied to Cole about why he wanted this maid so bad. That made sense to Cole because he'd always had trouble with the why of it—just as he was now having trouble with this line of thought, which he liked less and less. Yet it was becoming more and more compelling. And that being so, Cole knew he'd be smart not to dismiss something as nagging as this was. *Just how much money, and how much jewelry*, he now asked himself, *would that maid, Anne Candless, have to have stolen for them to make such a long train trip out here—when I'm already on the job?*

It would have to be an extraordinary amount. A sum Cole didn't think the Talmidges would just leave sitting around for a maid to steal. But even if she had, they wouldn't chase after her themselves. He was living proof of that. He knew firsthand that the rich didn't do their own dirty work. They hired men like him to clean up after them.

And that was exactly how Cole now realized he felt. Dirty. Like he needed to jump in the water and wash away the stench of how he made his living. *Well, dammit,* he told himself, as the carriage disappeared around a tree-shrouded bend in the trail. *If I knew how to do anything else, I would.* That stiffened Cole's stance. The woman in the carriage all but forgotten, Cole fought with the nagging desire for another way to earn his money.

He'd never experienced this before the past week. Before the kids. Before Kate. Had he? Well, so he'd thought. Cole frowned, checked his animals, seeing that they didn't overfill their bellies. Then he looked off toward the horizon, and found himself thinking . . . Who could blame him for being trail-weary? For being tired of always having to watch his back? For never knowing where home was, where he was supposed to hang his hat?

Suddenly, Cole found himself hoping that the lady he'd just seen was Norah Talmidge and that Mr. Talmidge was here with her. Because in that event, he'd give the man his damned money back and tell him to find himself another hired killer, since he wasn't about to shoot a woman. But Cole knew he couldn't do that, even if he could confront the Talmidges. Because giving them back their money wouldn't solve anything for him. He still had three mouths—no, four, counting Kate, and soon five, meaning her baby—to feed. *Son of a bitch.*

Tired of his thoughts, knowing he was getting nowhere, Cole pulled on the multiple reins he held and urged his horse and the mules away from the water's edge. "Come on now. Git up, there."

Cole headed back the way he'd come only minutes ago. Back toward Kate and the kids. That got a humorless chuckle out of him. Him. A family man. Then he sobered, shook his head. No. It wasn't possible. He couldn't even consider it. Too much blood on his hands. On his soul.

He then derided himself for thinking that that lady in the carriage was Mrs. Talmidge. *Hell, up close she prob-*

ably doesn't look a thing like Kate. But still, she'd been dressed exactly how Cole would love to see Kate dressed. He'd bet she'd be every bit as stunning as that other woman.

Hold on, Cole. And he did, blinking, surprised, much as if a bobcat had jumped out in front of him. What was he doing? he asked himself. And he meant his thoughts about dressing Kate. Well, he conceded, they were a damned sight better than his other thoughts . . . of undressing her. And tormenting himself with such images. She didn't want him. Or need him. And he felt the same way about her.

He had no room in his life for a good woman. Even if she was already his wife. But that was neither here nor there. Because she had her hands full, being with child and running from—Cole's eyes narrowed—whoever it was who wanted her baby. Looking now to his left, to where the landau had turned out of sight around the bend, Cole gave free rein to his thoughts. Kate had never said who it was who wanted her baby. And he hadn't questioned her about it, given everything else she was going through then. He'd figured it was none of his business. But that was before he'd gotten to know her better on the three-day trip here. They'd been through a lot and she'd never once complained or stinted on what she had to do.

Cole realized now that he'd come to respect and admire her. She looked so fragile and yet was tough as hell. But now that he thought about it, it seemed to him—that whoever was after her child would have to be pretty powerful. Someone like the woman who'd just ridden by in that expensive carriage? Most likely. Because Kate didn't strike him as the kind of woman who would have run, otherwise. But what kind of people would they have to be to take a child from its mother? Well, childless themselves, for one thing. And desperate because of it.

But desperate why? Well, there was only one answer that Cole could come up with. Money. A whole lot of money. More money than the people already had. Like an inheritance. Defeat tugged at Cole. There it was. He didn't like the next mental hurdle his mind was already leaping over. But circumstances forced him. From what he understood through the bits and pieces of news that made it out West, Edgar Talmidge's father was ailing. And Edgar Talmidge was childless.

Cole shook his head, refusing to believe, refusing to accept what seemed to be a simple and blinding truth burning behind his eyes. *No, it's just plain crazy.* The Talmidges somehow connected to Kate? He couldn't accept it. For one thing, Kate had come here from Kentucky. Or so she'd said—at the same time that she'd lied about being widowed. A tightness wrapped itself around Cole's chest. He fought against allowing his mind to take hold of such a notion. And yet, stubbornly, it did just that, telling him that maybe it wasn't as crazy as he'd first thought. Because everything seemed to be coming together out here, right now, in this vast and unsettled place.

It was true. Cole couldn't deny that. Kate's predicament—pregnant, penniless, unmarried . . . until he'd married her . . . and on the run—was the exact opposite of the Talmidges' predicament. Childless, rich, married . . . with a vast inheritance in the offing. Like an avalanche of boulders tumbling down a mountainside, the two sides were a collision just waiting to happen. Still troubling Cole the most was that Kate had never said who her baby's father was. Or who the people were who wanted to take her baby. And now, here Kate was, here he was, and here—he'd just bet— the Talmidges were.

Son of a bitch. It was far-fetched enough to be true. A sudden sense of urgency, of danger, had Cole hurrying back to the wagon. As his animals plodded tiredly along behind him, he accepted one thing. Only one person knew all the answers. And right now, she was on the other side of this stand of oaks. With his sister's kids.

As he neared the far and thinning edge of the thick stand of trees, he decided that he wouldn't accuse Kate or even question her directly. She'd most likely just lie to him. But

he knew he didn't have to say a word. Because the boys—
whom he still meant to have words with for taking off like
they had—had most likely already told her everything Cole
needed her to know about the lady in the carriage.

So all he had to do was see Kate's face. And then he'd
know. One way or the other. Cole emerged from the oaks
and sought his buckboard among the many wagons dotting
the landscape. And there they were. Kate was standing in
the wagon, her hand on Lydia's shoulder, Kitty at her other
side. The boys were holding on to the wagon's side. And
Joey was looking over his shoulder . . . back toward Cole.
Just then, the boy spotted him. He knew because Joey
pointed back in Cole's direction. And everyone else, including Kate, looked his way, too.

Kate saw him the instant he broke from the trees. Walking
slowly, his long-legged strides sure and firm as he led the
mules and his roan by their gathered reins, Cole strode toward her. Even from that distance, even despite the shading
provided by his Stetson, she felt his gaze upon her, could
see the grim slash of his mouth. Kate could only guess at
the nature of his thoughts, could only try to gauge his
mood. He'd seen the same woman the boys had, that much
she knew from what Joey and Willy told her. Apparently,
the lady had made a big splash among the men gathered
at the watering hole.

Even now, in their innocence, the boys regaled her with
tales of what the men said about the fine lady. Twice Kate
hushed Joey and Willy, warning them about repeating such
things in front of herself and Lydia. Much to their red-faced
chagrin, they'd finally settled on talking about how exciting
it was to be here at the actual border of the Oklahoma
Country. At any other time, Joey's enthusiasm and joy—
so different from his usual seriousness—would have glad-
dened Kate's heart. But right now her entire being centered
itself on Cole.

All too soon he was standing there at the buckboard's
side and was tying the mules and his roan to the wagon's

tailgate. To Kate, with her heart beating a steady tattoo in
her chest, it seemed he was avoiding looking at her. She
swallowed, wondering what he knew, what he thought . . .
and what had happened on the other side of those oaks.
Done finally with his task, he leaned into the wagon's
weathered wood and, with a thumb, nudged his hat's stiff
brim up until his black eyes were revealed. He then stared
into her eyes . . . and waited.

Even the children and Kitty quieted, no doubt sensing
the air of expectancy between the two adults. The boys and
Lydia divided their attention between their uncle's face
and Kate's. Next to Cole, his roan shifted his weight and
stamped a hoof. The mules nodded sleepily, their heads
drooping, their eyes half-closed. Even surrounded as Kate
and Cole and the kids were by the sea of humanity and all
its attendant noises, the quiet air around the buckboard told
its own story. Kate could stand it no longer and blurted,
"Have you given any thought to where we should set up a
camp for tonight?"

As if all it had awaited were her words, the quiet burst.
Filling the air now were strangers' called greetings to one
another, their shouts and laughter, a horse's whinny, a
child's cry, a mother's singing. Solid wagons rolled noisily
by, among them several cavalrymen, in military formation,
who cantered their horses alongside the newest arrivals.
Thoroughly impressed, Joey and Willy begged permission
to dart off for a better view. Cole looked away from Kate
to tell them, "You can go. But take your sister and Kitty.
Keep a hand on Lydia and stay to one side."

He wants to be alone with me, was Kate's fearful
thought. But having no choice, in light of his words, she
herded Lydia to the back of the wagon so Cole could hand
her over to the boys, who grumbled about having to take
the little girl with them. For his part, Kitty bounded easily
over the wagon's side and barked for all he was worth as
he pranced back and forth and waited for the children to
be ready. And then, they were, a brother to either side of

Lydia and holding her hands as they walked slowly off, allowing for Lydia's shorter legs.

Kate was finally alone with Cole Youngblood . . . who'd just seen a woman who looked a lot like her. Enough like her, in fact, to be her sister. Avoiding Cole's eyes, Kate put her hands to her waist and looked after the children. "You suppose they'll keep up with Lydia?"

"They will. And they'll be fine with Kitty along. He's not about to put up with any foolishness from anyone bothering them."

Kate nodded, shading her eyes with a hand as she watched the children's retreating figures . . . and worried her bottom lip with her teeth. She could not look at Cole, at her husband, who was going to make the land run for her. But after a few quiet moments passed, she had no choice. Taking a deep breath, she turned to him and plunged in. "Did you see her, too? The fine lady the boys told me about?"

"I did," Cole said, nodding and settling his Stetson lower on his brow. Then he undid the tailgate's hinged fastener and lowered it. Holding a hand out to her, he sought her gaze. "Why don't you come down out of that wagon, Kate? I expect you're sick of it by now."

And she was. Sick enough of it to cry. Sick enough of the fear and the lying and the worrying and the doubts. Sick of it all, and especially of herself. But she couldn't say any of that. The words just wouldn't come. So she took the three or so steps she needed to reach Cole and accepted his help getting out of the wagon. She put her hands to his shoulders and he circled her waist, gently swinging her down to the grassy, spongy earth. The land felt good under her feet. Solid and eternal. And Cole's hands on her were strong and his grip firm.

But to her surprise, he didn't release her and step back. Instead, he held on to her and looked down into her eyes. "I saw that woman, Kate. Except for her fine clothes, she could have been you."

Kate nodded, lowering her gaze until she looked at a

button on his shirtfront. "That's what the boys said." Only belatedly did she realize that she still gripped him by his shoulders, that she was still in his embrace . . . for all the world to see. But there was nothing she could do, nowhere to put her hands if she let go of him before he released her. And so, she stood there . . . waiting.

"I figured they would," Cole finally answered. Then, "Look at me, Kate."

Inhaling deeply of the clean Oklahoma air, dragging it into her troubled body, Kate did as he wanted. She looked up at him. His sober expression bracketed his mouth with tiny lines . . . and all but stopped her heart. *He knows.* "Yes?"

"Tonight, after the kids are asleep, I'd like to have a word with you. I think it's time."

All too soon, in the Oklahoma Country, daylight became nightfall. Stars filled the clear night sky's canopy. A full moon shone brightly on the hushed assemblage of waiting settlers. At the Youngblood camp, a cookfire glowed with embers. Filling their bellies was a supper of biscuits and beef stew that Cole had helped Kate assemble. She still wasn't that good a cook, but he was, having had to do for himself all his life. He'd been particularly pleased earlier to show up with the meat of a just-slaughtered steer and the fresh vegetables sold to him by the very merchants here with wagon after wagon of provisions they'd use in less than two days to open their stores.

After that, and availing themselves of the separate bathing areas, which were divided by canvas tarps strung by rope across the cold and shallow stream, and secured around two trees, one on each shore, Cole bathed in the men's area with the boys. And Kate, shivering and having to fight Lydia every step of the way, did the same on the women's side. But finally, the children were clean, exhausted, and bedded down in the buckboard. At one end of the wagon, Kitty yawned and settled in with them, turning and churning a scrap of blanket that Kate had given him until he had it just like he wanted it and felt it was good enough to sleep on.

And then . . . there was nothing to prevent that talk Cole wanted to have with her. Exhausted herself, but content for the moment, and sitting with her back to the fire so it could dry her hair more, Kate perched atop her little wooden box, the very same one she'd found in Arkansas City and had been sitting on when Cole discovered her crying her eyes out. To her right, his Stetson off, his gunbelt wrapped around itself and lying next to him on his unfurled bedroll, sat Cole. His knees bent, his arms resting atop them, he faced the fire, but sat far enough back that all she had to do was turn her head the slightest bit to see his face. His rugged masculine features were shaded with the night's dark and the moon's silver. His silhouette showed the acute tiredness of the man, his expression the heaviness of his thoughts. And the fire's light showed just how handsome he was.

"Kate," he began suddenly but quietly, startling her into tensing. "It's been a hard three days on you. I know that. And I admire you for all you've done."

Pleased and overcome with a shyness brought on by his kind words, which she hadn't expected, Kate faced forward and smiled into the night. "I didn't do anything but what I had to do. Same as everyone else." She cut her gaze over to him, found him staring at her. Her words stuck in her throat, but she finally got them out. "Yourself included, Cole. You got us here all in one piece. Well, six pieces, if you count Kitty."

He chuckled, his smile lighting his features as surely as did the moonlight. Kate's belly tensed with a gnawing want . . . for him. It always took her by surprise, her wanting this man. *Any* man. She'd never thought she would, after Mr. Talmidge. But she did. She wanted this man, her husband. And it was worse, this knowing and wanting. Worse than not ever knowing or wanting. It ached, it tore at her. And there was nothing she could do about it. She could only stare at Cole, could only soak up his presence . . . while she had him in her life.

Staring at him now, entranced by his deep voice, Kate suddenly realized he was watching her watch him. His gaze had warmed up considerably. A slow smile of heated recognition rode his features and challenged her to acknowledge it. Kate's mouth slacked open. *He wants me, too—just like I want him.* She wanted to jump up and run away. But she couldn't move. Nor could she run away from knowing the horrible truth between them. He was Cole Youngblood, hired killer, on the trail of Anne Candless—her, in truth. And that canceled out anything she might feel for him, or he for her.

Kate was quick to blink and smile and pretend to be distracted because of her tiredness. "I'm sorry. My mind is just so tired. Well, never mind. Go ahead. You were saying something to me?"

He sat quietly staring at her, his bemused expression communicating his thoughts to her as clearly as if he'd spoken them: *Pretend all you want that you don't feel it, too, Kate. But we both know the truth.* Then he inhaled and . . . picked up the thread of their almost-forgotten conversation. "I believe I was saying that I do count Kitty." Then he chuckled and shook his head. "That's the damnedest name Lydia gave him, isn't it?"

Kate grinned, glad for this talk of the everyday, even though she knew in her heart that he really didn't want to talk about the dog. "It surely is. And I feel like the biggest fool when I see the funny looks folks send my way after hearing me call out, 'Here, Kitty, Kitty. Come here, boy,' only to have that big old hound come running up and about knock me over."

Cole shook his head as he picked up a long stick and poked at the fire. "I've done the same thing a time or two. Calling out to Kitty and getting the funny looks, I mean. Not knocking you over."

In a rare moment of levity, Kate quipped, "Well, that ought to have folks fearing and respecting you even more."

The words, though, were no more than out before she realized how close she'd come to the real subject she was
avoiding, right along with him. "I mean the dog, too. Not
knocking me over."

Cole sobered . . . and Kate knew she'd given him the
opening he'd probably been searching for. When would she
learn not to let her guard down around him? "I know that's
what you meant. But if you're not too tired, I'd like to talk
to you about something else, Kate."

Feeling the warmth between them evaporate, and shivering in the cool April night air, Kate gave in to the finality
that seeped through her bones, weighing her down. "All
right. Go ahead. I've got to sit here, anyway, until my hair
dries." With that, she hugged her knees to her chest and
again stared out into the night—dismissing her growing
feelings for Cole—and wondered about her land. Would
she live long enough to see it?

"Are you cold?"

Kate tugged back a heavy wave of her drying hair that
fell over her shoulder. She stared at Cole as his gaze roved
over her, taking in her huddled posture. When his gaze
finally locked with hers, Kate raised her chin, feeling very
remote from him. And angry with him for being who he
was. "No. I'm fine."

He made as if to get up. "I can get you my coat, if you
like."

She put out a hand, urging him to stay put. "No. I'm
fine. Really."

He settled back down. "All right."

Wordless moments ticked by. Kate thanked the stars for
each one of those moments, thanked them for each breath
she took . . . since she had no idea how many more she had
left to her. It all depended, she supposed, on what Cole had
to say to her.

Then, breaking the silence, he said, "Today, as you
know, the boys and I saw that woman who looked just like
you."

There it was. Kate exhaled as quietly as she could. And

spoke cautiously. "They told me all about her."

"Yeah, I expect they did." Then a frown of vexation shaded his features. "Dammit. I never did talk to them about dropping the mules' reins and running off like they did."

"I'm not surprised you forgot. There was a lot going on this afternoon. I expect the kids are just excited about being here." Then she gave him a pointed stare. "So am I. And I need to thank you for making it possible."

Cole sobered, then looked away from her, gazing into the fire's slow-burning flames. "You don't need to do that."

"I don't? Why not?" Kate couldn't believe herself. Like a lamb to the slaughter, herself being the lamb, she kept moving Cole closer to her truths . . . and his. And yet she couldn't seem to stop herself, not even when his expression hardened. Obviously he'd heard the challenge in her voice. But inside her, it didn't feel like a challenge. Instead, every word she spoke felt more like a knife's wound in her soul. But nonetheless she was ready to get everything out in the open, no matter the consequences. "Why shouldn't I thank you, Cole?"

His fierce gaze bored into hers. "Because I'm not sure I've done you any favors bringing you here."

Kate cocked her head at a questioning angle. "What makes you say that?"

Cole exhaled sharply and shifted his weight, looking away from her. Kate could tell he was having trouble putting together the words he wanted to say. Finally, he turned to her—and asked her the one question, spoke the one name, she had been dreading hearing. "Have you ever heard of Edgar Talmidge?"

Chapter Twelve

Even though only moments ago Kate had called herself ready to finally deal with her truth, she found that the lies still came easier. Because they were now her truth. Which made them that much harder to abandon. But she shouldn't be so surprised, she chastised herself, as she sat there staring at Cole, her mouth dry, her body sweating, and dread filling her belly. Since she'd left New York, the truth of who she was and of the baby she carried had come to mean certain death. Only her lies had kept her alive and had gotten her this far . . . right to the edge of the Promised Land and her new life. Only now, it could all slip away. It wasn't fair.

And so, she said, "Yes, I've heard of him. I expect everyone has."

"That's true," he answered her. "A rich and powerful man like he is, everyone would know him. It wouldn't surprise me if he'd come out here to see the land run."

"Me, either." Kate felt fear seeping out of her pores, along with the sweat that trickled down her spine, a sweat unrelated to the fire at her back. Searching for something to do that didn't involve looking into Cole Youngblood's eyes, she reached back and fluffed her hair out, feeling it for dryness. It was dry enough. She swiveled her body atop the wood box, straightening her skirt as she went, until she faced the fire. Only then, when she was seated comfortably with her legs straight out in front of her and crossed at the ankles, did she venture onward. "Why do you ask about this"—she could barely get the hated man's name past her lips—"Mr. Talmidge? Have you seen him?"

Cole shook his head. "No. I wouldn't know him if I saw him. I never met the man."

Thank God, thought Kate as she exhaled a breath she hadn't realized she'd been holding.

"Or his wife," Cole suddenly added. "I never met her, either."

They were back to that—to the fine lady in the fancy carriage. Fear slammed through Kate and nearly had her blurting out everything she knew. *Damn you, Cole Young-blood.* His way of speaking all around a subject without ever bringing it up just ate away at a person's will—which was why he did it, she knew from countless conversations with him. Determined not to make it easy for him—oh, he may get it all out of her eventually, she knew that, but she didn't have to hand him her head on a platter—Kate clamped her jaws shut and said nothing.

"Have you ever met the Talmidges, Kate?" His question came right out of the still night, like a thieving, skulking coyote, intent on stealing instead of hunting for itself.

Kate's gaze riveted to Cole's. "Why would you ask me that? What would the likes of the . . . the *Talmidges*"—she all but spat the word out now—"have to do with me? I'm a nobody."

"You're hardly a nobody, Kate."

His soft-spoken words, in a voice so sincere, unhinged her. She looked down at her lap, saw that she'd been knotting her fingers together . . . over and over. With all her heart, Kate wanted him to take her in his arms and hold her while she cried it all out, told him everything. More than that, she wanted him to tell her it would all work out and be okay. But she knew better. It wouldn't be okay. And he wouldn't take her in his arms. And so, she sat there, alone, isolated on her tiny wood box, and sniffed . . . about a moment away from tears.

"Kate? Look at me."

She did. Then, surprising her, he reached over and brushed back a stray lock of her hair, even going so far as to tuck it behind her ear. Then he caressed her cheek . . . and smiled. Tears sprang to Kate's eyes, but she couldn't look away. Not even when he said, "You're *not* a nobody. And I ought to know."

She sniffed, bit at her lower lip . . . and raised her chin. "Why would you know? What makes you say that?"

He chuckled softly at that and then looked down and away for a moment. As if he were shy. That got Kate's attention. He was shy around her? She never would have suspected that. Just then, Cole swung his gaze back to her. "I know, Kate, because I've watched you for nearly a week now. I've seen what you put yourself through. And I know what drives you. Your baby. I have a lot of respect for what you're doing. Not every woman would have the strength or the courage to do everything you have."

That was quite a speech for him, Kate knew. Not only for how much he said, but for all he said, too. "I don't know what to say. Except that I believe every woman would do as I've done, Cole. She'd have to. She wouldn't have a choice. Babies don't just go away."

She heard herself and thought of her recent bleeding. And knew she was wrong. Sometimes babies do just . . . go away. But blessedly, hers hadn't. Then, something about the look on Cole's face told her he was thinking the same thing . . . about her bleeding and nearly losing her child. She knew what remained unspoken between them. The bleeding could start again . . . at any moment. It hadn't done so. But it could. *Why do things happen the way they do?* she wondered.

"Out loud, Kate."

She started, seeing now the bemused expression on his face. "What?"

"What you were thinking just now . . . say it out loud."

An embarrassed half-smile claimed her features, but she shrugged and said, "Okay. I was just pondering on why things happen the way they do."

He nodded encouragement. "Such as?"

"Such as. . . ." She hesitated, wondering if she really wanted to take Cole Youngblood into her confidence. But then she remembered that only a few days ago it had been her plan to have him get to know her so well that he couldn't possibly kill her or carry her off to Edgar Talmidge. She realized that now was the moment to act. "Well, here I am trying my best to get a piece of land and start a new life for me and my baby. Because, like you said, everything I do is for her—" Kate stopped, looked into his eyes. "Sometimes I think it's a girl child. That's silly, isn't it?"

"No, Kate. Who would know better than the mother?"

Warmed by his words, which said he respected her female intuition, Kate smiled at him and then went on. "Well, like I said, everything I do—everything I try so I can make all that come true—is bad for her." The baby suddenly became real to Kate. Always before, before this moment, she'd thought of the baby inside her as an *it*. But no longer. It was as if having spoken her belief aloud to someone had made the child real to the world, and not just to her. The eagerness of anticipation seized Kate. Her baby was a girl.

But suddenly she realized that Cole was frowning at her. "I don't understand, Kate. How's what you're doing bad for your baby?"

She coupled her words with a broad gesture meant to encompass the Oklahoma Country. "I mean all this, Cole. The jouncing around in the wagon. All the work. The hard walking I have to do. The bending and stretching. And lifting. The worrying—"

"What worries you, Kate?"

Wariness seized her. He'd certainly jumped on that. Even now, he was leaning toward her, no doubt in anticipation of her answer. Cautious, her chin raised, Kate shrugged, tried to play down her words. "Lots of things, I suppose. Like whether we'll get the land I want. Whether we get it registered on time. And build on it quick enough, like the law says. Things like that."

"Is that all?" He sat back with his question. But his posture was no less tense, Kate could see.

"It's enough," she allowed. "I've got the same worries as every other soul here, I expect. I'm no different from them."

Cole considered her a moment, as if he were digesting her words. But he kept to himself how he might feel as he next asked her, "What else worries you, Kate?"

He was attempting to goad her toward some confession, she was sure of it. So she spoke only of things he already knew. "Well, the baby does, of course. I worry I won't . . . carry her the full time. And then even if I do, she'll be born around the end of November. So I worry what the weather will be like then. And what the winters are like out here. And I worry about being alone when my time comes."

"Alone? No you won't. The kids will be here with you. I know they'd not be much help. But I'll try my best to be here with you, too. If you like."

Kate frowned, drew back, her eyes narrowing. "I appreciate that, Cole. I do. But why would the kids still be with me? What about that cousin of yours? You think it'll take you that long to find her?"

It was Cole's turn to look away and to look uncomfortable. He inhaled deeply, as if his chest were tight, and then again sought her gaze. "I don't intend to go find her, Kate."

Stung by surprise—this was exactly what she'd first feared, and had then hoped for, and now worried about— Kate sat up stiffly atop the wood box under her. "That's not part of our deal, Cole. You said—"

"I said a lot of things. So did you."

Kate swallowed, thinking he didn't know the half of it. Or did he? But still, she agreed with him. "Yes, I did. I said a lot of things. But that doesn't change the fact that—"

"That you're their aunt now."

For some reason, that most obvious relationship still startled her. She was actual kin to Joey, Willy, and Lydia. "I am, aren't I? But—"

"But nothing, Kate. It's better for them to be with you than it is for them to be with some cousin who's a stranger to them."

"Cole, *I* was a stranger to them a week ago."

"I know that. But they've"—his hesitation captured

Kate's attention—"come to care about you." He again looked away, staring out into the night.

Kate's heart skipped a beat. He wasn't only talking about the kids, she suddenly knew. He meant himself. *He'd* come to have warm feelings for her. She couldn't look away from him, from his strong and handsome profile. *Imagine that. Cole Youngblood, hired killer. He cares about me.* And even though as recently as only a few minutes ago she'd still hoped to get him to care, nothing could have made Kate feel worse. Because she feared she, in turn, cared very much about him. No, she didn't only fear it . . . she knew it. She cared so much that she could hardly picture a future without him.

Kate now acknowledged to herself that she'd been having these thoughts for some time. She recalled considering, some days ago, keeping the kids permanently. Yes, because she had genuine feelings for each of them. But also because she knew that if the kids were with her, she could be assured Cole would come by from time to time to see them . . . and maybe, one day, her. Kate sighed under her breath. Was she using Charlotte Anderson's kids to get her own way? She hoped not, because she truly wanted them with her. But more importantly, was she coming to love the woman's brother? Quite possibly. Kate scolded herself, saying she had to quit wishing for things because darned if she didn't keep getting them—and never in a good way.

But now that he had practically declared his feelings for her, Kate called herself a schemer. Because he didn't really know her, not who she really was. So whatever he felt for her was based on lies. That insight startled Kate. *Now where did that come from?* She had to stop herself from giving in to the urge to look around for a third person, some shadowy body standing behind her and whispering these truths into her ear. Because this wasn't like her, all this thinking about herself she'd done in the past week.

But maybe that was because before then she'd been an honest person. An innocent and honest person who'd had no need to question her every thought, her every action.

She'd never before had to weigh every response first to see how it would affect her past words or even her next deed. But no more. She now knew so much about the intolerable ways of the world that she'd become a part of it. The world had sullied her, she knew—not only her reputation, but also her body. And now . . . it wanted to claim her spirit with the lies it had forced her to tell.

Kate was confronted with another truth, one she couldn't allow herself to evade. If she did, she knew with blinding clarity, it would be at the steep cost of all that remained of that core of good nestled deep inside her. And that truth was . . . she couldn't blame a faceless world for her troubles. Because that would be yet another lie. She had to accept that she, and she alone, through choices she'd made, had created her present troubles, which had put her right here at this lonely place, at this fireside, with this man . . . who'd just said he cared about her.

Kate exhaled sharply, knew what she had to do . . . and found it was her turn to say, "Cole? Will you look at me, please?"

Slowly, as if he were reluctant to do so, he turned to her. He looked at her. He met her gaze, yet he said nothing. He didn't have to. It was there on his face. From his dark eyes shone the truth. He hated caring about her as much as she hated caring about him. There was no getting around it.

Which left her no choice but to try to set things right between them. She decided to start with the unraveling of one little lie from the tapestry of untruths she'd woven. Taking a deep breath for courage, she said, "You can't leave those kids with me, Cole. It wouldn't be right—even as much as I care about them. And I do. I care about them a lot. But . . ." Her hesitance now, right at the brink of a truth, disappointed her. She'd thought she could do it, but maybe she was so far gone that she couldn't. Shame had her looking down at the very earth of the Promised Land that lay all around her.

"But what, Kate?" Cole asked in his quiet way.

She looked up, met his gaze. "They could get hurt if they were with me. And I don't mean bumps or scratches, just growing-up things. I mean the truth is . . . they could get killed." There. She'd said it. And this tiny bit of truth felt good, like a return to honesty.

Cole narrowed his eyes, sent her a sidelong glance. "Is that so? They could get killed? Who'd kill them? Someone like the Talmidges?"

Kate gasped at his words, at yet another intrusion of that name into the relative sanctuary that was their campsite. It seemed such a violation in light of her present thoughts, in light of wanting to do the right thing by those kids . . . and by Cole. But maybe, it suddenly occurred to her, this way was the path, the path meant to be all along. Enemies. Her and Cole. It seemed so. It certainly seemed he'd been heading in this direction all along in their conversation.

Then, so be it, Kate found herself thinking. She raised her chin, but still said nothing, wouldn't answer him about the Talmidges. But her silence, she knew, spoke louder than any words she could say. Her silence damned her. But what difference did it make? It was already too late. For her. And for Cole.

Then Cole spoke again. "I've heard that Mrs. Talmidge has green eyes and black hair. Like yours."

Kate's heart thumped leadenly, angrily, in her chest. "Like mine? It seems I'm not all that remarkable, then, doesn't it?"

Cole chuckled at her words, a humorless sound, a sound like that of a pistol being cocked. "Oh, I'd say you're quite remarkable, Kate. Quite."

He didn't mean that as a compliment to her. She knew it. Yet she pretended to take it as such. "Thank you . . . I suppose."

He black eyes glittering with the reflected flames from the campfire, he ducked his chin in acknowledgment. "You're welcome." Then he shifted his weight, bending his knees, resting his arms atop them and folding his hands together. He stared out into the night, focusing just above the fire's flames. "You know, it's a sad thing, really, for the Talmidges. All that money. All that power. And no children. No one to pass everything along to."

Now he sought Kate's gaze again and held it. "A thing like that could make a man desperate, I'd expect. Desperate for a child."

He's only guessing, Kate kept telling herself, as she licked nervously at her dry lips and yet refused to look away. *He can't know unless I tell him.* "I suppose," was all she would finally allow.

Cole stared right through her. Anchoring an elbow atop his bent knee, he cupped his jaw and chin with a hand . . . and considered her. Then, when Kate's nerves were stretched taut, threatening to snap and shatter, he said, "Just tell me the truth, Kate. I think it's time. Because I think they're here. And I think you know it."

Kate startled even herself when she jumped up. "No," she blurted out, her voice no more than a hiss as she backed away, mindful of the buckboard wagon behind her. Cole was on his feet almost before she was. "No," she said again. "You don't know anything." Her breathing became shallow, her temples pounded. She had to protect her baby at all costs. "You know nothing, do you hear me?"

Cole put a hand out to her, as if he meant to touch her. "Kate—"

She jerked back. "No. Don't you touch me." Cole lowered his arm to his side and stood there, a deep frown bracketing his mouth with tiny lines. "Leave me alone," she warned, her voice breaking on a sob. She grabbed at her skirt, holding it up out of the way of her feet. "Don't say a word. You don't know anything. It's my baby. Mine. You don't know what I've been through."

"That's what I'm asking you, Kate. I want to know."

A derisive noise escaped her. She continued backing up . . . until she hit against the wagon at her back. "I expect you do want to know. The truth would mean a lot to you, wouldn't it?"

Cole stayed where he was, his chin coming up a notch,

his gaze scrutinizing her. "What do you mean by that?"

"You tell me," Kate challenged him as she glanced down, seeking his weapon. There it was, where he'd left it. On his bedroll and next to his feet. She saw too that he'd followed her actions and even now carefully considered her in light of that. Kate realized something else. She was losing control. And he had to know that. How could he not? But there was nothing she could do about it. Fear for her baby, more than for herself, and the realization that there was no longer a reason to pretend, had her on the edge of hysteria.

"What do you want me to tell you, Kate? I don't know what you mean."

She cocked her head at a questioning angle. "You don't? How about all those times you said you wouldn't shoot a woman? You want to talk about that? Here I am. And there's your gun. Shoot me."

Cole raked a hand through his hair. His every sharp-edged movement spoke of extreme agitation. "Why in the hell would I want to shoot you, Kate? You're my wife, for God's sake."

"Ha. In name only," she sneered. "And only because I forced you into the ceremony. And we both know that. So don't let that stop you."

"Dammit, Kate, stop me from what?"

"Stop you from doing your dirty work, that's what. I read that telegraph in your saddlebag, Cole. I read it. And I know what it is you have to do. And so do you."

Sickened by her very words, terrified over what might happen next, Kate turned and fled . . . out into the night. Out of the comforting light of the campfire, her only home-fire for now. Out past other wagons, other would-be settlers. Out past freedom and hope.

Out past Cole Youngblood's reach . . . but not his voice. "Kate! Come back. I'd never hurt you," he called after her.

"Dammit!" The angry word shot like a bullet out of Cole's mouth. His hands balled into fists, he kicked ineffectually at the dirt surrounding the campfire and continued to swear softly. Kitty's hound-dog head popped out of the back of the schooner. Peering around the slackened canvas above the tailgate, he stared alertly in Cole's direction.

Cole ignored him because Kate commanded his attention. She was rapidly disappearing from sight. As she threaded her way through the different encampments in the dark she was met by shouts of "Whoa, there" and "Hold on now, missy" from folks startled by her headlong passage. With practiced skill, Cole scooped up his six-shooter, unfurled the belt from around his holster, and strapped it on.

"Son of a bitch." He'd meant what he'd said to her. Didn't she know that? He wouldn't hurt her. He couldn't. Not ever. Because the truth was . . . he maybe loved her. That was as close as he could come to admitting it. But still, there wasn't much sense anymore in denying the possibility to himself. It just took something like this—Kate's endangering herself—to make him know it. Cole wanted to yell, because if something happened to her now, if she fell and hurt herself, he'd lose the only chance he had to find out. The only chance he had to tell her. And if that happened, he'd never forgive himself.

Cole hurried to tie the holster's leather thong around his thigh while trying to catch glimpses of Kate's retreating figure. She was at times swallowed up by the surrounding darkness, only to reappear moments later as she hit a patch of moonlight, or tore through yet another campsite. His gun finally on, his Stetson jammed on his head, Cole stepped over the schooner's wooden tongue and marked her retreat. If she continued on in that direction, she'd end up at the creek where that afternoon he'd watered the mules and his roan.

"Dammit." Cole looked back over his shoulder, sparing a glance for the covered wagon to his right. Inside were three sleeping children he couldn't leave alone in this sea of strangers. But Kitty was awake. Should he leave the hound in charge? Would the dog understand what Cole needed him to do? Or would he bound happily after Cole, thinking this a game of chase?

It was a chance he'd have to take, Cole finally decided. Because with each second he hesitated, Kate was farther away. That being so, he took the several determined steps he needed to get to the back of the wagon. Once there, he cupped the grinning dog's ears in his hands. And felt like a fool for speaking in so intelligent a manner to the dumb animal. "Stay here, Kitty. Stay with the kids. I've got to go get Kate. You understand? Stay here."

Kitty barked and wagged his tail. Could it be the dog understood? Cole stepped back from the wagon. Kitty stayed where he was. Cole nodded. "Good boy, Kitty." Kitty put his front paws on the wagon's tailgate . . . and showed a respectable amount of sharp teeth as he growled low in his throat.

Having to trust that this display meant that Kitty knew he was on watch, Cole set out after Kate, roughly following her meandering path across the crowded ground. His passing elicited the same reactions she had from the disgruntled settlers. But ignoring them as she had, Cole ran on, his thoughts more and more disjointed. Only troublesome words would come. *Talmidge. Saddlebags. Telegraph. Shoot a woman.* Cole's heart and mind seemed only to want to concern themselves with his present exertion, with keeping his steps sure and his feet under him. It was just as well. Because what could he say to her when he caught up with her?

She'd read the truth for herself. Right there in his saddlebags. He couldn't deny it. She now knew his next contract was to kill a woman. No wonder she was terrified of him. Hell, he scared himself sometimes. But what he couldn't account for was Kate's reacting only now to what she'd read. Of course, she hadn't said when she'd read the telegraph. And he had to admit, she'd had ample opportunity over many days to do so. But why now? Why tonight? What had prompted her strong reaction? Had it been his fishing around with her about her predicament and the Talmidges possibly being here? Hell, he knew the two things weren't related.

Cole jerked to a stop, much as if his last thought had been a brick wall he'd run up against. He *did* know the two things weren't related, didn't he? Gripping his sides, his hands to his waist, his lungs aching for air, Cole frowned as he looked around. He'd broken free of the close-packed wagons and was now standing in a flat stretch of unoccupied plains that sloped down to the creek's waters. Nothing moved in the unfettered moonlight. No sign of Kate. *Dammit.* And no, he didn't *really* know she had no connection to the Talmidges, did he? Only she knew. And he had to find her. And ask her. But the truth remained. No matter what her answer was, he'd never hurt Kate.

So now he had to find her and convince her. Before she got herself killed. But where to look? Which direction should he go? She could be anywhere. Frustrated in the extreme, Cole turned in a slow circle, his keenly trained gaze all but melting back the darkness in his quest to see his quarry. Then . . . Cole froze. Straight ahead. A shadow had flitted amongst the trees. Was it her? Could be. Could be a deer. Could be any one of the thousands of folks camped out here. Could be someone up to no good, too. Or . . . it could be Kate.

It was a chance he had to take. Besides, he was armed and knew how to take care of himself. Unlike Kate. Once again, Cole set out, loping easily, quietly, hunting her now, trying his best to hear a sound, a twig snapping, underbrush rustling . . . anything that would tell him she was within his grasp. Then he heard it—a cry. A whimpering cry. Cole stopped, frozen in position, listening, fearing yet praying he'd hear it again, just so he could get a bearing from the sound. Then . . . there it was again. To his left. Cole pivoted in that direction. Dread washed over him, weakening him. He'd heard that sound before, he now realized. Kate had made it when she'd been bleeding the other day.

Cole took off again, this time his entire being centered on the dark shadow stumbling blindly ahead of him, just

inside the protective cover of the scrub oaks. Whoever—
whatever—it was, it was hurting. That much was evident.
And one thing hurt animals and hurt people were was dangerous. Cole swore under his breath . . . and pulled his gun
from its holster. Holding the barrel up, keeping it pointed
to the night sky, he entered the cover of the trees, keeping
his back hugged up against the rough bark of one after
another of the tall oaks as he cautiously threaded his way
farther and farther in.

Then, before he could think, or even react, Cole was
blindsided. He had no time to do anything except grunt with
the force of the impact and clutch clumsily at whoever had
just hit him. Then . . . he knew. It was Kate who had collided with him and fallen into his arms. He knew because
slivers of moonlight that penetrated the trees' branches lit
up her pale and stricken face. Quickly he holstered his gun
and steadied her with both hands on her arms. "Kate, it's
me—Cole. What's wrong? Are you hurt?"

"Oh, God." A wrenching sob tore out of her as she
clutched at his sleeves and leaned heavily into him, her
cheek against his chest. "Why did you follow me? Why?
What do you want from me? I don't have anything left to
give. Nothing."

"What are you talking about?" He tried to hold her out
from him so he could see her face, but she resisted him.
Concerned to the point of fear—for her and for himself—
Cole relented and settled for stroking her hair as he held
her to him. "Are you hurt somewhere, Kate? Are you bleeding?" She nodded. Cole's heart almost stopped. "Let me
get you back to the—"

"No." She tightened her grip on him, as if her strength
could keep him in place. "Not like that. I don't mean like
before. Inside my heart, Cole. I hurt there. And it hurts so
bad."

Cole swallowed around the sudden lump in his throat.
And thought he knew just how she felt. He knew some of
the same pain. So, holding her close, caressing her silken

hair, Cole encouraged her. "Tell me about it, Kate. Tell me why you hurt."

"No." There was no longer a sobbing catch to her voice. She seemed to be calming down some. "Tell me why you followed me."

Cole looked off into the darkness above her head, which rested just below his chin. "Why? Because I—" He cut off his own words. He'd almost said because he cared.

So Kate finished for him. "Because you . . . care, maybe? Is that it?"

Cole stilled, felt suddenly heavy in his own clothes. The moment was here, the one he'd wanted only minutes ago when he'd set out after her. "Yes," he said, imbuing the one simple word with all the things he couldn't say, with all the things he'd never said before in his life to any woman. "Yes, Kate, I care. Is that so awful?"

She nodded against his chest. "It is, Cole. It's the worst thing in the world. And you don't even know why."

Cole stiffened. His arms around her felt cold, inside him insult mixed with injury. "I think I do, Kate. I think I know."

"No, you don't."

"It's okay. Really." He reminded himself of what he knew of this world and his place in it. A self-deprecating shake of his head told him he had no right to be either insulted or injured. Because no one but him had chosen his life's path for him. Not even his father who'd ridden off that day so many years ago, never to return.

Cole pulled Kate away from him. She turned her moon-silvered face, wet with her tears, up to him. Cole's heart melted . . . a woman like her wasn't meant for a man like him. He didn't waste time feeling sorry for himself. He had no patience with that. No, he was just saddened that it would be so. Because he felt certain that, given half a chance, he could make her happy. But the hell with it. It was too hard. "It's okay, Kate. I know who I am. You don't have to say anything."

She again shook her head. "No, Cole. Listen to me. The

problem is not with you. It's who I am. And it's everything that I've done. Not you."

Troubled in the extreme, Cole frowned at her. "What are you talking about?"

Kate shrugged out of his loosening grasp. She turned her back to him and raised her head, as if to stave off tears . . . or the truth. "I'm not who you think I am, Cole."

The cool, level tone of her voice shot through Cole like an arrow to the back. Something was wrong here. Very wrong. Suddenly, he wasn't so sure he wanted to know exactly what, either. Because he had a sense that the weight of what she had yet to say would crush him. But what surprised him the most about his own reaction was that he felt as if he already knew the truth of her unspoken words. As if on some level he'd always known or suspected she wasn't who she said she was. She'd been too complicated, too closemouthed. It occurred to Cole now that he didn't know the first thing about her. Only her lies. And that being so, could he take what she seemed on the verge of telling him now as the truth? Should he trust her now? But he knew he would. And it would most likely kill him. Thinking and fearing all this, Cole licked at his suddenly dry lips and ventured onward. What choice did he have? he asked himself. "Then who are you, Kate? That is your name, isn't it?"

She turned around to face him. Her chin rose a notch. She met his gaze. Her own was unwavering, her earlier tears dried. To Cole, she looked hard, as if formed of ice. Or maybe steel; there was a steeliness in her that perhaps he'd missed before now. "Yes. Kate's my name," she finally said. "But it's not my only name."

The wind sloughed through the branches. An owl hooted. And Cole gestured his frustration. "What does that mean, not your only name? Just spit it out, Kate."

"All right," she said, squaring her shoulders. "I'm the woman you're hunting. I'm the woman you know as Anne Candless."

Chapter Thirteen

"Goddamn you."

Kate flinched at Cole's curse. But felt certain he was right . . . God had indeed damned her. She also believed that the man standing before her would, at any moment, send her to meet her Maker.

But Cole apparently wasn't finished with her just yet. He stabbed the air between them with his pointing finger. "You're lying. You read that name in the telegraph. You don't know anything about—"

"Why would I lie, Cole?" Kate's hands fisted at her sides. "Why would I say I'm Anne Candless if I wasn't? Why?"

Cole looked everywhere but at her as he cast about for answers, as if the night wind or the stolid oaks surrounding them would give him the reason—one good enough to keep him from pulling his Colt and shooting her dead. His gaze locked with hers. "Because you saw it and got scared that I—your husband now—would be the kind of man who could shoot a woman. You wanted to confront me and challenge me."

She nodded. "You're right about one thing. I've spent a lot of time wondering just what type of man Mr. Talmidge would send. I wondered how low-down a critter the hired gun would be. And then, it did scare me that it was you, Cole."

He stared at her, his jaw worked, his frown deepened. "You're not Anne Candless. Your name is Kate Chandler."

Kate started to speak, but a sudden calm, like the eye of a storm, befell her. A new awareness settled over her. She frowned, seeing Cole as if this were the first time she'd ever seen him. No man could be stronger, more solid, more sure of himself. Yet somehow he appeared young and scared, possibly like the little boy he'd been many years ago. To Kate, he looked as if a stiff breeze could knock him over, or as if his whole world was falling apart.

Suddenly she knew, without really knowing, that the truth of who she was would save not only her . . . but him, as well. She had to convince him of her identity. It was her only hope . . . and his. Yet she didn't even know what she meant by that. She just knew it was true and, therefore, good. Still, when she spoke, it was with a quiet authority in her voice that surprised her, a quality she'd never heard before. "Your not wanting me to be Anne Candless doesn't make it the truth, Cole. And that's one thing that's been missing between us before now. The truth."

Cole pulled himself up stiffly, as if she'd slapped him. "I've always told you the truth, Kate. Always." He quieted. Kate employed his own tactic against him . . . she waited. Then, the words burst out of him. "Except about finding that cousin of mine. I intended to, at first. But then I realized . . . the kids are better off with you, like you said."

Kate struggled not to look down in shame. Those sweet, precious children. How could she face them? How could they be better off with her? Only through a sheer effort of will did she maintain a level gaze as she met his dark eyes, so glittery in the silvered night. "Only I won't be around for them to live with, will I? It's your mission to see to that."

"Dammit, Kate, *stop* this. It's not my mission. Besides, I know you. You're a good woman. You wouldn't even steal the time of day, much less money and jewelry."

A tsking sound escaped her. "Money and jewelry. I read that in the telegraph. And, you know, you're right. I wouldn't steal from him. Or from anyone else. I guess that's the only thing he could think of to get someone like you to take the contract on my life."

"I didn't want to, Kate. I had to. There wasn't anything—"

"Do you hear yourself? You're apologizing to me—*me*—

for taking the contract. Does that mean you believe me when I say I'm Anne Candless?"

His frown deepened. "Don't twist my words, Kate. And I don't believe you're her. All I'm saying is I took the contract against my better judgment. I have my sister's kids to feed and clothe. That takes money. So I had no choice in the matter—"

"I know something about that. I know about how your back gets to a wall before you know it. I might be young and all, but I'm not innocent of the ways of the world. Not anymore. You see, I didn't find my back to a wall. Rather, it was to a mattress. For days on end—weeks, Cole. Oh, it was the finest mattress available. Feather-stuffed. In a beautiful room. Inside a wonderful mansion—"

"What are you saying, Kate?" Cole stilled.

Kate swallowed, suddenly overcome with the memory and the emotion of what she'd lived through. "I'm saying . . ." The words wouldn't come. Taking a deep breath, she closed her eyes against the tears that threatened, against the awful pictures in her head. Then she opened her eyes and saw Cole hadn't moved. "I'm saying I'm Anne Candless. Only the message you got was wrong. My real name is Anna Chandler. Anna Katherine Chandler. Kate, to you."

Kate watched as several emotions played over Cole's face. Disbelief. Shock. Then, and slowly, dawning realization. Followed by denial. "You're lying. And I won't listen to another word." He turned on his heel, turned away from her.

Kate pushed forward, grabbing his sleeve and turning him to face her. "No. For the first time since you've known me, Cole, I'm not lying. I'm who I say I am—Anna Katherine Chandler."

"Youngblood," he said through gritted teeth. "You're a Youngblood now."

For long wordless moments, Kate could only stare at him. Then she exhaled . . . her breath felt hot and moist against her lips. "Yes, I'm a Youngblood now. And I couldn't be more sorry for you because of that."

"Sorry for me? Why?"

"Because now you have to face me with that knowledge. Or Mr. Talmidge. You have to do the right thing, Cole. But only by one of us."

"Son of a bitch," Cole muttered under his breath as he tugged himself out of her grip and again turned his back to her.

Kate died a thousand deaths inside as he struggled with his dilemma. She wanted to reach out, to touch him, to beg him to understand. But she could do none of that. His dilemma was as much of her making as it was Mr. Talmidge's. So all Kate could do was stare at Cole's back, at his broad shoulders, and wonder what he would do. Should she already be running away? Had she been a fool to stand here and spell it all out for him? Not that he appeared to believe her completely yet.

Just then, Cole pivoted around to face her. His features, in the moonlight, reflected a gunfighter's steeliness. "What did he do to you, Kate?"

Breathless, scared, Kate could only get out, "Then you believe me?"

"I don't know what to believe. All I know is I've had my doubts since the day I took this job. It seemed to me that money and jewelry, to someone like the Talmidges, shouldn't amount to a death sentence for some poor maid. I figured there was more to it, but I also figured it wasn't my job to question the why of it. Because the final decision was mine. If I didn't like the work, I didn't have to take the money. But I did take it, and like I said, I had to—for the kids."

Kate nodded. "I understand that . . . about the kids." She could see the reason in everything he said—even the part about doing what he did for his sister's children. After all, hadn't everything she'd done—every lie she'd told, every decision, good or bad, she'd made—been for her baby's sake? Almost unconsciously she put a hand to her belly in a gesture of protection.

Cole pointed at her gesture. "That's what I want to know, Kate. Who's your baby's father?"

Kate's hand fisted around her skirt's fabric, her chest hurt as she tried to take in a deep breath but couldn't. She raised her chin a notch. "The father doesn't matter. The baby's mine . . . and I love her."

"I'm not saying you don't. I'm just asking you if Edgar Talmidge is the father. He is, isn't he? And he's the one who wants your baby."

A yelp of hateful truth escaped Kate. She retreated a few steps, turned her face away from Cole's steady scrutiny. Instantly he stepped up to her, gripping her by her arms. "Look at me, Kate. What did he do to you? Tell me."

"No," she cried out, on the verge of sobbing.

Cole's grip on her tightened. "Dammit, Kate—tell me."

She twisted, fighting his hold on her. "No. I won't. You know what he did. What else could it be?"

Suddenly, Cole stilled. Something was different, something in the air, maybe. Or was it something between them? Whatever it was, Kate could sense it. She abandoned her futile struggling in favor of staring at him through the haze of her hair that had fallen across her face. Never before had she seen an expression like the one now on Cole's face. Murderous. Hating. Vengeful.

As swiftly as he'd grabbed her a moment ago, he now released her and stepped back. Kate thought sure she'd lost, that he would pull out his gun and shoot her. But his next words proved her wrong . . . and scared her even more. "I'll kill him," Cole said quietly. "I promise you that, Kate. With my bare hands, I'll kill him. That bastard son of a bitch won't live long enough to see the sun rise tomorrow."

And then, he turned away and stalked off, the underbrush rustling and snapping under his every step. Kate froze in position, her eyes wide, her knees locked against the heavy weakness invading her bones. She watched his retreating figure and knew she couldn't let him do that. Anything could happen. He could get himself killed instead. And if he succeeded in killing Mr. Talmidge—and she thought he would—he'd have to make his getaway and live the life of an outlaw or he'd be caught and hanged for murder. All on her account. But the worst aspect, to her, of each of those possibilities, was that she'd never see him again.

Which told her another truth about herself, one she was now ready to admit. She had to see him. Every day of her life. And so she chased after him, finally catching up to him and falling in beside him. She all but skipped along in her effort to keep pace with him. She thought about tugging on him, trying to get him to stop. But instantly discarded that idea. Because as purposeful as his every step was—and fueled as each one was by an awful anger—he'd only shrug her off. So Kate employed her only weapons—her thoughts and her words—instead, carefully chosen words that hopefully would influence him. "You can't do this, Cole. Think of the children. What would they do without you?"

"They'll have you." His tone of voice matched the terseness of his words.

"Me? I'm not so sure. I think Mr. Talmidge's family—and especially his wife—would make sure I was dead too. And in trying to get me, they just might get the kids too. That's why I said that Joey, Willy, and Lydia can't be with me." He didn't say a word. Kate exhaled sharply. "Cole, are you listening to me?"

"I am. And I think that's pretty far-fetched, what you're saying."

"No it isn't. It's about as far-fetched as your sitting around the campfire only a bit ago with me and reasoning out loud about the Talmidges and me—and being right about it all."

"That may be, but I've got to do what I think is right."

"Well, what is right, Cole? Tell me that."

But he didn't. In the face of his silence, Kate focused her attention on the tangled fallen branches that littered the ground and threatened to trip her . . . and the approaching silvered edge of the stand of trees that sheltered them now.

She realized they were heading toward the hills where the fancy people slept. Where the elegant gentlemen and ladies—especially one who looked just like her—resided for the night.

"You're asking me what's right, Kate? You have to ask that?"

His explosive words, coupled with his abrupt tone of voice, split the still night air like a knife's slashing arc, and made Kate jump in surprise. But she was ready with her answer. "I do. I have to ask. Because I'm the one who was wronged, Cole. Not you."

Finally, he stopped. Kate did the same, her heart pounding. "That may be. But you're my wife now—"

"No, Cole, you're not going to use that. Not for murder. Sharing the same last name is only part of our business arrangement. And nothing more."

He shook his head. "Maybe it was at first, Kate. But not now."

Kate's throat all but closed. What was he saying? "No. You don't—"

"But I do. And so do you. Are you going to stand there and tell me any different? I see how you look at me, Kate. I watch you."

Kate wasn't even sure the covering darkness could hide the heated blush warming her cheeks. "I watch you because . . . I don't have anybody else to look at."

Cole made a derisive sound, one that put the lie to her words. "Don't play games with me. We're both adults, Kate. I watch you. And you watch me. There's a reason for that. And I think you know what it is."

Kate's chin rose a prideful notch. "That may be true, Cole Youngblood . . . about me watching you. But I figure I've got good reason, you being who you are. But still, there's nothing between us—not what's between a husband and wife who, well, who . . . love each other. We don't have that."

"You mean I haven't touched you yet, like a man does a woman?"

Acute embarrassment—and a dose of lingering fear—had Kate looking everywhere but at him. "No. I mean, yes. You haven't. Not that I want you to, mind you."

Cole chuckled. "It's okay. I'm not going to try. I just didn't know you wanted me to."

Kate gasped, her gaze locked with his. "I never said I did."

He held up a hand, cautioning her, calming her. "It's okay. We're talking about me. Trust me"—his gaze slipped appreciatively over her, warming her—"it hasn't been because I haven't wanted to." Then he looked into her eyes. "But just when in hell have I had a chance, Kate? We've been on the move for days with three kids. And then there's been your sickness and your bleeding. How many reasons do I need? There's no privacy. We've only known each other about a week. All of that. But beyond that, I wasn't even sure you wanted me to touch you. I don't figure that some piece of paper gives me the right. I'm not that kind of man. Because, like I said earlier, I'd never hurt you."

Kate could only stare at this man standing in front of her. He'd probably said close to everything she'd ever want to hear him say. And at the worst possible moment, too. But she'd be darned if she was going to miss this opportunity not to use his words against him—in an effort to keep him alive now, so they could someday explore these feelings between them. "I appreciate everything you just said," she began. "I truly do. Your words mean a lot to me. Especially the ones about how you'd never hurt me. Because I figure that, right now, the only thing you could do to hurt me is to kill Edgar Talmidge."

Cole stiffened, his chin came up, his expression became granite. He looked at her as if she were horse droppings on his boot heel. "Are you telling me—after what that man did to you—you have warm feelings for him?"

Stung to the core, Kate's words burst out of her. "Dear God! *No.* The only thing I feel for him is hatred. And there's nothing I'd like better than to kill him myself."

"Then why—"

"Because it's wrong, Cole. Just like what you do for a living. It's wrong. If you kill him, or if I kill him, it'll just set off a chain of other killings. A man with that much money and all that family? Why, there's no telling where it would all wind up and who would be dead. Too many innocent people, I'm afraid. You have to understand that when I escaped that house in New York, I made an important decision, Cole. And that was to go on living. For my baby. I chose to put it all behind me and to face each new day as it came. Because I couldn't do it for myself. And I still can't."

He put a hand out to her. It was meant no doubt as a sympathetic gesture, but Kate flinched. She felt too fragile right now to be touched. He lowered his hand. "Kate, I'm sorry. I didn't know."

She nodded, sniffed back her gathering emotion. "I know you didn't. But it's okay now. I'm all right. And that's thanks to you, Cole."

"Like hell it is." He turned away, facing the beckoning hills shining just beyond the trees. His forbidding stance—hands to his waist, a knee bent, his shoulders squared—spoke volumes. Kate saw right through his pose, right through to the good man underneath, the one struggling to do the right thing by everyone, including her.

"You have trouble accepting yourself as a good man, don't you?" The words were out before she could stop them, before she even knew she was thinking them.

"No. I don't have any trouble with that, Kate. Because I know I'm not a good man. You just said so yourself not five minutes ago." He threw the words back over his shoulder.

Kate thought back and realized he meant her comment about how he made his living. "I didn't say you weren't a good man, Cole. I said what you do for a living is wrong."

"It's the same thing for a man, Kate. What he does to earn his keep is who he is."

"Maybe so. But you're still a good man, Cole. In fact, you're much better than most. Look at everything you've done for your sister and her kids. And look at what you've done for me—"

He jerked back around to face her. "What I've done for you? How can you stand there and say that? I've put you through hell, Kate, because of who I am. How long have you known that I had the contract on your life?"

Kate's mouth dried. She was about to test these warm feelings he said he had for her. "Only since the night before we came here, when I read the telegraph. But before that, on the day I met you and you told me your name, I've suspected you might be the man he hired. I knew you did some . . . work for Mr. Talmidge. So I suspected you were the one."

"Good God, Kate, why didn't you get away from me then? Why'd you stay?"

She made a gesture of helplessness. "I had no choices left, Cole. Remember? No money, no protection. No food. No place to sleep. Only that stupid little box I was sitting on. And with a baby to think about—and those drunks coming out of the saloon—I *had* to go with you. And then, I—well, I hoped . . . as time went on . . . that you might come to care about me some. And then if you did find out who I was, you might not be able to pull the trigger."

He didn't say anything. But he looked at her sidelong. "Well, I'd say your plan worked."

Kate exhaled cautiously. "You're thinking I used you, aren't you?"

He nodded, his tall Stetson only adding emphasis to his gesture. "Yep. You did. But that's okay. I used you, too. Neither one of us is blameless."

Kate felt a wretchedness seize her, one that wouldn't allow her to meet his gaze. Again she looked down. "I know. Only the children are innocent. Your sister's. And my baby. They didn't do anything wrong."

Cole's expression changed, softened somehow. "Is that how you can love it, Kate . . . because of its innocence?"

Through the shiny haze of sudden tears, Kate stared at him as his sincerely worded question filled her mind.

"Yes," she finally got out. "This child I carry did no wrong. She's mine. Just like your sister's kids are yours now and it doesn't matter how you got them." Then a sudden smile of realization found its way to her face and eased the emotion of the moment for her. "And now, I suppose, since I'm their aunt, they're mine, too."

Cole returned her smile with one of his own. "I expect that's true. And I guess each of those kids, including your baby, need us to be the best people we know how to be."

The man was a continual surprise to her. He was so genuinely good. All Kate could do was stare into his dark eyes—so hard to see in this dim light—and wish he'd hold her. For just a moment. "Yes, they do," she said, a remaining vestige of caution and uncertainty keeping her response short. She couldn't afford to misinterpret his intentions at this point, when so many lives, including his own, literally hung in the balance.

Then Cole exhaled his breath in a huff and scrubbed his hand tiredly over his face. "All right, Kate. You win. For now. I can't promise what tomorrow will bring. Or what I may be called upon to do if it turns out that the woman the boys and I saw is Mrs. Talmidge. I will tell you this—if it is her, and Mr. Talmidge is here, too, and they make a move—I'll put an end to the whole sorry affair. And I'll do it in one heartbeat. With no regrets. I want you to know that."

Kate nodded, wringing her fingers together nervously. "I understand."

"Good." His black eyes bored into hers, telling her he meant every word. "But for tonight, you win." He stepped over to her and took her elbow . . . turning her in the direction of the wagons and the kids. "There's just one more thing, Kate."

They broke out of the creek-hugging stand of oaks just then. Kate looked up at Cole, so strong and tall and handsome in the stark moonlight, as he stood there silhouetted against the backdrop of the plains behind him. The very sight of him made her heart all but skip a beat. "And what's that?"

"Do you think . . ." he began, frowning scarily but still managing to look endearingly unsure of himself. "I'll understand if you don't want to—or even if you can't—but do you think that just for tonight, just once, I might hold my wife in my arms while I sleep?"

Kate had never thought, after Mr. Talmidge's mistreatment of her, that she'd ever again be able to lie down with a man. And yet, she had. For here she was . . . in Cole Youngblood's arms.

And here the day was. One dawning full of pinks and yellows and promises. A wondrously bright and warm morning, the day before the land run. Curled up on her side, atop Cole's bedroll on the ground, with a warm quilt that covered them both, Kate lay there with her eyes open, still blinking sleepily, thinking this a miracle. Because Cole Youngblood snored softly at her back. His arm was draped over her from behind and held her to him, against the warm, muscled wall of his chest. She could feel his body's heat, even through his shirt. Yes, he'd remained fully dressed, down to his boots. All he'd removed was his gun and his Stetson, both of which rested at his head.

And true to his word, he'd only held her all through the night. He'd not touched her in any untoward or even husbandly way. Kate recalled now how tender and understanding he'd been of her, despite the desire that flared in his eyes, as she'd shyly removed her shoes and had crawled, fully dressed herself, onto his bedroll with him. After some initial awkwardness—mostly on her part—they'd settled into this position while the moon still rode the night's sky. And apparently they'd been so tired that neither one of them had moved.

If only every day would dawn so full of contentment and excitement. For the first time in many years, perhaps since her mother and father had been killed, leaving her a frightened orphan who'd eventually found herself scratching at the Talmidge mansion's back door begging for work, Kate felt safe and happy. She felt she could truly relax, could even look forward to the future.

Because all things now seemed possible . . . with Cole at her back, with his support. She was beginning to see that life she'd always wanted. Only now instead of just her and her baby, she pictured it with Joey, Willy, and Lydia. And yes, Kitty, too. And Cole. A family.

Kate frowned, hoping she wasn't jumping the gun. Because Cole had as much as said, last night, that. . . . *That he what?* Kate's frown deepened. What had he said? Only that he cared about her. He'd never said he'd give up his way of life and settle down with her and the kids. In fact, he'd said they were better off with her. Not with his cousin. Or with him. Kate's rosy picture of the future slipped away like a scudding cloud. In its place loomed a grim and gray reality. What would a man like Cole do without his gun and his wandering ways? Could he be happy in one place with a wife and kids? How would he make his living? He certainly wasn't a farmer.

Well, no matter what it might be, could she ask him to try? Did she have that right? Breathing in the strong, clean scent of the morning air, Kate's attention shifted. All around her, she heard the stirrings of awakening campers. All too soon she and her "family" would be up and doing the same things. But for now, Kate relished the quiet and took herself to task for the wayward nature of her thoughts. Was she thinking of asking Cole Youngblood to settle down? Why, she didn't even want him to, did she? She slumped back into his arms, felt his solidness at her back. Yes, she wanted him to. She wanted him to stay with her. Forever.

This past night had only proven it to her. She'd slept quietly and soundly in a man's arms. But did that mean she was ready to have a loving relationship with a man? In the marriage bed? Kate gave those questions due consideration. She imagined Cole's hands on her . . . his mouth, his tenderness, the words he might say. And instead of fear and revulsion, she found herself warming up, her breathing quickening. That was all she needed to know. If she was even thinking such a thing, it must mean she was healing—in her heart and in her mind, where it counted. And she knew something else . . . she had one man to thank for that. Cole Youngblood.

It was a miracle, one she wanted to share with him . . . when the time was right. Maybe after the land run. Maybe while he was building their cabin. And they were all helping. And Kitty was running around and getting in the way. Kate grinned, even chuckled . . . There she went again, picturing that happy little family—

"What's so funny?"

Kate froze. The husky voice at her back, the warm breath in her ear, the arm tightening around her middle . . . that was Cole Youngblood, her husband. He was awakening . . . and kissing at her ear as his hand splayed over her belly and rubbed slowly in circles. Kate's insides tingled. But despite her only moments-old vision of a loving physical relationship with this man, she panicked, jerking away and struggling to sit up. "Um, nothing," she said too brightly, as she peered at him over her shoulder. "I guess I was just . . . dreaming, is all. Did I wake you?"

Cole withdrew his hands from her and shifted on the bedroll, bending an elbow and supporting his head with his hand. From there, he looked her up and down . . . and smiled and said nothing.

Practically beside herself, Kate put her hands to her hair, then to her bodice, her skirt, and back to her hair. "I must look a fright, with my hair all mussed and my clothes—"

Cole captured her wrist and her gaze. "You're beautiful, Kate. Just beautiful. And I've never said that to another woman."

That did nothing to calm her down. Her eyes widened, she blinked, swallowed. As soon as Cole released her, Kate threw back the quilt and jumped up, all nervous energy and stuttering insecurity. For his part, Cole stayed where he was and watched her—in Kate's estimation, much like a cat watching a mouse it intends to pounce upon. "Um, before the kids awaken and want their breakfast," she finally came up with, "I'll go to the creek and wash up. I believe we need more water for coffee and oatmeal—"

"There's plenty of water. I got it last night." Then he became all business. "Besides, I'm not so sure you should go traipsing off by yourself, since we don't know who might be around." His pointed expression told her he meant the Talmidges.

"I see," Kate said, forcing herself to quit wadding her skirt in her hands. She just wanted to be away from him for a few moments, just long enough to collect herself. "Well then, I, um, at least have to go . . ." Her face heated up alarmingly, telling her it was probably beet-red at this moment. "Um, I have to tend to my personal business. In the women's area. I don't suppose you feel a need to accompany me for that . . . do you?"

Cole chuckled and blessedly shook his head. "No. Go on. I'll stay here with the kids, in case they wake up. I'm sure you'll be in good company at the creek bottom." Then he sobered and added, "You understand why I don't want you going off alone otherwise?"

Kate nodded. "I do. And I thank you for that. For caring."

His expression warmed. "I do care. Probably a whole hell of a lot more than I should. Certainly more than is good for either of us, Kate."

Kate didn't know what to say to that . . . despite her heart's soaring response. Staring at him, and fearing she had a silly grin on her face, Kate put a hand to her bosom, as if to settle her heart down. But to no avail. It insisted on thumping wildly . . . and was sure to betray her, given half a chance. "Then I'll"—she forgot what she'd been about to say, finally remembered it—"I'll just be a minute." With that, she turned, intending to make a hasty departure.

"Hold on."

Kate did, turning back to see Cole rolling easily to his feet. Her breath caught as he raised his hands to run them through his black hair. "Maybe you ought to take Kitty with you."

Kate frowned. "You really think that they're here, don't you?"

Cole shrugged. "I don't know. They could be. There's just no sense in our taking a chance we don't have to. If they are, they'll be looking for you as carefully as you are for them. And if they're not, then it doesn't hurt to be careful, anyway."

Fear shivered over Kate's body, raising the hair on her arms. She rubbed at it as she said, "I suppose you're right." Then she decided to tell him what else was worrying her. "You know, Cole, this—and I mean the Talmidges, my baby, and how they want it—won't be over today or tomorrow. Or even next year. They told me if I ran, then they'd kill me . . . and my baby. They won't stop until they do."

Cole stiffened, his expression hardened. "You think they'd kill you now, Kate? Or do they just intend to get you back to New York and keep you hidden away until the baby's born?"

She shrugged. "I don't know. They did set you after me. And you know what your orders are."

He had the decency to look down a moment, as if a twinge of guilt assailed him. "Yeah, I know. But I've been trying to figure out why they'd show up now themselves, if they think I'm on the job. I've never—well, not been successful. They'd have no reason to think I wouldn't be this time, either."

Kate realized he was right, and tried to forget they were so casually talking about her life being ended—and that Cole was the man to do that. "Then I don't know. Maybe they changed their minds about wanting me dead. Maybe, like you said, they want me alive until after the baby's born. After all, Mrs. Talmidge told everybody *she* was expecting, once they knew I was."

Cole's eyes narrowed in disgust. "Son of a bitch. That's sick. We're dealing with some dangerous people here, Kate.

But that could work to our advantage, her having told everyone she's with child. To me, that means they need you alive. But still, I'd think they'd be looking for me, as well as you, to head me off before I carry out my orders."

"Well, we don't know they aren't looking for you, do we?"

Cole considered her a moment, as if he were weighing her words. "No, I don't guess we do. But still, I'd think I would have heard if they were looking for me. Actually, though, you'd be easier to spot since they know what you look like."

His words stung her. Kate looked down. "Yes . . . they do. They know all too well what I look like."

"Oh, hell. Why did I say that? Kate, I'm sorry." It took Cole only three steps to reach her and enfold her in his arms. He kissed the top of her head, then bent down to kiss her forehead and her eyelids. "I'm so sorry, baby. I didn't mean it like that."

Kate felt silly for the tears that threatened to spill over. She turned her face up to his, intending to tell him that, but he surprised her by gently cupping her jaw with a hand and lowering his mouth to hers, smothering her words. His kiss thrilled her. It danced along her nerve endings and had her clinging to him, wanting more. A whimper escaped her, found its way into his mouth . . . He pulled back, stared into her eyes, apparently saw what he needed to see and again lowered his lips to hers. But just before he took her mouth, he whispered, "I love you, Kate Youngblood."

Kate gasped, stiffened, and then weakened, leaning into his chest as his arms stole around her back. Pressed against him as she was, all Kate could do was cling to his shirt sleeves and offer herself up, let him know she wanted him, too, that she returned his feelings for her. She stiffened. She returned his affection? She loved him?

The moment Kate stiffened, Cole's embrace softened, his kiss ended. He pulled back, his arms still around her, his mouth still wet with her kiss. His black eyes bored down into hers, looking right through her, to her soul. "Did I do something wrong, Kate?"

She shook her head, felt distracted, too hot, unnerved. "No. No, you didn't." She stepped out of the circle of his arms and brushed at the hair by her temple . . . and looked everywhere but at him. "I liked it. I did. I wanted you to kiss me. It's just that . . ."

"I understand, Kate. It's okay. I shouldn't have rushed you like that." Then, as if her silence unsettled him, he shifted his weight from one foot to the other, ran a hand through his hair, looking everywhere but directly at her.

"Cole?" she suddenly said, feeling she owed him an explanation. When he finally settled his gaze on her, Kate said, "I feel I ought to tell you that . . . I liked your kiss"— her face heated up, but she rushed on—"and I have feelings for you, too. I do."

His chin came up a prideful notch. "But . . . ?"

Kate frowned her bewilderment. "There's no 'but.' I just wanted to say that I don't worry so much . . . with you on my side."

His eyebrows rose a notch but his expression smoothed out and a calm seemed to come over him. "I'm glad to hear you say that. And just remember—the Talmidges don't know that I'm on your side now. Even better, they don't know what I look like, either."

"That's right. I didn't think of that last night. You've never met them. And yet you were getting ready to charge up that hill after them. How would you have found them?"

Cole shrugged. "A few well-placed inquiries would've located them."

"I suppose." And then she just stood there, feeling her hope for this new place, this new beginning, fade some. The Talmidges . . . here. It just wasn't fair. This was her corner of the world. Not theirs. How dare they violate it?

"Kate?"

She snapped to, realized she'd been lost in thought. "Yes?"

Cole's expression, along with his smile, warmed. "It will

be okay. I promise you. Just let me get Kitty out of the wagon and you can be on your way, all right?"

Kate nodded, too overcome with emotion in the face of Cole's tender handling of her to say anything. In only a moment, Kate had torn a strip of calico from an old dress of Lydia's, one that had no more wear in it, and tied her long and heavy hair up off her neck, the better to bend over the water and wash herself without ending up with wet hair all day. In the next moment, Cole had fished the dog out of the covered wagon and the hound had stretched and yawned and gathered himself enough to pad over to Kate's side when she called him. Together they traipsed off toward the women's area.

Chapter Fourteen

Despite all the other women ranged up and down the creek's pebbly shore and gathered in this one place to attend to themselves away from male eyes, Kate still felt alone. It was strange, really. All around her the women chattered, talking of tomorrow's land run, of their babies, their husbands, and their hopes for the future. Kate had even walked down here with two young women, strangers to her, one of whom had a baby girl perched on her hip. They'd talked of themselves, and Kate had shared a few friendly but neutral comments of her own. She couldn't afford to get too friendly. Because there was really nothing much she could say without divulging the awful details of her life to them . . . unless she wanted to lie to them. Which she didn't.

But it was true that, like them, she had a husband . . . one who'd just told her he loved her. Kate's tummy jumped with the giddiness as she thought of that revelation, but still she shied away from reflecting on what exactly his words and feelings might mean for her future. He could love her all he wanted, but would he stay around forever? She didn't think so and became aware that she was shaking her head, as if to push aside such thoughts. But she'd have to think later about Cole's loving her. Right now Kate preferred to concentrate on her similarities with these other women. Like them, she had children dependent on her. And a baby on the way. And high hopes for the run and the future.

But not quite like these other women. Well, most likely not. She figured if she talked long enough with any of them, she'd hear some pretty bad things about their lives, too. Still, while she might share some of the same dreams they had, she didn't really have anything in common with them.

And so, she made an excuse and moved down to a less crowded edge of the creek, toward the very same oaks where last night she'd run from Cole. Having already attended to her most pressing personal business, Kate now wiped at her face and neck with a clean piece of rag she'd found in that big chest in the schooner and had dampened with the stream's cold waters. She kept waiting for the morning sickness to hit her. But so far, it hadn't. She thought maybe that was good. Hoped it was, at least.

At first, she'd hated even knowing it was coming. But then, after she'd nearly lost her baby, it had comforted her. Kate chuckled. Right now she was just relieved that she wasn't sick. Then it struck her that she should have awakened Lydia and brought the child with her. Because now, once the little girl woke up, Kate would have to make the trip right back down here again. And there was still so much to do today in preparation for the run—

Kitty startled Kate by coming to his feet and growling low in his throat, his head lowered, his ears flattened, as he backed into her legs. A jet of fear coursed through Kate. What—or whom—had he seen? Kate immediately thought of the fancy lady the boys had described yesterday. Kate anxiously searched the direction the hound dog faced . . . to her right, toward the oaks.

Only sun-dappled darkness met her gaze, as the sunlight spilled between the high, thick branches to pour itself onto the forested ground. But she detected no distinct movement there to alert her. Raising a hand to shade her eyes from the bright sunlight beating down, she looked to her left, feeling her tied-back hair swinging over her shoulder with her movement. In this direction, she saw only the other women attending to themselves or visiting as they washed protesting small children. Still, Kate's heartbeat picked up and her pulse jumped as she turned back to the yellow-furred dog.

"What is it, Kitty?" She squatted down next to the hound, petting his big, square head as she again searched the edge of the oaks, just as he was doing. "What do you see? What's bothering you?" Then she had a thought that instantly relieved her of misgivings. She tugged the dog's head toward her and looked into his soulful black eyes. "Is it breakfast? A rabbit, maybe? Is that what you see?"

Kitty startled her again by twisting and jerking free of her—with enough force to knock Kate back onto her bottom. Instantly, without even looking back at her, the dog shot away, baying for all he was worth—right toward the darkened glade of the gnarled trees. Almost the moment the dog disappeared into the trees, Kate heard him snarling and growling. She heard tree limbs snapping, leaves rustling. Was someone running away? Or heading for Kitty?

Whatever it was, the dog was about to fight, that much was plain. And judging by the sounds coming from the thicket of trees, it wasn't a rabbit. No, it was something much bigger—and something Kitty didn't like at all. Kate realized that behind her, the women closest to her had quieted. No doubt the dog's baying and snarling had also caught their attention. She pivoted in their direction, whipping her face with the heavy ponytail of her black hair. From the distance, a thin blond woman called out, asking Kate if she was okay.

Kate quickly scrambled to her feet and called back, "No! It's not okay!" She pointed to the trees. "My dog! Go up the hill there to the two wagons parked in a vee and get my husband, Cole Youngblood"—she saw several of the women exchange glances—"and tell him to hurry. I've got to go see what's got after my dog."

Immediately two of the women—Kate saw it was the same two young mothers she'd walked down here with—separated themselves from the group and ran back up the hilly slope away from the creek. Relief coursed through Kate. They knew exactly where her and Cole's wagons were. She then turned toward the woods—

"Wait a minute! Kate, is that you? Kate Chandler?"

Kate whipped back around, again punishing herself with her heavy hair. She didn't know anybody out here, did she? She shaded her eyes and really stared at the woman who'd

called out to her a moment ago and who now was waving
frantically at her. She was so far away, it was hard to see—
then Kate gasped in recognition. "Is that you, Mrs. Jacobs?"
The nice lady from the train ride out here, the one who'd
wanted her to stay with her family. The lady with four
children, two of which were holding on to her skirt. "Yes!
It's me—Kate!"

"Well, hold on, honey." She pulled the little girls away
from her, shook a finger at them—no doubt telling them to
stay put—spoke to another woman close to her, and started
toward Kate. Her loud voice carried through the air as she
called out, "Don't you go in there after that dog. It could
be a bear is what's after him. You wait for me." She
reached into a pocket of her skirt. "I got me a gun right
here, and I'll help you."

"Oh, thank you—and hurry, please." Kate had no more
than gotten the words out and pivoted back around to stare
at the thicket of trees before she heard Kitty yelp horribly.
A deep, soul-wrenching sound that left her gasping.

And then . . . all was quiet.

Kate froze, her eyes widened. "Kitty," she breathed.
"Oh, no." No longer thinking of herself, of getting Cole,
or of waiting for Mrs. Jacobs, Kate hiked her skirt up out
of her way and, saying a prayer for her unborn child, gave
chase.

I should have known better, was all Cole could think as he
hurriedly strapped on his Colt and settled his Stetson on
his head. Facing him and jabbering away were two young
women, one with a baby riding her hip, and full of a tale
of Kate and Kitty and a fight in the trees down by the creek.
The women hadn't seen anything, had only heard the dog
yelp and had seen Kate running toward the sound. Hadn't
he heard it? they wanted to know. The fuss had been so
loud. But they thought Kate was okay. She hadn't been in
the fight. Just the dog.

Every time they said something about the dog being in
a fight Lydia screamed that much louder. So did Joey and

Willy. His teeth gritted, his jaw set, Cole struggled for control. First he turned to the kids, huddled behind him. "Now, you kids hush up. I'll go see about Kitty. You just stay here. I'll be right back."

"Is her dead, Uncle Cole?" Lydia wanted to know between sniffles.

"Kitty's a boy dog, Lydia," Willy sobbed as he put an arm around his baby sister.

"You heard Uncle Cole," Joey bleated, trying hard to sound grown-up. "Kitty's just fine. And so's Miss Kate." The boy turned his tear-stained face up to Cole and the two young women flanking him. "Ain't they, Uncle Cole?"

Cole exhaled sharply. "Yes, Joey, I'm sure they are." But he wasn't sure at all. Needing to be on his way, he turned to the women and focused on the plump and pretty brunette one. "I need you to watch these kids until I get back," he told her.

Her eyes widened. Cole hadn't meant to sound so abrupt, but he didn't have time for niceties right now. "Of course, Mr. Youngblood. I'll get their breakfast for them. You go on. My wagon is over yonder"—she pointed to the next encampment over—"and that's where we'll be."

Cole nodded. "Thank you, ma'am. I'm beholden to you."

She all but curtsied. No doubt, Cole reflected, she knew his reputation. Then he turned to the kids. "You mind this lady, you hear?"

Three dark little heads nodded that they would. Then Lydia tore herself away from her brothers and ran to Cole, wrapping her pudgy baby arms around his legs. The tiny little girl broke his heart every time she cried. It was a wonder she hadn't wrapped him around her finger by now. Cole leaned over and picked her up, giving her a fierce hug. "You stay here and be my brave little girl, okay?"

With her tear-dampened face nestled against his neck, Lydia nodded and mumbled out, "I don't want them to die, Uncle Cole. I love them."

Cole swallowed, patting the little girl's back. "So do I,

baby. So do I." Only belatedly did he hear his own words.

Stung by his own admission, he quickly handed Lydia off to their brunette neighbor, who held the little girl in her arms and, along with her red-haired friend, the one with the baby riding her hip, gathered the boys and told them she was Miss Nell and they were to come with her. She said she would introduce them to her own children and they'd all have a high old time.

With the children seen to, Cole was finally able to clear the wagon encampment and sprint for the wooded area down the hill, just as he'd done last night. Following the same path now, one much simpler to navigate by daylight, his heart in his throat, he rued every second that had ticked by. God alone knew what had already happened. But no matter what it was, Cole only hoped he wasn't too late.

Because if he was, if something had happened to Kate, then he couldn't live. It was that simple, and he was ready to admit it, ready to fight all her battles, face all her demons, slay all her dragons. Because, as he'd told her this morning—although the words had merely slipped out—he loved her. And he was glad as hell that he had told her. For no matter what had just happened to her and Kitty . . . Kate knew how he felt. Only now did Cole realize how much that meant to him. And how much she meant to him.

With that thought accompanying him, Cole arrived at the edge of the thick stand of oaks that shaded the gently gurgling creek. Plunging into the tangled undergrowth, dodging low-hanging branches, and calling for Kate—but getting no response—Cole plowed his way through the thick underbrush. In only seconds, he came upon a knot of men and women gathered around something—his heart lurched painfully—fallen on the ground. Whatever it was, he didn't want to see it.

A muttered "son of a bitch" slipped past his lips. Slowing his pace to a ground-covering stride, he waded into the crowd, all of whom stepped out of his way, pulling children aside as they went. Cole checked every face. Kate's wasn't among them.

His hope slipped another notch as he caught the bystanders' glances, and noted their subtly averted gazes. Again, Cole told himself he didn't want to see any more, even as the somber folks stepped aside. Then Cole saw what they'd seen. On the ground, appearing lifeless amid a torn-up patch of ground that attested to a vicious fight, was Kitty. Lying on his side, his head thrown back, his mouth slacked open, the dog—though not bloody anywhere—wasn't moving.

As he knelt on one knee beside the animal, a kaleidoscope of images of the dog from the day he'd taken up with them, flashed through Cole's mind. All his funny antics, his loving protectiveness. It didn't seem fair to Cole that the loyal dog should die like this. Again muttering "son of a bitch," Cole put his hand on the hound's shoulder. The yellow coat of fur and the skin underneath it still felt warm, as if he would get up at any moment.

"He's just knocked out, is all."

Cole looked up and saw it was a careworn blond woman, thin and plain, with two little girls holding on to her skirts, who had spoken to him.

Immediately she continued. "He's still breathing. I checked him over for broken bones, too. Didn't seem to have none." She nodded encouragingly. "I believe he'll come to directly and be as good as new."

Relief flooded through Cole and had him saying, "Thank you." Then he reached around the animal's rib cage until his hand pressed against Kitty's heart. The lady was right. He was breathing evenly and strongly. Like she'd said, the dog would soon be good as new. That was good. Real good. But uppermost in Cole's mind was Kate and her whereabouts. "There should have been a woman with this dog—"

"I know," the woman said again. "I seen her, too." Several other women nodded in agreement with her and murmured comments to that effect.

Cole's heart thumped hopefully. He looked from one

female face to the next. "Where is she, then? Do you know? Did you see anything?"

The same blond woman spoke for them again. "I purely didn't see a thing. All I know is she called out and said something had a hold of her dog and for someone to go get her husband, Cole Youngblood. I suppose that'd be you?"

Cole nodded, saying, "Yes," and wishing she'd just spit out her story.

"I thought as much. Well, anyways, then I recognized her from the train ride out here and told her to wait for me, seeing as how I've got me a gun in my pocket. No telling what manner of critter could've gotten after your dog. But before I could get someone to see to my girls for me, Kate heard this here hound yelp. And she lit out, running like the very devil was after her. When I got here, all I seen was the dog there. But I'm sorry to say, Kate weren't no-wheres around. Until you showed up, I thought she'd took out herself to get you."

"No. She didn't do that. I'd have seen her."

"I expect that's true."

The woman fell silent, no doubt thinking the same thing he was. Where, then, was Kate? Cole stroked the unconscious dog's shoulder, and considered the options, as the crowd of folks around him discussed what had happened and speculated among themselves. Tuning them out, Cole realized he knew only where Kate wasn't. She wasn't at the wagon. And she wasn't here with Kitty.

Only one other—terrifying—explanation made any sense. She'd run in here to see about the dog and had been grabbed and taken somewhere against her will. Whoever had been lurking in here had been after her, and Kitty had sensed the danger. That had to be it. Extreme agitation gripped Cole and had him running a hand over his mouth and jaw.

His first instinct was to rush away from here and run right into danger himself, to not give a damn about himself and just go find her and kill everyone who stood between

him and her. But what good would that do? He'd be no
help to her if he got himself killed instead, or if his commotion got her killed. No, this called for cool calculation
and a heap of caution. Because Cole thought he knew who
he was dealing with. And if that were true, then the only
comfort he could cling to right now was the certainty that
Kate wasn't dead.

Because it stood to reason that if whoever—whoever,
hell; the Talmidges—had her now wanted her dead, she'd
be lying here with Kitty. And she wasn't. Which meant she
was most likely more valuable to them alive. Thank God.
Small comfort, but still . . . comfort. Because alive she may
be, but she was also in severe danger. They could spirit her
away and seclude her somewhere. Cole knew enough about
the ways of the ruthlessly wealthy to know they effectively
swept their woes under a rug. Wasn't that his job, no matter
how he looked at it? To eliminate problems for them?

Cole's expression hardened. If what he was thinking was
true, then time was of the essence. Because Kate would
never be seen again . . . until she'd had her baby, and then
her body would turn up floating in a river somewhere. Cole
exhaled slowly, looking around at the concerned faces of
the murmuring crowd. Still, even with his need for caution
duly noted, Cole felt he was burning daylight just sitting
here beside the dog. He levered himself up to his feet and
caught the attention of two half-grown boys who'd edged
in for a better look and were even now reaching out their
hands to stroke Kitty's fur.

Seeing Cole staring their way, they jerked back their
hands and stood there, wide-eyed. "We didn't mean no
harm, Mr. Youngblood," one of them, a lanky, freckle-
faced kid said.

Cole wasted no time on pleasantries. "You two think
you can see to this dog for me?" They immediately began
nodding, and Cole kept talking. "Get him some water and
watch over him? Then, when he comes to, carry him up to
my wagon. It's—"

"We know where it is," the other boy, a black-haired,

fair-skinned kid, assured him. As Cole's eyebrows rose, the boy rushed on. "We didn't go looking for you or nothing, Mr. Youngblood. We wouldn't do that. It's just that everybody knows where you're camped." Cole narrowed his eyes. The boy's voice rose a notch. "It ain't like we been sneaking around, sir. We just—"

"That's enough, son," Cole said, his hand raised to forestall the boy. He was used to this sort of thing. Everyone wanted a look at a notorious killer. Cole had never been comfortable with his notoriety, and he liked it even less today. Especially since he had Kate and three little kids with him. Suddenly this reminder of why he should see her and the kids safely settled, and then move on, ate at the center of him. He was bad news, pure and simple. Because there was always some young punk coming around, looking to make his reputation by gunning down the best and the fastest. And that, Cole figured, was him.

Putting that concern aside, Cole focused on the boys as they knelt down beside Kitty, who was starting to twitch and whimper. "Whoa, Mr. Youngblood, I think he's coming to," the freckle-faced boy said excitedly, quickly turning to the black-haired boy next to him. "Run down to the creek, Sam, and get me some water, like Mr. Youngblood said."

Sam jumped up, no questions asked, and took off through the crowd. Cole watched him crashing through the undergrowth and then met the other boy's gaze.

"Sam's afraid of you," the boy said. "He says you're a natural-born killer. But I don't think so. I can tell you ain't mean at all. Why, you're just like every other man out here with his family and hoping for some land."

Cole stared hard at the boy, which made the kid look down, his attention trained on Kitty. Cole wondered which one of these boys was the smartest. The one who was afraid of him? Or the one who wasn't? He also wondered which one of them was right. But figuring that fretting over such notions wouldn't get Kate found, Cole turned from those thoughts to focus on Kitty. Renewed relief coursed through him because of the dog's apparent recovery. He hadn't particularly relished the thought of telling Willy, Joey, and Lydia that Kitty had been killed, any more than he relished the notion of telling them that Kate was missing.

But right now, he'd have to think of something to tell them. At that thought, he exhaled sharply. When he did, the boy raised his head, sending Cole an expectant look. Cole considered the kid a moment and felt he owed the boy something. "What's your name, son?"

"Jimmy Thomas, sir."

Cole nodded, somehow seeing his much younger self in this eager boy. "Do you need to let your folks know where you are, Jimmy?"

"No, sir. My ma's down at the water. Sam will tell her. And we already done our chores."

"Good. That's good." Cole knew he needed to thank the kid outright, but hesitated. Behaving in a civilized manner among law-abiding folks was proving hard business, he lamented. "I'm most appreciative of what you and your friend—"

"Sam's my little brother."

Cole nodded. "All right. I'm most appreciative—"

"No thanks needed, Mr. Youngblood," the boy interrupted him again. "I've got me a tale now to tell my own kids one day. About how I did a favor for the famous gunfighter."

Cole looked away from the hero worship in the boy's eyes, thinking he was no one to idolize. However, suspecting he'd never talk the kid out of it, Cole tipped his Stetson, as if responding to a compliment, but said, "Son, the best thing you can do for your future younguns is to not pick up a gun, except to defend yourself and your own. That's a lesson I wish had been passed on to me when I was your age."

The boy's expression sobered. He swallowed, his Adam's apple bobbing up and down in his throat as his gaze locked with Cole's. Then he ducked his head respectfully and said, quietly, "Yes, sir."

With that, Cole turned on his heel and made his way out of the woods. He'd given the boy good advice. Advice, Cole knew, that was unfortunately too late for him to heed in his own life. But he had one last good thing to do before he took up his old life. And that was to save Kate and her baby. He'd make the land run for her and the kids. Build that cabin for them. Then . . . he'd ride off. It was the best he had to offer them, even if that was the one thing he still hated his own father for doing to him and his sister.

Sitting on the cot where she'd been shoved, her hands tied behind her back, Kate felt her heart would nearly burst with fear and surprise when the spacious tent's flap was pushed aside . . . and Norah Heston Talmidge entered. Surprise because Kate had forgotten just how much she resembled the woman. They could be sisters. And fear because the woman was who she was . . . and because in her gloved hand, she carried a riding crop, which she slapped against her other palm. That threatening gesture awakened something inside Kate, something that said *No more.* Immediately, she struggled against her bindings and the cot's contours until she came to her feet. She'd be damned if she'd look up to this woman—in any sense of the words.

Norah Talmidge, dressed in a richly hued scarlet riding costume, allowed the flap to close behind her. An expression of amused disgust rode her features as she watched Kate's struggle to stand. The woman's smile reminded Kate of a snake's forked-tongue expression. "Well, well," the woman intoned. "If it isn't our thieving little maid."

Kate's eyebrows rose, not so much at the woman's lying words as at her voice. Gone were the dulcet tones Mrs. Talmidge had always used in her home. She now sounded cold and dangerous—more in keeping with her nature, Kate decided. And she knew, better than most, just how dangerous this woman could be. That being so, Kate reminded herself not to provoke her. Especially since the woman was flanked by the same two rough armed men who'd knocked Kitty out—Kate fervently hoped that was all they'd done—

and then had captured her and brought her here. She'd had a gun stuck hard against her ribs, but the men had managed to keep it from being noticed by the wealthy passersby up here on the hill.

Approaching Kate now, stopping in front of her as she looked her up and down—with much the same look she'd use to inspect a piece of furniture for cleanliness—Norah Talmidge finally met Kate's gaze and smiled. No warmth flowed from her expression.

"So, Kate . . . how fares my baby? I trust you've done nothing to harm him?" she said.

An impotent rage seized Kate . . . How could this woman even *dare* to mention the baby? Fear for herself evaporated, taking with it her trepidation regarding the other woman. "The child I carry is *my* baby," she said through gritted teeth. "It's a girl. And of course, she's fine. Because, unlike you, I would *never* harm her."

Norah Talmidge's gasp was followed by a hardening of her expression. A feral anger, diluted with a touch of insanity, flared in her green eyes—eyes so like and yet so different from Kate's. "Why, you little *bitch*," she snarled as she raised her riding crop and smote Kate across the cheek with it, wringing a cry of stinging, burning pain from the younger woman. "How *dare* you talk to me in such an insolent manner, you insignificant little . . . *hireling!*"

The riding crop had caught Kate from cheekbone to jaw, snapping her head to one side with the force of the blow. Her entire body rippled with a pain that raised the hair on her arms . . . and a horrific welt on her cheek. She forced herself to breathe, to get air into her lungs, lest she faint. Tears of pain filled her eyes . . . tears she refused to shed.

Stiffening her jaw, Kate straightened up and met Norah Talmidge's gaze. Triumphant green eyes locked with defiant green eyes. Kate didn't know where the words came from, much less the conviction behind them, but she heard herself saying, "One day soon, Mrs. Talmidge, I'll kill you for that."

Norah Talmidge's eyes widened in fear. Gasping again,

she pulled back, retreating from Kate, holding on to her skirt as she went. Looking over her shoulder—as if she feared to look away from Kate, as if she feared Kate would actually try to end her life right then—the hateful woman cried out, "Did you hear that? Did you hear her threaten me?"

Kate looked past Norah Talmidge to the two men she addressed. Big, burly, rough sorts. The kind of men loyal to the person who had paid them the most. What Mrs. Talmidge couldn't see, but Kate could—and it gave her a spark of hope—was their evident boredom with this little tableau between the two women. They exchanged glances that said as much and then faced their employer's back. "Yes, ma'am," the one in a black vest replied. "We heard her all right. You want us to do something about it?"

Norah Talmidge stopped where she was. A sly smile claimed her lips as she cocked her head to the side in a considering manner and again looked Kate up and down. Kate pulled herself up to her full height and pridefully raised her chin—which hurt, given the welt that ridged her skin. She realized she'd made a grave error in saying such a rash thing to Mrs. Talmidge. She should have remained quiet, should have concentrated on her concern for her child. Instead of stabbing at revenge with words.

While still meeting Kate's gaze, the wealthy woman addressed the two men. "Do I want *you* to do something about it?" She shook her elaborately coiffed head. "No. I think you've done enough by bringing her here. You've been paid. Now leave. I can handle her."

The men shrugged their shoulders and started to leave. Somehow Kate understood that these men were her only hope right now. Her conviction made her blurt out, "You won't get far, if you do leave."

Norah Talmidge stiffened, looking quite affronted that Kate had dared speak without being told she could. For their part, the heavily armed men stopped, allowed the tent flap to fall back into place . . . and turned to face Kate. The one in the black vest, his dark eyes narrowing, spoke for them both. "Is that so? How do you figure that?"

Kate swallowed, blinked . . . and plunged on. "Because I know how Mrs. Talmidge here thinks. And also because of who I am."

Norah Talmidge jerked around, swirling her skirt as she moved, and now faced the men who'd been behind her. "Don't listen to her. Go on. Get out. Right now."

But the men didn't. The second man, an unshaven sort wearing a dirty brown stiff-brimmed hat, wagged his finger at Mrs. Talmidge. "Now, just hold on there a minute, ma'am."

Kate was rewarded by Mrs. Talmidge's shocked reaction. Probably in all her life she'd never heard such audacity, Kate mused.

But the man the other woman had hired wasn't through with her yet. "I believe we'd like to hear what the girl has to say."

Norah Talmidge's hands fisted at her sides. Even from where Kate stood, behind the other woman and across the tent from her, she could tell her former employer burned with strong emotion. A helpless rage, maybe? Kate could only hope so. She wanted to say "How does it feel?" but wisely chose continued silence. Because she also realized that Mrs. Talmidge *was* powerless to stop these men, and therefore she was powerless to stop Kate. She'd been right to speak out to them, she assured herself.

A desperate hope coursed through her, telling her that she—unlike the pampered and coddled Norah Heston Talmidge—understood these everyday men. They were different, much more independent, more ruthless, much less pliable than the ruffians back East who lived daily within the dangerous reach of the Talmidge power. These men, by contrast, already had their one-time money and owed no one their allegiance. Too, they'd already been dismissed. They were now free to act on their own. Which they proceeded to do.

As one, with the wealthy woman effectively held in place unless she wished to directly challenge them, they turned to Kate. The black-vested man encouraged her to speak. "Go on, missy. Say your piece."

Kate didn't waste time hesitating. "It's true. You won't get far if you leave. Because she'll send someone after you to kill you. Just like she sent you after me."

The unshaven man shifted his rifle in his hands and chuckled. "But you ain't dead, missy. I don't expect we will be, neither."

"That's right. I'm not," Kate plunged on desperately. "But you will be. Because in taking her money and spiriting me away like you did, you just signed your own death warrants. And for more than one reason."

The men's expressions showed their sudden unease. "Go on," the black-vested one said.

"She's lying. She's trying to confuse you." Norah Talmidge took a step or two toward the men, drawing their attention her way—and blocking Kate from their view. "You're too smart for that, I'm sure. Such fine men like you—"

"Shut up, lady," the same man said. "You ain't been nothing but sass and disrespect since we hired on with you." Despite the richly dressed woman's shaking hand she lifted to her velvet-covered bosom, the man looked around her to again focus on Kate. "I said for you to go on. Give me those reasons why we're as good as dead."

Triumph flitted through Kate. "For one, you now know about me. Which means she can't allow you to live. She and her husband have too much at stake, through me, to take a chance on you talking."

"Talking about what?" The man nervously resettled his brown hat atop his head.

Kate licked at her lips. She was getting to them. She had no idea where her courage and the clear-headed thinking were coming from, but she prayed for it to sustain her just a few more minutes. Because, for all she knew, Cole was already on his way. It wouldn't be hard for him to put two and two together and to come charging up here. So all she had to do was stall until he came in, his guns blazing.

"She doesn't want you talking about my baby," Kate answered the man. "And she can't take the chance that you might."

"Lady, why in the blue blazes would we? What's so special about your baby?"

Good. The men were curious. Now she had them. "Because she and Mr. Talmidge intend to say it's theirs. And thereby they can claim his inheritance, instead of it going to his brother and his three sons. Before, only they and I knew about this. And they intend to kill me as soon as my baby is born. But now, you two know about it, too, because I just told you. Which makes both of you a danger to their plan."

The men's eyes narrowed. They focused on Norah Heston Talmidge, who'd stood quietly by . . . although not calmly. No, she actually simmered with rage. Hatred for Kate, so intense she could feel it, seemed to radiate from her very pores.

"Any of that true, Mrs. Talmidge?" the black-vested man wanted to know. "You intend to have us followed and killed?"

Norah Talmidge raised her chin and glared at the men. "I'm not accustomed to being questioned. Especially not by the likes of you."

As the men's eyes glittered with insult, Kate seized the moment. "It's true. All of it. Why else would she have had you bring me here? What do you think she wants with me? She told you I stole from her, didn't she?"

The men exchanged glances; some silent message passed between them. Kate's pulse leaped. Was it good news or bad? The black-vested man spoke up, his gaze traveling between Kate and Norah Talmidge. "We're washing our hands of the whole situation. You two women obviously got business to carry out. And we don't want no part of it. We been paid, like the lady said. So we're moving on."

"No," Kate whimpered, defeat a cold lump of dread in her belly.

Just as they'd ignored Mrs. Talmidge's earlier emotion,

they now ignored Kate's. Grim-faced and deadly serious, they turned as one and focused on the rich woman facing them. "Should someone follow us, ma'am," the man in the black hat said, "we'll come back. And we'll be looking for you when we do."

Before Norah Talmidge could respond, Kate, feeling the opportunity slipping away, again stopped the men's retreat. "Someone *will* come after you, all right. But it might not be anyone *she* sends. It'll be a lot worse. Because it could be my husband. And he won't be interested in talking."

Norah Talmidge pivoted sharply to face Kate. Her cheeks brightened with her temper. "You liar. You don't have a husband."

Kate almost smiled . . . and would have if her cheek hadn't hurt so bad. "But I do. I'm married now."

"Hold on, you two," the brown-hatted outlaw said, cutting in and drawing Kate's gaze—as well as Mrs. Talmidge's—his way. "I agree with my partner. We ain't got nothing more to do here with what's between you two. First you"—he pointed to Norah Talmidge—"insult us, and now you"—he pointed to Kate—"threaten us. This don't seem—"

"I didn't threaten you at all," Kate called out, interrupting the man. "I just told you the truth. Mark my words, my husband *will* come looking for you."

The man pushed his hat up on his head and looked more peeved than alarmed. "And just who is this husband of yours, that we should be afraid of him, sweetheart?"

Kate looked squarely in the man's eyes and said, "Cole Youngblood."

Never had two simple words ever given Kate more satisfaction. Norah Talmidge reeled back a step, her mouth agape, her complexion paling. "You're lying," she hissed.

Kate calmly shook her head. "No. I'm not. And I believe that all too soon, when he comes barreling in here with blood in his eye and his gun blazing, you'll find out just how truthful I'm being."

Kate then looked toward the two hired gunmen. For their

part, they couldn't seem to move, couldn't seem to muster a word between them. Although their skin did appear to be bleaching out right before Kate's eyes. No doubt with fear.

Kate couldn't help the smirk that played at the corners of her mouth. Never had she loved Cole more for being who and what he was than she did at this moment. She felt a moment's triumph—before she acknowledged to herself that she loved Cole Youngblood. Really and truly loved him. And knew he'd come after her. Because, as he'd said earlier today, he loved her. The realization rocked Kate, had her breathing shallowly.

Just then, the tent's flap abruptly parted. Kate jumped. Norah Heston Talmidge shrieked. And the two gunmen stiffened, their eyes wide, their rifles held tight enough to whiten their knuckles.

In stepped Edgar Talmidge.

Chapter Fifteen

Cole held his roan to a sedate pace. It was probably the hardest thing he'd ever done, he decided, as his fist tensed around the reins he held. Everything inside him wanted to raise hell and half the dust of Oklahoma as he tore through this tent city erected by the attendants to the rich. A murderous anger ate at him, one sharpened all the more for being intensely personal. Inside one of these tents was his wife. He meant to have her back, and he didn't care who he had to kill to accomplish that. Having nothing left to lose, Cole knew, made him a very dangerous man right now.

He wasn't oblivious to the stares coming his way. Even if these pillars of society did not know who he was, he looked out of place up here. His clothes weren't fine enough. His horse and his tack weren't sleek enough, not even for their servants. Besides that, there was his whole way of carrying himself, of slouching in his saddle. As if he didn't give a damn—because he didn't. As if he weren't impressed with or intimidated by them. Because he wasn't.

Therefore, he stood out. And that was how he wanted it, boldly riding right down the middle of the high-society tent city's main corridor. He figured his sober presence among them would cause a ripple that would spread rapidly throughout the camp. That was good. Because *they* needed to know he was coming. *They* needed to worry. *They* needed to have a care for themselves.

And . . . *they* knew who they were.

As he rode past, in the bright sunshine, not asking questions, directions, or permission, Cole had his Stetson pulled down low on his brow. He had no qualms about returning the open stares of those made of stern enough stuff to look him in the eye. Some were only curious, open and friendly-looking, stopping what they were doing and nodding his way as he passed. Some only spared him a glance before dismissing him and going back to their meals. A few women, though, stared openly, lingeringly. And still others, a few of the men, focused sharply on him, their expressions hardening.

As he rode on, his body rocking along with the roan's smooth gait, Cole found himself wondering just how many of these same men's names he would recognize, if he heard them. He wondered how many of them had hired him in the past, and would maybe do so again in the future, to do their dirty work. That was one thing that continued to surprise Cole—the amount of work that would come his way from men like these. Not all of them. Most of them were good men who loved their families and who lived their lives respecting the law and giving back to their country by helping others less fortunate.

Cole pronounced himself at least intelligent enough to know that much. Rather, in his experience, it seemed that a few men of this caliber—ones who, like Edgar Talmidge, repeatedly called upon him—held a heap of grudges and made a lot of enemies, most of them intent on escaping out West—only to run right smack into the business end of Cole's gun. Or the gun of any other hired killer who might be available. It always seemed there was one around. A gun looking for a contract. Cole shook his head, sparing a thought for this new territory. It would take a strong lawman to bring order, and to keep it, out here in a place used to making its own laws.

Until now, his place in this rich man's scheme of things had all been fine with Cole. Because he was able to remain anonymous. He remained faceless to them; and they remained faceless to him. He was no more than a name. And they were no more than a paycheck. But not any more. Trouble now had a face and a name—and these men harbored the rotten son of a bitch in their midst. Cole had no doubt these influential men would close ranks around Edgar

Talmidge, if they knew Cole's intent, which was why he didn't simply ask directions to the Talmidge tent.

A chuckle escaped Cole. He'd always wondered if it would come to this . . . him hunting one of their own.

And now, as he rode through their midst, searching for a telling clue that could lead him to Kate, he felt pretty certain at least a few of the men gaping at him knew who he was. But he didn't figure they'd do much about it. He wasn't after them, so why should they? Better yet, how could they—with their womenfolk and children around? And maybe even a mistress or two. There were always mistresses. These men seemed to marry for duty and money, and then philander for fun and love. But not Cole. All he wanted was Kate.

Cole's posture stiffened. He came close to reining in his horse. *All I want is Kate?* That wasn't what he'd meant. No, he'd meant that he wouldn't want to be one of these men because their lives were too complicated—by women and children and property and money. Cole agitatedly worked his shoulders, as if his shirt were suddenly too tight. Just being here around all these tents that reeked of untold wealth made him feel confined, tied down, constricted. It was not for him.

He'd always thought he respected his betters. But these men didn't seem the least bit better than he was. Far from it. Besides, Cole had a hard time swallowing the notion that anyone was his better. That wasn't the way of it out West. A man was known by how he kept his word, and not by the size of his bankroll. So these men here surprised him. They weren't bigger than life, as he'd imagined. In fact, they didn't strike him as smarter or stronger than he was. They were just men, men who had a lot of problems and a lot of meanness, most of it brought on by having too much money and too much time. And too much of a sense of their own power.

And here he had been helping them along for fourteen years. *Son of a bitch.* Cole fought the mirthless grin that twitched at his lips. He wasn't saying much that flattered himself, either. A sudden discomfort, more with himself than with the different breed of people who surrounded him, had Cole nudging his Stetson up and shifting his weight in the saddle. Well, hell, he hadn't come up here for a social hour. He'd come to find Kate. And he wouldn't leave until he did. Or until he was dead.

Cole turned his roan to the left at a break in the tent city's configuration. And again found himself unexpectedly amused—this time by the wagon-trampled curve in the main grassy thoroughfare he faced. Even out here on the prairie, among the rolling green hills and tall stands of trees, with over a million unexplored acres awaiting only the firing tomorrow at noon of the starter's gun to be claimed, these city slickers had constructed a city for themselves. They'd surrounded themselves with those they already knew, as well as all the comforts of home.

Such as, Cole noted as he rode by, the silver tea sets proudly displayed atop ornately carved wooden tables set outside some of the tents. All around Cole, servants abounded. Card games were in progress. Children ran about, their indulgent nannies close on their heels. Thus freed, the richly dressed wives visited and chatted, walking from one tent to the next. And that was another thing . . . there were some nice-looking women up here, too. But there was only one who interested Cole right now. And that was Norah Talmidge. Because she knew where Kate was.

If she were outside socializing, Cole figured, she wouldn't be hard to find, since she looked so much like Kate. But if Norah Talmidge held Kate captive, she wouldn't be outside engaging in social activities. She'd be occupied with her prisoner. Instead of faces, then, Cole concentrated on looking for anything out of the ordinary that would serve as an obvious marker for him.

He discarded the notion that he might find the Talmidges by identifying the fancy carriage the lady from yesterday had been riding in. Because everyone up here seemed to have one just like it. Cole shook his head in disgust. He'd seen carriage after carriage, with the fancy horses to match, being unloaded daily from the trains up in Arkansas City. Just brought their wealth with them, they did, rather than be inconvenienced.

Cole figured that Mrs. Talmidge—or Mr. Talmidge, because he knew he'd assigned more deviousness and blame to the missus than he had the mister—had to have had help nabbing Kate and spiriting her away. The Talmidges certainly wouldn't have sullied their lily-white hands doing the dirty work themselves.

And as Cole knew firsthand . . . where there was a hired killer, there was a horse. He searched now for that saddled, dusty, sweat-lathered animal, the one a kidnapper would have ridden hard as he'd taken Kate away. Cole's frown deepened. Something else bothered him about this other hired gun. And that was the simple fact that he had been hired. To Cole's knowledge, the Talmidges knew nothing of his own close association with Kate. So why hadn't they looked him up first when they arrived? And he knew they had arrived. He no longer doubted it, much less even questioned how he knew. He just knew.

Once they arrived, they could have easily found him with a few well-placed questions. Yet, they hadn't done so. Instead, it appeared they'd latched on to the first outlaw they could find to carry out their dirty work. Or maybe they'd spotted Kate on their own and, not wanting to risk the time and trouble it would take to locate Cole, had hired another gunman to get her instead. That would save them a heap of money, he had to admit.

But Cole shook his head and shifted his weight in his saddle. He had no answers, only questions. It was all mighty curious. And yet, the very way in which today's events had unfolded assured him that, had he not believed Kate's story about the Talmidges' misuse of her, then the existence of another gunman would have convinced him that the Talmidges had something to hide. He'd have known that obviously they'd lied to him about why they wanted her found and killed.

It appeared now—since they were right here on Kate's

heels—that it had been their plan all along to come out
here themselves after hiring him. Evidently they'd meant
to allow him to hunt her down . . . and then they'd take her
away after that. In essence, then, Cole realized, he'd been
used. And he didn't like being used. Not one bit. Or lied
to. Theirs was a breach of trust and confidence, when he'd
never given them a reason to think they couldn't trust him.

Dishonorable, that's what they were. All the more reason
not to like the man or his wife, Cole decided as he became
aware of the warm April sunshine beating down on him,
warming him beyond what his flaring temper already had.
He decided that maybe he'd ask the Talmidges for a few
answers to his questions . . . before he killed them. And he
would kill them. Kate would never be safe as long as they
were alive. So, they had to die. It was really that simple.

Having ordered that in his mind, Cole returned his attention to hunting for that horse or telltale sign that would
point him to the tent and the people he sought. *Like this
one.* Cole reined in his mount . . . and sat there staring,
wondering now what exactly had caught his wandering attention. Because he didn't see anything out of the ordinary.
Nothing so big as a horse, that was for damned sure. And
this tent was like all the others. Big. White. Surrounded by
all the trappings of wealth. Looking it over again, he finally
realized what had caught his eye. The door flap was tied
closed.

Now that's curious. The canvas flaps on all the other
tents he'd passed had been tied back, the better to catch the
breeze. But not this one. Cole's eyes narrowed as he looked
around.

No fancy carriage sat parked nearby, but that didn't
mean someone couldn't be inside. He looked down at the
ground surrounding the tent. Pretty chewed up. Looked like
horse activity. A lot of horse activity. *Interesting.* Of
course, he would have preferred to have real horses hitched
outside . . . horses whose flanks were still lathered. Because
that would mean a recent hard ride. In his head, Cole estimated the distance from the stand of trees below to this

tent up here. And figured the timing of a getaway was about right.

He had to hand it to whoever had pitched this tent here. He'd chosen well, if his mission had been one of secrecy. For one thing, the tent sat practically off by itself. The nearest tent was a good thirty yards away, Cole guessed. For another, this tent was staked around a bend in the tent city, away from the sight of the would-be settlers camped in droves on the prairie below. Which meant too that whoever had occasion to ride off through the trees that surrounded the creek wouldn't easily be seen before he was already away.

Still sitting in the aged-leather saddle, which creaked with his every motion, Cole turned toward the tree-sheltered stream below and plotted in his head the escape route 'he'd envisioned. And concluded his thinking was right. The lay of the land would have sheltered any fleeing horseman. Hell, only yesterday hadn't he himself lost sight of the fancy lady when her carriage had rounded the bend?

All this is mighty interesting, Cole reflected. *Mighty interesting.* His expression hardened as he dismounted and looped the reins around his saddle's horn. After settling his Stetson low on his brow and checking his gun in its holster, Cole stood a moment by his roan and kept an eye on the closed flap of the tent. After all, it could be flung back at any moment by anybody who might be inside. Considering what his best approach might be, Cole rubbed his horse's shoulder and listened for any sounds from within. Frustratingly, only silence and chirping birds greeted him.

There was only one way for him to know if someone, innocent or otherwise, was inside this tent. He had to take a look. He stepped back from his roan and pulled his Colt revolver. Even if this was the wrong tent, whoever innocently resided here, should they happen to be home, would be more inclined to listen to his apology if he had a gun in his hand.

And since he did, Cole didn't hesitate. Boldly stepping up to the tent, Cole led with his six-shooter and yanked the flap back, aggressively thrusting himself in through the opening and waving his pistol back and forth threateningly as he searched for a target.

None existed. The tent was empty of people.

"Damn," Cole fumed, relaxing his gunfighter's stance and holstering his weapon. He'd been so sure this was the correct tent. All the signs indicated it was.

It probably is. Maybe you're just too late. Maybe Kate has already been taken away.

Cole stiffened, hearing inside himself the whisperings of an ugly creeping fear. It gnawed at the rough edges of his confidence in his own abilities. He put a hand to his waist and rubbed his other one over his face. Could it be true? Could it be, for the first time in his life as a hired tracker, that he'd been too slow, too bogged down with Kitty and the kids and the ride out here and the need for caution? Had this newly learned caution of his cost Kate her very life?

"Son of a bitch." The curse slipped out of Cole along with his exhalation of a breath laden with sudden defeat.

He looked around the tent, turning slowly from where he stood in its middle. A thick, woven carpet under his feet cushioned each step. Greeting his contemptuous gaze were ornate but practical furnishings. A thick and inviting bed. A washstand with mirror. Two armoires spilling over with clothes—both men's and women's, he noted. A folding table and chairs probably meant for dining. And various closed-front cabinets, which no doubt held china, crystal glassware, and silverware. Everything a rich couple would need to pamper themselves out here.

To Cole's troubled gaze, the interior appeared painfully innocent. Nothing here even hinted of dark plottings or evil doings. Which had him wondering if the whisperings inside him could be right. Was he wrong about this tent? Were his instincts off? At thirty years of age, was he losing his edge—and at the worst possible moment? Cole fisted his hands in an effort to steady himself against any such misgivings. But, slowly, even a bit surprisingly to him, his hands relaxed. A change came over him. He realized that he was not in any way ready to accept the possibility either that he was wrong or had been too late.

Because he wasn't—wrong or late. It was that simple. Because anything else, with Kate's life hanging in the balance, was just too unthinkable.

Then, the thought of Kate uppermost in his mind, another emotion overwhelmed Cole. His chin came up a notch. His eyes reflected a mixture of fear for her and anger at her captors. A sudden and overwhelming sense of helplessness swept through him, something he'd not felt since he'd been a boy of seven and had watched his father ride away. Again seeing himself as that small boy crying and running after his father's departing horse, Cole erupted. Caution and calm and good sense fled. For once, in his adult life, Cole acted on gut emotion. And because he did, nothing in the tent was spared. Nothing was allowed to stand.

His face contorted with a helpless rage, he yanked clothes out of drawers and flung them aside. He tossed the coverings off the bed and kicked aside the carved folding table and chairs. With a glancing brush of his forearm, he swept gold jewelry and a silver-backed brush and comb set off the top of a bureau. He told himself he searched for anything that might be a clue, that might tell him at least that Kate had been here . . . that he wasn't wrong, that he wasn't over the hill. That he wasn't too late.

But in his heart, he feared the truth. He raged against every damned thing in his life that had ever held him helpless and shaking in its grip. He raged against every moment he'd ever felt lost and alone and scared. He raged against every hard and humiliating thing he'd ever had to do in the name of feeding himself and his sister and her kids. He raged against a fate that had made of him a killer of men, that had made him a man who—if he didn't find Kate—would never know the finer, more tender things in life. A man who would never have love. Goddammit, he raged against—

His father.

"*No.*" The hoarse cry was torn from Cole. And left him feeling alone in this world, this life . . . as always. It left him shaking. And hurting.

The storm of emotion abated as suddenly as it had erupted. "No," he repeated, this time quietly, as he shook his head. He looked around himself, at what he had wrought. The tent's interior was a shambles. The contents were all upended. And he was in the center of the ruin . . . squatting down, his weight supported on the balls of his feet, his fisted hands pressed against his eyes. For long seconds, he wasn't conscious of any thoughts . . . only that he was conscious. And sweating. And that he ached and hurt and his heart was thumping wildly. And he was, for the first time in his adult life, scared. Really scared.

Cole saw himself again as he'd been all those years ago. There he was . . . a skinny, dark-haired boy, terrified, watching his father ride off. Forever after, he and Charlotte had been alone, with only each other for comfort. Cole remembered how, for weeks, he had been too terrified to sleep and had clung to his sister. He'd promised himself, as he'd grown into his teen years and had become more independent, that he'd become the sort of man who'd never be afraid. That he'd be the one whom all other men would be afraid of. And now, years later, here he was . . . that man. The one all others were afraid of.

And yet, Charlotte had still died. He hadn't been able to stop that, had he? And afraid? He still was. Inside, in his heart, he was still the scared little boy, lost and alone. Helpless. Unable to understand his world anymore. Unable—after all his years of experience in tracking down all sorts of desperadoes—to find even one small black-haired, green-eyed woman named Kate.

"What am I supposed to do, Daddy?" he heard himself whispering. With great effort he blinked back the sudden tears in his eyes. "What am I supposed to do?" His voice was no more than a sick, weak whimper. And Cole hated it. Squaring his jaw, clamping down on his back teeth, he pushed himself up and stood tall amidst his ruined surroundings. He looked around, listened. But heard nothing. No one running to come see what the trouble was. No inner voice. No whispering back to him. No reassurances. Nothing.

"What am I supposed to do?" he asked again, his voice this time strong and resolute. "Tell me, damn you. Tell me."

And then he stood there, realizing his hands were fisted and raised in the air. He asked himself, *What is there left to do? Accept that I might truly be too late? That I'll never see Kate again? Just quit? Give up?*

He thought about how that made him feel. And slowly shook his head. *No. I'll search every son-of-a-bitch tent and wagon until I find her.* Cole lowered his hands . . . and chuckled, a somewhat erratic, watery sound. He inhaled several long, strengthening breaths in the moments he gave himself to tamp down his earlier fear and hopelessness. Since he'd decided to stay and fight, the only question remaining, then, was where to start.

"I could really use some help here, Pa," Cole surprised himself by saying aloud, even as he realized he was already slowly turning in a circle and again searching—for anything, in a place where there was nothing.

And then . . . he stopped. His gaze lit upon the cot in the corner—at the back of the tent. Everything inside Cole stilled and seemed to focus itself on the simple bed.

He hadn't noticed it before, not even in his rampage. And even now, there was nothing special about the cot itself that should draw his notice. Indeed, it was just an ordinary cot. Could even be standard army issue. But it wasn't the cot, really, that had arrested Cole's attention. No, it was what was lying atop it, strung over the wooden canvas-covered edge. There it was . . . the clue he needed, the clue that gave him back hope. A simple strip of calico cloth. Only this morning Kate had torn it from an old threadbare dress of Lydia's and had tied her hair back with it before going to the creek to wash up.

Cole couldn't seem to look away from the strip of calico.

He felt certain that if he did, if he looked away—it would disappear. Slowly, stiffly, he walked over to the cot and bent over, snatching up the piece of fabric and threading it between his fingers. Clinging to it were several long strands of Kate's black hair. Something murderous coiled inside Cole. Had this cloth been torn from her hair? Or had she somehow, unseen by her captors, left it for him as proof of her presence here? He had no way of knowing at this moment.

But one thing he did know, he assured himself, was that he meant to find out. He raised the calico to his nose, breathed in Kate's scent, and then stalked across the tent, ripped back the flap, and stepped outside. Daylight assaulted his eyes. Squinting, Cole searched the muddy ground around the tent. And finally looked closely at what before he'd only glanced at. The narrow wheel tracks of a rich man's conveyance ... some sort of carriage. Maybe a black landau, like the one he'd seen yesterday? Could be. At any rate, the wheel ruts and horse tracks led away from here, straight away from here.

Cole trained his gaze on those tracks, following them, until he estimated where this course would carry a vehicle. He raised his head to stare toward the horizon. In that direction lay the Cherokee Strip. That was all he needed to know. Cole wadded up the calico he still held and threw it on the ground. It had served its purpose. He then sprinted toward his roan, knowing he was about to find out just how fast this horse could run.

Terror coursed through Kate—terror for herself, terror for her baby—as twilight approached and she sat facing the Talmidges. The couple perched, shoulder to shoulder, on the seat opposite her in their enclosed landau carriage. As the driver kept the vehicle rocking along at a frightful, jarring pace, no words were exchanged. The occupants only stared at each other. Kate swallowed, half afraid her throat would actually close from the emotion constricting it. Of course, she could look away from the hateful faces of her captors ... but what was there to see? The passing landscape of Indian Territory?

She realized they were covering in reverse the same ground she and Cole and the children had ridden across only two days ago. Could the Talmidges mean to return with her to Arkansas City and the trains that made the runs back East? It made sense. But getting to the trains was a three-day journey. What would they eat? Where would they sleep? Already it was close to dark, which meant they'd soon have to stop for the night. To continue—with the horses unable to see their way—was to invite disaster.

But perhaps, Kate reasoned desperately, before they'd had her abducted, they'd managed to set up another camp deep in the wooded area somewhere out here. That had to be it. Because if not—Kate could barely get her fear-frozen mind around the words—then they simply meant to bring her out here and kill her ... and then return to their fancy tent as if nothing had happened.

The idea of such cold calculation stunned Kate. But which did she prefer, she asked herself? The quick death tonight? Or the one she'd know was coming once she delivered her baby? A wave of despair all but swamped Kate. Instantly she fought it, promising herself that she'd think of something, that she'd do anything, at almost any cost, to avoid either of those fates.

Afraid that her sudden conviction would show on her face, Kate finally did glance out the window. The passing parade of lurching and lumbering schooners, all traveling in the opposite direction from the landau, did nothing to cheer her. They were all headed for the Oklahoma Country. Which was where Kate desperately wanted to be. With Cole and the kids. She worried now about the children, about how Joey fretted over everything and felt everything was his responsibility. She worried if Willy would help his big brother keep up with Lydia. The little girl was always chasing off after Kitty and could get herself hurt. And who was fixing their supper and seeing that they said their prayers before going to sleep?

Suddenly, a heartsickness seized Kate and nearly tore a cry from her. Her concerns were those of a mother for her children, a mother whose children weren't being watched over.

Kate fought the helplessness in her soul. In only moments, though, she came to her own rescue when another thought occurred to her. She should forget about herself and worry about getting back to the children. After all, worrying about another child, the one she carried, had gotten her this far. Telling herself now that was exactly what she'd do, Kate affirmed for herself that Joey, Willy, and Lydia were indeed her children now. And they needed her.

Just like she needed Cole. *Oh, God . . . Cole.* Kate again looked out the window as she blinked back sudden tears. It was true . . . she needed him. And only God above knew where Cole was and what he might be doing to locate her. She felt certain he would come after her. Somehow he would. He'd get someone to see to the children, and then he'd come after her. Earlier, she'd dismissed an unsettling doubt that had her wondering if Cole might be in cahoots with the Talmidges—besides his contract to find and kill her. Even though he'd never said he wouldn't carry out his orders, the reality was . . . he hadn't done so. Because here she sat. Alive and—Kate stopped herself. She was alive, yes. But not well. She was far from well.

Because Mr. Talmidge held a gun on her. An unnecessary ploy. What could she do against the two of them and their driver who perched outside on his box? Besides, Kate's hands—swollen and tingly with an increasing numbness—remained tied behind her back. If only her hair were still tied back, Kate lamented. Long black waves of it insisted on falling toward her face. And her scalp still hurt from where Norah Talmidge had yanked her by her hair as she'd forced Kate to sit down again on the cot when Edgar Talmidge had entered the tent. In the violence, the threadbare calico strip she'd used to tie her hair back had come undone.

And how long ago had that been? Days? Weeks? It seemed so, to Kate, since so much had happened. But the truth was, she realized now, that only hours had passed. What an ordeal she had gone through! Once Mr. Talmidge had arrived to announce that their plans—plans, no doubt, for spiriting her away—were completed, Kate had been blindfolded and gagged and then hustled out and pulled, prodded, and finally tossed onto a horse, with someone— a big man—behind her in the saddle.

They'd ridden over jarring ground, hard, but not alone. Kate had heard, on either side of her, other horses' hooves. At the time, she had no way of knowing just how many other men on horses had accompanied them. But she found out soon enough, once they got to the waiting landau, which had been hidden in a forested area along the trail to the land run border. Once her blindfold was removed, she discovered that there were only two other steeds. Atop them sat Edgar Talmidge and his wife, Norah. And the hardships continued. Kate hadn't been given so much as a mouthful of food or a sip of water since she'd been abducted. And yet, she still had a painfully full bladder to remind her of her baby.

Through it all, though, she purposely hadn't raised a fuss. She hadn't fought, hadn't screamed, hadn't so much as kicked out. Nor had she said a word. Instead, she'd focused on her baby and had tried to conserve her energy and to shield her belly as much as possible. Kate believed now that the Talmidges wouldn't kill her. They wanted her baby very much. And until she delivered it, they'd be forced to see to her well-being. And that being so, maybe it was time to tell them a few things—a few things that wouldn't make them any happier, she supposed. But still, a few things they ought to know.

Kate pivoted, giving up her closed-off posture to face the Talmidges once more—two people she'd hoped never to see again. To Kate's unsettling surprise, their steady gazes were already upon her. And judging by their grim expressions, she could only wonder and guess at their private thoughts. As she looked from one to the other of them, and saw the flicker and dart of their eyes as they in turn assessed her, she wondered if people like them had thoughts—decent ones, anyway. And how they faced themselves in a mirror.

She further wondered what they said to each other in private. How they justified what they were doing to her. But most of all, Kate wondered what Norah Talmidge must harbor in her heart for Kate—a woman capable of giving Mr. Talmidge what she couldn't, what he wanted the most. A child. Not for the first time did Kate wonder who was the bigger monster here. Him. Or his wife.

"You look like you want to say something, Kate," Norah Talmidge said into the silence. "Feel free to speak. We won't harm you."

We won't harm you? Kate's mouth slacked open. She could only stare at the woman and mentally answer her own question. *Norah Heston Talmidge is the bigger monster.* Yes, Mr. Talmidge had been the one who had repeatedly raped her. But at least his violence had been straightforward. She could see it coming, could anticipate it, and could steel herself against it. But not so Norah Talmidge's brand of evil. The woman was much more deadly for being so underhanded and secretive. She was the one to watch.

Feeling certain of that, Kate proceeded cautiously, looking from one to the other of them as she spoke. "Yes, I do have something to say. I—I would like to know when we're stopping for the night. I . . . well, the baby"—acute embarrassment stained her cheeks—"is pressing on me and—"

"What about the baby?" Edgar Talmidge sat up stiffly, his cruelly handsome face a mask of suspicion as he leaned forward across the seat toward Kate. He gripped Kate's knee. "Are you feeling poorly, Kate?"

Kate stiffened at his touch and tried unsuccessfully, given the coffin-like confines of the carriage, to edge her skirt-covered knee away from him. Fearing Norah Talmidge's reaction to his touching her knee, Kate glanced at the woman who sat at his side and clung to his arm. There was a smirk on her face. Unlike Kate, she couldn't see that her husband's expression had changed . . . to one of concern. For Kate.

Nothing could have scared Kate more. She'd suspected toward the end of her ordeal in this man's bed, that he'd . . . come to hold some warm feelings for her. The mere thought of such a twisted thing left her weak and sick, forcing her to gather her courage in the space of her next breath. Then she blurted out, "I'm fine. I have to relieve my bladder, is all. The baby is pressing on it."

Edgar Talmidge jerked his hand away and sat back stiffly. Norah Talmidge reacted as if she'd just smelled a skunk. "Oh, how dreadful. What a crass thing to say." She buried her face against her husband's shoulder.

Stung, embarrassed, and resentful, Kate continued. "It might be crass, Mrs. Talmidge. But it's still the truth. I only hope your mishandling of me today doesn't cause me to lose this child."

Norah Talmidge's head popped up. She and Mr. Talmidge exchanged a panicked glance before the hateful woman turned a malevolent gaze Kate's way. "What are you talking about?"

"I've had some bleeding."

Mr. Talmidge frowned. "Bleeding? Why would you be bleeding? What have you done?"

In the time it took Kate to draw in a breath deep enough to sustain her protest, the man's eyes narrowed even more. Acting with blinding speed, he shook loose of his wife's hold on him and jerked forward across the airless space, grabbing Kate by her shirtfront and pulling her close to his face. His blue eyes iced over with wild emotion. "If you've been letting Cole Youngblood crawl between your legs, and he's hurt my child—"

"*Our* child," Norah Talmidge cried, sounding wounded.

The keening note in her voice startled Kate, but Edgar Talmidge ignored his wife in favor of continuing his harangue—a harangue tinged with an insane jealousy, Kate now realized. With his big-fisted hand still clutching her blouse front, he shook her and bellowed, "Answer me, damn you. Has he? Has Cole Youngblood—"

"No," Kate screamed, her tears hot as they coursed down her face. "But I've been bleeding, and I don't know why. And after the way you've tossed me around today, I could be bleeding again."

Edgar stared hard into her eyes and then shoved her back as he released her. Collapsing back against his own seat back and crossing his arms over his chest, he eyed Kate, looking her up and down as he said, "We'll stop here and see."

Chapter Sixteen

Kate knew the odds would be against her. The last of the evening's covered wagons had passed by more than a mile back. She feared she'd never be able to catch up to it, even if she did escape. So there she'd be—unarmed, afoot, and alone in the gray of the gathering dusk. She wouldn't even be able to seek shelter for the night. Because she'd have to keep moving, which meant fighting her way through the tangled brush since she couldn't risk being seen on the moonlit wagon trail. All that noise of her crashing about was bound to attract the attention of her pursuers, maybe some wild animal, and probably even an Indian or two.

All that to worry about while still trying to keep from getting caught by Mr. Talmidge and his driver, who'd most likely also give chase. The Lord alone knew what they'd do to her if she got away now and then got caught again. Like as not, they'd not be as . . . "kind" as they'd been thus far. Kate exhaled tightly, not allowing herself the added worry over possibly getting her feet tangled on a vine or a fallen branch that could trip her and cause her to fall. Because that could hurt her baby.

It was an awful plan. Kate knew that. Just take her chances and run? The odds of it working on this rough ground and with the night closing in were slim. But the truth remained, this was her only chance. And she had to take it.

So there it was. If she hoped to get away at all, she had to reach down inside herself right now and find the courage from somewhere. After all, what did she have to lose? Her life was as good as forfeit if she didn't try. And so was Cole's—if he caught up with them and had to face two guns to his one. Kate knew he was good and had probably faced greater odds and had come out okay. But in this instance, he didn't know what or who he was up against. And that being so, Kate felt she needed to do everything she could to get away and to prevent him from walking into a trap.

That's mighty big talk, came her rueful thought, *for someone squatting down behind a tangled thatch of overgrown bushes with her skirt up around her waist.* Done with her business, Kate wadded her skirt atop her thighs and turned her attention to surreptitiously searching the ground around her. She couldn't risk moving around too much, or making too much noise as she rummaged through the twigs and fallen leaves. Because Norah Talmidge stood on the other side of the bushes. Fortunately, Mr. Talmidge and their driver had gone off in the other direction to attend to their business.

All she needed, Kate thought frantically, was a rock. A good-sized one.

"Well, Kate?"

Kate froze at the sound of Norah Talmidge's voice and stared blindly at the tree trunk in front of her. Her hands fisted around clumps of dirt and twigs.

"You've been in there long enough to"—disgust accentuated the woman's voice—"attend to your business and to know if you're bleeding or not. Are you?"

Kate licked at her lips and then forced the words out. "No, I'm not." No one could be more relieved than she was about that. She had sincerely been worried that she might be.

"Well, thank *God* for that. Then stop your dillydallying and let's go."

Kate frowned. Hearing Norah Talmidge say "God" sounded so strange to her. She hadn't thought the woman knew who He was. "Um, just a another minute more. I'm almost ready."

There followed a moment of silence from the other side of the bushes. Then, speaking in a low and steady voice, Mrs. Talmidge said, "Don't try anything foolish, Kate. Edgar gave me the gun, as you know. I won't hesitate to use it."

Kate believed the woman *would* indeed hesitate, given that Kate carried the Talmidge heir in her body. But not looking to split hairs at this point, she dutifully called out, "Yes, ma'am, I'll be right along," even as she groped about in the dirt, hunting, searching, praying for just one rock, just one. Her hand bumped against something cold and hard. Kate froze, then instantly grabbed up her sought-after prize.

A relief so great it weakened her swept through Kate. She had within her grasp her freedom. And within her hand, a rock big enough to be a weapon, yet small enough for her to hold in her palm and conceal in the folds of her skirt. Breathing shallowly, Kate hung her head and closed her eyes, praying at once for strength and for forgiveness. She'd never in her life struck anyone for any reason. But this was different. This was for her baby.

Finally, swallowing her trepidation and her guilt, Kate stood up.

Norah Talmidge started, as if she hadn't known Kate was back there, and jerked her arm up until the gun was trained on Kate. She thought the other woman looked ridiculous, standing there pointing a big gun at someone. Ridiculous and young and unsure of herself. That surprised Kate. She knew Mrs. Talmidge to be twenty-seven, but right now, she looked like a fragile child herself and somewhat like a good wind could blow her away.

But the illusion—a sudden insight had Kate wondering if she'd really only seen a momentary reflection of herself in the woman—vanished when Norah Talmidge sneered and said, "What are you looking at?"

Kate shook her head. "Nothing. I didn't mean to stare." But uncertainty had her flexing her fingers around the concealed rock she held—an uncertainty born of her doubt that she had the capability of doing another soul intentional harm.

"Then, let's go. Come on." Mrs. Talmidge waved the

gun at Kate, encouraging her to move along.

Inhaling a deep breath into her fear-constricted lungs and exhaling it slowly, Kate set herself in motion. As she walked around the bushes she'd been behind, she still feared she couldn't do this—just bash the woman over her head. It was wrong. No less wrong than what had been done to her. But an even worse thought occurred to Kate at this moment, as she rounded the bushes and neared her adversary. What if she hit Norah and it didn't knock her out? What if Norah still had the presence of mind to fire the gun she held?

Norah? Kate blinked, sending a sharp glance the way of the other woman. Not only was she thinking of doing her harm, this woman who looked so painfully much like herself. But she was now also thinking of Mrs. Talmidge as Norah. Simply Norah. Which, surprisingly, took some of the fear away from Kate. It was her against Norah. Kate now stood in front of her foe. Green eyes met green eyes. And all Kate could think was . . . she needed to be behind Norah in order to give her a good whack. At least she supposed she should be behind her. After all, she'd never done this before.

What would Cole do? came the intruding thought.

"What *are* you staring at, Kate?"

Kate roused herself, blinking and shaking her head. "I'm sorry. I was thinking of Cole."

Norah tensed. Her finely shaped eyebrows veed downward as she leveled her aim with the gun. "I don't believe you, that he's your husband. Neither did Edgar when I told him." She chuckled at Kate's expense. "Cole Youngblood? *Your* husband? Hardly."

Kate's temper flared. She was mighty tired of this woman always putting on her uppity airs and looking down her nose at those less fortunate than herself. It was about time someone took her to task over it, too. "It doesn't matter what you think. Because he *is* my husband."

Norah laughed, but not a speck of good humor resided in the sound. "You little simpleton. Why would such a man marry *you*?" Her expression changed to one of casual cruelty as she leaned in toward Kate. "Especially since we paid him such a handsome sum to find you and kill you. Did he tell you that?"

"Yes, he did." Kate heard the restrained quiet of her own voice. And felt a moment's triumph as Norah's eyebrows winged upward with surprise. Feeling she had the advantage, Kate pressed her point, purposely trying to rattle the woman . . . as she looked for an opening for her attack. "And you *do* know he'll come after me, don't you? That even right now, he's on his way?"

Norah's mouth worked, she looked uncertain, even as she raised her chin and tried to sound superior. "Even if it's true, that you're married to him, it doesn't mean he cares all that much. After all, you can't have known him for more than a week."

"He cares." Kate said it with quiet authority . . . and realized she believed it, too. Cole did care. The knowledge warmed her, made her feel braver, stronger.

And Norah knew it, too, judging by her rising voice and the one step backward she took. "Well, he can care all he wants. It doesn't mean he can find us out here."

Kate's eyebrows rose. "You think not? On the one and only road between here and Kansas? And headed in the opposite direction from everyone else? With us in the only conveyance not a schooner or some heavy farm wagon?" Kate paused, allowing Norah to absorb all that before she added, "You *do* remember why it was you hired him, don't you? Those tracking skills, as well as that quick draw?"

Having said her piece, Kate waited silently, allowing her words to take their effect on the other woman. Rising fear and doubt slowly suffused Norah's features and leached from her that air of superiority that had always frightened Kate. She expected to feel triumphant, seeing this woman so disadvantaged. But surprisingly, as Kate watched her, all she could think was that for as long as she lived—and she hoped it was for a good, long time, the Lord willing—she knew she'd never forget how Norah Talmidge looked enough like her to be her sister. And yet they were such different women. Kate wasn't about to call herself the good one and Norah the evil one. But she did believe it was all that money, and being raised pampered and spoiled, that lay at the root of the other woman's desperate, if not evil, doings.

It seemed to Kate that Norah expected she was always to get her way. *Well; not this time,* Kate vowed. *Norah Talmidge will never hold the baby I carry in my body. Never.*

Just then, the wealthy, pampered woman quickly covered her uncertainty with an imperious tone and a haughty stance . . . and a steady aim with that gun. "Cole Young-blood and his attributes do not concern me in the least. Edgar will take care of him if he shows up. But you do concern me, Kate. So don't you *dare* lecture me, you little beggar. Why, you'd have nothing at all without us Tal-midges."

Any remaining fear or respect or servant's civility that Kate may have retained in her heart fled with those words. She stepped up to the woman, going eye to eye and toe to toe with her. Norah Talmidge was evidently so shocked at Kate's forwardness that she remained in place, her free hand resting against her bosom. Angry beyond anything she'd ever felt before, Kate still managed to keep her voice low and steady. "*I'd* have nothing without you? Is that what you said? What did I *ever* have because of you? Too much work, that's what. But not enough food or clothes to my name. And a dirty little cot in a musty old attic room was all I could look forward to at the end of a long day."

Warming up to her subject, Kate poured out all her servant's misery on this uncaring woman who faced her. "I never even had any money for myself. Do you know what that's like? No, you don't. It was hopeless, that's what. A life of endless cleaning and toiling ahead of me. And all for what? So I could be dragged off by your husband to his bed—all in the name of money—and be violated over and over by him until I was carrying a child *you* couldn't conceive?"

A look of intense pain contorted Norah's face. She recoiled, crying out and doubling over, holding herself. Kate's eyes widened as great sobbing, tearing sounds came out of Norah. Helpless, Kate stood there, feeling as if she were watching herself writhe in agony. Shocked and sickened at herself, at all the hatefulness and hurtfulness that had spewed out of her, she covered her mouth with a shaking hand. And wondered what she'd done. And if she'd ever be forgiven.

"Norah? Is that you?" It came from afar, the sound of Edgar Talmidge's calling voice. Kate stiffened and jerked toward the sound, off to her right, of a large man crashing through the undergrowth. "Are you all right?" he cried. "Where are you? *Damn* this wildness out here. I can't see a thing."

From the corner of her eye, Kate saw Norah, her elaborate coiffure all but undone, snap upright. Kate took a step back but the woman poked the gun's barrel right against Kate's abdomen, where the baby would be, and called back. "Edgar! I'm over here." She grinned maniacally at Kate—and then screamed as if she were being killed.

Kate jumped, her eyes widened, her hand tensed reflexively around the forgotten rock she still held.

"Norah? What's wrong?" Edgar yelled, sounding panicked.

"Edgar! Come quickly," Norah sobbed, while never looking away from Kate, never wavering as she aimed the gun. "It's Kate. Help! She's attacking me!" Then, with deadly calm, speaking in a voice low enough not to be heard by anyone but Kate, she said, "I'm going to kill you. And your damned baby. Because I hate you with every fiber of my being. I hate you for being taken into my husband's bed. And for being the one to give him a child. I never wanted you around. And I certainly didn't want you back."

"You didn't?" That made no sense to Kate. "Then why did you come out here—"

"I had to." Norah's face was a snarling mask of hatred. "Who do you think made it possible for you to escape my home and New York that night, Kate?"

Absolutely bewildered and flustered now, Kate heard her own halting reply. "It was . . . it was Hudson."

Norah laughed. "Hudson? Edgar's valet? Hardly. It was *me*. I did it. I wanted you out of my life. And Edgar's. I can always find another baby to call ours. That's not a problem. But it was *you* Edgar preferred. You. Over me. Afterward, when he'd been with you and would come to me, he'd say your name. He'd call me Kate."

Kate felt suddenly weak and defenseless, like her baby. This was too much. It was sick and degrading and . . . crazy. "I had no idea. I didn't—"

"I know you didn't. But still . . . you have to die. It's the only way."

Kate began backing away. Norah advanced on her. "No, Norah, you don't have to do this. Just let me go again." Another part of Kate's mind noted that Edgar Talmidge was out there somewhere . . . and getting closer.

"Oh, no, Kate. I can't do that. See, Edgar wants *your* baby. Yours and his. He wants part of you to be with him always. I can't allow him to have that. Why do you think he followed you out here? And why do you think I came with him? He came to get you back. And I came to make sure you never come back. You or your little bastard."

That was all Kate needed to hear. That and the metallic click of Norah pulling back the trigger hammer. It was now her life or Norah's.

"No!" Kate's howl accompanied a vicious swing of her right arm. Putting all her fear and her strength and her righteous anger behind it, she landed a resounding blow to the other woman's left temple that made her stagger to her right, sent the gun flying from her fingers, and took her feet out from under her.

Norah Talmidge never made a sound. For one horrid second, she righted herself, stood up perfectly straight, stared at Kate—and then simply went limp and wilted slowly, elegantly, to the ground, falling back as if she'd merely fainted. But blood pulsing from the crushing indentation on the side of her head put the lie to that. She was dead.

Kate, her eyes wide with shock, her body stunned into inaction, just stood there.

"Norah? Where are you?"

Edgar Talmidge was getting closer.

"Kate? Where are you, honey? Kate? Answer me?"

Numb, lethargic, not even bothering to look up, Kate told herself, *Well, that's just plain silly. That sounded like Cole. Only it can't be. Cole doesn't know where I am. It must be a trick.*

In the gathering dark, and feeling as if she swam against molasses, Kate ignored all else and stepped up to Norah, peering down at her body. The dead woman's eyes and her mouth were open, as if she were surprised. Blood pulsed more slowly from her wound. But Kate's only thought was, *So that's what I'll look like when I'm dead.*

She couldn't seem to rouse herself to move, to get away, to save herself. And yet, she knew she had to. She knew she had to find the gun that Norah had dropped and then kill Mr. Talmidge and his driver. And then she had to get back to the children. Because she was their mother. And because Cole loved her and would be looking for her.

If only she could move. Edgar Talmidge must be almost upon her by now. She could hear him charging through the undergrowth. But crazily, it sounded as if he were coming from two different directions at the same time. It didn't matter, Kate decided. Because he wouldn't be happy with what he found. Or with her. No. He'd be angry. Very angry. She needed to get away. Now.

Before she could take a step, though, a hard male body slammed into Kate's, eliciting a shriek from her and engulfing her in a bearish embrace as he took them both to the ground and rolled . . . just as a hail of bullets flew all around them.

*   *   *

"How's Miss Kate, Uncle Cole? Is she gonna be okay?"

Sipping at his morning coffee, and squatted down on his haunches in front of the campfire early that next morning, April 22, the long-awaited day of the land run, Cole pivoted on the ball of his booted foot to see Joey standing there between the wagons. Sleep-tousled and tucking his shirt into his britches, the dark-eyed boy looked concerned as usual for the world's woes. Nudging up his Stetson, Cole realized he must have been deep in thought because he hadn't even heard Joey climb out of the schooner and go tend to his business. "I reckon she'll be fine, son."

Joey nodded and adjusted his suspenders. "Where is she?"

Cole thought of Kate curled up like a baby in the back of the buckboard. He'd held her shivering body against his all night. "She's still sleeping in the wagon. Come on over here and get you some bacon and biscuits. It ain't much, and it's mostly cold. But it'll fill your belly."

"I reckon it'll do just fine."

Cole watched as Joey, never smiling, never complaining, approached him and took up a place on the thick branch Cole had only this morning tugged into their new, more remote campsite. Once the boy was seated, Cole picked up a clean tin plate from a stack and handed it to his nephew, who said, "Thank you, Uncle Cole."

A grin tugged at Cole's mouth. The boy was as sober as a cowhand a week after payday. "Where're your brother and sister? They up yet?"

Joey shook his head as he heaped his plate with the morning's vittles. "No. Not yet. I reckon they're still tired from yesterday. They ran and played all day, it seems, with Miss Nell's girls. I had all I could do to watch over them."

Cole cut his gaze over to Joey and wished just once this kid would cut loose and act like the child he was. Cole knew all too well that once Joey took on the trappings of being an adult, he'd be one for the rest of his days. "I expect you did a fine job of watching out for them, son."

Joey shrugged his thin shoulders and started on his breakfast. "I reckon. I had some help."

Cole nodded. "You mean Kitty?"

Joey swallowed a bite of bacon and said, "Yes, sir. He came right along just fine once he got good and woke up. Them boys brought him to the wagon, like you asked them to do."

Cole thought of the two half-grown kids from yesterday down at the creek. And realized that although they'd never forget his name, he'd already forgotten theirs. "That's good. I expected they would." He sipped at his coffee and then added, "I reckon ole Kitty's got a good-sized lump or two on his head."

Something tugged at the corners of Joey's mouth. Could it be a grin? "That he does. I reckon it don't feel too funny, but he looks most comical-like, if you ask me."

Cole grinned, heartened that Joey would find anything funny. "Where is he right now?"

Joey's mouth suddenly firmed, as if in disgust. "He's in the schooner. I'll be damned if Lydia didn't fetch that hound to sleep with us last night."

Surprised at Joey's cussing, Cole cut his gaze over to the boy, whose eyes were now wide as silver dollars. Cole took a slow sip of his coffee as he narrowed his eyes at his seven-year-old nephew. "I wouldn't let Miss Kate hear you talking like that, if I was you, son. Unless you like eating soap for your breakfast."

Joey put his biscuit on his tin plate and hung his head. "Yes, sir."

Cole bit back a grin. And took pity on the boy. "You're not going to tell me you've also taken up chewing tobacco, hard liquor, and cheap women, are you?"

Joey's head popped up. His cheeks were bright red. "No, sir. I only tried tobacco once, and I got sick as a dog."

Cole stared hard at this kid he hardly knew . . . and yet loved as if he were his own. "You did? When was that?"

Apparently realizing he'd told on himself, Joey again lowered his gaze to his plate and worked on picking apart that biscuit. "I don't recall exactly. Back when I was kid, I reckon."

Overcome with humor and pride at such a good kid being related to him, Cole chuckled and reached over to tousle Joey's hair even more. The young boy raised his head . . . and revealed he was actually grinning. A crooked, gap-toothed grin. Cole sat back, certain his chest would burst with this moment of happiness. He realized he owed the boy something. So he just spat it out before he lost his nerve. "You're quite the kid, you know that, Joey?"

Joey's sobering gaze locked with his. Cole rushed on. "I know I'm not a one to go around handing out praise. But . . . I'm right proud of you. You'll make a fine man one day, son. A damned fine man. The kind this territory is going to need."

Joey's mouth worked. He looked as if he might cry, but he never shed a single tear. Instead, he cleared his throat and set about eating again. After a moment, he quietly said, "All I want is to be like you, Uncle Cole." Now he looked up and met Cole's sober countenance. "You're a good man, too. And me and Lydia and Willy want you to stay here with us and Miss Kate . . . if she'll have us. We don't want to go to no cousin up in Kansas. Not if we don't have to. Not if we have a say."

Cole's heart constricted. "You have a say. And you don't have to go anywhere you don't want to. I believe Miss Kate and I have it worked out that you kids can stay with her for good. She's your aunt now, so it's okay," was all he could say . . . or promise.

Looking immensely relieved, Joey said, "That's good."

Suddenly feeling awkward, as if his clothes were ill-fitting, Cole shrugged his shoulders and stretched forward, reaching for the pot bubbling atop the grate over the camp-fire. He slowly refilled his tin mug and gathered his thoughts. Then, sitting back and sipping at the steaming coffee, he directed his gaze to the steadily rising sun and thought of the coming day. He had no idea in hell how to proceed with the inevitable events it would bring.

"You still making the run today, Uncle Cole?"

Cole cut his gaze over to Joey. "I was just pondering on that. I don't know how I can. Not with Kate—" He hadn't intended to worry the boy, but it was too late now. Already, concern had sprung into Joey's black eyes, so like Cole's own. "Well, not unless Miss Kate gets to feeling better."

"I thought you said she was okay." His voice was as high as his eyes were rounded.

"She is. She just—had a scare yesterday, is all." And had cried herself to sleep in his arms and had shivered and shaken until Cole thought she'd rattle her bones loose. He'd soothed her all he could, had kissed her hair, her face, her mouth, and had reassured her as best he knew how. But all she'd done was cling to him and say, "I killed her, I killed her, I killed her." If she was still like that today, then Cole knew he couldn't leave her. Not if she wasn't right in her head. But if he didn't go, then she'd never have that land. That would be a final blow to her, he knew.

Cole thought about that and decided he sure as hell wasn't about to be the one to deliver a final blow to Kate. She'd come too far to be defeated now. So how could he still do this for her? Well, it wasn't as if he was all alone, he suddenly realized. It wasn't as if he had to do everything himself and be everywhere at once. He had help. Good, reliable help. Cole frowned at that surprising thought, pausing a moment to allow it to sink in . . . For the first time in his life, he had help. Now he grinned, thinking this was quite something, this idea of not being alone, of having someone to turn to in times of trouble.

Suddenly, the day seemed brighter . . . and it had nothing to do with the warm yellow glow of the April sunlight shining down through the trees. The brightness came from within Cole, from the realization that with help, he could do this. The thought was a triumph of will and determination . . . and of a family united. Feeling good and strong, Cole turned to Joey. "You through with your breakfast?"

When the boy nodded and put his empty plate down, Cole grinned and told him, "Get your brother and sister up, if you would. It's going to be a long day, and we need to get moving."

Sudden excitement lit Joey's eyes. "Then you're going to do it, Uncle Cole? You're going to make the run?"

Cole still didn't know exactly how he would, given all the problems that still faced him—or rather, them—but he did know that he would. "You bet I am. I didn't come all this way just to sit here." Then, realizing that he was still just sitting there, Cole tossed out the dregs of his coffee from his mug and came to his feet. He put the tin mug beside the campfire and faced Joey. "I'm going now to see to the mules and my roan. I set them out to graze earlier. When I get back, I'll get Kate up."

"No need. I'm up."

Cole, along with Joey, pivoted at the sound of her voice. She stood back by the buckboard . . . holding on to it. While that made him frown—she seemed about ready to fall down—he also realized he really should expect nothing less. After all, she'd taken quite a beating yesterday during her ordeal. But still, afraid for this woman he loved so intensely, Cole looked her up and down. His hatred of all things Talmidge flared as his gaze lit on the angry welt raised on Kate's cheek by Norah Talmidge's riding crop. "How long have you been up? I didn't even hear you."

Her gaze lowered a second and then she raised her head, looking him in the eye. "A while. I've been up a while."

Her voice was strangely soft. That had Cole worried. "How you feeling, Kate? You look a mite pale."

She put a hand to her face and smoothed it across the cheek unmarred by the welt, as if she sought to feel the color there for herself. "Do I? It must be because I—I just woke up." She lowered her hand and met Cole's gaze. "I'm fine."

He didn't believe her in the least. His eyebrow arched to prove it. "You sure?"

"I said I was," came her testy reply. "I said I was fine. And I am."

Silence ensued. Cole watched her clutch at her dirty

brown skirt and stand there shakily—as if she were dizzy. Never looking away from her, he spoke to Joey. "Go get your brother and sister up, son."

"Yes, sir," Joey chirped as he jumped up and took off for the schooner. But surprisingly, the boy suddenly veered to grab Kate around her waist and hug her fiercely.

When Cole saw her wince and stagger back a step, he lurched forward, a hand held out to her across the distance. But she righted herself and hugged Joey in turn, tousling his hair and grinning down at him—all with painful effort, Cole observed. "Go on now, Joey. Do as your Uncle Cole says."

Joey scrambled into the schooner, instantly raising a noisy ruckus that had Kitty barking and Willy and Lydia fussing sleepily. As Cole heard Joey telling the two other children that this was the day of the land run—making it sound like Christmas—his gaze remained locked with Kate's. She'd again clutched at the buckboard to her left. Cole exhaled slowly, tightly. Just looking at her now, he called himself crazy for even thinking he could go off and leave her alone, even for the several-hour duration of the land run. He opened his mouth to tell her so, but she spoke first.

"Joey's almost as excited as I am." Her voice, to Cole, sounded unnecessarily loud, even over the din of the children's and the dog's waking-up noises. Could it be that even talking was a strain for her today?

"Yeah. It would seem so," Cole answered, responding to her words about Joey's excitement. Then he stepped up closer to her, the better to be heard without having to raise his voice. "Kate, I don't think you—"

The kids and the dog piled out of the wagon . . . in one noisy, rolling heap of arms and legs and squeals that interrupted Cole. Kate stepped back, staying out of the fracas. Cole's concern for her increased. She must be more beat up than he'd realized because she always stepped into the fray, sorting the children and issuing hugs and orders. But since she didn't this time, Cole took charge, quickly herding the kids together and setting them off, holding hands, with Kitty and Joey leading the way as always, for the nearby stream to wash up.

As they walked away, going slow to allow for Lydia's short legs, Cole watched them a moment and, unexpectedly, pictured the land run at noon today. He felt certain he could already hear the cavalry firing their pistols to signal the beginning of the run. *Now, why am I thinking about that?* he asked himself. Then it struck him—the kids. If he didn't grab those acres near Guthrie Station that Kate had her heart set on, then none of them—not him, Kate, Joey, Willy, or Lydia—would have anywhere to call home by this afternoon. They'd be no better off than they were right now. *Son of a bitch!*

He turned again to Kate. With tenderness for her tugging at his heart, he rubbed a hand up and down her arm. "Tell me the truth, Kate. Where are you hurting?"

A ragged sob escaped her, but her chin came up a notch and she shrugged away from his touch. "No one place over another. I'm just sore from yesterday." She then met Cole's gaze, her green eyes shadowed with weariness. Cole frowned, wanting again to comfort her. But again she resisted his touch. "I'm all right. I just got tossed around pretty good for most of yesterday, if you'll recall."

"I do. And I own a share of the blame for my part in that."

Kate lowered her gaze a moment and then lifted her face to his. Some kind of deep hurting edged her eyes. "There's no call to blame yourself. You did what you had to. We'd both be dead if you hadn't."

Cole nodded, even as he remained upset as hell with her paleness and her soft, injured way of speaking. Then something else that tightened his gut occurred to him. "Kate, you're not bleeding again, are you?"

She closed her eyes. When she opened them again, Cole half expected their green depths to be swimming with tears. But she was dry-eyed as she shook her head and answered him. "No. I'm not bleeding."

Cole exhaled the breath he'd been holding. "Well, that's one good thing." But still, upset in the extreme over her not wanting him to touch her today—after all, he'd held her in his arms last night while they'd slept—he could only stand there and watch her and pray he hadn't really hurt her last evening when he'd grabbed her up to get them away from Edgar Talmidge—*that rotten son of a bitch*—and his driver. But once Talmidge had all but tripped over his own wife's body in the dark, the chase had ended. At least for last night. Of course, by today, Cole suspected, the man had set the law—or a pack of outlaws—after Kate and himself.

Cole gave in to the sense of an impending disaster that had been nagging him since it had awakened him. "Kate, what are we doing just standing here and talking?" She flinched, no doubt at the suddenness of his speaking into the silence between them. Cole rushed on before she could interrupt. "We need to leave this place. And now. We're not safe. Not with three kids to worry about. We need to forget the land run and make our getaway. I have plenty of money. You can start over—"

"No." Kate's expression hardened. "I won't run." Then she slumped, all but wilting as she drew in a ragged breath—as if her outburst had taken all the remaining starch out of her. "I can't, don't you see that? I can't allow them to win, Cole. I won't be pushed out of my own life anymore by the Talmidges." Her chin quivered with her raw emotions. "They've cost me too much already, Cole. Too much. Don't let them take this land away from me, too."

Cole wanted nothing more than to hold her in his arms, but she wouldn't allow it. Twice now she'd shied away from his touch. He couldn't for the life of him figure out what was wrong with her this morning. "Kate, honey, I was just thinking of you. There's something wrong—"

"There's nothing wrong with me. Nothing to keep you from making the land run. So don't you go thinking any different."

Her denials and her insistence just plain angered Cole.

"I'll think what I will, Kate. And that means seeing that you and my niece and nephews are safe. Because, the truth is, we don't know where in hell Edgar Talmidge is. Or what he's up to this morning. He could be anywhere." Suddenly, to Cole, it was as if he'd only just heard himself. He put his hands to his waist and shifted his weight to his bent knee. "Dammit, Kate, if I had any sense, I'd hitch up the two wagons and get us as far away from here as I can— and right now."

He'd expected her to soften, to maybe at least see his side. But she obviously didn't—because her eyes narrowed with stubbornness. "You do that. You go on and take the wagons and the kids. They belong to you, anyhow. Just leave me the roan and that stake because I've got land to go claim. After that, I'll see that your horse gets back to you."

Chapter Seventeen

Cole hitched his thumbs in his gunbelt and considered her—her stance, her words, her determination. He knew what drove her, what ate at her. And he respected all that. But it was time she faced the truth. "I'm not worried about my horse, Kate. It's you I'm worried about. You honestly think you can make the land run yourself?"

"I do. I'm a married woman now, remember? The law says a married woman—"

"I know the law, Kate. I'm the one who told you about it. And you also know that's not what I mean."

A nod of her head accompanied her words. "I know. But if I have to, Cole, if you force me to, I will. I'll make the run myself. Somehow."

"Somehow?" Stubbornness to match hers rose up in Cole. This was not the time for a battle of wills—especially one he appeared to be losing. He gestured sharply her way, pointing out her own fragile stance to her. "You can't even let go of that wagon to stand on your own." Instantly she let go of the wagon and put her hands to her waist . . . and wobbled in place. Cole exhaled sharply. "Look at you, will you? You're beat to hell and weak as a kitten. You couldn't run that horse race across open land—even if you did know how to ride a horse."

Defiantly she said, "I'll do what I have to. I always do."

In an effort to calm himself, Cole concentrated on breathing in and out. Finally, he spoke quietly, firmly to her. "Yes, you do, Kate. You do what you have to do. I admire that about you. But it doesn't always work out like you planned, does it?"

Her chin quivered, her gaze wavered . . . but then she looked him in the eye. Her expression mirrored her pleading words. "Help me, Cole. Please. It's all I've got left. . . .that land. I can't lose it, too."

His heart suddenly melting for her, Cole could only stare her way, and give in to his own suspicion that he'd move heaven and earth to get her anything she wanted. Before he'd met her, he'd never known such a strong, determined, yet warm and loving woman as she was. In fact, he'd never admired another woman, except his sister, as much as he did Kate. One minute she was as strong as an oak, and in the next, she was as fragile as a weeping willow. But either way, she didn't hesitate to stand against a world at odds with her. Cole understood that; he'd had to do much the same thing his whole life.

When he didn't say anything, and she perhaps misinterpreted his silence, Kate turned away, showing him her slender back with a cascade of shiny black hair draped around her shoulders. Again she held on to the wagon and appeared to look around as she waited for him to give her his answer. Cole wanted nothing more than to reach out to her and take her in his arms and tell her everything would be okay. But he couldn't. Because there was a war going on inside him— not just the question of whether he should make the run or make their getaway. He felt he needed to understand and then win this bigger battle inside himself before he could help her with hers.

Before *I can help her?* Cole didn't like the cowardly feel of that. Why at this late date, he asked himself, was he hesitating about helping her? Especially given all she'd already done for him. *What all she's done for me? What does that mean?* Surprised to learn that he'd obviously been holding back, if not harboring actual doubts, Cole tried to think his way through this. He directed his gaze away from Kate's back, settling it instead on the ground, the better to concentrate on what was inside him, driving him. *What has she done to help me—except with the kids?* He gave his mind a chance to go where it would . . . and suddenly the truth burst before his eyes like fireworks. Cole's breath left him in a sharp exhalation of sound.

Kate immediately turned to face him. "What's wrong, Cole?"

Staring into her face, seeing his salvation there in her green eyes, and feeling his heart racing, Cole shook his head and said, "I don't know, Kate. I need some time to think."

Concern edged her eyes. "How long, Cole? The race begins at—"

"I know. At noon. I don't need long, Kate. Just a few minutes. Please." He'd never said please in his life that he could remember. But he was saying it now.

Kate considered him a moment, managing to look as if she still feared he'd take off the minute her back was turned and leave her pregnant and stranded with three kids. But then she agreed. "All right. I'll go check on the kids, while you think about . . . whatever it is that's troubling you." With that, she turned around and walked away, slowly making her way through the tangle of underbrush that would eventually lead her to the creek and the children.

Cole watched her go. He watched the swing of her hair and of her hips. He watched the way she held her shoulders so straight and square. He watched the sway of her steps, the very way she walked—until she was out of sight, swallowed up by the tangled oaks she passed through. Only then did he admit to himself exactly how she'd helped him. Only then did he allow himself to consciously think what only a moment ago had surprised him so.

What Kate had done was make him realize that *he*— Cole Everett Youngblood, a thirty-year-old hired killer— could feel love. The truth of it nearly crushed his chest. Cole suddenly wrenched around, setting his hand to any task he could find—banking the fire, straightening the scattered belongings they'd pulled out of the wagons— anything mindless that allowed him to concentrate on his thoughts.

If he felt love for Kate—and he did—then didn't that mean he was worthy of such love in return? He'd never before thought such a thing. Cole let drop from his hand the tin dishes he'd been stacking, and concentrated as hard as he could on the message taking shape in his head. A message that suddenly and clearly told him that the miracle of Kate, for him, was that never before—before her—had he thought he was someone a woman like her could love. Before her, he'd always kept his heart closed off, hadn't allowed anyone to get close to him.

Absently, Cole ran a hand over his mouth . . . and wondered if he'd kept himself shut off because everyone he'd ever loved—his mother, his sister, and of course his father—had been lost to him. His mother and his sister had died. But his father had abandoned him and Charlotte. Cole frowned and wondered if it was when his father left that a tender heart, a heart not afraid to love and to hurt and possibly even to lose, was just too painful? Had he decided then that it was better to tell yourself you didn't care—rather than to risk caring at all?

"Son of a bitch."

Cole stared now into the distance, seeing the horizon and the rising sun as a new day in more than one way. Suddenly, to him, his old way of doing things seemed downright cowardly. As it turned out, he hadn't been the tough loner all his life. No, he'd been the hurting little boy afraid to love. He now glanced in the direction Kate had gone—as if he could still see her there—and *knew*. Never again would he shut himself off. He knew that no matter how she felt about him—because she'd never really said— he loved her and would risk everything to win her love in return. It was that simple. And that hard.

He marveled now that all it had taken for him to understand this miracle of a tender heart was forgiving his father for leaving him and his sister like he had. Cole's knees stiffened. *Forgive him? Forgive my father?* The old hardness in his heart reared its head. Cole fought it, telling himself no, telling himself he had to forgive and try to understand. He owed the old man that much. Cole put a hand to his forehead and rubbed there as if trying to erase the notion that he owed his father anything. Could it be true? Had he been inflicting wound after wound, all these years, on his father's memory? He now realized yes, that was exactly what he'd been doing. Inflicting wounds.

And for that, he needed to ask for and to beg forgiveness. *I do?* Cole had trouble grasping this. Would seeking and offering forgiveness be easier to do since he now truly understood—in ways he never had before—his father's desperation and his fears? Could it be that Abel Youngblood, all those years ago, had simply done what he'd felt he had to in order to secure a better life for his family? Cole found he could now accept that it might be so. After all, wasn't that exactly what faced him today with his own little put-together family?

Yes, it was. Always before, Cole now realized, his father's decision to leave his children behind while he searched for a way for them all to be together had been to Cole a bad decision, one that had never made any sense. Only now did he grasp another outcome to that long-ago decision. If he and Charlotte had been with their father and something had happened to him, then they could have been killed, as well.

Cole frowned, looking inside himself . . . and suddenly knew in his heart that was what had happened to his father. The man had been killed by someone. Or had suffered some fatal accident. He'd always meant to come back for his children but had been prevented from doing so. For the first time since he'd watched Abel Youngblood ride off twenty-three years ago, Cole allowed himself to accept that perhaps his father'd had no choice—just as Cole now had no choice in this matter of the land run. Either he made the run, or he lost Kate because she'd never forgive him if he didn't.

So wasn't he preparing to do the same thing he'd held such a grudge against his own father for doing: leaving his family behind? And couldn't he be killed while hunting for that plot of land or when trying to stake it? Yes, he could. So how, Cole asked himself, was his father's plight any different from his own today? The answer was simple—it wasn't. What *was* different was Cole's adult understanding of his father's reasons for what he'd done, for how he'd gone about things. He realized now, from having to explain himself to three little kids—a first in his life—that they couldn't always understand the reasons behind what he did. But he knew why he did things the way he did. And he always acted with their best interests at heart. Just as his father had done.

Cole shook his head. *Son of a bitch. The old man didn't leave because he didn't care. He left because he did care.* With that conclusion, one Cole had never before accepted because he'd never before today risked his own heart, a great weight was lifted from him. He suddenly felt strong and whole. And he had Kate Chandler Youngblood to thank for that. At once overcome with what he felt for her, with his fears for her, with his love and respect for her—no matter how she might feel in return—Cole saw again, in his mind's eye, her warm and loving face. He looked up now to the blue sky above the tree-lined horizon . . . and saw a wheeling eagle high overhead.

He watched it a moment and then said, softly, directing his words skyward, "I've been wrong. Can you forgive me, Dad?"

Then . . . he waited. Within moments, a warm beam of sunshine seemed to settle on him, bathing him in its yellow glow.

Almost immediately upon its heels, he heard someone coming through the underbrush. Cole quickly swiped a hand under his nose, denying the emotion clogging his throat, and turned to see Kate coming back his way. Straining for composure, not wanting to be seen like this, Cole adjusted his Stetson and then sought her gaze, latching on to those green eyes that had set his world on fire.

"Are the kids doing what they're supposed to be doing?" he asked, managing to impose a gruff tone into his voice, one that didn't betray him.

She nodded. "They are. Like always." She stopped a number of feet from him and stood there, looking everywhere but at him as she twisted her fingers together . . . and waited.

Cole smiled, his heart going out to her. He knew for what she waited. Still, right now he wanted nothing more than to stroke her cheek with his fingers and tell her how much he loved her. But he did none of those things, instead staying where he was as he softly called out her name. "Kate?"

She jerked her attention back to him as if he'd yelled. Her eyes were rounded with expectancy. "Yes?"

"I did my thinking."

"And?"

"And you win. I'll keep my promise to you. I'll make the run and get you that land."

Closing her eyes, as if immensely relieved, Kate nodded and exhaled. Finally, she opened her eyes, smiling shakily as she stepped up to him and went into his embrace . . . at last allowing him to hold her close. "Thank you, Cole. That's all I've ever asked you to do."

So it had all come down to this. The land run of 1889. About an hour away, as best Kate could figure it. And in the end, she was going to miss it. A humorless chuckle escaped her. Life sure seemed to turn in funny ways, she decided, thinking now of life as a living, breathing thing that purposely set out to throw your plans and dreams right back into your face—when you least expected it.

She felt she had proof of that fanciful notion, too. Because, less than a week ago, when she'd finally arrived in Arkansas City, she now recalled, she'd wanted nothing more than to claim her own land herself. But then she'd found out how impossible that was—and had forced Cole to marry her before he made the run for her. But once she'd gotten married, she'd decided again to make the run herself, thinking that was the only way she had to spare the children, should some hired gunman come looking for her and take out his wrath on them, too. Only that killer turned out to be Cole.

But he hadn't been the only one. She'd become a killer, too.

Kate swallowed, overcome again with the horror of what she'd done last night. She could never have foreseen that she'd take the life of anyone, much less Norah Talmidge. Kate scrubbed her hands over her face, barely able to withstand the words—"I killed Norah Talmidge"—or the thought of the act behind them. For as long as she lived, Kate didn't think she'd ever forget the sound of that rock thunking against Norah's skull. Or the sight of all the blood. *There'll be a price to pay for all that,* she reminded herself.

Because the murder of someone of Norah Talmidge's wealth and social prominence wouldn't simply go unremarked. Even if she survived Mr. Talmidge's wrath—he may have fancied her in his bed, but he'd not forgive her for taking his wife's life—then surely the law out here would have something to say about murder, even if it was committed in self-defense. But who would believe her, a penniless maid on the run from New York City?

Kate finally lowered her hands and turned her face up to the sun, gulping into her starved lungs great draughts of fresh air. It was all falling apart—her plans, her life, maybe even her sanity. She wasn't sure she could stand here another minute, atop the crest of this gentle slope of a hill where they'd made camp last night, and do nothing. Especially in light of all the activity going on below. Down there, on the plains for as far as the eye could see, was all the excitement and pageantry she'd been used to seeing in the huge parades in New York City. Only out here on the plains, with nothing as witness but the open land itself, it was all too much to take in.

Kate didn't know where to look first. She could scarcely believe the sheer numbers of would-be settlers here for this event. Thousands upon thousands of folks milled about below as they readied themselves for the run. Even up here she could hear their noise and bustle, could almost taste their excitement. Somewhere among them was Cole. Kate

wondered what that was like, being him and sitting there
atop that tall, long-legged roan and taking in everything.
She wondered if he thought of all the other folks surrounding him as his adversaries, since any one of them might
end up trying to stake the same hundred and sixty acres he
meant to claim for her.

That thought frightened Kate. She sure as heck hoped
he was the first one to stake that section close to Guthrie
Station that they'd talked about. Already in her heart that
plot of earth was her home. She wasn't sure she could stand
it if she lost that, too. Kate fought back the tears. *No. I
won't think about that now. Later. Not now.* She ought to
rest, to lie down, she knew that. Her body needed the quiet
time to heal. But she just couldn't bring herself to do it.
Even as tired and wrung out as she was, why should she?
There was no more point to conserving her energy.

Besides, right now she had too much else to worry
about. She looked behind her and saw a sprawling campsite
chock-full of three kids playing, four mules grazing, two
wagons hunkered down low to the ground, and a napping
dog named Kitty. An unexpected and perhaps lifesaving
chuckle escaped Kate. She decided that maybe she'd been
looking at this all wrong. She should—instead of counting
the tragedies—be counting her blessings. That seemed like
such a hard thing to do. Especially today of all days. But
maybe she should try. Because she had many blessings in
her life. Many.

Kate bowed her head and swore right then that from here
on out, she'd be the best and most loving mother and fierce
caretaker of everything in her keeping that she could be.
She had to be, she felt, or maybe they too would be taken
away from her. She looked up, feeling the tightness in her
chest, like iron bands wrapping around her and constricting
her breathing. If that happened, if she lost one more thing
she held dear, well, then, she wasn't sure she'd want to
live. As if hearing her own maudlin tone, Kate rushed to
assure herself that she wasn't being an overwrought miss,
by any means. Just a practical one.

After all, if she couldn't even hold on to one tiny thing that mattered to her, if she continued to lose everything and everyone who did matter, if she was never right, no matter how good and kind she tried to be, well then, maybe she just didn't know how to live. It was really that simple. And that hard. Because sometimes, it seemed to her, certain folks just didn't make it. They got eaten up by their troubles and never seemed to recover. They just dried up and blew away in a wind very much like the one blowing now. Was she one of those lost people? she wondered. Or could she go on?

She had no idea. She just figured that the day-to-day living would bear out her fate. And her measure of toughness. Kate paused there a moment in her thoughts. She'd never thought of herself as tough. That word, to her, seemed more likely to fit someone like Cole. Kate smiled. Cole. He was such a good man. Before he'd ridden off for the border, he'd given her strict orders to stay here and stay hidden until he got back. He'd then handed over his rifle to her and had even shown her how to fire the weapon. Her arms still hurt from the rifle's weight. She hadn't proven very good with firearms, but Cole had told her if worst came to worst, just aim and shoot. It'd make an impression on anyone threatening her, he'd assured her.

Also before he left, as he'd sat atop his roan and had looked down at her—surrounded by three kids and an old hound dog—he had told her again that he loved her. Just right out loud and in front of them all. The boys had gasped in embarrassed surprise and Willy had poked at Joey until Cole had told him to settle down. With Lydia wrapped around her legs and caught off guard like she'd been, Kate had lowered her gaze to the ground . . . and nodded. That was all. A nod. She hadn't known what to say. He'd quickly covered the awkward silence by telling them all to stay put and that he'd be back as soon as he could.

Kate took the time now to think about her feelings. Did she love Cole Youngblood . . . her husband? She did. His nearness made her yearn for his touch—and she'd never thought, after Edgar Talmidge, that she'd ever want a man to touch her again. But she did. She wanted Cole's touch on her skin, his kiss on her mouth . . . and only his. The truth was, she wanted nothing more than to be able to lie in his arms for the rest of her natural days. She wanted every morning and every night to hear his words, his voice . . . they were music to her ears. And his laughter healed her.

Yes, she loved him. But she couldn't afford to allow herself to be taken over by her love for him. Because he didn't intend to stay with her once her home was built. A stab of pain knifed through Kate's heart. Of late, she reflected, her life had been about losing—everything and everyone she loved. Especially Cole. It was plain to see that his home was his saddle. And his comfort was his gun. She knew that and had no reason—his professed feelings for her aside—to believe that he'd stay forever. And that being so, saying those three words aloud to him and thereby making them even more real and hurtful to live with once he was gone from her life—well, it just made no sense.

Exhaling her cares and woes, as well as her thoughts of Cole, Kate focused on the moment and all its problems. Looking about and turning slightly, she hit her foot against something. Looking down, she saw the loaded rifle she'd laid beside her on the spongy ground when she'd come up here for a few minutes by herself. She certainly hoped she didn't have occasion to use the gun today. It seemed to her that she'd lived through enough excitement and horror in the past two weeks to last her a lifetime. So hopefully today would come and go without a hitch, and by this evening, she and Cole and the kids and Kitty would be resting on her land.

Her land. It was hers—despite its also being in Cole's name and despite him being the one to actually make the run. And yes, she painted a pretty picture in her head of how it would be, she knew that. But the truth was that as the day wore on, she hardly cared if it rained or shined. She hardly cared if Cole got the land for her or not. She'd said she cared. She'd told him the land meant everything to her. And it did. Or it would . . . later. But not today. No, today—on a morning already too full of loss—all she wanted to do was lie down and cry and think about her baby. But if she did that, if she began crying, she feared she'd never be able to stop.

Just then, the mid-morning April breeze blew cool and lifted the long hair off Kate's neck and shoulders. Its kiss felt strangely like a warning and made her shiver. Heeding it, and recalling Cole's warning to be on the lookout for Edgar Talmidge, she again looked all about her. But nothing out of the ordinary met her eye. She hadn't expected it would . . . because poor old beat-up Kitty wasn't barking. When he was quiet, all was well. Still, Kate chastised herself for relying solely on the hound as her beacon.

Because hadn't she only just counted, among her responsibilities, remaining vigilant over these three kids, four mules, and one ornery hound dog? *That Kitty, I swear.* Kate said a silent thank-you that, mercifully, Kitty sported only a lump on his head but no other injuries from his attempt to protect her yesterday. Today he seemed fine. Kate wished she could say the same thing about herself.

No. No feeling sorry for myself. I need to be more like Kitty and not think of myself. I need to stand prepared to do whatever it takes to keep us all together and to let the children know they're safe and loved. Hearing herself, Kate took a moment to bask in the rightness of that sentiment. It was a good way of thinking. She liked herself for thinking it. And thought maybe Charlotte Anderson would, too.

A smile came to Kate's face. She felt certain that she'd somehow formed a covenant between herself and Cole's deceased sister. This filled her with a sense of wonder . . . and told her that perhaps all was not lost. Because Charlotte Anderson's children were now hers, and in ways she hadn't even understood until this morning's . . . event. In ways she couldn't even think about yet. Too much else was pressing in on her right now—in much the same way that her hand was pressing against her swollen belly, Kate belatedly realized. Evidently, while she'd been lost somewhere in her thoughts, a part of her mind had allowed her hand to stray there. *My baby*. Kate's chin came up. She closed her eyes, slowly shaking her head . . . *my baby*. And wanted to die.

Just then, a childish scream—Lydia's—rent the air. Wrenched out of her sad reverie, Kate jerked around, looking down the back slope of the hill to where the children had been moments ago when she'd last checked on them. She expected to see one or the other of the brothers messing with the little girl. That always got a squeal out of Lydia—

Kate gasped . . . and froze with fear. Her heart leapt painfully in her chest as a cold numbness seeped through her. Her warning for the boys died on her lips. She lowered her hand.

At the base of the hill stood Edgar Talmidge . . . with a howling Lydia clutched tightly in his arms. Next to him, holding the reins of their two horses, stood his driver, a surly, rough-looking fellow who, Kate knew firsthand, had no qualms about his employer's underhanded goings-on. Yesterday, more than once, he'd been pleased to handle Kate roughly.

"Good morning, Kate," Edgar Talmidge called out to her, a triumphant yet conniving smile on his face, even as he fought to keep a hold on the crying and protesting Lydia. "Did you sleep well last night after murdering my wife?"

Kate licked at her lips, felt her chest tighten. Edgar Talmidge looked plumb crazy. All wild and dirty, much as if he'd spent the night in the woods, perhaps digging a grave with his own hands. While one part of Kate's mind paid strict attention to the danger that he posed, another part insisted on running through a litany of fearful concerns that crowded her consciousness. *Where are the boys? Where's Kitty? Why didn't he bark? What's Mr. Talmidge done with them? Kate, pick up the gun. Use it—no, be careful. He might shoot you before you can pick it up. Watch out for Lydia. I can't shoot at them. I might miss and hit the baby. Oh, Cole, where are you?*

Spurred by Lydia's cries, and by all her worries, Kate

lurched forward . . . toward her hated and very dangerous enemy. But his driver instantly pulled his gun and trained it on Kate. She stopped, afraid of what he'd do, afraid he might choose to shoot one of the children instead of her. Kate cut her gaze back to Mr. Talmidge. With his arms wrapped around Lydia, he looked as threatening as a big poisonous snake.

"Let her go," Kate called out. "You've got no quarrel with her. Just put her down and leave her be." She couldn't believe the calm steadiness of her own voice—or the pleading note that came into it with her next words. "She's just a baby."

Mr. Talmidge smiled . . . an evil sight, to be sure. "A baby, huh?" He turned the scared and sniffling little girl about in his arms, looking her over as if he'd not realized it before now. "I believe you're right, Kate," he called out, again directing his gaze up the hill to where she stood. "I came here to get a baby. And look . . . now I have one. Imagine that."

He means to keep Lydia. Fright burst through Kate, weakening her knees. Fighting it, she fisted her hands, digging her nails into her palms. "I said let her be. It's me you want. Not her. Just put her down."

As she watched—and agonized over her own helplessness, even with such a powerful rifle so close at hand—Edgar Talmidge, a bearishly thick man of light coloring, again held Lydia out at arm's length and looked the little girl up and down. Kate feared he meant to dash the crying child to the ground. *Over my dead body, he will,* she thought . . . as she surreptitiously eyed the rifle at her feet.

A metallic click—a trigger hammer being pulled back— accompanied the driver's called-out warning to her. "Don't even think it, missy. I see you looking at that gun up there with you."

Kate tensed, meeting the gunman's gaze. His eyes were shaded by his floppy-brimmed hat. But Kate remembered from yesterday that his eyes were watery blue and empty-looking, much as if he had no soul. He wouldn't care what he did or who he shot, she believed, because he had nothing to forfeit to the devil. "That's a smart girl," he said. "Now keep your hands where I can see them." He then turned to his boss. "Go ahead, Mr. Talmidge. Say your piece."

"Thank you, Hedges," Mr. Talmidge responded . . . as if this were a drawing room and they were all polite society. He then turned to Kate. "Now, Kate. At last, it's just me and you. Like old times, isn't it?"

A surge of hatred swept through Kate. "There never was a me and you," she told him. "Never. There was only you taking from me. And I'm not going to let you do it again."

Looking at him now, watching the effect of her words on him and even seeing his expression harden, Kate wondered why she'd ever been afraid of him. Because suddenly she wasn't. In fear's place, a murderous hatred now coursed through her, a hatred that meant his death—if she got even half a chance.

"*You're* not going to let *me*?" His chuckle rang derisively. "I don't need your permission, Kate. The Talmidges take what we want. You should know that by now. Especially since it's *my* seed already growing in your belly."

Leaving Kate to seethe in her helplessness, Edgar Talmidge turned his attention to Lydia and wiped at her tears as they coursed down her cheeks. He cooed some quiet words at the baby . . . words that didn't quite reach Kate. Words that didn't succeed in quieting the child.

Kate's breath caught. To have that man's hands on this child almost killed her. No doubt, he'd made the gesture to prove to Kate that he still had the upper hand . . . because he still held Lydia. The message wasn't lost on Kate. Her chest constricted with fear for the little girl. Just then, Lydia shoved Edgar Talmidge's hand away from her face and shrieked, "No. I don't want you. I want Kate. Her's my mommy."

She called me mommy. Kate's heart nearly tripped over itself. She looked at the girl's red contorted face as she renewed her struggles against her captor. She expected Edgar Talmidge to be angry and insulted. But instead of frowning, he was grinning at Lydia. An illness engulfed Kate. She'd been right. He meant to keep her. *Oh, dear God.* She had to do something—and now. Divert his attention somehow. "Where are the boys? What did you do with them?"

Mr. Talmidge shifted Lydia in his arms—the little girl fisted her hands and rubbed at her eyes while sobbing quietly—and exchanged a glance with his driver, who looked this way and that around the campsite. Then Edgar Talmidge turned to Kate. "Boys, Kate? I assure you, I don't know what you're talking about."

For some reason, Kate believed him. Relief coursed through her. The boys were okay. But where were they? Had they wandered off and didn't know what was going on? She immediately rejected that. In the time that had elapsed between her last check on them and Lydia's scream, they couldn't have wandered far enough away not to have heard their sister's piercing yell. Perhaps, having a good hold on Kitty, they were hiding and watching. If so, Kate hoped they stayed hidden. The last thing she needed was *three* children being held captive.

"But that brings up a fascinating point, Kate. Tell me something," Edgar called out, jerking her out of her fearful thoughts. "Tell me about this fascinating ability of yours to attract children to you. How do you do that?" When Kate didn't answer him, he let her know his displeasure. "What's the matter, Kate? You don't feel like talking to me? Maybe the cat's got your tongue."

Kate swallowed, feeling a trickle of sweat run down her back. She focused on her enemy now, knowing the moment drew nearer when she'd have to risk everything—or lose it all. "Nothing's got my tongue, Mr. Talmidge," she finally called out as she started down the hill . . . slowly putting one foot in front of the other. She divided her attention between the man she hated most in the world and his armed henchman, who still had his six-shooter trained on her—and could at any moment pull the trigger. "I'm coming down now. And I'm leaving the gun where it is in the grass. I'll go with you—"

"No, Miss Kate! Don't do it. Don't go with him!"

Horrified, Kate lurched to a stop and jerked around. Behind her, not twenty feet away, stood Joey at the top of the hill. Willy, wide-eyed and struggling, was next to his older brother and had his arms wrapped around Kitty's neck. For his part, Kitty strained and jerked against the boy's hold on him and snarled in the direction of Mr. Talmidge—who held the dog's beloved Lydia. *They must have crawled through the underbrush and then skirted the hill to get behind me,* Kate thought.

Before she could move or say a word, Joey did the most heart-stopping thing Kate could have imagined. He grabbed up Cole's rifle, hefted it to his shoulder, and cocked it. Gasping in fear because she knew that all the men standing below her had to do was move over a few feet and Joey would be their target, not her, Kate stretched out a hand to the armed little boy and yelled, "Joey, no!"

"Get down, Miss Kate," he yelled right back. "I mean it. I aim to shoot that man holding on to my sister."

"Joey, for God's sake, put the gun down!" Kate grabbed up her skirt, meaning to run up the hill toward the boy. But her legs didn't seem to work right. With her muscles locking and burning, she fell down on her stomach. Pain surged through her, but Kate's only thought was for the boys. *Dear God, help me,* she cried out in her mind. *Don't let me lose these children, too.* She struggled to her feet and again held out a cautionary hand to Joey. Even though sheer terror for all of them coursed bone-deep through her, she noticed her hand wasn't shaking in the least. Could it be that her prayer had been heard?

She had to believe that it had. Anything else was unthinkable. And so, she gained in strength and calmness—a calm that allowed her to talk rationally to the scared but brave little boy trying to defend his family. "Listen to me, Joey. I want you to think about something. How would you feel if you missed him and accidentally shot Lydia?"

With the rifle held steadily at his shoulder, Joey sighted down its length, his black eyes never wavering from his intended target. "I ain't about to miss and hit Lydia. Now, get out of my way, Miss Kate."

Kate licked at her dry lips and shook her head. "No, Joey. I'm not going to do that. I can't."

Joey exhaled sharply. "Why not?" he wanted to know.

. Kate wrestled for the right words, even as she wondered why the two armed men behind her were so quiet, why they hadn't already killed the lot of them. What were they waiting for? Then, with blinding clarity, it came to her. They didn't shoot now for the same reason that Edgar Talmidge, after hiring a killer to end her life, had apparently changed his mind and come out here himself to stop Cole from killing her. This greedy man, with his father dying and his wife dead, desperately needed Kate's baby to inherit his money. Therefore, he still needed Kate alive. Although not these three children.

Kate exhaled, felt the day's growing warmth and her strength's steady waning. She looked into Joey's black eyes—so like his uncle's—and knew she had to find the right words to convince him to put the gun down. Those words, she knew, would have to be the hardest ones of all, the words from her heart. "Joey, honey, I won't get out of your way so you can kill that man. I can't."

His frown said he didn't like her answer at all. "Why not?"

"Because, Joey . . . because I love you. It's that simple. And I don't want anything bad to happen to you. But it could if you don't put that gun down right now." He didn't move. The rifle didn't even waver. Kate swallowed, felt the renewed pounding of her heart. "Please, Joey? I'm asking you to do this for me."

Tears sprang to Joey's eyes. He sniffed loudly and cried out, "I can't, Miss Kate. I'm scared to. He'll hurt my sister. And all of us. I just know he will."

Desperation ate at Kate. "No he won't, Joey. He just wants me."

Tears spilled over and ran down Joey's cheeks. "Well, he can't have you. My Uncle Cole loves you and went plumb crazy when you were carried off yesterday. And so did we. See, me and Willy and Lydia, we love you, too. And I ain't letting no bad man cart you away again."

Kate's heart had never felt warmer . . . or colder. The children loved her. And were about to get themselves killed because they did. Her worst nightmare come to life. Kate's pride in Joey's bravery warred with her urge to shake the stubbornness out of him. How long *would* the men behind her remain patient? she wondered. After all, as she'd already told Joey, the only one Edgar Talmidge needed was her. Kate felt certain time was slipping away from her. She feared the men would simply sidestep behind her and—

Two shots rang out.

They came whizzing by Kate . . . from behind her. The bullets missed her, but she screamed and stumbled, falling forward to the hard ground. Immediately, she struggled to regain her feet, clawing at the grass and dirt, crying out and fighting her long skirt, which became tangled around her legs. She feared another bullet would end her life at any moment. But she feared more what the first two bullets had already done.

Because at the top of the hill, she'd seen Kitty take off and had seen the rifle go flying—as if it had been torn from Joey's hands. At the same moment both boys had yelped as if with pain and had fallen down the other side of the hill.

Chapter Eighteen

Poised at the starting line, in the front ranks of the would-be settlers, Cole intently watched the mounted cavalry officer off to his right. Slowly and deliberately, the uniformed man raised his six-shooter into the air. Excitement shot through Cole, even as he licked at his dry lips and tightly held the reins to his prancing roan. In only seconds, at the stroke of noon, the army officer—like so many others ranged up and down the various borders edging the Unassigned Lands— would fire his gun and signal the beginning of the land run.

Coursing through Cole was the same anticipation that rippled through the surrounding throng of folks. Excitement was a living thing that settled a quiet hush over them all and held them frozen in a moment in time and history. Every muscle in his body tensed as he hunched over his roan's neck and thereby got his weight off the animal's hind quarters, the better to allow the horse a sudden burst of speed.

A grim smile came to Cole's lips. This roan was used to racing. More than once, Cole had put him up against the horses of men who'd thought they had a winner. Every time the roan had beaten all comers. Every time. Cole had no reason to believe this time would be any different. The roan was rested and ready to go.

Under him, the nervous horse pranced in place, fighting the bit, his muscles quivering with anticipation. A sudden jostle from another rider who crowded in too close to them had the roan snorting and whinnying, his head raised and his teeth bared. Instantly working the reins to circle his horse, Cole shouted to the other rider to mind his animal and then, with his own mount again steadied, he freed a hand to stroke the long-legged roan's neck. Into the horse's ear he crooned, "Easy, now. Easy. Don't let him worry you. Save it for the race. Save it for getting that parcel of land for Kate."

As if Cole's words had been the signal, the army officer fired his gun. The land run had officially begun.

A hushed and frozen second followed the hollow, booming sound. And then, all up and down the miles-long line, echoing reports of other cavalrymen's shots could be heard. In that moment, everything was forgotten—the hardships, the despair, the worries—as all hell broke loose. Cole, along with every man, woman, and child—whether atop a horse, in a wagon, or on foot—broke free of the starting line and surged forward with whoops and prayers, and plenty of hope . . . for a chance at a plot of free land and a new start in life.

Cole was at the forefront of the massive surge, which he felt resembled more an ancient army charging out to meet an enemy than it did the impossibly crowded horse race that it actually was. He let out the reins, gave the roan his head, and leaned over the animal's neck. Lifting his weight out of the saddle, with the roan's long and coarse mane whipping his face and neck, Cole centered his weight in the stirrups and held the reins taut.

Time seemed to stand still. It was the eeriest thing to Cole, this dulled quiet all around him. He'd heard about this from his father, who'd fought for the North in the Civil War. The noise of battle, he'd said, seemed to occur only at the edges of the action. But in the thick of the fighting, all was quiet and slow and drawn out almost painfully. This race was no different, Cole now realized. He felt certain that just by flying along so fast, he and all the other riders had slowed their passage through time . . . a gauzy moment that blurred the edges of reality.

Then as suddenly as it had descended, the quiet and the blurred slowness lifted, leaving a bright and startling quickness in its place. Cole now heard every whooping cry raised and became aware of every rider around him urging his own mount onward. It seemed to Cole the very ground rolled with a thunder all its own under the roan's flying hooves. The horse's stretched-out gallop ate up the prairie ground and carried them across the open land. Exhilaration ripped through Cole. His heart pounded in time with each thundering hoofbeat.

Suddenly he became aware of something else—and quickly glanced over his shoulder. *Son of a bitch!* The roan was pulling ahead of the pack. The big-hearted horse was leaving the crowd behind. And then, in the next second, Cole let out a whoop of his own for they *were* the front-runners. He glanced again at those behind him . . . and saw wagons rolling through the raised dust, saw teams struggling over the very hills and low-lying rills that the roan had easily cleared. Some behind Cole made it, some floundered and their dream died. Other men and women yelled encouragement to their mounts.

But up front, ahead of them all, it was a clear and glorious day. A stab of pure joy grabbed Cole and had him grinning and cheering the roan on. Nothing could stop him now. Nothing but time and miles lay between him and the hundred and sixty acres that Kate wanted. Nothing. It had all come down to this—a horse race that wasn't even a challenge for his roan.

Then, seeing where they were and recognizing the landmarks—from hours of studying his brother-in-law's map—Cole tugged on the reins and guided his horse to the left. In that direction lay the staked-out soon-to-be city of Guthrie. But more importantly to Cole, Kate's land was there, too, just shy of the city and to the north. Suddenly Cole realized he'd never been more proud of himself than he was at this moment. This was a good thing he was doing, and it had nothing to do with killing. It had to do with new life. Just like Kate's baby was a new life.

And here he'd stepped in and accepted the challenge, as well as the responsibility for her and for Charlotte's children. He was doing this for all of them. And it felt good. It felt right. As he slowed his roan some, feeling now he could save the animal's stamina for the distance yet to go,

Cole began to wonder if he could, after all, leave this place. He'd always said he would, but Kate and the kids and this land were starting to feel like home to him. The settling of this Oklahoma Country was something he wanted to remain a part of. It was that simple. And that hard.

Because as Kate had told him earlier this morning, making this land run was all she'd ever asked him to do. She hadn't asked him to stay on afterward. He could. The land would also be registered in his name. He knew that. Just as he knew that he wouldn't stay if Kate didn't want him to. He wasn't someone to force himself on a woman. He'd told her he loved her. He'd told her twice. And she'd said nothing in return. He wasn't surprised. She'd been through hell at the hands of Edgar Talmidge . . . and now carried the man's child. The last thing a woman would want after that experience, Cole expected, was another man.

So that all meant only one thing: after getting Kate's land for her, and after building her home, he'd be leaving . . . just like he'd said all along.

To Kate, the feel of the mule's bare back was hot, bony, sweaty, and itchy-hairy. Its rambling, bone-jarring gait was a trial to withstand, especially for a body as raw and hurting as hers was today. But still, she was grateful for the animal. And for Willy. Unscathed except for some scratches earned while evasively rolling down the hill a few minutes ago, he sat perched in front of her and handled the reins as Kate held on desperately to his narrow waist and tried her best not to fall off or to drop Cole's rifle, their only weapon.

Kitty plodded along on their right. And to their left, atop one of the other mules, sat Joey, who reined in his mount and fussed at his five-year-old brother. "Are you sure you saw which way they went, Willy? 'Cause I didn't see 'em, and you fell down that hill just like me and Kitty did when them bastards shot at us."

Startled by Joey's cussing but figuring this was no time—with Lydia's life in the balance—for a lesson in etiquette, Kate kept silent and held on to Willy as he sawed back on the reins of their mount. When he got the long-eared animal stopped, he turned enough to face Kate and his brother. "I seen 'em, Joey. I did. That man flung Lydia atop his horse like she was a sack of flour and then the two of them men took off this way."

The little boy, a black-haired miniature of his Uncle Cole, pointed in the direction they were already headed. Kate exhaled sharply. *West. They have Lydia and they're headed west.* "All right," she told the boys, "you two hold on a minute and let me think. Just sit here and be quiet for me."

When they minded her and fell silent, Kate attempted to divine Mr. Talmidge's reasoning. Why hadn't he, back at the hill, simply stayed put and allowed Kate to trade herself for the little girl? Certainly he knew he couldn't go back East with Lydia and claim her as his child. No one would believe him. *So why—?* Then it struck Kate . . . Edgar Talmidge took off because he hadn't known where Cole was. The awful man had meant to quickly snatch Kate and get away. But it hadn't worked. He hadn't expected resistance.

In light of that, Kate thought she could now see his plan. It was pretty smart of him, too. And awful for her and the boys. Because the mule she rode with Willy was now standing on the very border of the land run. Of course, it stood abandoned except for them. Only churned-up earth and grass attested to the tumultuous traffic that had passed over it about fifteen or twenty minutes ago. But already littering the way west were a few broken or overturned wagons, their precious cargoes littering the prairie. Here and there soldiers worked to help right the vehicles.

Weary and sore, and feeling she now knew the odds against them, Kate slumped behind Willy. Talmidge meant to catch up to the tail end of the throng of settlers and lose himself among the multitude of folks swarming willy-nilly all over the prairie. Because once he was lost to them, he had surprise again on his side. Plus, in the sweet and innocent person of Lydia, he had his bargaining chip: Kate for Lydia. He could afford to bide his time and wait for the right moment. Because he already knew that Kate loved the child and would exchange herself for the girl.

The horrible truth, then, for Kate, was if she didn't locate Talmidge and Hedges before they lost themselves on the prairie, then the odds of finding the little girl at all were very slim, indeed. After all, the men had those two sleek, fast-looking black horses that yesterday had pulled the landau. And here she was atop an ornery mule, accompanied by two little boys who were very lucky to be alive. No one had to tell her that they were still breathing only because the men probably hadn't intended to shoot the children, just scare them. Which they'd surely done.

They'd scared Kate, too. She recalled now her heart pounding in her throat, how she'd forgotten her own belly pain and the danger to herself as she'd bounded over the hill, only to see the boys sprawled on the hillside, staring wide-eyed up at her. She had panicked and skittered down the hill to grab them up and frantically check them for wounds, which they'd rushed to assure her they didn't have. Then she'd just as quickly grabbed up Cole's rifle from the ground where Joey had dropped it and had whipped around, thinking to kill at least one of those evil men who preyed on women and children. She'd decided it would be Hedges, since he wasn't holding Lydia.

With the boys, she'd crawled to the crest of the hill and had seen Hedges a good distance from Mr. Talmidge. With the boys showing her how, she'd sighted on the man and had fired . . . and had missed terribly. But it had been enough to spur the men into firing back. Kate and the boys had ducked back behind the hill again. When they'd risked another look, they'd seen the men bolting onto their horses and using Lydia as a shield. It now occurred to Kate that by firing at them, she'd really left them no choice but to do exactly what they had done . . . take Lydia and run.

As guilty as she felt about that, Kate knew all wasn't yet lost. Because their taking the little girl would probably prove to be the worst mistake either of them had ever made. Yes, they thought to use Lydia as a means of drawing Kate out. And that had worked . . . she was already on their trail and prepared immediately, should they find the men, to give herself over to them in exchange for the child. Wisely, she hadn't told the boys that. No sense worrying them with such an outcome now. Kate figured she worried enough for all three of them, especially over what Edgar Talmidge would do to her when he realized that she no longer—

No. Kate shut off her thought. Maybe it wouldn't come to that. Because what Edgar Talmidge and that awful Hedges didn't know was the little girl was the niece of hired killer and expert tracker Cole Youngblood. Wait until he found out about this—

"That's it!" Kate said excitedly, drawing the boys' attention her way. "We've been foolish about this. We don't stand a chance of finding those men and your sister—I know it, and you know it. But your uncle can. He can do this. I think we should find him and tell him what happened. Then I can stay at the land and protect the claim . . . with this rifle and you boys helping me. And Cole can go hunt for Lydia."

Joey's eyes lit up. "That's powerful good thinking, Miss Kate. Let's go." He started to dig his heels into his mule's sides, but then he slumped and faced Kate again. "You do know where this land of yours is, don't you?"

That was a fair question, Kate decided. She didn't suppose she blamed him for being doubtful of her skills. After all, so far he'd had to help teach her how to cook, shoot a rifle, drive a wagon, and ride a mule. "I have a pretty good idea. I've seen it on a map your father had. It's a little bit north of what's going to be the town of Guthrie, which isn't too far inside the border of the run. I figure we can ask some of these soldiers out here to direct us—"

"And tell 'em about Lydia and those men," Willy piped up. "They can look out for 'em, too."

That was just plain inspired. Kate tousled the boy's hair and hugged him to her. "Willy, you are so smart. That is exactly what we'll do. Let's go."

As they rode off, heading for a knot of soldiers up ahead

of them who were helping a family pick up their spilled belongings, Kate considered Willy's suggestion. For one thing, it would take a heap of convincing to get these or any soldiers to hunt after a man of Mr. Talmidge's reputation and wealth. And for another, she herself was guilty of murder and was reluctant to tell the soldiers—the only law out here—the reason for Talmidge's actions.

Kate kept silent and held on to Willy for dear life. She only hoped Lydia was doing the same, clinging to dear life wherever she was. Kate also hoped they'd reach Cole in only a few hours and that he would indeed be on the land she already thought of as hers. Because if he wasn't . . . what then? Despite what she'd told Joey, she wasn't sure she would recognize the specific plot of land Cole meant to stake. What a piece of land looked like on a map was one thing. What it looked like firsthand was another.

But if he wasn't there, and since they hadn't really discussed where else he should sink their stake if that plot of land was taken, she'd have no idea where else to look for him. Or for Lydia. And with her body already protesting, with crampy pains still riddling her abdomen, she would have no strength left to try again . . . if she even made it as far as her land and Cole without first simply dropping off the mule and dying by the wayside. After all, she'd lost a goodly amount of blood this morning when she'd miscarried her baby.

With folks thundering by all around him, with every one of them holding a flagged stake and intending to plant it in a good piece of soil, Cole clutched his own numbered stake in his hand and vaulted off his tired roan. Exhausted but triumphant, he sank to one knee, the better to jam the numbered piece of wood into the damp spongy ground. With one mighty swing of his arm, Cole brought the stake down . . . and instantly owned a hundred and sixty acres of land just north of the Guthrie Station.

As he was supposed to do, he pulled up the government's white-flagged stake and immediately secured it in his saddlebag. This was the prize everyone sought. Because only these white-flagged stakes, with surveyor's marks on them designating the boundaries of an exact piece of property, would be accepted to legally register any claim next to a man's or a woman's name in the land office's books. So, only then, only when the all-important stake was firmly in his possession, did Cole exhale in relief—and call it a miracle that this claim hadn't already been poached ahead of time.

Because a number of the claims he'd seen had been staked out as early as last night by dishonest folks who'd come in sooner than they'd been supposed to. They were pretty brazen about it, too, having already set up armed camps in places that Cole had been the first legitimate rider to pass by. Seeing the way of it, Cole had quickly decided that should such a squatter be camped on this land, he would deal with him accordingly. But that hadn't happened. So to Cole's way of thinking, the squatters were the government's problem. Not his.

Thus, his work done, the stake secured, the land as good as his and Kate's, Cole could now only stand back and stare at the stake. In the day's cooling breeze, the red strip of cloth tied around the wood unfurled and fluttered to life, much like a flag would. Overcome with satisfaction, Cole nudged his Stetson up and swiped his forearm across his sweating brow. Such a simple thing, that stake, to mean so much. All across this prairie land he'd seen some crazy things, as folks fought for the land they meant to claim over the objections of someone else who arrived in the same place at the same time. He'd already seen men shot and a few knife fights break out. He expected there'd be more, but he didn't think he'd have any trouble.

All for a plot of land. A week ago he'd thought these same people were misguided and foolish. But not now. Not today when he understood them and was one of them. Well, at least for the time being. He supposed that what happened after he got a home built out here for Kate and the kids would be up to Kate. *The house. That's it.* Cole took a second to look around and wonder where the best spot for that would be. But after sighting on several acceptable locations, he decided to hold off, figuring Kate should have the say in that.

He then chuckled, wondering what she would have thought of all the unlikely conveyances folks had used to make the run in. He'd seen folks chase across the million acres with covered wagons, buckboard wagons, landaus, surreys. On horseback, muleback, atop ponies, and on foot. He'd even seen a few desperate souls running along with their belongings in front of them—in wheelbarrows. But the most surprising—and the slowest—contraptions; the ones that had shied his roan more than once, had been the bicycles. Before today, he'd seen a few of them in his travels, and still thought of them as the strangest thing he'd ever seen. Weren't likely to catch him atop such an ungainly invention, that much he knew.

Just then, a sudden grin came to his face for no apparent reason. He put his hands to his waist and raised his face to the sun. The bright warmth bathed him like a benediction. And then he knew the reason for his happiness. He'd done it. It had been easy, and it felt damned good. He'd gotten the land that Kate had wanted—the same land that Mack Anderson had meant for his family to settle on. This was one good thing he'd accomplished, Cole told himself, and could always point to in his misspent life. He'd helped settle a territory and had settled his own family—by blood and by marriage—on it.

Yes, he'd done it. And in a little bit, after he rested the roan some and got him to water, Cole knew he'd have to start back the same way he'd just come to go get Kate and the kids and fetch them back here. They'd all be so excited. He hoped Joey, Willy, and Lydia weren't being handfuls this afternoon. Kate hadn't looked like she felt good today. Not that he was surprised, given everything she'd been through yesterday.

And yesterday's events were another matter that still weighed heavily on Cole. Edgar Talmidge. Cole feared that

Kate would never be safe as long as that son of a bitch drew breath. And here he still didn't know what the man looked like. It'd been too dark last night to get a good look at him. But seeing Edgar Talmidge had been the last thing on Cole's mind as he'd made his dive to bring Kate down and save her from being killed. Just recalling how that bastard had shot at Kate had Cole narrowing his eyes and succumbing, for a moment, to the murderous hatred that coursed through him.

He'd remedy that little problem as soon as he got Kate and the kids out here. He'd have Kate describe the man and then he'd go find him and kill him—no discussion, no mercy, no sneaking up on him to do it, either. Right out in the open. Let the son of a bitch know why, too. And who. Cole knew there'd be trouble when he did. He couldn't just up and kill a man like that—filthy rich, influential, tied to politics and banking as he was—and not expect the law to have a thing or two to say about it. But Cole had already made his peace with his decision to commit murder.

Before, he'd given his targets a fighting chance, which they always took. But the law, if there'd been any in the area, had looked the other way. For one thing, the lawmen themselves hadn't wanted to face Cole's gun. For another, usually the men he'd sought were the scum and dregs of society, anyway, and their deaths hadn't particularly upset the good citizens of a town. But not Talmidge. This one was different. A pillar of society. Cole made a scoffing noise. *To hell with him.* Talmidge was a walking dead man, as far as Cole was concerned. And once he killed him, Cole knew, so was he.

But it didn't matter. If he couldn't be with Kate and the kids forever, then he just didn't care where or how he spent the remainder of his life, no matter how short a time that might prove to be. He had to do this, had to call Talmidge to task for his evils—before the man got another shot at harming or finally killing Kate. It was true, sometimes wrong was just that—wrong. And it had to be stopped at any cost.

* * *

Several hours later, as the afternoon shadows lengthened and the day cooled, Cole could finally turn his roan's head back toward the border area. He'd just registered his claim in the land office at the Guthrie Station. As satisfying as that feeling had been, he'd been more fascinated with what was going on around him. Cole shook his head again with the wonder of it all. Out of a grassy prairie had arisen a city of tents and actual wood buildings, which were apparently partially constructed elsewhere and brought in on the heavy wagons he'd observed unloading the various sections.

Streets and general stores and homes and office buildings—all in one afternoon. Despite his pressing desire to get to Kate and the kids, and to assure himself of their well-being—and despite his impatience with the long line he'd been forced to wait in—he'd been dazzled by the sights around him, as was everyone else. But now, filling his mind were the obligations closer to his heart—again, Kate and the kids. He'd been worried about them all afternoon. But no more. Finally, it was time to do something about it, now that the roan had recuperated enough from its miles-long land run dash to carry him back home.

Home? Cole frowned as he heard his own thoughts. Slowly his frown turned to a smile, one of loving acceptance. He chuckled and edged his Stetson up a notch. *All right, then. It's true. Kate is my home. Wherever she is, my heart abides. I'll be damned.*

He suddenly laughed out loud—and realized folks were staring at him, and waving to him. Cole stared back. Who was that thin blond woman with a bunch of kids all around her? Then he remembered—Mrs. Jacobs from yesterday. The lady who'd seen to Kitty and had told Cole she knew Kate. Cole grinned and waved back, thinking, *Well, how about that? It appears she'll be a neighbor. Kate will like that, having a female friend so close by.* Other folks, from the safety of their claims, also called out and greeted Cole. He realized he liked it, this feeling of being an accepted part of society, even a newborn one. He'd not experienced this before, not since he'd been a kid.

That brought him around. He'd had acceptance before and had abandoned it. Now it appeared he would do so again. Cole sobered and set his gaze on the road ahead. There was no sense in getting used to being a part of something permanent, he reminded himself.

But still, he had today. It was all he could count on, really, since he meant to end Talmidge's miserable life very soon and would most likely get himself arrested, if not lynched first. What troubled Cole now was the realization that he probably wouldn't be around to build Kate that cabin he'd promised her. At least there were carpenters and builders aplenty in the area whom he could pay to see the job done. Well, there it was—just one more detail. Having settled that for himself, and feeling that his affairs were in as good an order as he could get them, Cole put his heels to his roan, urging the rangy horse into a steady canter. He had miles to go, so there was no sense in wearying the roan now.

But he hadn't been riding long, and wasn't too far out from the land he'd staked, when he hauled back on the reins and brought the roan to a stand. *What the hell? It can't be.* He nudged his Stetson up and stared hard. Because if he was seeing what he thought he was seeing, he wouldn't have to wait at all to see Kate and the kids. Because they were coming toward him, riding at a fast pace atop two mules and waving and hollering. Kitty ran right alongside them, his long ears flapping in the breeze.

Cole's insides tensed, his heart thumped leadenly in his chest. Their being out here couldn't be good, he knew that much. Cole dug his heels into the roan's sides and rode out to meet them across the rolling prairie land. In only moments, he was abreast of them, his roan's head even with Kate's and Willy's mule's tail. Joey, atop the other mule, sat his animal on the other side of them. Kitty circled them all, barking and baying. Before Cole could say a word, Kate was leaning over and clinging to him . . . and crying. She looked like warmed-over death, white as a sheet and about ready to drop.

Confused, stunned, hardly able to believe they were really here, Cole looked from one stricken face to the other—and yelled over Kitty's excited uproar. "Joey, quiet that dog." The boy instantly dismounted and called to the hound, who slunk over to him, wagging his tail as he sank down at Joey's feet. Cole turned his attention to Kate. "Honey, what's wrong? What the hell is going on? What are you doing out here? I thought you and the kids—"

"*Lydia*, Cole." Kate turned her tear-stained face up to him. "It's Lydia. Edgar Talmidge has her. After you left, he found us. I tried to stop him—"

"She did, Uncle Cole," Willy interrupted. "But he and another man shot at us."

A murderous anger seized Cole. "He shot at you? At you two boys and Kate?"

"Yeah," Willy said. "And them men wanted Kate. But Joey told 'em no and to give Lydia back. But when they wouldn't, Kate shot at 'em and they grabbed up Lydia and took off. We think they headed this way, too."

Rage against those men and fear for Lydia boiled through Cole, but Kate grabbed his attention by pulling weakly on his shirtfront. He looked down at her, meeting her gaze . . . and noticed the fearfully washed-out appearance of her green eyes.

"You've got to find him. He has Lydia."

Not even asking himself why he did, just knowing he wanted her in his arms, Cole gently tugged Kate over in front of him on the roan. He held her tightly to him, wrapping his arms around her to keep her securely in front of him. "I will, Kate. Trust me . . . I will. But what's wrong with you? Are you hurt somewhere? Did Talmidge—"

"No." She shook her head, her chin trembled . . . as if despair ate away at her. "I lost the baby, Cole. This morning."

Cole's expression contorted with sadness and a surprising sense of loss. This baby had meant everything to Kate.

"Damn, Kate, I never would have left you today if—"

"I know. That's why I didn't tell you." Then she clutched at him, pleading, "Please, Cole, I want to see my land. Is it far? Will you take me there now?"

Cole went still and cold inside. It was beginning to sink in. She wasn't sure herself she was going to live. *Son of a bitch.* Despair almost got the best of him. But pulling himself together, he set about doing as she'd asked. He turned to the boys. "Joey, mount up. And Willy, you keep up, too. We're going to the land I got for you."

Joey vaulted up onto the mule's back, righted himself, and then said, "For *us,* Uncle Cole. You got it for all of *us.* That means you, too."

Cole's gaze locked with Joey's determined one. "We'll talk about it later, boy. Right now, Miss Kate—"

"We know. She told us. She lost her baby." Joey's expression never changed, but he sniffed loudly. "We didn't know until we were almost here, and she fell off the back of the mule."

"Ah, Jesus." The words tumbled out of Cole. He held more tightly to Kate, who was softly whimpering now.

"We did the best we could getting her here, Uncle Cole," Willy added, always worried that he wasn't doing the right thing.

"You did fine, son," Cole assured the little boy. "Just fine." *The goddamned ride nearly killed her,* was the thought Cole kept to himself.

With Kate held in his embrace, with his own heart in his throat, Cole turned his roan and told the boys to follow him. Having to proceed slowly, given Kate's precarious condition, it took Cole a little longer than he'd expected to get them back to the claim. But finally, in the afternoon's long shadows, there it was. The land. It was a somber, quiet homecoming. Kitty dropped under the nearest tree and lay there, his big head resting on his paws.

Taking advantage of the same shade, Cole reined in his roan and kicked his feet free of the stirrups. With Kate still in his arms, he swung his leg over the roan's head and slid down the horse's left side. Then he laid Kate down on the ground, next to Kitty, who reached over and licked her pale, sweat-glistening face. Brushing the dog aside, Kate somehow found the strength inside herself to pull up onto her elbows and look all around her. Then she met Cole's gaze. "It's beautiful. Just like I knew it would be."

"Yeah, baby. It's beautiful. Just like you." Cole watched as Kate smiled and then sank back down, turning on her side and closing her eyes. Her outstretched arm supported her head. More afraid than he'd ever been, Cole called out, as always, to Joey. "Take my horse and your mules to the water, son."

Joey instantly dismounted and signaled to Willy to do the same thing. "There's a creek—you can hear its waters now—on the other side of these oaks," Cole told him. "After you boys drink your fill, wet down your shirt and bring it here so I can cool Kate down with it."

"Yes, sir." Joey began unbuttoning his shirt. Cole then ripped off his Stetson and tossed it to Willy. "Here, boy, fill this with water and bring it back."

The hat sailed past Willy's grasping hands, but he caught up to it and quickly plucked it up off the ground. "I got it, Uncle Cole."

"Good." Cole ran a hand through his sweat-matted hair. "Now go on. Do as you were told."

The boys took off. Kitty hauled himself to his feet and padded after them. Only then did Cole turn his attention to Kate, the person he loved best in all the world . . . and feared losing the most. As if sensing their aloneness, Kate opened her eyes and managed a shaky smile for him. "Cole, I have something else to tell you."

Feeling tears clog his throat, Cole smoothed her hair away from her face and said, "Save your strength, Kate. You can tell me later."

She licked at her dry lips and swallowed. "No. I'll be fine. I'm just . . . tired. All I need is rest. But there's something I want to say."

Cole sighed, not wanting to argue with her. "All right, baby. What is it?"

Kate blinked wearily and then, as if summoning the last of her strength, reached up, her hand shaking, to stroke his cheek. Overcome by the feel of her touch on his skin, Cole grabbed her hand and held it to his lips, kissing her palm. "Don't leave me, Kate. I love you. Jesus, how I love you. I'll do anything. I'll—"

"Cole . . . honey. I'll be fine. I promise. Just listen to me now." She looked him square in the eyes. "I love you. And I always will. All my life, I'll love you, Cole Youngblood." Speaking had taken all her strength. She wilted back down, weak and breathing shallowly . . . but breathing.

She loved him. Then somehow . . . the rest would follow. With his heart all but bursting with joy and fulfillment, Cole couldn't stop himself . . . he gathered Kate in his arms and sat down, his back against the sheltering oak tree, and just held her as he stared out over their land.

Chapter Nineteen

April 23, 1889, could very well be his last day on earth, Cole realized. Somehow that didn't seem fair, now that he had everything in the world to live for. He had Kate ... she loved him and was doing much better this morning. He had good neighbors ... Mrs. Jacobs had been more than helpful last evening in seeing to Kate and assuring him that, yes, she was young and strong and healthy—and would live. It had been hard for Cole to go asking favors, his hat in his hand. But the Jacobses had thought nothing of it and had even brought a meal over for them last night and blankets for bedding.

Then, this morning, Mr. Jacobs had come in his wagon to take Kate and the boys back with him to his claim ... until Cole got home. Assuming he did. Cole had told the couple, out of earshot of their kids and his nephews, enough about what was going on so that they could decide if they wanted to accept the possible risk to their own lives, should Talmidge skirt Cole and make his way here. They'd assured Cole they'd have a care for themselves. Mrs. Jacobs had even pointed to the six-shooter strapped to her waist and said she'd take good care of those two varmints if they so much as showed their faces around here.

Then, Mr. Jacobs had offered to take the boys and head back to the border to get Cole's wagons before they got ransacked and looted. Cole hadn't known what to say in the face of such generosity ... but he'd finally agreed to allow it. And so, off they'd all gone. Thinking now, as he rode into Guthrie, of his nice neighbors—and liking himself for realizing that he'd have done the same for them in return—Cole turned his thoughts to his nephews. They were definitely among his blessings. They were good kids, knew how to take care of themselves. They'd be a big help to Kate.

And he even had Kitty, Cole realized, thinking about the big old rawboned yellow hound. Probably a good hunting dog. All Cole knew was the dog loved Lydia. And that brought Cole around to what he didn't have. He didn't have his niece. His eyes narrowed. He wanted his niece back. He hadn't slept much, not knowing where the child was or how she was being treated. Last night his only option had been to stay with Kate and the boys. Still, Kate had tearfully begged him to leave right then and go find Lydia. But he hadn't. He couldn't. Not with Kate so perilously sick. She'd needed him more, whether she knew it or not.

Which meant that Cole had to accept that whatever had been done to Lydia, if anything, had already been done. His rushing off in the dark with no clue where to begin looking wouldn't have changed the little girl's fate. But truly, in his heart, Cole didn't think that Talmidge would be stupid enough to harm even one hair on that child's head. Because if he did, death would come instantly to him. Instantly. Kate had told Cole that Talmidge—whom she'd described to him, along with Hedges—hadn't known whose niece Lydia was when he'd taken her. But Cole figured he probably did by now. Lydia would tell him. She had no problem making herself heard and her wishes known.

At this point in his thoughts, Cole rode into Guthrie proper. He'd already rejected the notion that Talmidge would head for his fancy tent back at the border. For one thing, it was too far to travel back to quickly, especially while trying to hold on to a squirming little girl. And for another, Cole figured that Talmidge was smart enough to realize that Cole would think of the tent, too, and so wouldn't go there. A grim smile came to Cole's face. He'd always believed that successful tracking was like a good game of checkers. You never underestimated your opponent, and you thought four jumps ahead of him before making your first move.

And so, looking at things from Talmidge's point of

view, Cole had decided that Guthrie was the place to begin his search. In Cole's estimation of Talmidge, he figured the man would know that every settler out here, at some point or another, would have to come into Guthrie, the only city out here. The land office was here. The building supplies and the workmen were here. The dry-goods store was here. So was the doctor. So all Talmidge needed to do was keep a hold on Lydia and sit tight . . . until Kate came to him. Now, the only thing wrong with Talmidge's plan, as Cole saw it, was that Kate hadn't ridden into town. He had. Which meant a world of hurt was coming to that Talmidge son of a bitch.

Cole tamped down his rising temper. Now was not the time for hotheadedness that could get him and Lydia killed. Taking a deep, calming breath, he forced his thoughts toward a more practical bent with regard to Talmidge and Hedges. Where out here on the wide-open prairie would two inexperienced city slickers like them go to hide, except to a city? Cole had seen the Talmidge tent. All the comforts of home. Talmidge and Hedges wouldn't know the first thing about fending for themselves, much less for a child— a three-year-old child who would need things like food and a bed. Only a few weeks ago, Cole had been at a loss himself over how to care for three kids. So he now figured that the men he hunted would fall prey to the same fumbling shortcomings he had and would seek the comfort of what they knew best—city services and the help of paid servants.

So, when put together like that, it just made plain good sense for him to be riding into Guthrie like he was. Just then, he rode by a makeshift saloon, no more than a big white tent with its opening flaps tied back. Inside he could see a long board atop two oak barrels serving as a bar. And business was booming. Men already, at this early hour, stood in a long line outside. Cole shook his head. It wouldn't surprise him if, in less than a month, there were more hotels and restaurants and stores here than a man could shake a stick at. Oklahoma Country was certainly the land of opportunity. Just ask any surveyor, land attorney, or speculator toiling hereabouts.

But such things weren't Cole's concern today. No, today he hunted two sleek black horses . . . and two slick men. Manuevering the roan through the bustling crowd filling the streets, and lacking patience with the holiday spirit of those hanging red, white, and blue bunting in preparation for the upcoming official celebration of this territory's opening, Cole made his way toward a blacksmith's shop and a stable. Beyond it was a huge corral filled with dozing horses.

Cole shook his head, still marveling at how all of this land yesterday had been standing silent and unclaimed. And today, it was a noisy, crowded town. A town that a man like Talmidge would run to. He'd want a bath and a bed and a meal, all things he could get here. And for his horses' care . . . he'd need a blacksmith. Cole reined in his horse at the corral and dismounted.

A big, muscled blacksmith, shirtless and wearing a leather apron, immediately came out to meet him. "Sorry, mister," he said, swiping at his sweating brow, "but I'm all full up with horses right now. I ain't got any room, what with all the touts being here in town. You might try over at—"

"I'm not looking to stable my horse. In fact, I just need to look over the ones you already have here."

The blacksmith frowned . . . and sized Cole up. But apparently something he saw in Cole—perhaps his stance or the look in his eyes—had him instantly cooperating. "You looking for any horse in particular, mister? Mayhaps I can tell you if I've got it here. Might save you some time."

Clearly, the man didn't want whatever trouble was coming to happen here at his establishment. And so he wanted Cole gone. That was fair, Cole decided. "I'm looking for two matched sleek black carriage horses. Owned by a man name of Talmidge. He would've had another man with him and—"

"And a little girl not the least bit happy about being with him?" Sudden excitement had the blacksmith wide-eyed and telling all he knew. "I *knowed* there was something going on there. That rich man couldn't make her happy no way and no how. She kept saying she didn't like him and wanted her mama. Would that be him, mister?"

"That would be him." Relief coursed through Cole. He exhaled with the knowledge that it was definitely Lydia that the smithy had described. After all, how many times had she said the same thing to him? "You wouldn't happen to know where I could find this Talmidge, would you?"

Again the blacksmith looked Cole up and down. "There going to be trouble, mister?"

Cole raised an eyebrow. "Between you and me?"

The smithy's eyes bulged as he sucked in a breath. "No, sir. I don't want any trouble. I meant between you and Mr. Talmidge."

"That'll be up to Mr. Talmidge," Cole said. "Now, where'd you say he was staying?"

"I didn't. But are you the law? I heard the government officials are looking for a sheriff for the territory."

"I'm not the law," Cole assured him, just as he'd had to do with Kate the day he'd met her. Cole wondered what it was in his bearing that spoke to folks of authority. Whatever it was, he let it go for now and decided on a more direct approach for getting the information he needed out of this gossipy blacksmith. "On my ride through town, I noticed more than one clapboard hotel already up and accepting guests. So, what I need from you, Smithy"—Cole smoothed his six-shooter out of its holster and pointed it at the startled man's knees—"is the name of the one where Talmidge told you he'd be staying, should you have any trouble with his horses."

Pale under the grime of his occupation, the blacksmith blurted out, "I don't want no trouble, mister—"

"Mr. Youngblood. Cole Youngblood. And neither do I."

The man's mouth slacked open. Then he swallowed hard and told everything he knew on the subject. "The Hotel Moran, Mr. Youngblood. It's right up the road a piece. You can't miss it. And I'm sorry, I didn't know you were in town, or I'd have—"

Cole held up a cautioning hand to stop the man's babbling. He looked the silenced smithy in the eye. "Let's keep it that way. You don't know I'm in town. Got it?"

The smithy nodded and nodded. "Yes, sir. I got it. I haven't seen or talked to you. Never met you."

"That's good." Cole then tipped the brim of his hat to the man and said, "Much obliged to you, Smithy." Turning away, he remounted and rode off, heading for the Hotel Moran.

But he hadn't gone far, maybe past the doors of four or five other businesses—he noted one was an attorney's office and another a good-sized dry-goods store teeming inside with women who had children in tow—when a shot rang out and Cole's Stetson went flying off to his left.

Son of a bitch!

Instantly, screaming and crying and running feet accompanied Cole's rapid dismount. "Get out of the street. Take cover," he yelled, staying close against his agitated roan's side, using him as a shield as he guided the animal with the reins in his left hand and aimed his Colt over the saddle. Again he warned the running folks, "Get off the street. It's me they want. Hurry. Move it."

Whoever had fired on him—and he thought he knew who it was—had been across the street on his right. Sweating now, with his blood pumping furiously through his veins, Cole effectively looked in every direction at once. He searched for any quick and furtive movement between buildings. He looked for the glint of sunlight off gunmetal, anything that would point his enemy out to him. But nothing moved. And all was deathly quiet now. The busy Guthrie street had emptied of all but horses at hitching rails. That was good. No sense anyone else getting hurt. This was his battle.

When Cole had the roan out of the middle of the street and close to a building, he glanced up to read the sign. He didn't want to take refuge where there might be innocent

women and children. Howard Undertakers, the sign read.
A grim shake of his head accompanied Cole's thought.
Won't be far to go, should this end badly. Having gained
the building's side now, Cole let go of the reins and hit his
horse's rump, sending him trotting around the corner where
he'd stay until Cole whistled for him. Cole immediately
flattened himself against the side of the building, his drawn
gun pointing out of the alley toward the quiet, sun-drenched
street. He looked this way and that, and called out, "Talmidge? Is that any way to greet a long-time employee?"

From his left side, here in the narrow alley with him,
came his answer. "No. This is."

A hard punch with a meaty fist, a direct blow to his
kidney, left Cole gasping and sent his gun flying out into
the street. Immediately, before he could recover or catch
his breath, he was hauled up by his shirtfront and punched
in the jaw. The blow knocked him out into the street where
his gun was. Dazed and staggering back limply, Cole
caught sight of his attacker. Pugnacious and thick and snarling. *Has to be Hedges. Should have thought of this . . .
there're two of them.* The man charged him again, his arms
out as if he meant to grab Cole in a bear hug and squeeze
him until his spine snapped.

Cole shook his head to clear it and gulped in air. Even
though he expected a bullet in the back at any moment from
Talmidge hidden across the street, he sidestepped the burly
man's grasp and rammed his fisted right hand into the
man's gut, doubling him over and sending him to the
ground. But apparently only barely fazed, the son of a bitch
rolled onto his back and, fumbling inside his suit coat, came
up with the gun that had bulged out under the fabric.

"Jesus," Cole croaked, diving for the ground and rolling
over and over himself. Something hard stabbed into his
back. Cole rolled again, this time landing back first against
a water trough. He looked down at what he'd rolled over,
hoping only for a big enough rock to hurl at the bastard.
But what he saw renewed his faith. His gun. He yanked it

up, aimed, saw the big man's eyes go wide—and fired at the same time Hedges did.

Hedges missed . . . by about two inches. The bullet lodged in the trough just above Cole's head. But apparently he hadn't missed . . . because Hedges was mighty quiet now. Cole jerked his gaze to the man lying in the street and figured that probably the neat round bullet hole in the yahoo's forehead had something to do with his sudden silence. Cole had only exhaled when a door opened, directly behind him, on the other side of the trough. Leading with his pistol, Cole came suddenly up and over its thick wooden side. There stood a thin and balding—and startled— shopkeeper.

"Son of a bitch." Cole jerked his gun up, pointing it to the sky. "Get the hell back inside right now."

The frightened man wordlessly stepped right back inside and slammed the door. Cole again flattened himself on the damp ground beside the trough and, exhaling sharply, ran a hand over his eyes. Supporting himself on his elbows, he again searched for any movement that would give away Talmidge's position. Cole's biggest fear was that Hedges's attack had been a diversion to allow Talmidge to escape with Lydia. Just the thought of that rich bastard getting around him and making his way out to the claim—so close by and where there were only women and children—gave Cole a sinking feeling in the pit of his stomach.

"Youngblood? Where are you?"

Cole started . . . and then stilled, listening. This had to be Talmidge. In the dead quiet, while he waited for the man's next move, his aching kidney and swelling jaw seemed to hurt all that much more.

"Come on out. I got something you need to see."

Son of a bitch. He had to mean Lydia. "Dammit," Cole raged, his teeth gritted around his whispered curse. He had no choice.

Cole stood up slowly, dropping his gun to the ground and raising his hands . . . as instructed by Talmidge, who'd just stepped out of the Moran Hotel doorway up the street.

The man was armed with a Colt Peacemaker, which he had aimed at Cole's heart. But the gun was of no consequence to Cole. Because Talmidge, the cowardly bastard, had Lydia pinioned in his grip . . . and was using the little girl as a shield.

Cole had never felt so helpless. He took a second to assess his niece. She appeared to be okay. Scared, to be sure, and not understanding what was happening. And crying . . . which was to be expected. As soon as she saw Cole, she flailed her chubby baby arms and legs and sobbed loudly. "Uncle Cole, Uncle Cole. Come get me. I don't like him. He's mean."

Cole's chest tightened as he heard Talmidge tell the little girl to shut up. Lydia only screamed all that much louder. Terrified beyond belief, Cole called out, "It's okay, Lydia. Just be still, honey. And everything will be okay." *If I have to die making it so,* Cole added to himself. "Just be still, baby."

Amazingly, the little girl did settle down some. She stopped fighting and resorted to a quiet sobbing that ate at Cole's heart.

"Where's Kate?" Talmidge called out to Cole—who locked gazes with the crazy bastard. "I'm prepared to trade you your niece for her. All I want is Kate."

Talmidge had just said exactly what Cole had thought he would. He also believed that the last thing Talmidge would expect from him was his cooperation. "All right. That's fine with me." Cole put his hands down and added, "Let's go. Kate's out at her claim. I just need to get my horse and my hat."

"Stop right there."

Cole did. His gun now lay on the ground right next to his left boot. Cole wondered how good a shot he was with his left hand.

"Is this some kind of a trick?" Talmidge wanted to know. "Kate said you'd married her. Is that true?"

"It is." Just hearing this man call his wife by her first name made Cole want to choke him with his bare hands.

"You're married to her? And yet you're willing to give her up so easily?"

Not in a million years, asshole. Cole shrugged. "Hell, yeah. Why not? Our marriage was only a business deal. I knew at the time that she was carrying your child. So why would I want her?"

There were two things Cole couldn't let Edgar Talmidge know: that he loved Kate and that she no longer carried Talmidge's child. If he gave away the first of those two things, then Talmidge would know he could more easily manipulate Cole. And if he knew that Kate had miscarried, then Lydia became worthless as a pawn. In this game, worthless meant dead. "So what do you say?" Cole challenged Talmidge. "You coming with me or not?"

Talmidge looked everywhere but at Cole as he licked his lips and shifted Lydia around in his arms. He actually appeared to be thinking about it. But then his gaze snapped back to Cole. Only now did Cole see the flatness and the too-bright shininess there that spoke of insanity. Cole couldn't believe that he'd done this man's bidding more times in the past than he cared to think about. And each time represented a life taken. "I don't trust you," Talmidge suddenly shouted to Cole.

Cole eyed the man. Perhaps losing his wife and then losing Kate had pushed him over an edge. Cole knew that nearly losing Kate yesterday had almost made him crazy. So why not Talmidge? Still, Cole exhaled his breath slowly and urged himself to proceed with extreme caution. "What difference does it make if you trust me or not, Talmidge? You have my niece. And I'm unarmed." Never looking away from the man, Cole toed some dirt over his gun, trying to hide its nearness to him from Talmidge's sight. "I'm cooperating fully. So it's your call."

"I'm not going anywhere with you, Youngblood. That was a nice try. But like you said, I've got your niece. So you go get Kate and bring her here. And I'll wait here with this little girl. You have until noon to show up with her.

Or I'll kill Lydia." Making his point, he put his gun to the little girl's temple.

She instantly grabbed at the gun's barrel, trying to push it away as she shrieked, "No! I don't like you. Put me down. I want my Uncle Cole."

Swept by fear—Lydia's antics could cause Talmidge to mistakenly fire the gun—Cole cried out, "Lydia, don't do that. Be still, baby." He was dying inside. He had no idea what to do at this point. He was losing . . . and Lydia's life hung in the balance. So he appealed to a madman. "Just . . . take the gun away from her head, Talmidge. You don't want to do this. I'll do what you want. I swear it. Kill me instead. Right now. But for God's sake, man, don't hurt that child."

Talmidge's expression changed, became strangely thoughtful . . . as if the notion of self-sacrifice had never occurred to him. He cocked his head to the side and stared at Cole. "You really mean that, don't you? That you'd rather I killed you than her?" Then he grinned and his eyes gleamed.

Cole's knees weakened, nearly giving out on him. *He's going to do it. He's going to kill Lydia just to torture me.* That meant Cole had nothing left to lose. A low growl in his throat came out with his words: "Don't even think it, bastard."

Talmidge's eyebrows rose, his expression became mocking. "Brave words for an unarmed man, Youngblood." Then he shifted his hold on Lydia, pushing her up more into his arms. His right wrist, his gun hand, edged almost up under her chin—dangerously close to the scared child's mouth. And all those sharp baby teeth.

Hope surged through Cole. He now addressed his niece. "Lydia? Remember what you did to Willy when he pulled Kitty's tail and made him yelp? Do you, baby?" The little girl's pouty mouth and wide-eyed expression stiffened into remembered belligerence toward her brother. "You do remember, don't you, honey?"

"What are you trying to pull, Youngblood?"

Cole ignored Talmidge and kept talking to Lydia. "You remember, don't you, baby?"

"Yes," she said, her sweet little baby voice a precious sound to Cole. "Willy hurt Kitty."

"That's right, baby, but he didn't mean to. But that mean man who's holding on to you did the same thing to Kitty. Only he *meant* to hurt him."

Lydia's eyes rounded like saucers. Her mouth turned down with determination—and she grabbed Talmidge's arm and bit the hell out of the unsuspecting man. Instantly, he howled and his gun fell from his nerveless fingers. In the next instant, Lydia shrieked and also fell from his grasp, only to hit the ground hard on her chubby belly.

"Stay down, Lydia," Cole yelled as he dove for the ground and his gun. Lying flat on his belly, pretty much as Lydia was, Cole fished his weapon up with his left hand— *Son of a bitch.* He jerked toward Talmidge, who had his gun in his hand again and was reaching for Lydia. Cole had no choice but to play the hand dealt him. He fired the pistol left-handed.

With Cole's aim off, the bullet took Talmidge in the left shoulder, forcing a cry from him as he spun with the impact. "Stay down, Lydia," Cole yelled again, even though the little girl hadn't moved since she'd hit the ground. Cole saw Talmidge right himself . . . and point his gun at the helpless little girl.

"No!" Cole yelled, firing his weapon over and over and over . . . until Talmidge lay bleeding and dead in the street.

Instantly, Cole was on his feet, reholstering his gun as he ran for Lydia, who still lay facedown in the dust. Reaching her, Cole stopped so suddenly that he raised a small dust cloud. He dropped to his knees and gently turned Lydia into his arms. As he brushed her hair back from her dirty little face, Cole heard his own prayer: "Dear sweet God, no. Not this child."

Lydia's eyes opened and she gasped when she saw it was Cole. Then, crying, she held her arms out to him, wanting him to hold her. Cole immediately hugged her to his chest . . . and cried and thanked God and rocked with her right there in plain view of all the citizens now opening their doors and slowly refilling the main street of Guthrie.

Two and a half months later, July Fourth dawned bright and sunny in the Oklahoma Territory. The daylight itself seemed to smile, to anticipate the promise of the coming holiday celebration. Birds chirped, the stream's waters gurgled, and a cow mooed, making known its wish to be milked. But inside, in the Youngblood home situated on one of the choicest claims in the area, Kate still lay in bed. She stretched, yawning, feeling warm and safe and secure. Yes, she needed to get up and get breakfast and hurry the kids along for the coming trip into Guthrie and all the festivities. She knew that . . . and so did Cole, that devil. A grin captured her features.

With his arms wrapped around her, with her snuggled up against him in their wide, comfortable bed, with her cheek against his bare chest, and with him stroking her hair, Kate knew that breakfast and kids and celebrations would just have to wait. Grinning, she wriggled upward in Cole's arms, kissing her way up his chest, his neck, his jaw, until she was within range of his lips. At the last moment, before she could capture his mouth, Cole pulled back and stared down at her, grinning also, his hand lovingly stroking her cheek. "Last night wasn't enough, Mrs. Youngblood?"

Suddenly shy yet feeling playful, Kate gave a dramatic shrug. "It was enough then." She met his gaze, hoping the burning she felt inside for him shone forth. "But not now, Mr. Youngblood."

Her seductive grin, her arms going around his neck, arching her body against his, wrought an immediate response from her husband. His sharp exhalation and the stiffening of his naked body told Kate everything she needed to know. He pulled her more closely into his embrace. And Kate knew she'd never tire of the feel of this man's hands on her body. Every day he healed her spirit more. Every day the nightmares in her heart and in her mind receded a bit more. Every day they were replaced by Cole's love, by his touch, by his steadfast faithfulness.

And in the time since her body had mended, in the time since they'd worked side by side to build their home and a life together with the children, Cole had proceeded slowly in showing her how to love. He'd allowed her to set the pace and to mark the moment for their first coupling. Since that first tender time, he'd shown her that love such as his for her arose from respecting her during the daylight hours. And at night, he'd taught her that gentleness and tenderness weren't only found in a man's touch, but also in his heart. Most importantly, he'd shown her what it was to be with a man whose touch she wanted and whose love she needed.

Like now. Desire for her husband fired Kate's senses as she responded with abandon to Cole's deft caresses, to his kiss that hungrily ravaged her mouth, to his searching hands that seemed to be everywhere at once on her body. Kate writhed with the now familiar heat that instantly and feverishly consumed her senses with his first touch. She murmured words of love to him, which only spurred him on. In an instant, Kate's nightgown was over her head and tossed aside, leaving her naked body pressed up against his.

A sharp inhalation was wrung from her at the feel of his muscled chest against her bare breasts. She clung more tightly to him, caressing his shoulders and arms as Cole dipped his head down to her breast to capture an already taut nipple. The heat of his mouth, the swirl of his tongue, as he moved from one nipple to the other, forced a soft cry of desire from Kate's parted lips. And then he dipped lower on her body, kissing his way down her belly, past her navel, until he found her secret place and swirled the same kisses there.

Just as she thought she'd pass out from the pleasure, Cole pulled away, now trailing his kisses back up her body. "My God, Kate, you're beautiful." His voice was breathless and tight with passion. "I could never, in five lifetimes, get enough of you. Never. I think I've known from the first moment I saw you that I'd love you."

Kate's answering smile came from her heart, a heart filled finally with love and happiness, two treasures she'd never thought she'd own. She stroked his face, gazed into his eyes. "I love you, Cole," came her whispered words. "I love you so very much."

As if he'd been waiting only for those words from her, he pulled himself up and over her. Holding fast to his arms as he held himself above her, Kate welcomed his weight atop her, welcomed the feel of his hips pressed against hers, welcomed his sliding into her, his coupling with her. She bent her knees and raised her hips, meeting his every loving thrust with one of her own. Finally Cole lowered himself more fully onto her, holding her close, embracing her, dragging kisses over her ear, her temple, her cheek. Kate wrapped her legs around Cole's middle and her arms around his neck, urging him onward, feeding her own desire as much as she knew she did his with every kiss, every caress, every whispered word of love.

Inevitably, the tightness inside her coiled. The heat firing her blood combusted, warming her cheeks and raging throughout her body, seeming to settle in a tingling warmth in her thighs. She gasped and clung to Cole, all but burying her face in his shoulder, suddenly unable to help him or herself to increase their mutual pleasure. A gasp escaped her.

"Oh, Cole, I need you so." Her whispered words were hot. Her biting kiss on his neck wrung a cry from him. "Now, Cole, now," she urged, holding fast to his muscled and sweating back.

Cole responded. His thrusts increased, became a pounding and steady pace that coiled the tightness inside Kate to such a turn that, even inside herself, she could feel Cole's desire thicken and harden even more. The moment was near. Kate could barely breathe. Cole's weight pressed her into the bed . . . and she wanted more of him, wanted to feel him from her head to her toes, wanted to drown in this expression of his love and desire for her.

And then . . . Kate stiffened. It burst, sending her over

the edge of sanity, beyond reality, beyond the moment and the time and the bed. Her head thrown back, her toes curling, a wanton cry bubbling up from her throat, Kate's body danced across the rippling undulations, the hot sweet intensity that threatened to have her out of her mind. From Cole, who now held himself rigid over her, as his body pumped its seed into hers, she heard his own hoarse cry of fulfilled desire . . . and felt whole again. Felt alive. Loved. Cherished. Wanted. As if she'd just come home. Where she'd never been before.

Epilogue

Later that July Fourth morning, now dressed and ready to go, Kate put her hands to her waist and stopped, standing in the upstairs hallway and looking right and left into the children's opened bedroom doorways. She swore the new house was already too small. Eight rooms and two stories . . . too small? Maybe, she decided, it simply seemed as if it were in all the high-spirited and hectic confusion of this hot and sunny day.

Well, standing here isn't getting anything done. Instantly going into action, and moving from one bedroom doorway to the next, Kate clapped her hands together and set about individually encouraging the freshly bathed Joey, Willy, and Lydia to rush around a bit. "Come on, now. Hurry it up. You don't want to miss the big get-together in town, do you?"

"No, ma'am," Willy called out, garnering Kate's attention. She stepped over to his doorway to see the little boy's black eyes dancing with happy anticipation of the holiday. "I just got to get my shoes. And then I'm done."

Kate smiled as the five-year-old stuffed his treasures— a piece of rawhide, a bent coin, and two rocks he fancied— into his new britches pockets. "Good for you, Willy. You'll be the first one ready." Kate moved away from his door—

"Kate?" he called right back.

Kate stepped back into view, trying not to see the appalling heaps of clothes and bedding all tossed about. "Yes, baby?"

"I can't find my new shoes."

Chuckling, Kate sagged against the door frame and crossed her arms. "I don't doubt that, Willy. Have you looked under your bed?"

Realization dawned on his lightly freckled face and he dove, head-first, under its metal frame. "Here they are," came his muffled call.

"Good," Kate called over her shoulder since she'd already moved on to Joey's doorway. She peeked in—stopping short and trying to cover her gasp.

Inside his neatly kept room and standing at his dry sink, with water in the basin and his skinny little back to her, shirtless, shoeless, and his pants' suspenders dangling to either side of his legs, the boy's mirror-reflected gaze locked with hers. "Joey," Kate gurgled. "You're . . . shaving."

Eight years old now, as of two weeks ago, and in love with ten-year-old Meredith Jacobs, whom Kate knew would be in Guthrie with her family for the festivities, Joey's rounded eyes begged her to take him seriously. He slowly swirled his uncle's shaving brush around in its soap mug. "Well, not yet. I'm just getting ready to start."

Kate tried desperately to think how to handle this, before the boy began carving the flesh off his face. "Joey, I think shaving is a fine idea, but in about five more years. I've always heard that a man needs to wait until he has a beard coming in. That way, he doesn't cut himself so bad."

Surprisingly, Joey looked relieved at her intervention, much as if he'd gotten himself into a situation he now regretted. "Yes, ma'am," he agreed readily, putting the razor down and mopping at the suds on his face. I suppose I can wait a bit to try it."

Relieved, Kate swallowed and nodded. "A smart decision. Now, you get yourself dressed. I'll just go check on Lydia. Your uncle says you're to come straight down when you're ready and help him."

"Yes, ma'am," Joey said obediently, tugging on his suspenders.

With that, Kate turned away, heading for Lydia's room, across the hall from Joey's. Suddenly there was a great fuss in that direction. Kate got to the little firebrand's bedroom door and saw only the top of the child's head and her bare chubby legs. In between was the daffodil-yellow dress she struggled to get over her head. Chuckling, Kate stepped inside and assured her, "I'm here, baby. Shhh, now. Let's see what we can do. Hold still."

Lydia did and Kate set about trying to sort out arms from armholes and finally managed to pull the dress down into place. With her riot of dark curls now a fuzzy halo about her face, Lydia gave Kate her best pout. "I want Kitty to go with us," she said—for about the twelfth time this morning. "If Kitty can't go, I don't want to go." She crossed her arms defiantly and poked out her bottom lip.

Kate instantly mocked the little girl's expression and her stance. "Then that settles it. You get to stay here all day and chew on an old bone and drink water out of the creek with Kitty—while I go into town with the boys and eat all the pies and see the parade and dance with your Uncle Cole—"

"No!" Lydia cried out, putting a tiny hand over Kate's lips. The little girl's black eyes widened. "Me, too. Me, too. Kitty won't mind, huh? He'll stay here and be brave and make sure the bad man doesn't come back, won't he?"

Edgar Talmidge's hateful face suddenly swam into Kate's mind. She sobered and immediately swooped the little girl up into her embrace, holding her as close as she could and rocking with her. "The bad man won't ever come back, baby. Ever. He's gone for good. Your Uncle Cole made sure of that, remember?"

With her little face snuggled against Kate's neck, she nodded. "Uh-huh. I do. But . . . he still scares me."

"I know, baby, I know," Kate soothed, aching for the child who still had occasional nightmares and stole across the hall in the night to sleep with Willy or Joey. Or cried until Kate or Cole came upstairs from their bedroom downstairs to get her. Kate tugged Lydia back and smoothed the child's hair away from her face. "But it's all over now, and Uncle Cole is here to protect us all. No one is going to hurt you ever again."

"Yeah," Lydia instantly agreed, smiling now, very proud. "And Uncle Cole's the sheriff. So the bad men have to do what he says, don't they, Mama?"

"You bet they do, sweetheart." Kate tenderly flicked the tip of Lydia's button nose and smiled, her heart overflowing every time Lydia called her Mama. She still insisted on calling Cole her uncle . . . but Kate was Mama. Kate stood up now and turned the child's back to her. "Let me button you up and then we'll get those pretty ribbons off your dresser to put in your hair. How does that sound?"

"Fi-ine." Lydia drew the word out. Then, "Can Kitty have a bow, too?"

Not the least bit surprised, Kate just laughed. "Why, of course." Done now with the dress's buttons, Kate helped Lydia into her stockings and button-up shoes. After that, she brushed and plaited the little girl's long hair, running the promised ribbons through each braid. When finally Lydia stood ready, Kate handed her another length of satin ribbon and said, "Here. Go tie this around Kitty's neck— not too tight, now."

Lydia's eyes lit up as she took the long red ribbon from Kate. "I won't. Kitty likes when I give him bows. Big ones."

"I know," Kate cooed, even though she knew that Lydia would only hopelessly knot the satiny length and it would have to be cut off the dog. "He'll be so pleased you thought of him."

Lydia smiled smugly and nodded—obviously very pleased with her own generosity—and then, with Kate following along behind her, skipped toward the doorway, calling out to her brothers. "Willy, Joey, come go with me. I gots a ribbon for Kitty."

From Joey's room came a muffled, "Ah, hell. Not again. That poor dog."

But from Willy's room came running feet. "Wait for me, Lydia. I'll help you knot him up again."

The children met up at the stairs, going down together, Lydia one step at a time and holding on to the bannister, Willy assisting her. And Kate followed behind them, close enough to hear their do-not-do-too litany on bow- and knot-tying all the way down. Once they reached the last riser and hit the hallway on the first floor, they raced off through the house, down the hall and out the back door, Willy ahead and Lydia squealing about it. Downstairs herself now, Kate closed her eyes and smiled . . . and stood in the hallway, her hand on the bannister as she reveled in their childish joy and abandon. Pure music to her ears.

Suddenly she was hugged from behind, a hard masculine body pressing warmly against her back. She hadn't even heard Cole's footfalls. He must've stepped out of the carpeted parlor and onto the runner in the hallway. Warmed by his kiss on her neck and by his murmured words of love, Kate instantly relaxed, caressing the square-palmed hands clasped together at her waist. Smiling a secret smile, she reached a hand up behind her and cupped Cole's cheek as he covered her upswept hair with kisses. This man's touch simply melted her . . . and he knew it. "I love you so much, Cole. You make me so happy."

"Good," he said, nibbling at her neck. "I want to. For the rest of our lives." After another moment of nuzzling, he rested his cheek on her hair and said, "Have you decided what you want to do about Justis Talmidge's letter? You've had it a week now. The man deserves an answer."

Kate sighed and nodded. "I know. And yes I have decided." She turned in Cole's embrace so she could face him and flattened her palms against his chest. "Please don't be angry, but I think we ought to take his offer, Cole. It's a lot of money, I know—more than we could ever spend. But I think we can do a world of good with it. Especially for the children."

Cole's expression hardened. "Sounds like you have made up your mind, then."

Kate hated this. They'd disagreed from the outset, ever since the letter from New York had arrived at the post office in town. "Please don't be angry, Cole. Justis Talmidge offered it in the right spirit. I never knew him to be anything but a good and decent man. I know he had no idea what was"—Kate looked down at a button on Cole's shirt—"going on in his brother's house until Hudson, the valet, told him."

Cole instantly pulled her into his embrace and kissed her forehead. "Honey, you're right. Don't think about that." Then, by her arms, he held her out away from him and met her waiting gaze. "It's all settled, then. If that's what you want, then that's what we'll do."

Kate had never loved him more than she did at this moment. She closed the gap between them and laid her cheek against his shoulder. "You're not angry with me?"

She felt Cole's negative shake of his head against her forehead. "No, sweetheart. I'm not. What you've decided only makes good sense. I suppose his aim is to make up for what his brother did. I can respect the man for that. Besides, if he hadn't stepped in when he did in the investigation of his brother's and his sister-in-law's deaths, you and I might not be standing here having this little talk."

Knowing the truth of that, Kate hugged Cole tighter. "I was so scared, Cole. I sometimes . . . well, I still have bad dreams, like Lydia."

"I know, baby. But I'm right here, and I'm never going to leave you. Ever." He kissed the tip of her nose. "Even after I die, I'm going to come back and haunt you."

Kate pulled back in mock horror. "Oh, please don't. I just said I have nightmares."

Cole chuckled at her. "Speaking of nightmares, I've got the wagon all packed. The food, the blanket for the picnic. It's all in the buckboard. All I need is my family. But first—" He held Kate out at arm's length, whistling his pleasure. "Look at you, Kate Youngblood, in your new Sunday-go-to-meeting dress."

Suddenly shy and embarrassed by her own husband's

attention, Kate looked down at herself and fussed with the flower-sprigged cotton skirt. It was the prettiest dress she'd ever owned, and she was so proud of it. But she'd never learned to preen, so she simply asked, "Do you like me in it?"

"Only slightly less than I like you out of it."

Pretending shock at such a decadent turn of phrase, Kate playfully smacked at his chest, hitting the shiny sheriff's badge affixed to his black vest. She worried about him; his job was such a dangerous one. But still, every day she thanked God for this opportunity for Cole to do good with the one thing he knew—a gun. Instead of taking lives now, he was keeping the peace. And speaking of that: "Cole, I'm afraid I have a bit of tattling to do."

He adopted a mock ferocious expression and tugged at his gunbelt. "Which one? And what did he do?"

Kate pursed her lips and planted her hands at her waist. "Well, it's Joey. I don't know what to do. I caught him getting ready to shave just now."

Cole glanced up the empty stairwell and laughed. "That boy, I swear." Then he focused on Kate and, putting his arm around her shoulders, walked them toward the back door and the waiting wagon. Over his shoulder, he shouted up the stairs to Joey. "Let's go, boy. You can't keep the ladies waiting all day."

Kate tugged on Cole's vest. "What are we going to do about him?"

Cole shrugged. "I'll talk to him. I still need to talk to him about chewing tobacco, anyway."

Kate stopped, forcing Cole to do the same. "He chews tobacco, too? Cole, he's eight years old. And he cusses. I'm worried about him."

"I can tell." Cole started them again toward the wide-open back door. "But luckily he's sweet on Meredith Jacobs, from what Willy says. So she's our best hope with him."

"She is? How?"

"Well, it's been my experience that the love of a good

woman can completely turn around the life of even the hardest of men." Cole grinned down at Kate. "So maybe Meredith can do for Joey what you did for me."

Basking in Cole's love and praise, and feeling suddenly playful herself, Kate turned her face up to the only man she would ever love and quipped, "You mean make him the sheriff in a new territory?"

Cole laughed with her as they stepped outside, out into the warm sunshine of a beautiful day in Oklahoma. Only to have Joey slam the door behind them and, with Kate's fresh-cut flowers from the parlor fisted in his hand, breeze by them and head for the loaded wagon. Only to see Willy sitting quietly in the wagon's bed, the crude fishing pole he'd made himself in his hand. Only to see Lydia standing defiantly in the back of the wagon—between Willy and, of course, the ribbon-bedecked, tongue-lolling Kitty.

Kate sighed and Cole shook his head as they made their way to the buckboard. Cole handed Kate in and then stepped around the mule team to climb on board himself. Sorting out all the reins, he set the team on the road for Guthrie. As they passed through the opened gate that signaled the boundary of their property, Kate's heart constricted . . . as it always did. A tear came to her eye . . . as it always did. But through it all, she smiled and blew a kiss at the hand-lettered sign she'd made a couple of months ago and Cole had nailed up for her on a gate post.

Melissa's Acres, it read . . . named after the little girl Kate never got to hold. But would always love.